THE
INHUMAN
PEACE

Also by Yudhanjaya Wijeratne

Numbercaste
The Inhuman Race
The Salvage Crew

YUDHANJAYA WIJERATNE

THE INHUMAN PEACE

HarperCollins *Publishers* India

First published in India by
HarperCollins *Publishers* 2021
A-75, Sector 57, Noida, Uttar Pradesh 201301, India
www.harpercollins.co.in

2 4 6 8 10 9 7 5 3 1

P-ISBN: 978-93-5357-477-2
E-ISBN: 978-93-5357-478-9

This is a work of fiction and all characters and incidents described in this
book are the product of the author's imagination. Any resemblance to actual
persons, living or dead, is entirely coincidental.

Yudhanjaya Wijeratne asserts the moral right
to be identified as the author of this work.

Typeset in 11/14 Scala (OTF) at
Manipal Digital Systems, Manipal

Printed and bound at
Thomson Press (India) Ltd

MIX
Paper
FSC FSC® C010615

This book is produced from independently certified FSC® paper
to ensure responsible forest management.

'Thus, from the war of nature, from famine and death, the most exalted object which we are capable of conceiving, namely, the production of the higher animals, directly follows. There is grandeur in this view of life, with its several powers, having been originally breathed into a few forms or into one; and that, whilst this planet has gone cycling on according to the fixed law of gravity, from so simple a beginning endless forms most beautiful and most wonderful have been, and are being, evolved.'

—Charles Darwin, *The Origin of Species*

INTRODUCTION

I magine that the British Empire never fell.

The Great War never happened; Britain conquered all that stood in her way, destroying the rebellions of the Americas and the British Raj; the old hegemonies remained, untouched by the fire of revolution.

Now the Commonwealth flies the flag of the Empire, many of its colonies stripped bare in the name of British interests. The world clashes with guns, germs and steel. On the surface, the dreadnoughts known as the Tin Soldiers march on all who stand in Her Majesty's path; while in the skies, the Angels Interitus orbit the Earth, ready to wipe out entire cities at a moment's notice with their tungsten bombs.

Who dares resist? To the Far East, the Second Song Emperor rules China, and meditates upon an electronic empire built behind the Bamboo Curtain. To the West, the French and the Ottomans bicker after the failing of their great alliance; German knights prowl the borders of their Empire, fearful of the advances of Catherine IV and her Russian nobles. In dark corners, scientists, especially of the Russo-Nipponese alliance, still dream of a worldwide network uniting all nations, but the Vatican disapproves of this heresy; from Rome, the Babel Machine computes the algorithm known as the Echo of God, endlessly reconstructing and flooding the airwaves with background radiation of the Beginning of the Universe.

In the middle of this grand and great drama, a little island called Ceylon floats in the waters of the Indian Ocean. Seen from above, it is just a grey-green dot; a speck sheltered in the watery shadow of great India. If it lusts for empire, it is only in the dreams of what few monks committed their scrolls to memory when the British destroyed their temples.

A handful of lights glitter on Ceylon's otherwise blank skin.

Look at those lights, now. Most of them are Kandy, the old, overpopulated hill capital in the heart of the country. Very few other cities exist – a state maintained, partly by wit, partly by incompetence, with the net effect of preventing the natives from gathering, from rebuilding their art and thought, from forming too complex an economy to govern. Yarl, that first bastion of resistance, has been obliterated; Colombo, the seaside market city, crushed in the tug-of-war between Britain and China, before the peace treaties were signed.

In the books of those who rule this realm, Ceylon is part fortress, part factory, part abandoned green, part trade hub. From China come robotics, rice, tea, synthsilks, construction technology. From the British Raj come education, silver, medicines, drugs to increase lifespans, surgeries to change the shape and function of the human body and the famous network of banks and insurance underwriters that form the beating heart of capitalist-colonialism. They slip through Ceylon's grasping hands and leave laughing. Who cares if the locals are happy? The British Empire is content, and there is peace. A country is a small price to pay for the New Silk Road.

But Ceylon is far from peaceful. If the invader had actually learned the history of the place they trod on – if they had actually paid attention to those monks with their endless tales and parables, instead of just turning them into fodder for Kipling's tales – they would have learned of the slow political poison that grew in this country. They would have understood how every single attempt to unite this land under a single coherent government had been met with abject failure; they would have seen the rot that crept in, the dynasties that rose, again and again, first to cripple, then to supplant, sowing graft and servitude in lieu of law and order; they would known that emperors and kings and governors alike were doomed to this great head-first tilt into chaos.

And so it is now. It is 2024. The British think they have a government in place. The people who live here know that the British control the courts, and perhaps the military; certainly not the police, not anymore. Five families have ruled this misaligned roost for at least a generation now.

Take, for instance, House Bandaranaike, the largest and richest of the lot. A tidy little coalition of fathers, sons, uncles, mothers, aunts, nephews and nieces that went to the most elite Kandyan schools and promptly became directors of some state-owned operation or the other. Interests: minerals, ores, weapons. Behind every grain of titanium sand and every ton of graphite is a Bandaranaike. Punish one, reprimand a couple, and the island's electricity workers would immediately go on strike, the thorium miners would announce fasts unto death and armed mobs would suddenly appear.

Or take Molligoda. The Molligodas command all the armed forces the British are too busy to administer, especially in the unruly South; and only a very good accountant, able to freeze the entire island, and study all the motions thus suspended, could have calculated just how many men and guns that actually meant. Ever so often violence would break out between the Bandaranaikes and the Molligodas – sometimes a duel with swords, sometimes a lover spurned – but by and large these things were settled under the justice of the Maha Sangha, and not the sweating judges the British sent to watch over this far colony.

And what of the monks themselves? The Sangha, who have always written themselves into history, are no less powerful a government; their words hold where law will not; their messages carry where official channels fail; they represent, though unelected, and choose who falls and fails.

This is not immediately apparent to the very tall, very thin man who has just appeared on the rooftop of what appears to be a construction site. The sun has already brought a rosy glow to his candlewax face, and in a few moments, will begin roasting it. The dirigible that brought him here is a thin, hungry-looking affair, with the words HMS CARADOC painted across its bow. It signals to him, rises, and is lost to the sky. Only the pale man remains, surrounded by concrete dust and scaffolding.

Presently another man, perspiring slightly, makes his way through a maze of stairwells and to this top floor. This second man is bald and built like a tank; only good tailoring, it seems, prevents him from spilling out of his suit like a mound of flesh. In one hand, he carries a silver-tipped cane.

'Ah, there you are. Edgar Drake the Second,' says the mound, sticking out a hand. 'A pleasure to meet you, Penhaligon. We've heard great things about you. Sorry about the delay, I had to sort out a meeting with a roboticist. You know how they are – love to hear themselves talk.'

'The pleasure is all mine, I assure you,' says Nigel Penhaligon. The proffered hand is clammy and uncomfortable to the touch. 'There are roboticists here?'

'One,' says Drake. 'Well, you know how it is. Not officially. Local chap, not with the Royal Society. Bit ... unorthodox, shall we say, but between you and me, half the units we shipped out to Kashmir (he pronounced it "Cash-mee-yur") all came from his lab here. Decent stuff. Decent stuff.'

'You're not the real Drake, are you? You'd be much older.'

'As I said, the second. I'm afraid my original is, indeed, much older. And possibly in better shape.' His large hand gestures at the city around them. 'You could say Colombo and I have that in common.'

Nigel Penhaligon looks out over the ruins that lie strewn about, as if God Himself has reached over and tossed His toys about, and seems to struggle with himself. He settles for a very mild, 'Half this city seems to be missing.'

'A bit more than that, I'd say,' says Drake. 'Look over there.'

To the West, in front of the setting sun, looms something that looks like an eggshell making a passable attempt at imitating the Moon. Even at a distance, it is taller than anything else in the city; it sits utterly still, dominating the horizon. The sea churns and froths around it. Workers swarm over its pockmarked hide. Occasionally, something glows from within. In front of it is something that could have once been a beach, but is now a jagged expanse of blackened and fused glass. Behind it, keeping careful distance, is a fleet of black ships.

'That's one of their port cities, isn't it?'

'Smashed right into the harbour here,' says Drake. His fat fingers sketch over concrete dust and steel, spilled across the roads and ruins like snow, and into melted-looking rubble beyond. 'New breach weapon ... they call it the Divine Wind or something. We've seen this on the Nepal border, but never mounted on a sea vessel before. Troops landed, went straight in. South – we think they had another landing planned; there's another port there – and east to the perimeter, and the rest straight into the governor's residence. Local forces didn't stand a chance. Mostly normal troops and Tin Soldiers,' he says to

Penhaligon's raised eyebrow. 'It took maybe a day to take the entire city.'

'That doesn't account for all the damage.'

'Well,' says Drake, and for the first time his gravelly voice loses some of its bluster, 'that was us, I'm afraid. Angelstrike.'

They both look up, as if they could see with their own eyes the satellite that brooded on the other side of the blue sky.

'You fired an Angels Interitus,' Penhaligon's tone is flat, 'on a civilian city.'

'Spare the rod and spoil the child, Penhaligon. You know how it is. We can't allow Her Majesty to look soft, can we? One solid blow wiped out all those Chinese Marines and their tanks and set that bloody thing on fire, and everybody wants to talk civilized again.'

'A full Angelstrike.'

'Yes, yes. Cost of doing business, I'm afraid. Anyway, the Chinese backed off, everyone shook hands, we've all agreed to put this misunderstanding behind us and get on with it. As of two days ago, everything's signed and ready. You, sir, shall be the one to get on with it. You can thank me for dealing with the mess.' He waves his hand at the horizon. 'Come on, we'll do fine. The country has two more harbours.'

Nigel Penhaligon, Knight Grand Cross of the Most Honourable Order of the Bath, does not move, but stares at the ashes of Colombo, once the commercial capital of this little colony.

'Don't worry, we've already moved the orphans and the trade routes into Kandy,' says Drake impatiently, as if offering a conciliatory prize. 'That's the other city, up there in the hills, you know – bloody annoying to get to, but it seems like we'll be operating from there from now on. Come on, let me tell you about the tea here. We're having some problems with the topsoil ...'

Many years later, a girl arrives in a crate. Or at least, she looks like a girl. Only when the moon peers out from behind the clouds can you see the glint of metal bones, and the rags wrapped around them in a crude approximation of skin.

The light falls on her face – a cracked visage where the synth-skin has peeled away, revealing the ceramic plates underneath. But her mouth looks new, as if someone has lovingly pasted new skin there, stretching it over the gleam of clean white ceramic and fresh steel. One of her arms is broken – a reject welded on casually, perhaps the last of a rush order.

It is April, the cruellest month, breeding not lilacs out of this dead land, but thorns and weeds. No spring rain for this country – not this close to the Equator – but memory and desire mix well enough even under the scorching Ceylonese sun.

The guards shepherding her are tense, and their movements practiced. They're not quite sure why they have to deal with this last-minute addition – it was dangerously close to T-zero, or Activation Time. Silently, they trudge past the decrepit shells of dead buildings and the bodies carefully parked there – little human dolls with ticking counters inside their minds; eyes open but unseeing.

They take her, purely by coincidence, to where Nigel Penhaligon once stood. The crate is cracked open, the girl carefully prised out. Automated standby systems keep her upright, sleepwalking to a halt on the ghost of Penhaligon's footsteps. The fingers on her good hand are pried open, a makeshift spear stuffed into her fist. Instruments are checked, a thumbs-up given, and the guards fade into the twilight, not wanting to be anywhere near an activated bot.

A counter ticks. The sun crawls hesitantly up the sky, turning it blue first, then pink, then swift gold. Tick, tock, tick, tock, and as the light touches her, she begins to wake up. She chatters to herself, low and musical, turning the spear this way and that. Something startles her from across the street; frowning, she balances herself, with her bad arm stretched out and back, and with one smooth motion tosses the spear at a little warehouse on the other side.

Several somethings – very much like her, but male – catch the spear, chatter back, turn it this way and that and begin studying it. Then, as if by silent consensus, they split off, running on swift metallic feet through the bones of a broken city, hunting for more things to make spears with.

The girl sits back on her haunches, watching them go. Outside, the sound of pianos begins drifting through the dull air: Chopin's Piano Sonata No. 2 in B flat Minor, Op. 35, the 3rd Movement, a dirge that spoke of dust and ashes and loneliness.

Things are about to change.

I: Connection

ONE

In the city responsible for all those glittering lights, a messenger took a turn at a little over sixty kilometers an hour. Ordinarily, given the topography of Kandy and its roads, this should have resulted in him falling to his death and bouncing off several curving roads on the way down, but the messenger in question was from the Ministry of Reconciliation, and the Ministry chose only the best riders for this kind of work.

His motorcycle, a Royal Enfield Bullet-E, skidded just enough to put the fear of several gods into him, but kept going, cutting through the crickety stillness of the Kandy night. He rode past rings of houses that grew progressively shorter and wider – land was a luxury, and the more you could build horizontally, the better off you were – and stopped at a lane where they were just two storeys tall and the owners rich enough to have actual courtyards in between.

One of these houses belong to Kushlani de Almeida, PhD. It was the only house in the lane with its lights still on. It was six months after the October Massacre; many years before Kushlani would fight the combined political might of Kandy's old Houses in a court case and lose, and so commit the act of desperation that would see her die in a pool of her own blood, with a bullet in her belly. Her hair was still black and her face had yet to take on that expression she became famous for in her later years; the one that made people feel as if something immensely old and incredibly furious had picked them up and pinned them like butterflies to a corkboard.

She was, in short, still Assistant Two on the payroll, Assistant One in theory, and had just moved out here, very much against her parents' wishes.

If asked why she was up, she would have responded first with the automatic complaint of all Kandyans – the nights were getting warmer, even in Kandy; this was absolutely unheard of; it was those bloody idiots and their plantations and factories, turning the topsoil to desert and the clouds into smog.

But it was not just the heat that kept her awake. For months now, the October Massacre had played in her mind.

In hindsight, it felt like the plot of a bad science-fiction novel. The Colombo Entertainment Zone, the ultimate in post-apocalyptic, high-stakes television, a city-sized set for killing machines. Aritha Bandaranaike, gormless villain #1 and playboy aristocrat, deciding that the Conductor robots that prevented all hell from breaking out were better used as a party prop. The Explorer, the chief antagonist; a bot designed to test the boundaries of the Zone, the situation, to discover and exploit weak spots, largely as a diagnostic tool, arriving at exactly the right time to exploit this loss. The train to Kandy, which *had* to be on a supply run at just that time.

Bystanders #12–13, innocent people, on the way back from the Wednesday market, their bags stuffed with whatever pola vegetables didn't look too diseased, suddenly finding themselves on the receiving end of all the violence they usually only saw on their televisions. And Kushlani de Almeida, #1 protagonist, forced to dissect something that, for all her time in robots, had made her actually think about the lives of the things they made and destroyed in the name of profitable entertainment. All this chaos, lining up perfectly.

Karma, her father had said. *Karma,* as if that explained the madness, as if it was a story written out in advance, with everyone playing roles proportionate to their sins. Kushlani had long stopped believing in karma. There was no order to history; only moments of order interspersed with chaos, and people trying to make sense of it afterward.

But the dreams remained.

At first it had been just the panic of knowing that something had gone wrong, that bots meant to stay in Colombo had escaped, and they were coming here, heading to Kandy. Then the dream had changed. First to sitting in front of her parents' old television, watching the news – three dead, twelve injured. The memory of monks ranting about robotics and karma.

But as of late it had changed again. The dream now began with the last act of that tragic drama; the memory of cutting into that little girl's body, slashing away the steel and the wires and the clever cabling underneath the fake skin. In real life, she had performed the autopsy with flawless precision, falsified the report just enough to let everyone keep their jobs, and moved on. In the dream, however, instead of the precise cuts with the 1-2 scalpel, she slashed into the body with a knife, an ugly and rusted thing, and the body screamed and twitched and bled, and the head, separated from the corpse, whispered *can speak, can speak, can speak,* and opened its mouth in a rictus of terror.

Kushlani de Almeida was not a superstitious person, a fact that her family often deplored. But as of late she had taken her father's advise and wore a *panchayudhaya*. The little golden disc, worn around her neck, held tiny avatars of the traditional bow and arrow, sword, trident, conch and disc. And because she was practical, it also had the decidedly nontraditional radio ID chip that signed her in and out of the office. And here she was, unable to sleep, turning that little golden disc over and over in her hand.

She heard the gutter whine of the bike before the lights washed over her windows. There was that initial moment of panic – it was, after all, quite late – but she recognized the voice at the gate, so she made her way downstairs and opened the door.

Sure enough, it was Jagath.

'Miss,' he said, holding out a little voice recorder. She played it.

'We've got trouble on the project,' said Hewage's voice in the hot night. 'Come. Immediately.'

≈

Thirty minutes later the sun crept over the grey hills, cutting into the sweltering heat with lances of red and gold. It had done so long before humans came and claimed these hills as theirs and set up temples, and by now had gotten into the habit of things. The sacred city of Kandy, having sat still in its own shadow for almost a thousand years, had also gotten used to the sight.

The Ministry of Reconciliation, arguably the worst-named government body to ever exist, hummed with activity. Beyond the initial warren of buildings, the Watchtower, the ever vigilant seat of the entire bot operation, stretched giant solar cells, unfolding them lotus-like to catch the sun.

Jagath's bike crawled up to the gate and whined in. Kushlani de Almeida, having gotten off a little before, followed a few minutes behind; her parents would have a had heart attack if she was seen on the back of a bike. The guards waved her onto the path that led to the Watchtower.

Two more gates followed; then, in front of the surprisingly normal-looking entrance to the Watchtower, was a game attempt at plastic grass, one of Hewage's endless attempts at sprucing the place up. She kicked them aside and strode in. They had meant to have the entrance tarmacked, but with one thing and another, and government budget being spent on frivolities, it had never happened.

The production lab was running. An endless stream of body parts, shaped like children's limbs, clattered past her on the conveyor belt. Bay 17 – where the editors and sound mixers lived – was lit up. A few dozen interns – gangly, overexcited graduates lured from the nearby University of Peradeniya by the promise of a government pension – floated between offices, flocking around researchers like the glorified carrier pigeons that they were. It was all rather ...

Normal.

That surprised her.

The carpet led her to the glass elevator and upwards to the very top, to Hewage's dominion: the dome-like command and control centre from which every inch of the Watchtower's workings could be operated. Within, the stench of smoke and ash hanging like a stale toxin, and at the centre of it, Hewage – a thin, grey-haired man in the black and white of a government servant. Next to him, on the one empty tabletop, a mug full of coffee dust and cigarette butts.

She had never really probed into how Hewage got his position there. To run the entire Watchtower, to sit there with his cigarette and his crumpled shirt and bark out orders and have a hundred men and women jump to do his bidding in their crisp shirts and white sarees. It was the kind of position you got only if your family was, as everyone said, 'connected'. But Don Hewage had no friends, and the only family he had was dirt poor and in crippling debt. He had an engineering degree and a stint at the University, and then red lines on his record – that would be the Peradeniya insurrection. Nobody knew him outside the Ministry of Reconciliation. He even had that scar of a name: Don Hewage. No ancestral names, no lineage to declare his place in society – just the accusation of having bent over to the Portuguese, most likely because he was from a poor family that had taken money in exchange for their dignity. But somehow he had wrangled himself in here – a roboticist in this highest of offices, to head the single largest source of pure profit for the government.

One of life's mysteries.

The lab doors opened. The familiar dome beyond, banks of outdated computers lit up, an image across their screens: a child, or something that looked like a child, bathed in oil and dust, standing on a field of bloodless corpses. The king of a dead hill. The killcam broadcast swerved into its face, marking the tribes, the flayed skin, the metal beneath and its mouth open in a triumphant scream. Viewership counts: Ceylon, India, Australia, Malaya, Maldives. All the colonies south of the white noise broadcast by the Vatican's stupid Babel Machine. The ultimate daytime show.

'Everything's normal,' she said by way of complaint.

Hewage blinked owlishly at her. 'No need to start a panic, neh?' he said. 'Tea?'

It was odd not having One here. The guy was an inbred idiot, but he made good tea with just the right amount of milk and sugar and a dash of ginger, something he'd picked up on a work rotation at the Hambantota harbour. So instead, she sat down and watched Hewage potter about with his stooped shoulders.

Eventually, he handed her a piece of paper. Old school, that was Hewage. Wasting trees.

Hewage, it began.

I'll get to the point. I'm not happy with the new developments on your side of the pond. I've been seeing scattered reports in the Ceylonese media about some robots from the Crofton–Kandy entertainment complex being used in a private show of some sort by some Bandaranaike toff. Then I have Sir Nigel Penhaligon claiming that your bots are glitching and heading up to Kandy to slaughter innocent people in the streets.

Where do I start? This is a clusterfuck, as the Americans say, and you, my good man, are up front and centre. Bots being used for private entertainment – which idiot authorized that? Those bots are the property of the Crofton Institute, and Lady Crofton is a very influential member of Parliament – NOT to be trifled with.

But far more worrying is this business of a technical glitch. There should be NO technical glitches anywhere. Not on the bots, not on the broadcast, not on the reporting and certainly not on containment. That was our arrangement with you.

I don't want excuses. We are dispatching two people to sort this out once and for all. One will evaluate all the software and hardware running on those things. The other will exterminate any aberrations.

Assign your best and brightest to assist the evaluator. The exterminator will sort out his arrangement with Sir Penhaligon and the Inquisition.

No tricks. If you try what you did in Singapore, I'll have you transferred to the bottom of the ocean with concrete shoes. I expect this to be completely sorted out and forgotten in six months.

Regards,
Edgar Drake III
Permanent Undersecretary of State for Foreign Affairs

'Fuck,' she said.

There were several things that deserved the curse.

Hewage dumped a mug in front of her and started pacing about. 'The Bandaranaikes are going to suffer,' he said. 'Drake's ordered all of Aritha Bandaranaike's land to be turned over to the Crown. He's the heir immediate, so House Bandaranaike loses half of everything they have. That House is being decimated. Rambukpotha and Madugalle are over the moon."

'When?'

'Yesterday.'

Such great shifts meant periods of intense and ugly change. They would see the changes soon: ministry boards being reshuffled, public-private enterprises suddenly restructured, mass firings, anyone even remotely related to the Bandaranaikes being swapped out for whoever from the other Houses could sneak a foot through the door. She reached for the mug, troubled. The tea was surprisingly generous, heavy and sweet, almost like her mother's.

'What do we do?'

'Nobody's happy about it. Bandaranaikes in courts. Bandaranaikes sending petitions to the Queen. And bloody Aritha seems to have slept with the daughter of the Minister of Defense. Anything about him brings us up. Right now the biggest problem is that every time they call me up to explain, I have to tell them we can't really predict the bots, and that's what makes for good TV. Then they talk about putting up fences and getting the army to contain them, and then someone shows them a budget. There's a motion circulating in the governor's office saying we're a danger to the whole country. Report from a Lieutenant

Kanishka, same bastard who's been handling coordination down there. Whole laundry list of manure: iterations get more dangerous, complex battle formations, all that bullshit. And a counter-motion saying if they shut us down, the government loses so much bloody international tax money that they'll be running back to the Crown, hat in hand—'

'Hewage?'

'Yes?'

'What do we do? And why the hell is Edgar Drake involved?'

Hewage stopped pacing. 'We do as Drake says,' he said. 'You're the liaison to the evaluator. Give them access. Let them do their crap', he waved a hand, 'And roll back changes when they're done.'

'Hewage.'

'Yes?'

'We just finished putting them back together.'

He gave her a look and lit his cigarette. Blue smoke puffed out, filling the air. 'So?'

These last six months, whenever the autopsy of that girl-bot came up, she would try explaining things to Hewage.

'She felt alive,' Kushlani had said, over and over again. 'Imagine being born in an urban warzone, having to fight every day of your life. Imagine what you would grow up to be. You would be violent. You would be savage. But you would still be human, wouldn't you? You would still be brave and afraid and sometimes cruel and sometimes kind and sometimes just tired. And he had said, "Wipe her."'

He read her. That was Hewage, all over again. 'You repaired the girl,' he said. 'Wiped her memories, reset her to factory defaults?'

'Yes.'

'Same difference, at the end of the day.'

'Hewage?'

'Yes?'

'Why is Edgar Drake involved in this? What did you do in Singapore? And why did you call me up? What do I do?'

He didn't smile; not quite. But there was a twitch; not the kind that was amused, but the kind that suddenly made him seem older, crueller and a lot less like the absent-minded manager she knew.

'We're out of milk powder,' he said. 'Run down to the shop and get us some, will you?'

TWO

How does one describe British India? A vast explosion of people, and colour, and the smell and texture of a billion bodies and minds toiling. A subcontinent reduced to being a province, thanks to the guns that spat remorseless pieces of metal, time and time again, into brown and white bodies alike. Picture empires and billions soldered into a slave-nation that rules half the world in trade and arms.

And in this madness was Goa, a city-state once created by the Hindu sage Parashruma, then remade by the Portugeuse captain Alfonso de Alberquerque, and then ground down and recast again when the Portuguese handed it over to the British as a gesture of desperate friendship during the Napoleanic Wars. And over the military constraints of its design, Goa layered its many addictions: its bazaars, its beaches. In Goa the sheer chaos of India met the pomp and infinite rulesets of British governance, and, over decades, bowled it over, knifed it in a dark alley and tossed its dead body into the sea. This was the only place in the world where the tourists were more local than the locals. And in this dry heat stood the Goa Mathematical and Military University.

'What is it that separates mankind from the animals?' said the man at the pulpit.

It was cold in those dark halls. Despite the heat outside, the students huddled, wrapped in their warmest, surrounded by the old stone of the lecture room. The wooden door that lay between them and freedom bore a sign that said Psychohistory.

The man the door belonged to looked like the word itself. He was young and old at the same time, like a philosopher hitting middle age. He had a salt-and-pepper beard and crow's feet around the eyes; but the eyes themselves were bright, and alert, and sharp, and somehow *hungry*. It was he who decreed both the temperature and the syllabus in these halls.

'Anyone?' he tried. This was a question he always asked in his class; it was useful to gauge how good a particular batch was, and how open they were to having their beliefs broken down and substituted with knowledge.

A few hands went up. 'Intelligence,' said one of the furry creatures.

'Dreams.'

'Religion.'

'Genocide?' tried a fourth.

'Good, but not quite there,' said the professor. 'Intelligence, not really. We know we're probably the most intelligent on Earth, but the margins are actually pretty small. Apes are intelligent. We've seen how they can easily learn languages and complex symbols. Whales have their own language ... dolphins ... cats ... and octopuses, if we understand them properly, are intelligent tool-users.

'What of dreams? Animals dream. Genocide ... yes, we've observed plenty of instances among our close genetic neighbors, such as chimpanzees, where one tribe will wipe out another, so the only difference is that we have larger tribes to do this with. Religion ... interesting hypothesis, Miss Watson, but I submit to you that religion is a by-product of the real reason.

'And the real reason, ladies and gentlemen, is ... extelligence.' He wrote that word with a flourish on the wallscreen behind him. It had a neon glow in the amber light. 'Extelligence. We have the ability to record, preserve and share our thoughts, our dreams, our religious convictions, our plans for what to do to that nasty sabretooth cat that keeps prowling around the cave ... extelligence. A body of knowledge that often outlives us. We experiment with the world around us and transmit what we know through books, videos, culture, religion, so that the next generation can stand on the shoulders of that knowledge and do even greater things. Our holy books, written thousands of years ago, laid out tried and tested standards of behaviour so that we won't have to start from scratch. Our engineering manuals describe engines, electricity, mechanics, so that anyone around the world can learn engineering without having to rediscover the wheel. We are basically the sum of our intelligence plus our ancestors' knowledge.

'In this way, we evolve faster than our genetics would otherwise indicate. The real difference between us and the monkeys, people, is that if a monkey discovers gravity, it has no way of making sure that knowledge outlives it. Every octopus, born alone on the seabed, must learn from scratch what its predators are and how to make those little shell-like structures they live in. We, on the other hand, have Newton's books and colleges and old wives' tales to tell us about the world. So when studying the world around us, when trying to predict how countries and cultures will behave, we have to remember that our individual intelligence does not matter. What we have to study is the several thousand years of extelligence that a culture has built up. Right there is the key to our future.'

This earned the customary impressed nods from the audience. He always enjoyed this part. A bit of theater to get them in the mood before the coursework piled up.

'So we're going to start by looking at and predicting some limited and fictional cultures before we head into the complexities of the real thing,' he said, warming up. 'Download the excerpts from and—'

There was a knock on the door.

'Come in,' he said, irritated.

There was a creak from the wooden door and the Dean poked his head in. 'Am I interrupting?'

Well, obviously, you idiot, but I can't tell you that because you're the Dean. 'Not at all. What can we do for you, sir?'

'There's someone waiting for you,' said the Dean enigmatically.

'Alright, carry on with the Foundation excerpts,' he said to the students, and followed the Dean out. 'What's this about, Henry?'

There was a strange white man there. He was bald and built like a tank, and in one hand he carried a silver-tipped cane. 'Edgar Drake the Third, Foreign and Commonwealth Office,' he said, sticking out a hand. 'A pleasure to meet you, Professor Bengali. That's an odd surname, isn't it? Bengali?'

'Not at all, I assure you,' said Jacob Bengali, feeling a slight chill. The proffered hand was clammy and uncomfortable to the touch. 'My family's from Calcutta. You're not the real Drake, are you? You'd be much older.'

Drake smiled. 'As I said, the Third. I'm afraid my original is, indeed, much older. And possibly in better shape.'

'What can I do for the Foreign Office?'

'There's a small situation we need some advice on, Professor,' said Edgar Drake, holding out a document. Jacob took it. At his touch, the paper transformed itself from a blank sheet into an ornate invitation. 'We'd like to invite you for tea at my office on Thursday.'

'Has the Office run out of psychohistorians?'

'They all pointed me to you, Professor,' said Drake. 'Something to the effect of your theories laying the foundations of their work, so I thought I'd save us a lot of time and come straight to the source. I'm authorized to tell you that there will be an offer made to you tomorrow, and should you accept and turn out successful, you might be making enough to retire in comfort the moment you return. You might even have an entire field to write about – I'm sure none of your colleagues have as yet been involved in mechanical warfare. Should you excel, tenure and your own department at any college of your choosing could be arranged. The Crown is never ungrateful.'

Bengali saw the Dean's face turn into a comical mask of surprise. He kept his own very still. The Office often recruited civilians, but not for such reasons.

'Let me guess,' he said. 'You came to me, a non-specialist. Which means your other practicing psychohistorians are either incompetent, too specialized or employed elsewhere. You could have run short of practitioners, but that's unlikely.'

'True.'

He cycled through the names and places he knew. Psychohistorians were ferociously protective of their domains; he would have heard some noise if so much as a consultation was happening on someone else's turf. 'Not the Russian or German fronts; you've got Canard and Walker there. Can't be the American colonies, or the Spanish, or the Portuguese ... there's du Marek and three others in the Royal Society for that. This can't be China or India. What is it? Something new?'

Drake smirked, as if satisfied. 'Close, but no cigar, as our American cousins say,' he said mysteriously. 'We do need your expertise, however, and it *is* a place untouched by your colleagues. We're ... ah, hoping that your Indian connection might serve a purpose. I'll see you on Thursday.'

Bengali watched him go, curious. 'Strange man,' he said to the Dean. 'How do you know him?'

'Sometimes, a man needs friends in low places,' said the Dean. 'Bengali?'

'Yes?'

'You can do whatever you want with this chance,' said the Dean. 'In fact, I'd advise you to take it. Get out of the classroom a bit, do some new research, publish something new for God's sake, before you're buried under people doing all the fancy footwork with your theories. But be very, very careful what you say to a Drake.' He leaned closer, and whispered, 'Don't behave as though you're their equal.'

That evening, Jacob Bengali sat awake, reading the letter over and over again. He looked around his little apartment. Shelves of books lined every wall – actual paper, heavy books with titles like *China and Hong Kong: Predictions for 2054* or *Indian Wartime Simulations*. All of them written by fellow psychohistorians – some of them former students – who had greedily gobbled up bits and pieces of his work and applied them to countries that could make their name. They added a weight to the darkness that had little to do with their actual size on the shelves.

He had a love-hate relationship with his field. It was their lot to live at the very edges of history, economics, sociology and mathematics, and more often than not the work they did was more science fiction than actual predictions. They oversimplified complex systems, fell in love with their own narratives and waved away the truth with wordplay. A lot of the books on his wall did exactly this. There were very few he could take down and be satisfied with.

Be rigorous, he'd tell his students over and over. Question the stories you weave out of the data. Remember that we often get it wrong.

And yet, they were fortune-tellers, prophets, all these men and women on his wall. If they missed the mark of prediction, they generally missed it less than others; and to those who failed by a only small margin came all the spoils of the man who can tell a government, 'I told you something like this would happen.'

He could have shared the fame. He could have taken the lead, gone out on to the field and actually made some predictions instead of sitting around and thinking about those things in the abstract, waiting for a rigor that would never exist in the subject. He was just a citation at the back of these books, earning nothing save a pittance at the university.

There was a time, he thought ... fresh out of school, top marks. Pride of the Goa Mathematical and Military University – the first real roboticist India had cranked out. He had written his thesis on the machines from the Russian and German fronts. Walker, who had designed said machines, read his work and wrote to the Royal Society, praising this promising young Da Vinci.

He had been particularly blunt: *I consider it a mere accident of birth that Bengali was born Indian rather than British; surely it falls to us to correct God's error in this matter.*

Bengali still had Walker's letter. He had pictured himself, like Shelley's Frankenstein (but not as timid, no!), standing back from a sparking bench and screaming out his triumph to the world.

But no. A recommendation like that could only get you so far. Sooner or later, it would come down to you standing in the London cold with the Secretary of the Royal Society of Roboticists giving you that brittle, condescending smile; that code for 'You're a little too dark for this, son, but I'm not supposed to say it, so could you finish your tea and get out of my office and shut the door behind you? There's a good lad.'

So he had taken the next thing that came along: the University. A career built on doing the teaching that

Canard, Walker, du Marek, Trembliss were too important to do.

He flipped the invitation over and over and over in his hands, watching the message flow smoothly to keep itself pointed at him. *Dr. Bengali,* it said. *Ceylon. Will you accept?*

But there was something that needed checking up on first.

≈

It was impossibly hot outside. Bengali, having carefully locked his door, checked himself – spectacles, testicles, wallet – all there – and walked through the thronged roads, inhaling both the sea breeze and the slight smell of rubbish that came with it, his white shirt sticking to his skin. Buildings melted before him, the strange Goa air turning them all into one looming Indian-Portuguese-British protobuilding that lined every road and sidewalk, and blocked out the trees that lay beyond. Every so often, a glass spire rose, skirted in sloped roofs.

The human tide pushed him and he pushed back, making his way to the nondescript building that housed the local chapter of the general staff of the Indian Army – specifically, the intelligence operations. Very few civilians were supposed to know where it was. Naturally, this meant everyone knew everything about it.

The C.O. looked up as he walked in. 'Ah, Dr. Bengali. Here, take that chair, go sit under the air conditioner.'

The air conditioner rattled and sang and cooled him. They waited a bit. This was India: everyone waited a bit. Finally, the C.O. looked at his hopeful face, and said as gently as he could, 'I'm afraid we've had to turn down your application again, Doctor.'

Bengali could feel his face sag. 'Who made the cut this time, sir?'

'Emerson. Good chap. Solid.'

But Emerson was terrible at his job. He knew it. The C.O. knew it. The only qualification he had was that he had been born to the right people, in the right country, with the one passport that trumped them all. Something small inside him broke.

'It's been three years.'

'There's concern about your expertise.'

'I speak four languages. I've literally written the bloody book on the subject. My PhD was at Oxford. And—'

The CO, who was British, but not an unkind man, listened gravely and let him run out of steam. 'Not my call, Doctor,' he said. 'But perhaps you can bulk your resume a bit. Make up for your—'

Nationality, went the unspoken word between them.

'There's a small assignment in Ceylon. Field op. Straight from Lord Drake. I recommended you to him. Won't hurt to get in with the right people, what?'

Bengali, crestfallen, looked down at his feet. Joining the general staff could have been his one way out, the one ticket to something more than just ... sitting there, writing theory, doing all the hard work and then having others steal his thunder.

He mumbled something and left the office with his fists clenched. His feet went on autopilot, taking him out of the office. Out into the madding crowd. Out, out, out, past the holograms of Christ and Vishnu, past the park, past the faces. His legs trod the known path back to the university and parked him in his office. The rest of the day went by in a blur; it was dark by the time he looked up from his papers.

He sent for the driver. 'Bar,' he said.

The driver, who everyone called Pindulu, looked at Bengali and sympathetically offered him a small half-bottle of arrack. Ceylonese stuff. Pindulu's beady eyes tracked his swig anxiously and looked relieved when he stopped at just two shots.

The alcohol was excellent. It dissolved into his bloodstream, setting off a dull, burning fire in his heart.

What was the point, he thought as Goa flashed by in silence, neon lights and holograms emerging from the dull white buildings. What was the point of being capable, of being educated, of publishing some of the greatest breakthroughs in the field, of never failing to salute the right way, when all it got you was this far, and no further? What was the point when some East London reject could waltz in and take your throne?

The cab veered off the main road and onto a side street by the beach, and Pindulu, bless his heart, let him have one more sip before he got out. The flag of the British Raj glittered in the night sky: the Union Jack and the Star of India in an ugly compromise. Underneath it, men and women partied, lit by neon, the dull thump of the beat creeping over his mind. Tourists swirled and laughed.

And thus it was that Jacob Bengali, bitter and disillusioned, decided to go to Ceylon.

THREE

In the films, of course, the hero, having decided his course of action, dashes off. One scene sees him pensive and brooding; the other sees him descending into a market several thousand miles away with a smile on his face and adventure in his eyes.

Real life required a lot more documentation.

Drake the Third, having taken it upon himself to occupy Bengali's office, began by handing him a stack of gazettes.

'I didn't think you'd use this much paper,' said Bengali.

'Bureaucracies are slow monsters, Dr. Bengali,' said Drake. 'Very few of these documents were ever digitized. Whiskey?'

'Not this early, thank you,' said Bengali politely. Drake seemed to inhabit the room in a way that he found profoundly intrusive. Perhaps it was the fact that Drake had clearly fiddled with everything, and to no apparent purpose. The coat-rack was in a slightly different place;

the chairs had been swapped; the little Ganesh figurine on the desk placed next to the computer terminal instead of on top of it. It made Bengali feel like an alien in his own domain.

He shuffled the papers over the desk and began to read. All were of Ceylonese origin. One, dated 2010, declared that the domains of the former city of Colombo were to be handed over to the Kandyan government. The next declared that the Kandyan government would partner with the Crofton Institute to form a new organization that would oversee the development of 'The Colombo Entertainment Zone', whatever that meant. The third shuffled this Crofton–Kandy instrument and its management under a large body called the Ministry of Reconciliation.

'Largely created to fund the local Inquisition and run re-education camps after the Yarl rebellion,' said Drake. 'Most of their job is to put down ethnic dissent.'

The fourth gave this supposed Ministry some very odd broadcast and licensing permissions.

Crofton. Anyone worth their salt knew that name. The Crofton Institute was a military-science kingdom masquerading as a corporation. Its labs took the cutting-edge work of the finest roboticists – people like Walker – and perverted and commodified the hell out of it. Specialized one-off regimental units became cheap cannon fodder unleashed in the Balkans. Minesweeper bots built in the Ottoman theatre turned into vacuum cleaner designs. Bengali had had no idea they worked in Ceylon, too. Odd.

Next came a series of financial statements from this Ministry of Reconciliation. Whatever this thing was, there was plenty of money in it – more than tea.

'What do you make of it?' asked Drake, peering at Bengali over a pair of gold spectacles.

Bengali puzzled over the documents. They appeared to be hastily assembled; a trail of political minutae that seemed at odds with the finances and the actual nature of the operation. He told Drake so.

'Good, at least you're paying attention,' said Drake. 'Ever heard of a chap called Don Hewage? Roboticist.'

'Hewage. Hewage. Wait. The self-learning machines guy? The crackpot?'

'Precisely. On paper, Dr. Bengali, the request is simple. After Colombo got the shit bombed out of it, Hewage got some funding from the Crofton Institute and started tinkering. Set up a gladiatorial show using some old commodity bot designs that nobody was really using. Turned that into a public entertainment spectacle; it's been running for a few years now under the government, and they make quite a bit of tax money from the broadcast. They're having some code issues. They want an expert to help redesign their software, make sure it measures up to the safety standards.

'The unofficial request is the kind that cannot be sent in writing. Hewage made a breakthrough. It was funded by us, through the Crofton Institute, with the highest levels of authorization. To see if we could train machines that can learn, adapt, fight under all circumstances, approximating human behaviour, especially for urban warfare scenarios.

A ruined city just so happens to be the perfect training ground for urban warfare.'

'I've never heard of this.'

'Your clearance has never been high enough for you to hear of it,' said Drake. 'Look at the screen. We've got some footage.'

A file. Locally stored from a SingNet location. Grainy footage of a group of young boys dressed in rags. They ran towards each other in what looked like a blasted and shelled out neighborhood, screaming. Many carried crude spears.

As Bengali watched, the boys impaled each other on the spears. No, not boys; now he could see the metal beneath. Transfixed, he watched them hack, stab and cut each other to pieces, often picking up whatever was around – rocks, fallen weapons, even their own severed limbs – to smash at each other.

'Studies conducted with terrorist groups showed that they were less likely to fire if they thought they were fighting children,' said Drake. 'Empathy. The human brain has too much of it sometimes. Turns out they were right. Hewage's operation has been broadcasting the training process this entire time. Turned it into reality TV. The income alone is enough to pay for the labs. Two birds, one stone. Bread and circuses in one go.'

There was a pregnant pause.

'Those were fully automated?' asked Bengali.

'Fully.'

'I've never seen machines move like that.'

'Even more progress has been made,' said Drake. 'Six months ago, two, just two of these bots broke out of the test environment in Colombo, made it all the way to the Ceylonese capital, navigating entirely on their own, and encountered humans. There were ... casualties. Twelve civilians, a small squad of Ceylonese soldiers killed. To those of us who set this experiment in motion, this is unexpected progress. To those on the receiving end, that is the locals, this is an unfavourable outcome, so they need reassurance. Experts were called in to make the right noises and write the right kinds of reports. The Ceylonese set great faith in foreign experts. Which, Doctor, is where I'd like you to come in.'

'I don't understand,' said Bengali. 'This has to be a trick. Some code hack.'

Drake ignored him. 'What I want you to do is simple. Forget the safety standards. I'd like you to evaluate their capabilities. Conduct for us an independent audit, if you would, benchmarked against our most public hardware on your Tibetian scenarios, set A through F. We understand they're considered the best in the field.'

'I'll need the source code, of course.'

'I'm afraid you'll have to obtain it yourself. Hewage is a bit of a tight bugger and isn't exactly communicative on this stuff. Our understanding is that he feels a bit stiffed by the Royal Society and is waiting to publish through Crofton, and make a name for himself there.'

I know how that feels, thought Bengali.

'Obviously, we want to see if this has military applications first, given that half the funding is ours,' Drake continued. 'You're the expert, of course, so I trust you'll be able to tell us what we've paid for. I'm sending one of my men to help you. I think you'll find him more than satisfactory.'

'This isn't exactly ethical, is it?'

Drake paused. 'War isn't ethical, Bengali. You think Walker became who he is by pondering the ethics of the machines he built? You think du Marek has clean hands?'

'Sir.'

'In an ideal world, men would treat each other with kindness, guns would be nothing more than forgotten doodles by mad inventors and we would all hold hands and live happily ever after. But we don't live in an ideal world, do we? This world works because violent people stand ready to deal death on those who would do our countrymen harm. Cigarette? I know you smoke.'

Bengali hesitated, then broke his tradition of not smoking in the office. 'And there's nobody else?'

'You happen to be the closest on this one and I'd rather not waste time,' said Drake. 'This is a real situation, Bengali. If this experiment works out, we're talking about a new age in warfare. Beyond the sawhorses and bloody bones jobs we've got right now. There's a limit to the human, and we mean to go beyond it. It's critical that Hewage be left alone to continue his work, but also critical that we get the current tech he's working with. You understand, of course.'

'No,' he said, thinking fast. *A way in.* 'I mean, yes. I'm in.'

'Good. You'll have help. Here.'

No paper this time, but a sleek datapad, completely unmarked. He thumbed it open. There were two names, highlighted: Eliott Grimme. A photo: a thin, pale man with feral, clearly artificial eyes dressed in military fatigues. Very little information. He'd never heard of Eliott Grimme, but then again he'd never heard of a lot of people that worked for the office. Perks of being on the outermost circles.

The next name was Don Hewage. Again, very little: a photo of a short, old man with graying hair and a severe expression, staring away from the camera, and a short code that identified him as the Director of the Colombo Entertainment Zone Project, Ministry of Reconciliation, Kandy.

'The only other set of documents you'll get is the official request put in by Ceylon,' said Drake. 'That'll happen ... whenever. Bureaucracy. It's not important.'

Bengali looked out of the window again. The reflection of his face stared back.

A lifetime of being Igor. But finally, a chance to be more.

'Why bloody not,' he said, almost to himself, and lit another cigarrete.

≈

Three days later, Jacob Bengali found himself on board an aircraft carrier headed for Ceylon. It was quite possibly the largest ship he had ever been on, one of such tremendous size that all merchant traffic ground to a halt and their captains signalled to each other in fear and doubt. It spat out a smaller craft, a military hydrofoil that whispered across at a deceptively brutal speed. Various harbour officers rushed to it as it drew closer, and were completely ignored by the faceless Indian sepoys that poured out. Unlike their commanding officers, they had not yet earned the privilege of taking off their masks. One or two wore turbans, but otherwise it was one stream of khaki fish that bore him down to the security terminals at the dock. He could see eyes widen as he went past, with people trying to figure out if he was some kind of international criminal. But which criminal warranted an entire aircraft carrier? Worse, was he some kind of VIP? Should they have paid more attention?

He merely smiled and nodded, enjoying the moment while it lasted. Of course they hadn't sent an aircraft carrier just to pick him up. This was a regular trick in Her Majesty's deck – randomly sending in the military to remind the colonies that she was there, she was watching, ready to protect the Empire from all threats, foreign and domestic. The carrier was probably one of those that haunted international waters between Australia and Ceylon, a constant reminder to the Chinese not to stretch their legs too far. A few drones circled idly overhead. A professor he had studied under had worked on the algorithms that made the drone fleets align, cohere and separate. He squinted. The name leaped into focus: HMS CARADOC.

As he drew close, he realized why the aircraft carrier hadn't drawn closer to the harbour: it was old, this thing, scarred and rusted forward and astern, a clear clone of the even more ancient Russian Sakharov-class. Perhaps it could be an air superiority vehicle, capable of launching a support fleet of surveillance/refueling blimps and fighter drones, but nothing that could rock up to a colony and threaten to blast it into submission. Easier to let people imagine the threat than manifest it.

The sepoys poked and prodded him into a dinghy, and from there to the ship itself. Bengali had hardly gotten used to the rocking before they pushed him up an automatic ladder onto the bow of the carrier. The rest was a blur. He watched a sky-camouflaged cargo zeppelin land with majestic pomp on the deck; it looked like a great carbon-fibre whale, the cross-like helicopter-swingarms looking like awkward bones sticking out of its belly. Sepoys loaded it. With what, he had no idea.

The crew patted him down. Your room key. Your bridge pass. Keep this on you at all times. Then he was shown to the coxswain: a fellow with a long, hooked nose and an exceptionally lean and powerful body fitted very neatly into the white uniform of the Royal Navy in the tropics. A mechanical hound, large and exquisitely worked, lounged near his feet. Junior officers swarmed like ants around him.

'Bengali,' said the coxswain, with genuine pleasure. A Bangalore accent, hidden beneath the carefully cultivated mid-Atlantic voice that many Indians adopted in the service. A rough and calloused hand shook his own. 'You're looking thinner, old chap.' The other hand came out with a datapad, field issue. 'I've been instructed to give you this.'

Bengali struggled to remember the last time he had seen this man. 'Yadav,' he recalled finally. 'Burma, wasn't it? I was on a training assignment.'

'But I didn't know you were in the university now,' said Yadav. 'And Ceylon next? Glamorous. So you finally got to travel without joining the forces, eh?'

Bengali shrugged modestly. 'I'm technically part of the Home Office.'

'Good, good. Always good to see one of us getting out there without having to scrub floors and wear stupid uniforms. Come, let's go introduce you to the captain.'

'I'd rather not trouble him, honestly—'

'No, come on, he gets bored down there.'

They fell into an easy rhythm, Yadav crossing the deck with an easy grace and Bengali following, thankful that the ship was big enough for him to keep in step without having to think twice about where he put his feet.

'I'm thinking of retiring to the Americas myself when my contract's up. Plenty of land in the Free States,' Yadav called over his shoulder. 'Watch the railing. You ever thought about it?'

He had. Several hundred times, in fact. But while the Americas might have had land, they already had their economists, mostly Austrian, and their roboticists, mostly home-grown, and thus their own ladders to climb. It was fine for Yadav, who being a Navy man could fit in almost anywhere, and had no aversion to hard labour. For Bengali, however, it would mean starting right at the bottom as a sub-sub assistant to some decrepit professor or military contractor, and the thought galled him.

The railings and decks gave way to closed corridors far away from the open air. Uniforms changed from the tropical whites to the ominous black of the Inquisition, and salutes to Yadav grew less frequent, replaced by nods and stares from visored helmets. A thump-thump-thump built up, slow at first, turning into a great metal heartbeat that shivered the walls around them; Bengali shuddered in sync.

At last they came to the brains of the ship; that great dome where once navigators would have stood and captains barked out orders from. Yadav keyed in a complex combination into a set of blast doors, and knocked gently on the final one.

'Come in,' said a rich baritone that echoed around them. The door unlocked itself with a series of ugly clanks.

If Bengali had to choose one word to describe the space inside, it would be 'captainly', almost to the point of it being a stereotype: a beautiful wooden cabin, lined with dark, polished wood, lit by inset lights on every surface; an exceptionally beautiful desk, which looked as if it could have been stolen from a university professor's study. A portrait of Tin Lizzie hung at the back, as well as an almost life-size rendition of the Queen back when she had fair hair and white skin; before she had gone under the knife and emerged with that sculpted metal face that so terrified both subject and enemy alike. A man sat in front of the portrait in a large swivel chair. He had grey hair, swept back, and a strong lined face with hints of a beard, and a crisp white uniform. He was smoking a pipe.

Then the hologram flickered and Bengali saw the room he was actually in: a nightmare of metal and screens and rubberised cabling. At the heart of it, crucified in a glowing tank, was the captain. His face a wasted white, the skin pierced and shredded by the control interfaces that plunged into it, and his eyes were open, blank and blind. In front of it, an Inquisitor, helmless: a pale face set with lenses, and more arms than Bengali wanted to see. No doubt tasked with maintaining its once-human kindred.

'Excuse the visuals,' came the voice again. 'It's been a while since we maintained our more trivial systems.' The wooden floors reappeared and the man in the captain's uniform swiveled, smiling, instead of the dead thing in the tank. The Inquisitor became the table.

'Sir,' said Bengali awkwardly.

'We met Dr. Bengali in Burma, sir,' prompted Yadav.

The man in the chair blinked and smiled. 'Aye, the roboticist. We were having a spot of trouble with the Shan. Tough chaps.'

'Tough, sir,' echoed Yadav.

'Will you sit down?'

Bengali sat. The chair felt reassuringly real. 'You can call me the Caradoc,' said the captain. 'I'd give you my Christian name, of course, but that doesn't matter, does it?'

'No, sir,' said Bengali. Captains were bonded to their ships for life, and very rarely moved.

'You're excused, Mr. Yadav.'

'Sir,' said Yadav, who saluted and was then gone. The hologram captain leaned back in his chair.

The Caradoc sighed and leaned back.

'I take it you're one of Drake's men,' said that rich voice.

'I work for him, yes.'

A cigar appeared, lit, and Bengali watched, fascinated, as the hologram took several puffs from it.

'I have an old friend in Ceylon. Nigel Penhaligon. Ever heard of him?'

'No, sir.'

'He runs the Inquisition there. You'll make his acquaintance, no doubt.'

'Oh.'

'He told me about an experiment in Ceylon. Training little machines of war, eh? No doubt that's what you're there for.'

'I've been asked to do some design work, yes, sir. Mostly safety features.'

'And you believe a machine will take the place of a human brain and a human heart?'

Not really, no. 'Well ... I have my doubts, sir.'

'Children,' hissed the Caradoc, the beautifully textured voice giving way to a harsh metallic growl. 'Those bastards designed them to look and act like children.'

The hologram flickered again. Metal paneling replaced the illusion of wood, and Bengali was left staring at the wasted figure in the tank, its hands splayed as if to reach him and dead eyes open and staring. The wires trailing from its back and sides twitched, as if caught in the grip of a powerful emotion.

'Yes, flinch, stare, grovel,' it said. 'You see us as abominations, but we made sacrifices for honour, Dr. Bengali, for the Queen and for the country. Drake and his goons would see us all replaced by these mockeries, these toy soldiers.'

Bengali gulped. Something seemed to be expected of him. 'I've just been asked to make them safer, sir,' he said. 'I'm completely on your side, sir.'

'Make them safer, you say,' said the Caradoc.

'That was the request.'

The wires twitched again. 'Drake hasn't trained you very well,' said the Caradoc. 'Never try to lie to one of us, Dr. Bengali. You baselines just aren't built for it.'

'I'm just a consultant with the office, sir. You should really take this up with Mr. Drake—'

The Caradoc sneered. 'Just a consultant,' it said. 'Of course. Well, Dr. Bengali, go with God, and do whatever it is your superiors told you to do. I'll make my displeasure known to those authorized to receive it.'

≈

That night, Bengali tossed and turned in his bunk. The data pad glowed in his face; he thumbed through its contents with the kind of restless boredom that prevents sleep.

'Runway twelve cleared for landing,' crackled a not-quite-British-not-quite-South-Indian accent.

On the Value of Ceylon to the Empire, read the pad. Whoever had prepared the document had carefully circled 'thorium', 'graphene' and 'titanium'. For entire chapters they harped on about the importance of trading with China. There was production value, trade routes, impact on industry, key political players. Links spiraled out like a confused spider web, from every paragraph to more extensive articles on the factories of Ceylon and its history of rebellion.

It was practically a bloody tourist brochure. Bengali skipped it and went to the video section. These he put in a playlist, skipping through them rapidly. He saw China, extending tendrils from Australia. A fleet of Chinese Marines in power armor, disembarking in a city that looked like it was in the throes of growing up. A reflex shot fired by a British soldier. Both sides slugging it out. Towers crumbling under gunfire. A satellite marked with the wings of an angel spun with careful precision and fired a tungsten shell – a single warning shot that leveled the entire fledgling city.

'You fired one of the Angels?' a reporter was saying.

'Her Majesty's orders, I'm afraid,' said a shadowy voice. 'Show the Chinese we're not playing silly buggers. She's been a bit touchy these last fifty years. Still ...'

Deals, news radiograms, photos – the videos flitted through past in a high-speed blur, flick flick flick flick. The Chinese bowed and asked to build a port in Colombo. A nexus of trade between Her Majesty's Empire and the subjects of the Song Emperor. Agreements. Ships dredging up sand from the waters. An island-city rising next to the ashes of the ruined city.

And, somewhere down the line and not recorded on these videos, the Crofton Institute had looked around at the ruins and decided it would make the next generation of weapons and disguise it as hyper-violent gladiator drama. And here he was, decades down the line, being sent in for what was essentially industrial espionage.

No sleep tonight, he thought. And on the heels of that: *this better be worth it.*

Outside, the sea stretched out under the moonlight, black and endless, and took him and the Caradoc to Ceylon.

FOUR

Many thousands of miles away, a man received a package. Unlike Bengali's, it was hand-delivered by a messenger who quaked with fear and promptly forgot that he had ever delivered such a message. It was a single sheet of digital paper, on was a short, brief scrawl: 'TRUST THIS IS SUITABLE.'

The man reading this letter sat in a cafe under gloomy North Irish skies, thinking. He was thin and lanky, and wrapped in his greatcoat. He had a memorable face, but not a particularly handsome one: it was too square, too rigid where it should have been soft. His eyes were set too far apart, his forehead wrinkled, not with age, but in thought. Certainly not the image of the handsome captain returning from war. His name was Eliott Grimme.

'You look racked,' said the waitress, passing by on her rounds.

'Long day,' he said. It was as much as he spoke here.

She didn't say anything else, but poured into his cup. He nodded his thanks and sipped, feeling the filthy black sludge burn its way down his throat. As he sipped, he decrypted the text; the scrawl vanished, and the paper began to fill up with details.

It was indeed a strange case. *You are no doubt aware of the safeguards commonly put in place by the Royal Society of Roboticists and the Crofton Institute to ensure that no machine shall approximate life in a blasphemous manner*, it began, and went on to detail the laws and codexes of advanced machinery; these he skipped, scanning for the salient bits.

There.

Ten years prior, the Crown had authorized the Ceylonese to run a novel form of entertainment: cheap humanoid bots set loose in a ceaseless sort of battle royale within the ruined city of Colombo. Most novel of all had been the realism exhibited by the bots: there had been talk of great profits, and possibly taking this format out into the rest of the world. The papers were filled with reports and financials.

He skipped them. Alright, someone figured out there was money to be made. Circle of life. It was what came next that was interesting. A profile of a roboticist called Don Hewage. A list of academic papers. *Dynamic risk profiling using n-ward Bayesian inference. Mutating random decision trees in the application of intelligence. A computational method for feedback control optimization*. There were repeated uses of the phrase 'machine learning' highlighted.

Interesting indeed.

Last year, the first incident. One bot had escaped the game area and made it almost to the command centre, slaughtering a few civilians in the process. There were cryptic reports from the local Inquisition chapter. The locals had gunned it down and raised a hue and cry.

Obviously, someone had screwed up. He could read between the lines well enough. There was a number at the bottom of the text. He asked for the bar's radiogram and called it.

'Might be bit of a hog, even by your standards,' said Drake without preamble. 'It's all in there, but the long and the short of it is that we seem to have a robot colony running around in the old city of Colombo.'

'Like Hong Kong.'

'Not like Hong Kong. These things can learn.'

Eliott processed this, tracking carefully over the map while tuning Drake out. He checked his instructions thrice, very carefully.

He knew the logic for this kind of thing. It was easier to send a man than a regiment; easier to deny one soldier than a submarine.

'And how are you doing, Grimme?' Drake asked.

'I haven't drunk much in a while,' he said. 'Just a bit of beer every now and then.'

'Oh, I know. Three pints of Guinness a week, on average. Always the same bar. Very machine-like of you.'

It wasn't the first time he wondered how much the Drakes knew, and how.

'Alright, then,' said Drake, back to business. 'We're sending you with another fellow for assessment. His job is to figure out who the most interesting beasties are. Your job is to find and capture them, and make sure the mess is contained. Make a parade out of it every time you take down something. Let the public know we're doing a good job. Nigel Penhaligon will be your point man for the job. You'll be using his men.'

Interesting indeed. He folded everything up very carefully, finished his coffee and stepped outside. The wind was cold, the cobbles matter missing and sky grey. His British greatcoat was painfully obvious in its navy-blue wrapping. A half-rotted board on the pub across the street said: *God created whiskey to keep the Irish from conquering the world.*

No, he thought. God created the Lewis gun for that.

A gang of teenagers – all underfed frames with sharp eyes and dyed hair – lounged menacingly around the corner of the coffeehouse. They looked at him like dogs might look at a steak that had decided to walk around.

One of them made a faux lunge at him, looking to startle him perhaps, but he stared at them until they felt uncomfortable and turned away, sneering. Basic challenge dynamics: escalate or lose.

And what did he have to lose? Twenty years of service to Her Majesty and this was what it came down to: walking through a city he had helped suppress, haunting the one coffee shop that would take his money. Staring daggers at teenagers who knew no better, who were just as lost as he was, trapped in a grey world with no beginning and no end.

'I'll take it,' he said to no one in particular.

≈

Drake's package, as always, had been precise. Duty assessment and physical at Musgrave Park Hospital,

Belfast, just a little bit North from where he was. Straight to London afterwards. Musgrave was one of the best orthopaedic outfits in the Commonwealth, and also one of the best rehab centres. He hoped he didn't need rehab.

He was met at the gates of Musgrave, given a few respectful salutes – the men still knew his name here. He couldn't hear the whispers trailing him past the gate, but he knew they were about him. Eliott Grimme. India, Hong Kong, Africa. The Grimme Reaper: the soldier who swapped the gun for the pen and had more blood on both than most would ever see in their lifetimes.

He was escorted to the assessment unit, which was huddled up in the far corner of the Musgrave grounds like an interloper. There was a barrage of tests. Psychometric profiling in a cold, sterile chamber where lights gleamed like dead neon eyes. Cleared fit for duty. The neural safeguards were still in place.

'Nobody wants the Reaper on the loose, eh?' he said to the machine attached to him.

'Just routine checks, sir,' said a disembodied voice. 'We've had problems with your line, you know, just some reinforcement algorithms. Now, this won't take a second ...'

Then he was ushered to Withers Ward, where the bone surgeons plied their trade. The buildings loomed in the fog, warm lights adding slight haloes to the white columns – a calculated effect, he was sure.

'I haven't seen a Mark-III skeleton in years,' said the surgeon, who looked too young. Like everyone else. 'Now these were real combat frames. How long have you had it for, sir?'

'It's in my file,' said Grimme.

'I like to ask questions,' said the surgeon mournfully. 'It's boring when you know everything.'

Grimme disagreed. *Ever been dropped into a hot zone with no intel, Doctor? Ever walked in expecting a few villagers with pitchforks and heard that bone-chilling scream 'Aayo Gurkhaliii!' echoing through the mountaintops just before the bullets begin and men shed red blossoms of death?*

But then the drugs began taking effect and the memories became fuzzy. 'I'm reading a lot of damage on the skeleton, sir,' said the young surgeon from a distance. He sounded disappointed. 'Lots of bullet scarring, a few cracks in the outer layers.'

'Leave the skeleton,' he managed to slur before he went under. It had served him well. The Mark-IIIs had been built for bullets. You don't throw away a good tool.

When he woke up, there was with a little more oxygen in the lungs and a little more fibre muscle all over. The skeleton was activated, cleared for duty. He didn't complain.

'Take you a day or two to get used to the weight,' said the young surgeon. 'Fill in the form on the way out, sir.'

He shook his head, knowing it would take him much longer. It always did.

And onwards, to the last port of call, to a location no map would divulge and no Interitus would see. A man and a woman met him there. The man was large and well dressed, wearing the clothes of a public servant, though an infinitely superior one. His suit was an unassuming black, but the cut and the silver-grey shirt underneath spoke of the finest tailors England could offer. He leaned on a silver cane.

The woman wore the colours of steel, with her Majesty's Rose – white, black and red – pinning a red cloak that hung around her like a shield. Occasionally, the wind would blow and the cloak would shift ever so slightly to show the metal underneath. She carried a long, ancient rifle that might have been ceremonial, but looked like it could still put a bullet through anyone who assumed otherwise.

Behind her loomed a wall, so vast and pitted and scarred that it looked like someone had stolen a chunk of the moon and planted it there in the gloom.

'Grimme,' said the man.

'Drake,' said the Reaper. 'You're not the original, are you?'

The grey sky swirled and peered at them.

'My ... original wanted to retire,' said the cloned Drake, public servant. 'Takes a toll, you know, this business of empire.'

'No rest for the wicked, eh?'

'You have the message?'

Eliott offered the message to the woman. It pulsed a soft white as soon as her fingers touched it. She unlocked her visor, read the message with inscrutable eyes and eventually nodded to the soldiers above. A subtle tension left the air. Snipers powered down, auto-defenses lost interest in Eliott and two vertical lines appeared in the scarred wall behind her, the section between them slowly sinking into the ground. She turned and appraised Eliott with lenses that had long since given up all pretenses of being human eyes.

'Drake,' she said. 'I hope you know what you're doing.'

'Don't we all,' muttered Drake. 'Grimme, shall we?'

'Does it have to be this way? Can't I take a bloody airship or something?'

'The edict will not be argued around,' said the woman, stiffly. 'You travel in pieces, sir, or not at all. The auto-surgeons will reassemble you. Should you renege, one of mine will come for your head.'

The edict of Hong Kong, that bloody legacy.

Eliott Grimme sighed. 'Fine,' he said. 'Just make sure there's enough painkillers on the other end.'

FIVE

On the other end sat Nigel Penhaligon, Knight Grand Cross of the Most Honourable Order of the Bath. He was well over a decade older than when he had first set foot in Kandy as its first chief of police.

Many things had changed since then. Governors had come and gone. Very few had lasted or managed to escape Ceylon alive. Ceylon, after all, was bit of a conflict zone, and the situation with the Chinese had to be handled carefully. And someone watching from the outside would have noted, with an increasing degree of sarcasm, that it was such a blessing that Penhaligon had existed in these turbulent times, maintaining order despite the ever-increasing burdens of his post, forced to pick up one institution after another to keep the government from failing. Surely it would not be too much of an irregularity if the charter lapsed here and there and the oddly religious post of 'Chief Inquisitor' became necessary, nay, critical, even more so than the Governor. Surely Penhaligon could be given some leeway to have his best men and women modified, because the job did have its dangers after all.

Surely even the stodgy bureaucracy that had put Penhaligon there would have noticed him becoming a superpower in his own right.

But men do not become powerful without first being able to assume control over the narrative around them, and Nigel Penhaligon had most quarters convinced that he was, in fact, the perfect man for the job. Most.

And thus the most powerful man in Ceylon sat there, supremely confident in his fiefdom. Time had made him paler and turned his suit into a sarong and a shirt, a combination that he normally wouldn't be seen in, but it was damn hot these days and sacrifices had to be made.

He sipped his cooling tea, staring through the window at the crumpled mess of a man that the doctors had dumped on the operating table. His subordinates came to him with news several times, but each time he shooed them away, distracted. His eye fell on the fine blue streaks of the porcelain cup in his hands, now empty, and he spent what felt like many years thinking about how fragile it was, how hard to make, how easily broken.

'That's the leader?' asked someone behind him, staring at the body being assembled before them.

Penhaligon turned. Bailey, the youngest of the novices.

'No,' said Penhaligon. He thought about sending the boy away, like all the others, but why not let him watch? He might learn a thing or two. He gestured to a seat next to him.

'He doesn't look like anything special.'

'That's because he's not,' said Penhaligon. 'He's a decoy. Damned terrorists never show their face,' said Penhaligon. 'Look,' he pointed to the part of the face where the surgeon was removing skin, exposing the artificial muscle, carbon-weave and metal underneath. 'Look at that. They took the face of the man we wanted to catch and built a copy on this one.'

But this one had armor, is what he didn't tell the boy. *Damned clever assassin, taking on the face of our mark just to get close to us. Damned expensive one, too, judging by all the bodywork.* He had a feeling he recognized the subcutaneous armor: Chinese tech, hastily assembled in a local factory.

The boy peered at the glass, brought up a display, zoomed in. 'Huh.'

Penhaligon watched the boy. A decade ago he would have taken some pleasure at this corruption of innocence. Now he was just tired. The Lanka Resistance Front was a dangerously annoying development. He had a sneaking suspicion that they might actually have a mole in his operation, and sorting out this whole robot episode had been a chore and a half. And the heat was the straw that broke the camel's back. There was only so much enthusiasm left.

The intern looked nervous. 'Sir, is it true what they say?'

'What do they say, boy?'

'That he, uh, the Reaper's coming. Here.'

'Indeed,' said Nigel Penhaligon. 'It'll be quite the party.'

He turned back to the twitching body, remembering it all – Pestilence, War, the Reaper. Charlotte Plague, built to bring down the IRA. Biological warfare packed into a thing that walked like a woman, talked like a woman, but would never be touched by the diseases humanity could suffer. Gregory Mars, sent to India to quell the Gurkha Rebellion. Both, after months of massacring the enemy wholesale, switching sides, cutting devastating lines into British troops before the Tin Soldiers finally took them out. And Eliott Grimme – the Reaper, the last of the lot, the most faithful, the one who cleaned up both the IRA and the Gurkha messes – ordered to Hong Kong and condemned for taking the only course of action that would have actually worked. The Order's greatest triumph and its greatest failure, all in three bodies that twitched and bled, but could never really die.

He thought about the long chase, both man and machine exhausted by the end of it, and that terrible final battle – all those years on the shores of Goa. Grimme, obsolete and wounded, under fire by an entire platoon, and still charging, still charging ...

The surgeon was cutting the armor now, his fingers carving fireflies in the air. The body twitched like a puppet having its strings cut.

'Ah. Sir,' said the boy. 'The meeting, it's starting. Mahanayake wants to know if you'll be there.'

Penhaligon gave him the empty cup. 'Waste of time. Tell Swan to fill in. Tell him to put a few people on the Zone, just in case someone tries anything funny. We'll have the Reaper figure out how to sort this out from the lab, and everyone goes home happy. Tell Mahanayake the whole thing will be over in a month, at most. And call Hewage. Tell him we have the Reaper.'

'Yes, sir.' The boy saluted and sped away. Penhaligon went back to staring at the corpse on the chopping block.

He had a bad feeling that things were going south, and not in a way that involved beaches.

At least, he thought, like a man reaching for the gun under his pillow, he would have Eliott Grimme.

SIX

Jacob Bengali's arrival went unnoticed by most of Kandy. Dr. Kushlani de Almeida, however, was not most of Kandy, and had stayed up precisely for this. As per custom, she checked her list of things to do after waking up and pushed the windows of her room open.

Outside, Kandy gleamed – a city of gables laid out like a tablecloth over several hills and railway lines. It was Poya, the day of the full moon, and therefore a holy day. But the clouds were bad these days – thick and angry and choking – and so the Fake was being prepared for the night: a giant blimp that often ran election campaigns, this time reconfigured to look like the lunar surface, bathing the city in a soft white light. Every shop was shut, every supermarket and restaurant abandoned, and the temples struck back, reclaiming the darkness from the commercial neon with their prayers. Only the hotels stayed open. One, not too far from her window, ran pink and blue tracers against the clouds, sketching out the Union Jack over and over again. The lightshow crept closer to the Fake Moon until it settled right on the blimp. The British claiming yet another land as their own.

The antique pendulum clock struck 5 a.m. The room was dark against the lit city outside, and the old furniture somehow made her feel curiously removed from what she saw outside the window, as if she was in a bubble of time in which she could hide forever.

She made herself some tea – not the horrid perfumed English breakfast stuff, but silver tips; something clean and light to keep her head straight. Then she went down to the Post Office and called the office radiogram. The operator put her through to Hewage.

'The evaluator is here,' she said without preamble. 'I've got him a room at Queen's Court.'

The sound of music drifted through the speaker. Violins, frantic, trumpets, a complex interplay. It was the kind of music they played for the bots.

'Tchaikovsky, 1812 Overture,' he said. She heard him typing on the other end. 'So. Best we can do?'

'And cheapest.' Though they had probably felled a small forest to produce all the paper for the permission and visa forms. 'I've a breakfast invitation with you. You'll have to manage the rest.'

'Understood,' he said, surprising her. Then he sighed. 'You know what happened today?'

'What?'

'Wife's leaving, taking the kids.'

She was at a loss for words. 'Why?'

'Word of the court case filtering down,' he said. 'In a stupid way. I think one of her brothers works for the Bandaranaikes. She seems to think we controlled the bots that killed all those people.'

'I'm sorry.'

'She called me a murderer.'

'If she believes that—'

'She's smart,' he said, cutting her off. 'If she believes it, more people will, soon. Let's get this done. I'll invite a few people who need to be there, a couple of journalists as well. See you in six hours.'

Over the line, Tchaikovsky fired a cannon.

Queen's Court was upmarket. Kushlani deliberated over a saree, picked the black one with a dash of gold and borrowed the family car. Her father would grumble at her later, but she couldn't just walk up to Queen's Court. The car was smooth and electric, and she was tired. Her mind was on random access, rifling through the most useless things buried among her neurons. This combination turned the ride to Kandy into a series of impressions, half-formed – the endless traffic by the lake, crawling around a protest; an electromech policeman waving its arms futilely, whistling; a young man and a young woman furtively holding hands as they walked out of a restaurant; a score of government servants pouring in and out of the administrative quarter, a sea of white shirts and black skirts and sweat and empty wallets, too hot and too poor for avant-garde tech fashion. They blurred together, dreamlike.

And then she was there. A wide driveway trimmed with green. An old colonial palace-mansion, renovated with smiling greeters and unsmiling Army types who checked her car for bombs and ran her blood profile ID. Inside, a different world – all marble and royal purple and soft lights; complexions became fairer, dresses shorter, jackets more pretentious.

'He's here?'

'Just arrived, miss. Olive Lounge.'

'Doctor,' Kushlani corrected, attempting to be gentle about it, but it came out like a whipcrack. The hotel receptionist became even more confused than she no doubt was on a daily basis. She almost rang up the hotel doctor before Kushlani brushed onwards, irritated. Feeling out of place in her saree, she found her way to the Olive Lounge, which was a stupid name for a room that had no hint of green in it whatsoever.

Hewage had beaten her there, the old fart.

'Ah, Kushlani. This is Dr. Bengali.'

A dark-skinned man with a large, stooped frame darted forward. His hand was fortunately warm, his smile a bit strained. Probably travel fatigue.

His accent was very difficult to place: English, but that slight over-perfect English from Singapore and the upper tiers of Indian and Sri Lankan society.

'I was hoping to brief you, but—'

'Oh, no need, no need. Mr. Hewage and I had a long chat over the basics.' An inscrutable look passed between the two men. 'Sit, please. Will you have some breakfast?'

They had breakfast. Polite and professional, with Hewage speaking, snake oil salesman on full blast.

'So in one month, the Big Match begins,' said Hewage, sketching out the general scenario: at a specific time each year, every bot tribe would be driven into battle, spurred on by a training cycle carefully overseen by army men on the ground. A bloodlust among faux-children, a brutal and ugly battle painted over with scoreboards and live commentary. Entire nations would bet on which tribe would remain standing.

'That's an odd name for an annual bloodbath.'

At the Hub, they called it 'rebuild time'. The 'dead' would all be gathered, dumped on a supply train and shipped to Kandy, and for the next six months, Kushlani, along with her techs, would labour night and day to repair, rebuild or replace. The techs never watched the matches. 'It hurts to see something you built die over and over again,' one of them had told her on a lunch break. 'I can't describe it.'

'Now, whoever your favorites are, a lot of them are going to die. The rest we're going to capture, eh? This will be the last season of this particular model. We're going to rebuild them to be safer. We're going to rebuild our systems so we can track them better. Come January, a new version of the bots we all know and love will be in Colombo, perfectly controllable from the Hub itself, certified safe.'

'Well, this is interesting,' said Bengali, over a forkful of egg. She could see that he wasn't quite buying Hewage's pitch. 'Of course, I'll have to examine the bot code ... you know, certify it to make sure out-of-bounds behaviour, like the stuff you experienced, is truly rare.'

'Surely observational evidence is enough? Watch the bots in the field, log their behaviour, look at the outliers -'

'Well. Drake did ask me to vet your code, Dr. Hewage.'

Hewage's legendary secrecy kicked in. 'Without the right documentation in place, you'll be staring at it for decades without being able to make head or tail of it. It's not even written in a language you're familiar with, Bengali. Observation will tell you more.'

This clearly displeased Bengali. He tried to steer the conversation to safer waters. 'So tell me what you do, Dr. Almeida.'

'Kushlani.'

'Then I must be Jacob to you.'

'The plan was simple,' she said, taking back the credit. 'The Big Match happens. That's when, traditionally, we've got the most number of bots in one place, so it's easier to monitor a large population of them collectively. We look for behaviour we don't want, regardless of whether a bot survives or not. We bring those back to the Hub.'

'Local Inquisitions are helping with that,' added Hewage. 'The others we repair and send back out. Maybe with some kind of system that lets us reset to a baseline model.'

'And maybe we add in some code to make sure certain behaviours are off bounds?' Bengali looked at Hewage.

Hewage evaded the question. 'We'll see,' he said. 'Coffee? We're talking about monitoring ten thousand of those little bastards, you know. It's a pretty big job, though you're going to be here without much to do until the Big Match is over.'

Bengali murmured something about Crofton coffers running deep and raised his coffee to a toast. She swiped a pastry, excused herself and retired to the balcony outside, feeling lost. She had the impression of wheels in motion – too many, too soon. All her carefully laid plans had, it seemed, prematurely begun.

The balcony outside was marble and mostly uninhabited. It looked out over a steep drop, and you could see the railroad that snaked from the far distance and stopped right at the border of Kandy city, before dissolving into a network of roads – like a guest too polite to enter without taking off his shoes, she thought. The sun, now high in the sky, made the steelwork shimmer and flash. Traffic hummed around the tracks and grunted its way around the lake at the centre of Kandy, like animals around a watering hole.

Somewhere out there, past that horizon, were the bots. She thought of the girl she had dissected, such as the Explorer – the one that had lived long and hard, and learned enough to be almost human in her own mind.

Were there others like her? She had thought of those fantastic little learning engines, initially a hack solution, but one that had genuinely become something special over time; something different.

'What's wrong?' asked Hewage, appearing suddenly in the doorway.

'Just thinking,' she said. 'You didn't tell him about the learning stuff, did you?'

'He knows,' said Hewage, darkly. 'Or he suspects, the bastard. Drake wouldn't have sent him without some background. We'll figure something out.'

'How'd you get the Inquisition on board?'

He walked over and lit a cigarette. 'Penhaligon insisted. I don't have the political clout to refuse them. I think they want to keep and eye on everything, make sure we don't do something stupid. You and I are going to spend the entire bloody month pimping the Big Match and then we'll try to sort this bloody mess out.'

'Wife get back to you?'

'People aren't machines, Number Two,' he said, taking a long, slow drag from the cigarette.

'Sure they are. Same principles. Incentive. Reward.'

'Some things can't be fixed', he shook his head. 'Bloody mess ... seeing that young pup remind me I've done enough work for ten PhDs here.'

'The bots?'

'The bots,' he said. 'You interested in my job?'

She suddenly felt overwhelmed, but with excitement, bordering on some kind of fear. 'That implies you're moving on,' she said.

Hewage snorted. 'That was the plan. Looks like Drake's just put his foot down on the pedal, now,' he said, throwing the cigarette butt over the railing, and it fell smoking into the undergrowth. 'Never mind. Forget it. Let's get this stupid thing over with.'

SEVEN

Exactly one day and thirteen hours after Kushlani de Almeida met Jacob Bengali, the contents of a very suspicious shuttlecraft were delivered to a secret place in Kandy.

Eliott Grimme woke up. Unlike Bengali, he had a rather unpleasant time doing so. It was cold, *so* cold. Every muscle screamed in agony, and he felt like a plank of wood with a thousand carpenters hammering nails into him. He knew this waking, as well as the pain that would come next. His eyes burned as the frozen retina-optics woke up. His skeleton rebooted, screaming and vomiting error messages. He curled into a foetal ball, twitching against the agony that had once been familiar.

He tried to move and found that he couldn't, except for his neck. There were time-limited blocks on every limb that apologized and told him to wait for the surgery to be complete.

How long had it been? Seconds or centuries?

Parts of him activated in a flash of bright, searing neural agony.

A distant voice said his name. The voice sounded wrong somehow – too many cadences and frequencies folded into one, like three voices overlapping through a bad speaker. He opened his eyes. Darkness and gloom, and in the darkness, a shape with glowing red eyes. It reached out with long hands and unfolded him, pulling him to his feet. For a brief moment, he thought about fighting back – a thrust to that actuator joint on the shoulder; a brief twist of the neck. But what would be the point?

The voices resolved. First: a whip-cord-thin runt whose skin shone with lines of copper and silver, and a fat, perspiring man with red lenses for eyes. Inquisitors, definitely from the colonies: good manners did not permit such open modification in England. He had arrived, then.

'Reassembly shipping', Eliott said to them, 'is shit.'

They smiled, faded. And then came the man himself.

He dressed like a British fop – tailored suit, hat, gloves to hide his inhumanity. A face that was mostly hard angles and leathery skin. Neither particularly handsome nor particularly ugly, but striking in a very powerful way. There was silver on his temples, but otherwise he looked exactly like he had when Eliott had first met him face to face, all those years ago. Grimme nodded at the man who had once hounded him over two continents, earning him his immortality and the terrible weight of being one of Her Majesty's select.

'Grimme.'

'Penhaligon,' said Grimme.

'Cold in here, isn't it? Temperature, boys.'

It became less cold.

Eliott rotated his view and turned – white wall, spider. The image froze.

No, not spider. Doctorbot. Black, menacing arms – dead, dormant. Glass screen – Penhaligon. The image froze again, shattered, dissolved into noise.

Error. Rerouting.

When it reformed, the Chief Inquisitor was sitting in a chair next to him. And Penhaligon suddenly looked old, like a corpse that had crawled out of its grave and put on fake skin. He produced a cigarette and lit it. Interesting.

'You didn't use to smoke,' Eliott said.

'Spare me the lecture,' said Penhaligon. 'Not all of us run on electricity. How do you feel, Grimme?'

Eliott consulted himself. Everything was functioning. Full system diagnostic, he ordered.

Error. Rerouting.

'We had to freeze your motor functions, sir,' said a voice behind him.

Helpless, he turned his head back to Penhaligon. 'I'm getting too old for this business. I want a chartered plane next time. Where the hell are we?'

'Kandy. Capital of Ceylon. I'm sorry about the discomfort, but we wanted you here as soon as possible. Don't worry, we'll get you out of this place as soon as the setup's complete. The weather's a huge step up from Ireland, let me tell you that.'

'You've been good since the reconditioning, I take it? You did a really good job of Dublin.'

As good as could be once your entire neural structure has been remapped. 'How long has it been, Penhaligon?'

'Twenty years, give or take? I don't quite keep track of time anymore.'

It was a lifetime ago.

He was surprised when the preliminaries came back positive. Muscle status: relatively weak, but primed. Conductive fluid status: not just fine, but completely refreshed – some compound he'd never had in him before. Feedback in the skeleton. The pain vanished. A small glitch in the neural interface calibration – there, fixed. Now he could see better.

There was a sign that said 'AVOID CONTACT WITH THE NEWLY DECANTED'.

Error. Rerouting.

Penhaligon peered down at Eliott. A grimace in the darkness. 'Hang on,' said Penhaligon. 'We need to take these blocks off. We've pumped your system with Lace.'

'I don't know what that is.'

'After your time, I suppose. Came out of Nippon. High-grade machine fluid. Some of the best around, supports custom commands. One of my clones in Hong Kong got it for me, ironically enough. I've had your system completely flushed and set up with it. Hold still.'

The doctorbot hissed, pulling out cables, undoing restraints, scurrying over his body. Ice ran through his skeleton. The neural blocks dissolved. Eliott's skeleton, designed to keep the body moving even under complete loss of muscle and neural connectivity, popped off its own diagnostics. The doctorbot scuttled over him, making some last-minute love taps. Eliott fought the split-second urge to smash it, and instead brushed the various spines and cutting instruments out of the way.

'I'm surprised I'm on this job,' he said.

'It was a predictable choice,' said Penhaligon meditatively, watching him. 'Drake thinks we hate each other, you know.'

'Does he?'

'Getting a bit annoying, our dear former employer.'

The irony. 'Queen's favour not doing you much good?'

'People are people,' Penhaligon said, simply. 'You do your part, retire to a nice place like this, make sure the Chinese are happy and trading with us ... and then that arsehole realizes the political value of the posting.'

'I can't imagine.'

'Can you walk?'

He could. Penhaligon gave him a robe and stood back as he balanced himself onto his newly reassembled feet, letting the neural agony fade. The darkness lifted slowly, showing him the cold and sterile room he was in.

Penhaligon had opened the door. Eliott limped out after the Inquisitor. Cold hospital tiles turned into wood, wood turned into something like stone and the light went from dim white to sunlight. A squad of dark-skinned Ceylonese guards saluted Penhaligon and Eliott, flattened themselves out of their way, and marched back into the building. They did not break step, and had the look of men who had just walked out of a minefield.

A gentle breeze began to register on his skin.

They emerged onto a balcony of some sort. The sunlight turned the Inquisitor into a younger man, giving some colour to those bloodless cheeks and a dull metal shine to the few parts that peeked out from the black clothes. It turned the black rose on his chest a deep red.

Eliott looked up at the sky – an infinite thing of red that stretched on into the sunset. 'If this was what you were after', he said, 'you should have come with me to Ireland.'

'It's better in the mornings.'

'That's what they all say.'

Something crept into Eliott's mind. Error. Rerouting. An annoying little glitch that wouldn't go away, that came with a ghost of memory, creeping past the neural blocks. The pounding of his feet on sand ... gravel? Through the Gurkha valleys and ghost towns and cities thronged with people and holograms, and always the man with the hat following him. Penhaligon, younger, chasing him across continents – an impossible predator chasing impossible prey. Penhaligon, sitting through years and decades and centuries, watching Eliott in a cage, his mind split into a million fragments.

Unbidden memories of Hong Kong. Of an enemy that played an n-dimensional game of chess with the lives of men and machines; not too powerful to be modelled and predicted, but good enough that all Rassilikov logic chains were exhausted, the standard tactics database had gone out the window, and all that was left was Eliott and a few thousand men too afraid of him to refuse orders.

And at the end, that exhaustion and relief of a game well played; that empathy for an enemy that had done its best; the arrest –

'Obviously, I know Drake's paying you the good stuff,' Penhaligon was saying. 'But I'll make you an offer worth considering. You work for me, full benefits ... you'll be treated like a king, and you'll retire here. The people are good. You'll spend your last years a legend instead of being sent out like a lapdog.'

Full system diagnostic again. A few small blocks popped; nothing he couldn't ignore. Nothing the shrinks would have flagged as 'below operational standards'.

It was good to be somewhere, anywhere, out of that dreary place. 'What's the first job?'

Penhaligon smiled for the first time. It was a face unused to smiling. 'Just like old times.'

The sun, setting through that grim sky, painted it in rose and gold, and the city in shadow-light, making Kandy look like some great, inverted bloodshot eye.

II: Emergence

II: Emergence

ONE

Broken Arm woke up.

The sunlight peeked through the tattered cloth she had hung in her room. Little rays broke through and made tiny motes of dust dance in front of her face. She tried to catch them, but her hands closed on nothingness. She thought of them as her friends.

Outside, the soft evening sunlight lit up the ruins of Colombo in a fierce glare, sketching out the world she had always known – buildings toppled over, roads cracked, weeds and twisted trees exploding out through skeletons of shattered concrete. From her window, she could see everything, all the way to the sea, which was the only thing that stayed unbroken.

A few birds – mutated monsters that bred fast, lived large and left behind horribly bloated corpses – saw her face emerge from her building, screamed, and flapped away.

The forager party had already gathered outside. They hung back, as awkward as the birds. At a nod from her, they entered the building, single file, crawling over beams and girders and horizontal staircases and the smashed-up ruins of diagonal floors to get to her nest. They left their weapons at her door as a gesture of respect and huddled around her.

Broken Arm had learned a way to be useful long ago. Her left arm, which had always dangled awkwardly, had been cut off by a fast spear many years ago. She had learned to make weapons. She had learned to listen to the others and put together their stories, fragment by fragment, and thus know more than everyone else. The others, in turn, kept her alive and came to her when things outside their ken happened.

'Cinnamon,' whispered Sky. He was called Sky because he spent hours looking up at the great blue dome and the white clouds beneath.

The story was that four bots from the Place Beyond had walked Inward. No, not bots: Big People. She was not quite sure how she knew this, only that she recognized the similarity in Sky's description.

This was odd. There was nothing in the Beyond but the barrier that could not be climbed, the one that hummed with terrible lightning. These newcomers had somehow made it through the barrier.

Sky, curious, had gone with three others to meet them, waving their spears high and openly, so as to show themselves coming from afar.

The newcomers had seen them, and attacked. Nobody was quite sure how. Something had struck Cloud straight in the chest, where the power cells were. She had detonated instantly, a death of a kind they had never seen before. Sky had lined up the newcomers and thrown his spear well, with such force that it stapled two of the enemies to the ground. Road charged the others. The newcomers had retreated, but not before attacking again. They had spears in their hands that spoke lightning and could kill from afar.

Sky showed his hands to Broken Arm. The tips were badly bent, because he had used them to batter one to death.

Moonlight, Road and Water?

'Dead,' said Sky. 'Dead, dead, dead.'

But now the real question: 'Did you find food?'

Sky shook his head.

'Port City?'

Again, nothing.

≈

If Broken Arm worried, it was with reason. Just six moons ago, they had brought metal to the Port City that lay just outside their home; and out had come Big People, lots of them, making her and the others form queues, taking their metal in exchange for that dark nourishment that they so craved. They knew not the origins of this arrangement, but merely that this was as it was, as it should be.

But as of late, the Port City kept its gates shut, mute to their entreaties. The mountain of scrap metal piled outside by starving tribes went by ignored.

She did not know, of course, that this was due to a longstanding agreement – the opening moves of a Big Match, repeated from time immemorial, happening with clockwork precision by order of a man named Hewage in a city far beyond the one they knew. The first move was to starve them, with the Port City witholding the cakes of fuel they burned for energy. At first, the bots would line up, dumbly disappointed, but then they would begin to forage wider, becoming more desperate, and the first clashes and deaths would begin. Supplies were sometimes airdropped, based on viewer polls, at specific locations where the terrain and the camera setups were particularly good.

In Kandy, they called this the 'First Innings'.

Broken Arm knew nothing of Hewage or Kandy or the drama that would unfold. All she knew was that they were beginning to starve, and that for some strange reason, Big People were killing them. She held them all close, even the new ones.

'You should go check again,' said Sky.

There was murmured consensus.

The Thing that Spoke in Music crackled feebly. Whoever ran it had long since given up on the pianos and violins: now a gentle Pali pleading filled the air. 'Buddhang saranang gacchami ... dhammand sarang gacchami ...' Words she had never understood, words that spoke of refuge in a tongue long since forgotten.

She stalked out of their building and into the silence of the evening.

As the moons had gone past, the other tribes had begun pulling back from the strip that connected them to the Chinese Port City. Why wait, after all, for a thing that clearly did not benefit them anymore? But she, for some reason, had stayed, haunting this place and hounding the Port City.

Had she been aware of the fine machinery that made up her thoughts – the software that made up her soul – she would have described it in terms of attention cycles and backpropagation and feedback loops. Instead, she just walked, a little lopsided figure making its furtive way down what had once been called Galle Road, to the brown desert that had once been the Galle Face Green.

As always, the Chinese Port City was waiting. Its lights were shining bright like miniature suns, reflected on the little strip of water between it and the bank she stood on.

'WARNING,' it told her in its strange, rambling voice, like it did to all the others who came to talk to it. It used to suffix this with 'MAINTAIN DISTANCE FROM STATION', but as of late it had started to say something different.

She sat under the moonlight in Galle Face Green, now Galle Face brown, amidst the shattered roads and tumbled towers. The sea lapped away, eating at the edges of Colombo.

'NO FOOD TODAY,' it told her in its strange, rambling voice, like it did to all the others who came to talk to it. 'CONTRACT FOR STATION HAS ENDED.'

'I know,' she said.

There was silence. She wondered how the Port City ate. There were people in there. Some said they were Big People, like the ones Upwards, but some rudimentary classification had been made, and now she thought they were more like the tribes. They were metal and they did not bleed. They could not be fought; they could not be talked to. The Children of the Taj, once the greatest of the bot-tribes here, had found that out.

'How do you live?' she asked it. 'Who gives you food?'

'STATION IS SELF-SUSTAINING.'

'I don't know what that means.'

She felt the Port City shift to its own language. Images played across its moonlit skin. Symbols. A tribe standing in the sunlight. A tribe eating the sunlight. Something like the sun inside the Port City. The Port City, a tribe unto itself, eating its own sun, but the sun never ran out. A maze of symbols she didn't understand.

She stared at it morosely, watching the waves lap at it. Always the same message.

A runner arrived. It was from Sky. One of the tribes had heard there was food beyond this place, in Colombo 01. Should they go? There would be a fight. Probably several.

What else was there to do?

'WARNING,' the Port City said. 'NEW AGENT ACTIVITY DETECTED.'

'I don't know what that means.'

'NEW AGENT ACTIVITY DETECTED. THIS STATION IS NOT PERMITTED TO SHARE ADDITIONAL INFORMATION OUTSIDE CLASS-3 CONSTRUCTS,' it said, gibberish she didn't understand. 'RECALIBRATE AUTONOMY.'

And then it fell silent. No amount of pleading could coax an answer from it. The great floodlights dimmed, and all went silent in the ruined city of Colombo.

TWO

Kushlani de Almeida watched the broadcast screens, sipping her tea. Or rather, Hewage's tea.

He knew she didn't like watching the carnage, and in a rather unexpected gesture had set two of the three screens to the stats: viewership, local, international.

That she enjoyed. It displayed years of work, and this year was more successful that the last three years put together. Indonesia was watching. Siam was watching. Burma. Most of Tamil Nadu. Two hundred million people had tuned in, including, she knew, her own parents, and this was her triumph. Almost all the undersea lines from here to the British Raj must be jammed full of the data from this stream.

And this month would be night shifts all the way through until the end, so watching the numbers climb was a favourite pastime.

It was the other screen that she hated. This one she had set to track a specific bot. The girl – the Explorer model she had autopsied, patched up and sent out.

It was ... not heartbreaking. She would never have allowed herself a feeling *that* melodramatic, but she felt both a perverse sense of pride and a sickness in her stomach. Pride, because that little bot had turned out to be such a capable leader – an underdog good enough to seriously flip the balance – and she knew a lot of people had a lot of money riding on her. The sickness came from when she saw it caring for others. Talking to them. Making sure the bots were armed and equipped, and when a bot fell, dragging it back to safety and trying to repair it. Kushlani could still remember the memories it had. Watching the sunset. Helping that other bot learn and adapt to the ruins of Colombo. So much love in so alien a thing; so much humanity in wires and printed circuit boards and processor cores provided by the lowest bidder.

The viewership jumped every time a repair scene came on. She knew that her friends – or at least the few she didn't actively despise – were all at watch parties in the big hotels, drinking Nipponese sake and flirting and cheering for the crowd favourite. Broken Arm was one of the biggest draws of the year. The audience loved her.

Survive, Kushlani willed in her mind. *Just survive.*

THREE

Jacob Bengali woke up and tried to swing himself out of bed. Something was odd ... the bed was a lot larger than it should have been. He flailed about, disoriented. His hand hit wood, smashed a glass off something ...

And then he realized he wasn't in Goa anymore.

He opened his eyes cautiously. A net. A white expanse resolved itself into a four-poster bed, and beyond that, wooden walls; real wood, not fake. A cavernous room, dimly lit by a soft gold filtering through heavily curtained windows. Motes of dust danced in an errant sunbeam lancing across his new abode. It touched the broken porcelain on the floor – the tea had spilled out onto the red cement beneath, taking on the colour of blood.

He pushed the curtains aside, saw a slope of dark grass that fell away, and beyond that, mountains wreathed in dark clouds, turning gold and pink in the dawn light.

'Ah, bugger,' he said softly to himself, because he couldn't think of anything else to say.

It took him a while to get ready. The bathroom mirror showed a worried man. Toothpaste. Shave? No. Clothes. A shirt, freshly ironed. Pants. Shoes? Yes. He pushed open the heavy, creaking wooden door and began his descent.

They had moved him out of the hotel and put him up in some sort of massive colonial bungalow not too far from the Kandy Fort. Bengali had never paid much attention to architecture, but he'd heard the name Minnette de Silva enough to appreciate the history of the place, if not the subtler nuances of design. It was a far cry from the kind of quarters you got from the India Mission.

And to top it off, Penhaligon had assigned Bengali his very own Inquisitor. As he made his way downstairs, cringing slightly at the old wooden creaks, smelling the strangely still oldness of the house around him, a vision materialized: a breakfast table laid out for a small village, with seven clay pots of curry orbiting a vast mound of—

'String hoppers, sir,' said the Inquisitor. Mason, the thin one who had served them dinner. One of the more human ones. His copper-streaked face glinted dully when he moved. 'There is also milk rice and roast paan, if sir wants.'

He came forward and began to pour himself a cup of tea with milk in it.

'Have you eaten?'

'I was waiting for sir,' said Mason.

The Ceylonese clearly knew how to treat a guest, thought Bengali, biting into his potato curry and string hoppers. And, for good measure, there was the milk rice with the fish curry, both of which sat in his belly like ballast. It was just like Indian food, yet different, the coconut milk making every curry subtly crisper. Bloody hell. Even if he got nothing out of this trip, the chance to wake up in such a house and eat this much made it all worth it. Mason watched him.

'If sir is done,' he said politely, 'we should begin.'

Every day began the same way. The waking and the fumbling, and then what he thought of as purgatory, that was the preparation before he descended to the real task at hand: watching the streams of what these people called the Big Match.

He watched, first with sickness, then with fascination. It was slaughter and carnage, hundreds of child-sized bodies throwing themselves at each other with wild savagery. Presumably while entire families cheered in front of their televisions and called bets. He watched them kill each other, over and over again.

He had never seen machines move like this before.

The first order of business was to get Hewage to tell him what exactly he had done to make the bots behave like this, but the first few days went by and nothing happened. Except, perhaps, his waistline gaining an inch or two. Invitations to lunch went unanswered. Requests for documentation were answered with the same canned statement: the government of Ceylon had a lengthy and complicated process for making its intellectual property available to auditors. The process had been set in motion, but it would take a while.

Fine. He was no stranger to red tape. He turned to Kushlani de Almeida. Interesting background: local university, no formal robotics training as far as he could make out, and if she knew about the finer workings of the models, she certainly wasn't discussing it with him, certainly not over daily radiogram calls.

But Bengali had dealt with students and staff, after all. He began asking how the Big Match was doing. How many bots were out there? How did they handle repairs? What were their timelines like? The answers she gave were too specific to be that of a government PR person: she clearly knew a great deal about both the hardware and the administration side of things.

Very well, then. "If the hill will not come to Mahomet, Mahomet will go to the hill," he told himself, and, summoning the Inquisitor, went off to find Kushlani.

This proved to be a little more difficult than he had anticipated. The university, for all its flaws, had generally been a model of order. Project plans and key information discussions were confirmed days in advance, and whoever he was supposed to be meeting presumably had the same knowledge. Here it was a lot more chaotic.

For starters, it seemed like there was some sort of court action going on that mysteriously took Hewage and Kushlani completely beyond his sphere for a week. The various sub-functionaries they left behind seemed to have absolutely no idea who he was or why they should bother helping him. There was a huge to-do involving some high-ranking government official – or was it just some rich fellow? The name 'Bandaranaike' came up repeatedly, and every so often Mason would vanish, only to return the next day, shaking his head. 'No luck, sir. Tomorrow?'

So he did the rational thing, which was to scrounge this half-mansion guesthouse for books, find a decent chair, and read. After all, Drake was footing the bill, and it was nice to stretch out for once and not have to think about classes.

But the books he found were dull. Half of them were of caricature, written by British explorers licking their lips at the exotic. To understand a country, one had to read what its people wrote of it, not what tourists saw. The one local history he found on Ceylon was a long essay on kings and the temples they built, and reservoirs and princes and princesses and miracles, and then, suddenly, around the seventeenth century, it switched to tactics, geography, incursions, tales of traitors and byzantine political games. Then it leaped centuries and began talking of rebellion: one from the North, led by scholars from Yarl; one from the South, led by fishermen. And then it stopped.

Frustrated, he went outside.

The guard at the black iron gate was an amicable old man. In exchange for a couple of cigarettes, he popped the gate open and let Bengali out with a 'Mahatthaya gihilla ennawane?' Bengali didn't speak the language, but the tone was clear. Yes, he assured the guard. Just a walk to stretch his legs.

The road cut diagonally downwards, offering him the option of going either back upwards to even more remote climes, or further downwards to Kandy. He set off downwards. At first it was it had been pleasant – sloping roads, coconut trees, a sense of silence that was completely unlike what he was used to in Goa. Then it became oppressive. The city centre might have been worth seeing, but between that place and him was an endless string of little villagelets that seemed to be made entirely of salons, barbershops and grocery stores, all stuffed to the brim with people who paused and watched Bengali labour with mild amusement. Houses painted with hideously bright colours perched precariously along roads that wound around far too often. Packs of motorbikes – most of them looked Indian – overtook him every so often. Packs of excessively friendly dogs leaped out of the many bends, sniffed around and left. Wedding reception halls appeared to grow in this wilderness like fungi. The heat of the sun was not a pleasurable bite, but a heavy, dull siege against the senses.

When he did manage to cross this great waste, he found a city equal parts colonial nostalgia and nationalism. A veneer of police control had been laid over anti-British graffiti in the process of being scrubbed off. Faux colonial-era lamps lined the pavements, and in places gave way to a darkness lit by ancient LED signage piled higgledy-piggledy over one another, advertising everything from doctors to dresses. These, too, tapered off, and then it was the temples and hotels that competed with each other. Everywhere he turned, there were Chinese or English tourists taking photos of themselves next to Buddha statues.

He tried a hotel. The lounge was full. Screens had been set up on grassy lawns; arrack flowed, and parties clustered around tables, drinking loudly. He saw millions being traded, and bookies in suits and their patrons watching the televisions hung everywhere, cheering mightily.

Time passed in cigarettes, burned one after the other, until Kushlani de Almeida invited him to dinner.

FOUR

'He says he's been writing a book,' said Kushlani. 'About the bots. Well, mostly about the bots, but mostly about himself as well. We're celebrating a good run for this Big Match. I suppose he felt generous.'

She showed up at the house in a magnificent red and black saree, and in the shielded privacy of the car, Bengali had found himself wanting to ask about her, but not daring to. So he had asked about Hewage and his annoying secrecy instead.

'I see,' he said, trying not to let his disappointment show. Books were PR. He flipped through the pages on the microchip she had offered him. Tracts of text; nothing that looked even remotely similar to code or equations or even a complex diagram. Layman fluff.

'I understand you're busy,' he told her. 'All I need is the source code and compute, and I'll be able to function pretty much independently. Figure out what to do, make recommendations, and, you know, you decide whether to take me up on them or not.'

'Again, I'd like to help you, but only Hewage has the source.'

'If this doesn't happen soon, I'm going to have it to report to Drake.'

'Don't be silly. Look around you.'

He did.

'What do you see?'

'People celebrating ... party of some sort?'

'Semi-final of the Big Match,' she said. 'Everything's running smoothly, everyone's caught up in it. This is probably one of the best we've ever pulled off. People are enjoying themselves, Jacob. You're not going to get anything right now.'

'What do we do right now, then?'

'Food,' she said. 'Because we've got maybe a month before all the bots end up back in the Watchtower, and I'm enjoying wearing this saree and having a nice dinner while I can. And if you want to make this nicer, you can tell me about your university and how it fits into all this. And if you do a good job, I might bug Hewage on my way home on your behalf. Here. This is where we get out.'

The doors opened to a gray sky and a Kandyan hotel, stretching its verandahs out towards them. The wind blew at Kushlani as she emerged from the vehicle, making her saree trail its long tail. For a moment, she looked like a dragon.

'Well?' she said.

≈

And so the next day Mason rumbled up the hills in a long, black car – a hearse more than anything.

'Kushlani miss sends her regards,' he said.

Bengali smiled and climbed in. The car took him past the maze of shops and hotels he had seen so far, up into the hills, and beyond, to a place where the houses fell away and the buildings seemed to hide behind large walls and autocannon and barbed-wired fences. They passed one embassy, then another, then another. Then came a dreary grey building, stark and Brutalist, shaped with rings upon rings of concrete reaching up like a giant funnel planted there to catch the rain. There was an electrified fence outside it – a new addition, apparently – and an ugly gate with armed guards in front of it.

'Ministry of Reconciliation,' it read. It looked like a hotel built by a man who had spent his entire life designing bunkers.

This, Mason assured him, was where the entire bot operation had been run from. 'Around are normal ministry work buildings,' he said, clearly struggling with English. 'Inside, big building and here,' he gestured at the big Brutalist spiral – 'Watchtower. Big Match laboratory, operations, transmission.'

So *this* was where everything happened. Bengali eyed it critically.

And then he was being marched inside. Past gates, ID verification systems and then into a long hallway that went past massive glass-fronted machine workshops the size of aircraft hangers. Peering in, he saw row after row of white-suited engineers, assembling children's skeletons out of metal, fitting batteries, crafting faces. Kushlani saw him and waved him over. She was wearing engineer whites.

'This is what we call the engine room,' she said. 'This whole place used to be a factory for Lanka Leyland – that's the local subsidiary of British Leyland. They used to make parts for fighter planes here during the Nippon war. Because of how critical it was, the Nipponese kept sending banzaicraft here, so they ended up turning it into a fortress. The workers stayed, most of them.'

He saw a man painting a thin ceramic mask with great care. 'The bots are handmade?'

'Well, we're all government employees, so we have to keep them on a payroll. Unemployment's up three percent. We're not going to be automating anything anytime soon.'

'And the bots themselves? Model?'

'Crofton Institute HumanKind 45s. You know the model? We got the license to build them here. Revenue share.'

He knew the model. It was ancient, at least two decades old, barely worth licensing. Originally designed to be household servants. Sturdy, repairable, but about as mechanically complex as a graduate thesis. Some latent peer-to-peer shortwave ability so that newcomers to a household could quickly learn their human master's preferences the moment they walked in the door. A tremendously basic operating system that could be called smart only if you compared it to a dog. So that was Crofton's game here: bundling off their old and infirm tech to the Ceylon.

But HK-45s were never able to move like the ones he'd seen on television.

He followed her past the engine room. Double doors on the other end swung open, and they were inside an atrium, presumably on one of the outer levels; there was a thin glass strip in the ceiling, and through it he could make out other rings rising above. 'Most of our shortwave transmission infrastructure is also up here. Old Nippon stuff. Radius is about a hundred miles, enough to broadcast to TVs and track and control our sensors without clogging up the data pipes. The broadcast signal is duplicated into the data pipes and sent off to the station in Trinco – that's where our undersea cables connect. It's pretty old tech, but also very stable.'

How crude, he thought, and how complex. Robots being hammered together by a few lads in a workshop. Nippon-war era transmitters. And here, the site of one of those most intriguing robotic breakthroughs in recent years.

A little past that was another hallway. A blue light flickered, painting a strange, clinical scene. Row upon row of servers stood like bookshelves, flickering; some lay on their sides with their guts exposed. It smelled of decay – something dusty, with a whiff of something darker underneath ... something rotten.

Cells. To call them cages would have been a lie, but they gave off a powerful impression, even in concrete, of wanting to be cages. Most were empty. In one was a fat Inquisitor, a huffing creature with red lenses for eyes. In another were three, sitting, facing each other, all identical in stature, their faces hidden behind black masks. There was a certain delicacy to their curves; the slightest hint at their chests that made him sure they were women, or had been at some point.

And standing outside, as if to guard the open not-quite-cells, was a giant, dressed in a manner more ornate than anyone Bengali had seen there. The giant was easily eight feet tall and wore a chest piece with a lion's head as a sigil. In one hand he carried a mace that sparked and spat angry lightning. It gave Bengali a terrible headache just to be near it. One hit with that thing and he would be dead.

The thing's face was an unbroken sheet of metal, a single crude melon that sat astride those shoulders like a mockery of a human head. The face turned to them. Bengali almost jumped.

'And we, uh, do upgrades and additions to the Inquisition,' said Kushlani, embarrassed. 'Ignore Angulimali here. We're just passing through, Anguli. Hewage mostly handles all this stuff, Jacob. This way, please.'

For the first time, he wondered what the hell Ceylon was really like to need such monsters. All the colonies had Inquisitors: it was known. But he had never seen so many out in the open before. In India, there was at least some civility, some token pretense, some attempt to package the thing into a veneer acceptable to society.

He let himself be led to an elevator, glad to be away from that strange glare.

'And you run all this?' he murmured softly as the elevator took them up, revealing level upon level of workshops, offices and at least one food court.

'I work on the broadcast and research fronts,' she said. 'Although ... well, like I said, I can give you some of the information you want, but source code, for that, you need to talk to Hewage. He calls the shots on everything. Here, this is our stop.'

The elevator stopped at a bland floor lined with what looked like offices. A door said 'DE ALMEIDA – PRIVATE'. Inside was a white room, almost clinically sterile: two racks of compute hardware took up the back, and at the front there was a desk, a medical operating table, a tea machine and a terminal connected to the guts of some machine. None of them new, but there was enough – he counted, with a slight twinge of envy – to outpower anything the university had given him in recent times.

A face peered at him from the desk. He started, but it was just a bot, like the ones he'd seen on the televisions. Up closer, the illusion of it being a child disintegrated somewhat. He could clearly see the metal jaws, the lenses, the carefully placed striped of fake-skin that hid the seams and frameworks.

'What am I doing here again?'

'On the table, Dr. Bengali. The machine on the table has got all the data I can share with you: hardware, statistics from previous broadcasts, footage, b-roll, highlights. If you need anything else, drop me a message. I'll be down shortly – I've got to get started on the prep work for tomorrow's broadcast. Also a draft copy of Hewage's book. It's not really complete. I don't think it'll be worth much, but he said he wanted you to understand.'

A thick book – real paper, bound and scribbled over in an untidy scrawl. He opened it to the first page and read:

In the early 2000s, a friend of mine conducted an experiment: could a machine design a circuit?

We were at Dartmouth, I was doing my master's. Several months before M dropped out and caused all that scandal. My friend set about creating a circuit design that would take in an input signal, and if it was more than five volts, would light a bulb with it. She took the design around and we all had a crack at making it as efficient as could be.

She then wrote an assembly program which had what we felt was a strange directive – shuffle components about in random configurations and zero in on circuits that met a goal. It was 'rewarded' for getting closer and closer to the goal – again, we had arguments over how the points were allotted, which seemed a bit arbitrary. She went ahead and did it anyway.

'Is there, ah, a smoking area nearby?'

She tucked the bot head under her arm. 'Balcony down the hall, on the right.'

He watched her flow out of the room with the disembodied head tucked under her arm.

'Of course,' he murmured, and shook himself. Surreal.

The first design produced was fabulously stupid. It was so far off that we joked that a random assemblage of circuit components could have done a better job. The hundredth was the same.

The thousandth learnt to light the bulb.

By the two thousandth, it was taking in a signal and lighting a bulb.

By the four thousandth, it was doing exactly what she wanted it to do. Except here was the kicker: it ran on a third of the parts we used for the original lab-designed circuit. Some parts weren't even connected, but if you took them out, the circuit stopped working. Somehow, the assembler had, by trial and error, figured out how to use fluxes in the various wires to produce a working circuit.

She died before she could publish. Suicide. It took me years to replicate her work, but eventually I had it: proof that if one let a goal-based machine learn and evolve towards a target, not only would it eventually reach the desired outputs, but that it also might do so with a third of the cost of components. And of course, once the desired output was achieved, we only needed to store the output, not the design program.'

He sat down and began reading.

≈

Evening fell. One of the servants, possibly worried about him missing lunch, brought him a gin and tonic and sandwiches. Someone else brought him a packet of cigarettes. He looked up once or twice, and even wandered out looking for Kushlani, but the corridors were too eerie, so he came right back to the book, engrossed.

So what had Hewage done here? The technical documentation on Kushlani's machine was sparse on the software. They had kept the HK45 base operating system, sure, but the way things trailed off into obscure technical details made him suspect that a lot to do with the software had been redacted. What was *backpropagation*? Why was there an entire side note about bias-variance tradeoffs? What was this heap of binary named 'default model' that seemed to take in input and produced output, but lacked any kind of *if > this > then > do that* logic, and mostly seemed to be setting and resetting states?

He puzzled over this, at times digging into Hewage's weird little autobiography to see if he ever spoke of these things.

Why was this operating system sandboxed, with the command buffer sealed, except to this hodgepodge of—

Wait.

The first inklings of the design struck him. So Hewage had taken the old HK45 and its safe, predictable operating system. He had then installed this strange batch of code and fooled the OS into thinking that this other code, running right there in its own head, was actually a *human*, talking to it.

As Bengali traced the command paths, he began to notice the little touches of genius. In front of the machine learning system was a module called TC/TCITR that siphoned outputs from what the selfish-state model 'saw': damage done, power loss to the system, and so on. TC/TCITR maintained a log of all orders sent by 'the human' to the selfish state, calculated a 'confidence interval' based on the history and results of such decisions and deleted orders that it deemed too stupid. At higher levels of confidence, the TC/TCITR module started reducing the number of decisions it actually checked, and let most of them through.

The end result was charmingly intelligent: initially, the fake 'human' code would be deemed too stupid to obey, and the base programming would run the show. Which meant –

The code – this part of the machine – was *learning*.

And as the machine learned and its decisions became smarter, it gained more and more control over its decisions. More and more confidence in its judgements. It delivered these judgements to the operating system, and bit by bit, the base programming would give way.

Bengali flipped the autobiography open. There were pages he had skipped. Hewage had developed an interest in biology, it seemed:

We think of the human brain as one unit. The terminology we use – souls, minds – belie the underlying nature of the actual design. The mind is not one seamless device, but many minds constantly talking to each other. The frontal lobe thinks, plans, issues commands. The temporal sometimes accepts, often fine-tunes, sometimes argues, sometimes acts on its own. The parietal lobe watches, understands, passes information.

A biologist would no doubt be able to describe the brain better, but this for me was enough. Why reinvent the wheel? All this time, we in the robotics industry have been obsessed with building parietal lobes and trying to tack on functions of the frontal lobe in ever more complex and hand-crafted decision trees, often slowing down the overall processing.

Nature has a design that works. I think we should adopt it. Hardwired instincts, flexible, long-term planning that can learn, uncertainty—

He felt a surge of excitement.

And here were other command lines, things that could trigger overrides: the operating system could talk back to the machine-that-learned, and 'ask' it to think about power, repairs. Or it could panic if everything dropped too low and run screaming for the hills.

And here were behaviour deviances: a standard module – custom-tuned parameters for social attention and low appetite for risk. The Explorer module, greyed out, that turned down the social attention parameter, turned up the risk.

Was that by accident, or by design? Where the hell did these parameters come from? If by design, this was a complexity beyond what he'd seen in the code. He murmured to himself, thinking of how to explain this to Drake. No, Drake probably knew. The question was of what military significance was this? Sitting there, in that ugly remodelled fortress in a backwater colony, Hewage had made breakthroughs that would send shockwaves through the Royal Society of Robotics. How to validate this model? And how the hell had this come about in the first place, given that none of it was actually in the documentation?

'Incredible,' Bengali murmured, and felt unpoetic. All this work, and only Hewage, and maybe Kushlani de Almeida, knew. Unpublished. Unheard of.

He could take it. His hands trembled briefly. He could take this. Publish it under his name. Bengali, J, 2035. Walker, du Marek – they would initially resist, of course, but he could raise funds. If it worked out, he would be a god. Given enough time and students—

No. No. Drake knew. Drake must have sanctioned this, of course. Bengali then came down to Earth as he finished the documentation. The machine-that-learned itself. Hewage talked around it, theoretically. But he never, as far as Bengali could see, described its actual implementation. Every diagram had it as a black box in a standard flowchart.

And the book. The autobiography. Hewage had it sent to him. Which meant he knew exactly what effect it would have.

Bastard. Like stout Cortez, with eagle eyes, staring at the Pacific. And Bengali, like all of Cortez's men, wild-eyed, silent upon a peak in Darien.

Bengali threw the books aside and fumbled for a cigarette. The balcony was nearby. He smoked furiously, barely taking in the city outside, and started when the door opened midway through his smoke.

It was Hewage. Wordlessly, the Ceylonese man lit his own cigarette and joined Bengali at the balcony. It was silent for a few minutes, as they inhaled the promise of cancer.

'So,' said Hewage, at last. 'Did you copy the books yet? Don't pretend you weren't instructed to take what you could. You should have enough to send to Drake now.'

'But not the meat of it.'

Hewage grinned. It was a very feral grin. 'No, not the meat of it. They won't be able to replicate it even if they sleep with those damn books for a year. I'll publish my way, by God. Ten years here, running the grandest experiment of all time, just so idiots at the Royal Society can't argue back. I'll work for Drake, but after I get my dues in the field, not before. You understand what I'm doing here now?'

'Not all of it,' said Bengali. He felt like saying more – that he thought it was genius, that he thought it was madness, that he was profoundly jealous, that he wanted in ...

'Good,' said Hewage. 'So what will it take? A nice blank certification for my stuff, some breadcrumbs for Drake ... how much money in the bank is that worth for you?'

Bengali gaped. 'You know I can't take a bribe.'

'You'd be surprised how many people said that when I started and how few continued saying it a little later.' Hewage flicked ash off his cigarette. 'There's a few more years of work to go before I publish, and it definitely has to be public. There's two others – Chinese roboticists, doing little behavioural experiments out of the Port City.'

'You invited *the Chinese?*'

'Why not? You people think they're playing around with little toys, but in reality they're far ahead of anything du Marek and the others are on. Their Port City systems alone are incredibly sophisticated. They're dying to do more with the tech. Even if the Royal Society stiffs me, China certainly won't.' Again, that feral grin. 'Besides, what do you think pays for all the fuel we feed the bots?'

'That'd make you a traitor!'

'The only thing I have sworn allegiance to is myself,' said Hewage. 'Of course, if you report this conversation to Drake, I'll just say you were jealous and making things up. I'm far more valuable to him than you are.'

Bengali had the sudden, fleeting urge to kick the man off the balcony. He admired Hewage now, true. He was clearly a genius. But still, a punch in the face—

'Seven million rupees.'

'No. No. Absolutely not.'

The Ceylonese man stubbed out his cigarette and flicked it over the balcony. 'There is a tide in the affairs of men', he said, 'which, taken at the flood, leads on to fortune.'

'I'm not taking a bribe, no matter how much Shakespeare you quote.'

'Well,' said Hewage. 'Pity. Because until you do, that's all you'll ever see. Enjoy the Big Match. We're coming up on the Second Innings now. And tell Drake I said hello.'

FIVE

Meanwhile, harsh yellow sunlight lanced down upon the ruins of the old city of Colombo, touching briefly on a small gang of tiny figures cleaning garbage from a road.

It was Broken Arm and her tribe, or what was left of it. The days had not been kind to them. Three-fourths of all the tribes they usually allied with were gone. All the large groups had crumbled beneath the mathematics of too few resources divided by too many. Half of the Sons of Cinnamon dreamt uneasily in shadowy halls, watching their batteries trickle down, unable to move or cry out. The Children of the Taj had left. The Dockhands – the roving maledict that usually raided heavily into the centre of Colombo – now confined itself to the port territories and the pieces above. Any remaining machines, dead or alive, had been beaten, scavenged for the last bits of fuel-food in their machine guts, and left to die.

All around Kandy, bets had been made, post-match drinking already planned, and now people sat, glued to their screens, watching the carnage unfold. It was entertainment at its finest.

Under Broken Arm's guidance, the tribe dragged all manner of filth – from polythene to rusted iron to chipped, stained concrete – from the mountain of trash that sat squat behind them to home, to mutant crows and pockets of gas that burst every so often. Since time immemorial, they had taken things to the mountain, cleaning up the streets of this ghost city. They knew exactly where to look for iron, for heavy things that could be thrown, for padding that could be turned into shields.

Because they were in battle.

It was with a group they had generally avoided in the past. No names had been exchanged, no callsigns established. They had come in the darkness of the night, cutting down the Cinnamons, gutting them for food and turning whatever buildings remained into outposts. They fought with rocks and traps. Across the face of the Galle Face Green, stretching all the way into Havelock, were webs of plastic and old nylon, some of them still containing the struggling figures of bots who had wandered in.

Broken Arm had to intervene. The Cinnamons were allies. Her tribe took what weapons the Cinnamons were willing to part with – spears, most of the time – and fought back in fierce guerilla battle. Early on she had established the idea of ambushing the enemy when they came to check on their traps. Her forces had now taken seven outposts from the Sons of Cinnamon, and the battle damage showed. The sun, with its cutting lance of heat, fell on legs that sparked and pseudoskin so badly flayed that some of them looked like grinning skulls crowned by flaps of flesh.

Sky, who had scouted around, had brought back the numbers, the locations, the enemies. Steel rods, bent by patient, painless hands, became hooks for tearing down walls. When they were ready, the tribe charged out of camera range and towards their new enemy.

'UNWISE', said the Port City as they passed it. 'UNWISE. NEW AGENT ACTIVITY DETECTED. UNITY IS STRENGTH.'

Broken Arm did not understand what this meant.

SIX

Eliott Grimme, like Bengali, had a job to do. Unlike Bengali, he went to work immediately.

One of the greatest military strategists to ever walk the earth had pointed out that all warfare was based on calculation. 'Before doing battle, in the temple one calculates and will win, because many calculations were made,' Sun Tzu had written, referring to the need to withdraw and think things through before commitment.

Through the ages, men and women had hewed to this word, though with varied results – the humans, too biased, too limited by their norms and principles and hatreds; the machines, too inflexible, too prone to constructing beautiful plans of such great complexity that they fell apart at the desertion of a single brigade; and then finally, him.

The midpoint. The organizing principle. The machine that bled. The Reaper.

Every morning, he woke up to grey concrete. The room was comfortable and came with the two Inquisitors who would wake him up. He would pace the corridors outside, following the rambling corridors, stopping short whenever the prospect of the outside came into play. The thin copper-wire runt would follow. The fat one would guard his door.

This hospital was a part of the greater corpus of the Inquisitor headquarters in Kandy, and had been designed for efficiency, not intuitiveness. Sometimes, he would emerge onto an assembly point, empty except for Inquisitors guarding the doors. Other times, he'd emerged onto a training ground, where dozens of tuned bodies in camouflage fatigues drilled in that strange native martial art of theirs called Angampora – all leaps and grapples and holds, modified to work with pistols and rifles.

Penhaligon ran an odd ship – part mafia, part police station, part elite commando corps. Sometimes Grimme would emerge in the police-like heart of this operation – endless halls of humans processing cases, reporting to Inquisitors that lounged lazily and stalked between lanes of tables like vampires sniffing their prey. At the long end of these halls was an office with Penhaligon's name on it. The rich and the powerful apparently came to pay obeisance there.

Ceylon, Taprobane, Serendib. He flipped through every single piece of information Penhaligon could supply him – histories, population reports, weather. Island-nation, Crown colony, tropical temperatures, very high humidity. Seven million people. Two main hubs: Kandy, where he presumably was, functioned as the seat of government, while the Trincomalee port was the commercial centre.

What used to be Colombo was now dust and shrapnel. The rest of the island was either a factory – there were tons of those automated farms that extracted everything from tea to titanium – or a homestead; a feudal village handed over to some harmless Brit who had earned a second-class retirement. Some of them bred and multiplied and ran their villages like slaveshops. Others went native and took local mistresses. Or maybe the local mistresses took them.

Axiom one: *Know Heaven and Earth.*

Grimme set up a preprocessor and went to sleep.

It was the first trick he had learned after that very first operation, where he stopped being Captain Eliott Grimme and started becoming the Reaper. The processors spliced into his brain were old now, but they still let him design the commands he needed, and translate those commands for his brain cells to work on. Not everyone survived being able to manipulate your own brain, of course – War and Plague had been the best examples of how badly things could go wrong.

But he was the Reaper, optimized for this kind of thinking, the last and arguably the greatest of his lineage. His brain still worked, and the processors still ran their firmware, and the preprocessor began its work. In the darkness, it sifted through everything he had, extracting, reordering and unpacking information. Maps unfolded in his mind. Information. Knowledge banks slowly packing themselves into his head. The parser, glitching all the while, dipped into the stream of history, pulled out images like fish. He saw an island, green and dotted with strange white domes, where people came to worship. He saw ships visit, all creaking timbers. He saw brown men in ridiculous dresses – all tassels and gold and silk – being visited by white men in iron. The ships were fought off, the men in iron killed. More ships came, more men, until the last of those in tassels whimpered in a cell barely large enough to contain them.

Then came geography. For this, he had the Inquisitors turn the cooling all the way up in the room. He slipped into the bathroom, took off his clothes and curled up gingerly in the bathtub, waiting for his skeleton to start sending the first of many thousands of overheat warnings. Geography compute was a serious task.

He spent the next twenty hours in a terrible fever, every available neuron press-ganged into service, every synapse overclocked. His skin burned. Water rose from the bathtub in a dense fog. What little intelligence remained misfired, struggling feebly to keep his heart pumping and his head above water. Several times he came to find himself numbly reciting lines that had once struck him on the field of battle, lines tied to the flicker of flame and the charnel stink of the the trench:

> What are the roots that clutch, what branches grow
> Out of this stony rubbish? Son of man,
> You cannot say, or guess, for you know only
> A heap of broken images, where the sun beats,
> And the dead tree gives no shelter, the cricket no relief

The preprocessor burned through every single map at his disposal, gobbling up landscapes, spitting out terrain markers. Choke points. Cover. The roads that snaked from Trincomalee in the east, from the harbour, to the city of

Kandy. The railroads that ran down from there, single-minded, into Colombo. The roads that followed, ever winding. It pulled out the hills of Kandy and quantified the steepness of the climb. The swept down rivers and established flood markers—

A knock on the door. 'Sir, Penhaligon would like to see you for lunch.'

'Later.'

'Sir, he—'

'Later!' he growled. The knocker retreated hurriedly, and then there was only ...

> *There is shadow under this red rock,*
> *Come in under the shadow of this red rock*

And last, it came to Colombo – Colombo by the sea, a city of a million people reduced to rubble in a single instance. A great, corrupt oasis of steel and tar and concrete, warped and twisted, home now only to poison and weeds and a sea breeze that carried the cries of things that had once been seagulls.

> *And I will show you something different from either*
> *Your shadow at morning striding behind you*
> *Or your shadow at evening rising to meet you*

A mountain of trash, inexplicably dumped in one corner. Buildings toppled and old tanks parked in the streets, blocking off almost all the exits. A few embassies whose main structures had survived the Angelstrike, and automated cannons running long after the humans inside had been reduced to bone powder. A post-apocalyptic set piece of city-sized proportions.

I will show you fear in a handful of dust.

And beyond Colombo? The Chinese Port City. Here there was emptiness. He felt the preprocessor and its army of worker neurons rummage hard. There were no schematics anywhere, but he had seen these in Hong Kong. Great floating domes made of what looked like glass, but in reality was a translucent nanoweave skin, self-healing, that could double as an armor and solar array.

It would have the usual precautions, of course. Spore-cannons capable of spraying that entire city with nerve gas. Banks of conventional guns that could send uranium-tipped rounds through anything in their line of sight. Banks of Chinese Marines – vat-cloned off a perfect model, power armor, nasty hundred-kilo railguns. One of those Confucian AIs running the show. This one probably just played courier, trading Chinese goods for British ones, running up shipping and handling bills, a genius reduced to playing shopkeeper.

It must be bored out of its shell.

The preprocessor, which had sensed his thoughts, slowed itself down patiently until his reverie was over. It read the legal agreements and staked out a no-fire zone, then neatly packed away the irrelevant, the unnecessary and the bloated, leaving him with what he needed: a battle map.

'I will show you fear in a handful of dust,' his lips said to the choking, humid cold.

It was late when he rebooted again. His skeleton had thrown him into battle conditioning and gotten him out of that tub. By the time his higher functions came online, a dozen repair processes were crawling through his body, checking subsystems for nonexistent damage. He shut them down and fumbled his way downstairs, top-heavy because of the changes that damn surgeon had made. A few days, bah. It always took longer. Reflexes trained over decades for a lighter, faster body almost threw him off balance and were shelved for retraining.

The fat Inquisitor was outside the door. He didn't seem to speak much, and he just led Eliott to the belly of the building. A series of entrances. An airlock. Two more Inquisitors – young, Ceylonese-English mixes by the looks of them – opened a door. A smooth carpet, a stuffed lion head beneath the Imperial crest, a table set for lunch, untouched. It smelled of fresh paint. Sixteen chairs stood before the captain's table, like supplicants praying to a wooden god. There were people in there, most of them in uniform, some obviously drunk, all in a careless ring around Penhaligon, who stood like a dark vampire in their midst. There were soldiers playing cards in a corner.

The reek of arrack hit his system. Officers angled away from the circle, curious, but not curious *enough* to welcome him in.

Penhaligon smiled; a thin tightening of the lips. 'Gentlemen, meet Eliott Grimme, the man you've heard so much about,' he said, guiding Eliott gently from one circle to another. 'Captain ... ah, this is Colonel Wattegama, Perera, de Andrado. Ratwatte, here, come talk to Mr. Grimme.'

A chorus of rituals – how-do-you-dos; pleased-to-meet-you-sirs. Hands stretched out to be shaken. Eliott spurned the automated human contact, ignored the looks they gave him, half-offended, half-afraid. There were shades of white skin, Eliott noticed, and even where the Ceylonese name held higher rank; the whitest went first.

'Pleasure to meet you, sir,' said a cultured voice with a thin veneer of a London accent on top. Eliott found himself shaking hands with a dark, heavyset, bespectacled man who squeezed his hand like a python strangling its prey. 'Thank you very much for helping us out with the situation here. Whatever you need, come talk to me.'

Penhaligon gave the man a pointed glance and led Grimme away, murmuring, 'It would have been better if that bloody family hadn't caused this mess in the first place. Fucking Bandaranaikes think they own the place. And try not to make Khan suspicious; he's obviously here from India. How's progress?'

'On schedule. I have the topography. We need to talk people, supply trains, transport.'

'Good. Mason, take Mr. Grimme, show him around.'

Mason was the thin Inquisitor. 'Food,' he said to Mason. 'I need food.'

Mason hesitated. 'Rice and curry, sir? Or bites?' A man, dark-skinned, uniformed and sober, sprung into action, and seemingly produced a plate from thin air. Sandwiches – trying very hard to be polite, but there was too much butter, not enough meat. Eliott ate a few anyway. It was inefficient, but the body could extract some useful elements out of the mess.

Penhaligon tapped his glass gently. The circles closed around him, the conversations slowly descending into silence.

'Gentlemen', he said, 'before we begin dinner, let's go over the situation a bit. Firstly, Ceylon. Lovely place. Crown colony. We've got a lot of resource operations here, but I think we all know the big picture here. Some of you ... Molligoda? You were around when the Chinese first came here and the whole madness exploded in Colombo, yes?'

'Yes, sir. And then we flattened them, sir,' said an old man who sagged heavily over a bloated belly. He beamed around at the table. 'Angelstrike took out the entire city, heh!'

Your city, though Grimme. *Sellout*.

'There you are. God bless our souls, gentlemen, we fired an Angels Interitus down on a city of a million people just to prove a point. The Chinese got the message, asked for permission to dredge up some land off the ruins and set up a trading center. So now, the real point of this island is to serve as a neutral go-between zone between the Chinese and us. There's a delicate balance to keep here, and we've kept it so far, so before I go any further, a toast to us for a job well done.'

They cheered and raised glasses the colour of tea. Molligoda was the first to down his drink.

'Now, unfortunately, we have a situation,' said Penhaligon, suddenly quieter. In the hush, they all leaned forward, the cheer wiped from their faces. 'You all know the situation with the bot business. A few glitches, huge to-do. Two of them got into Kandy right here and killed a few good citizens. Our Bandaranaike's uncle was involved, weren't they?'

Dark glances. The one named Bandaranaike, decked in the livery of a major, flushed a deep purple.

'No one's blaming you, Bandaranaike. Shit happens and flowers grow on it.'

'Sir,' said Bandaranaike, who seemed to have some difficulty speaking.

Penhaligon tutted, like a disappointed parent. 'But I'm afraid it's time for some professionalism in this circus. Her Majesty's government have demanded that we test, certify and pass through all manner of red tape, and the upshot of that is we may not have a Big Match next year.'

Eliott was surprised at the dismay on people's faces. It seemed genuine.

'But we do have to try and get each and every one of those little machines hauled back here and tested before we send them out again. I've brought in one of my associates, Mr. Grimme, who you've now met. He's much older than I am, and dare I say very, very good at his job. Some of you may already know who he is, some of you may not. All I can say is, don't bother looking up his files, gentlemen, it's far beyond your place to do so. I'll handle the politics. If things go according to plan, this is basically just an exercise in collecting puppets. No shots fired. No heroes, no martyrs. We play this game until every one of those bots are recalled and back in Dr. Hewage's lab, at which point the technicians figure out safer ways of doing things.'

People tried not to look Eliott in the face. Someone muttered, 'Hong Kong'.

'And by the way, nobody tries to shut Hewage's operation down. Nobody interferes. No scapegoating this one, or Mr. Grimme here may pay your families a visit. Clear?'

'Sir,' said Molligoda. Others nodded and agreed. Penhaligon's expression brightened immediately and he clapped his hands.

'Wonderful. Wonderful. I always told my boys that you were men of reason. Dinner?'

Eliott looked at the strange concoction that was put in front of him. A smorgasboard of colour on white; browns, yellows, greens.

The arrival of food seemed to trigger something in the small crowd. Everyone sat down to eat, some less steadily than others. More sober, dark-skinned men turned up to serve them. There was an odd dynamic between them. Though they were soldiers, they seemed more like servants – slightly stooped, nodding eagerly at the officers, who turned back and ordered as though they were talking to children.

'They're Tamil, sir,' said Mason, who had seen Grimme staring. 'The Yarl affair got them all demoted.'

This meant nothing to him, but he filed it away for reference. The Indian major, more polite than the rest, sat down next to him. Everyone except Penhaligon ate with their hands. He watched them carefully and mimicked them. Large portions. No food above the second digit. Doable.

The rice was ridiculously rich, loaded in carbohydrates; he could break that down for energy. More protein was required. He sent Mason back for more, and more, until most of the guests had stopped eating and began staring at this pale, thin waxwork of a man who had demolished six plates of rice, and was now well into his seventh.

Penhaligon coughed discretely as he began to order the eighth. Grimme looked at the stares around him. Of course. Among humans, he would have kept the energy intake low. The Tamil soldier, instead of food, brought him a bowl of water with a lemon in it, and he washed his hands like the rest of them. The soldier seemed startled to be thanked, and scurried away.

≈

'That was sharp,' Eliott said that night, as he followed Penhaligon down the winding corridors. It was almost midnight, if time meant anything. Behind them was a motley crew of men and women in uniform who had followed them from the room. There was a cook among them, and what looked like a maid. None of them were, of course, what they seemed to be – they were all Inquisitors; they were human only when you looked at them sideways. 'You think they'll do what you want them to?'

'Of course they're going to do what I want them to. Men like this are predictable, Grimme. By the way, I got you what you asked for. Can you make it quick?'

'Sure,' said Eliott. They emerged onto a yard – a dark thing that opened up to a night sky overhead, with only the artificial moonbeams for company.

Penhaligon nodded, satisfied, and pulled a cigarette out of the long folds of his suit. 'You think we can have this over with in a month?'

He thought about it. One city. Slightly under a thousand machines, sandwiched between the Ceylonese and the Chinese. A few pesky no-fire zones in between. There would be a lot of poking and prodding to do, of course, a few opening gambits to be made, but on the whole ...

'We'll try for a month, maybe two,' he said. 'That's my best estimate so far. You know, you didn't even need me here. Get yourself a battle computer from Hong Kong and that'd do just fine.'

'Drake give you any funny orders?'

'Yes, he asked me to kill you when this was done.'

'And are you? Going to?'

The question hung between them. Eliott let it drag out a little longer, just to the edge of cruelty. 'I might be interested in this retirement plan of yours,' he confessed. 'I like what I've seen of the place. You'll need to make me vanish, of course. And I need maintenance.'

'Fallen in duty. Tragic accident. Gone rogue. The possibilities are endless. And you've seen our equipment and the boys we keep around. I think we can support you quite well.'

And just like that, a deal was struck. Penhaligon grinned. 'Switching sides became easier for you once you crossed over, wasn't it?'

Eliott looked up at the night sky, at the dark clouds that swirled around the moon. Those words stirred up memories from inside him – data points, tagged by the preprocessor as useful; memories he had not recalled in a while. Machines he had fought with; machines he had fought against. Hong Kong, yes, but buried under that, the ghost of Gregory Mars. War: simple, direct, honorable. The perfect battle-axe, until the day he flipped sides and fought alongside the Gurkhas. And Charlotte Plague – engineered to be the perfect, the most beautiful of them all. Charlotte, to whom men handed their kingdoms on a platter, besotted. Charlotte, who dismantled the IRA by merely crossing her legs, and then vanished, sowing the seeds of her deadly retrovirus in her wake. And himself, the Reaper – master of the long game; the ultimate secret weapon.

But he had changed too, hadn't he? They all had. And it was he, Eliott, who had been sent to clean up the mess, and then Penhaligon had been sent after *him* – an endless dance of plays and counter-plays and hidden motives.

'Once you see the futility of it all', he said, 'it really doesn't matter what side you're on.'

Mahasen Wijeratne, who everyone called Mason, lay in his isolation chamber, a utilitarian enclosure of concrete and glass, and thought about Eliott Grimme. A tall, narrow thing, with a face that might as well have been carved out of pale candlewax; so corpselike. Only the eyes, he thought, showed life. There was a curious restlessness to them – they roved over faces with a surprising intensity, and rarely stayed still, moving with a certain economy, a certain wariness.

So these were the prototypes, he thought.

Mahasen had seen the specs for War, of course. Gregory Mars had been the poster boy – the simplest of the lot, the straightforward Uberman, the man-tank-supersoldier. The kind you put on recruiting posters. The kind whose internals boiled down to insane amounts of torque and neurons tweaked so impossibly far that it was practically precognitive when it came to shooting things down and chopping them up. Mars was, in a sense, the template of what had eventually become both the Colonial Inquisition and the Special Operations Executive.

But Death was a different beast. This one they had always kept mum about. It was only after Hong Kong that the word really leaked. And then they caught it and sent Grimme back for reconditioning – Penhaligon's career had really kicked off there. Who knew what else they had added?

Still, Penhaligon caught it, he thought. That old man. So not an impossible mark. Not too fast. As long as it didn't do anything stupid, this was an easy ride.

And so he was not ready when Grimme knocked on the door.

'You're supposed to see this,' the man-machine said softly. 'Penhaligon's orders.'

'Hang on,' said Mahasen, strapping on his handguns. The stims kicked him fully awake.

He followed Grimme down those weird corridors. They came by winding paths to an isolated corner of the building, where there were thirty men, stripped down to only their basic gear. A mix. Ceylonese soldiers, officers. They stood at attention. Only their eyes betrayed their nervousness.

'This is it?' asked Eliott Grimme, sounding disappointed.

'As representative as I can get,' said Penhaligon, who did not seem to relish this either. A cigarette hung from his fingers, trailing ash. 'As much as I can spare you.'

'Alright,' said Grimme.

And the torture began.

They took them out one after the other. Led them like cattle to a locked room, soundproof. Locked them in with Grimme and Mason, who tried not to look, who tried to shut down the implants that took those terrible screams, processed them and made them too clear and audible to bear.

When it was done, Grimme got up, blood splattered on his pale face. 'Next.'

There came a point where Mahasen could take it no more. Grimme looked down at the chokehold Mahasen held it in. The waxwork face looked completely unsurprised.

'Know thyself,' Grimme said, as if explaining to a slow, dim-witted child. 'I need to know how these systems perform under stress. I need to know where they break and why and how.'

'Damn you,' Mahasen cried over the moans of the ruined thing that wept and wailed on the chair.

Grimme kicked Mahasen's feet out from under him, tossed him lightly against the blood-splattered wall. For a second, he saw Grimme as it as it truly was: a monster in human flesh, a rude simulacra, as much machine as the things they were supposed to fight, a reaper designed to do what even Penhaligon could never bring himself to.

He almost shot it to bits then and there. He guns were already out, aimed right at that pale face.

'Next,' it said. And when Mahasen did not move, it walked out calmly, to where the last soldier stood, practically shitting his pants in terror. From the other room came the sound of grunts. And then the screaming.

When Grimme returned, it looked thoughtful. It looked at the guns Mason pointed at it. 'A word of advice,' it said,

almost gently. 'Treat those things like a penis. It's fine to
have one, but if you pull it out and start waving it in my
face, we're going to have trouble.'

No wonder, he thought to himself as he lay in his bunk
that night. No wonder they never spoke of Hong Kong. No
wonder they kept this thing secret. No wonder Penhaligon
wanted it buried when the job was done.

≈

The next few days passed in a blur for Eliott Grimme. Or
maybe it was time that stood still and he who moved; he
could never tell.

In the mornings, he helped sort out the army he would
take down south once the machines were done killing
themselves. Penhaligon ran his Inquisitors with an iron
hand, but the 'army' that he had inherited was a ragtag
mess, a bunch of peasants press-ganged into holding
rifles up ceremoniously when white men passed. The
last time this country had seen an armed conflict within
its borders was in the 1980's: the ill-fated Yarl Rebellion.
The Governor at the time, one H.S. Beckett, had kept the
Ceylonese men away and deliberately undersupplied,
fearing that they might switch sides, and sent in troops
imported from India.

Which means the damned Ceylonese Volunteer Rifles
were running around with guns older than their fathers.
Most of the troop transports ran on petrol. The plantations
and farms hadn't prepared proper field rations in decades.
It all came down to a standing army of ten thousand,
probably less once you accounted for dead people on

payroll, all poorly equipped, poorly trained, and basically about as useful as a well-aimed rubber duck.

He marked out a twentieth of the best. At best estimate there would between a hundred bots and two hundred bots left over, so he would have a five-to-one advantage: decent odds. Then he began digging into the leadership.

Generations of Governors and Inquisitors had placed over them a bunch of secondhand aristocrats whose chief achievement, as far as Eliott could figure out, was to have attended the right school. This whole colony was a nation of sheep. Held down by a handful of slightly better-fed sheep.

Molligoda, Bandaranaike, Dissanayake. These he had to work around.

'Announce a game,' he said to Penhaligon. 'This Big Match will be special. Truly special. We'll have our folk enter the tournament. Bets on whether the humans will win.'

The announcement rippled like a shockwave through the population. And then came a show of force. The pain test had showed him men who broke too easily, gibbering out command secrets and passcodes at the slightest hint of pain. He had Penhaligon dump the bodies from the pain test where the command aristocracy would find them. No explanations. Fear and guesswork did to men's minds what certainty could barely hope to achieve.

Then, while panic and gossip spread like wildfire, Eliott got Penhaligon to point out a few of the most disposable aristocratic henchmen, armed them to the teeth, and packed them on a transport to the outskirts of Colombo.

The pretext was that they were going out on reconnaissance and to establish supply routes.

A small group of the bots had strayed past camera range, occupying five crate drops just at the perimeter of the Colombo zone. The henchmen took four, were cut down, fell back and held three. Just enough victory. Just enough dead to make sure surviving meant something special.

It worked perfectly. Men would come back bearing trophies and exaggerated tales of their own gallantry. People became superstars, albeit briefly. There would be medals. Promotions. Pats on the back. All these silly baubles that guaranteed that other humans would gladly put their lives on the line now. They had been shown the carrot as well as the stick. The donkey would do exactly as expected.

'Fear in a handful of dust,' Eliott said to Penhaligon. They were in Penhaligon's cavern of an office; empty of people and servants, it looked 'Humans are predictable, Penhaligon.'

Penhaligon smirked. 'I remember you used to write poetry,' he said. 'Always thought it passing strange. You know that your case file, when they gave it to me, had all your poems cited as evidence that you might be going mad?'

Eliott struggled to remember. Much of specifics of those times had been erased from his memory during the reconditioning; only ghost trails remained. Her Royal Majesty could not suffer a servant to remember their defection. There were no other poems in his head.

III: Expiration

ONE

The old woman leant heavily on her rake, panting in the heat.

She could feel the rain in the air. It was in the heat that wrapped around her like a living thing, the sun's angry glare picked up by the humidity and turned into an insufferable monster. It was in the way the shirt stuck to her back and her collar stank every time she went indoors for a sip of the precious water.

A month ago, she would have had some company, at least – lines of farmhands outside her little shop, ordering hot, sweet tea and playing checkers and sharing bootleg beedis. But now, the Maha harvest was done, the harvest harnesses packed up and returned to the Tower and the farmers vanished. Now, the fields around the Tower lay barren and bare.

Occasionally, a handful of those who worked at the Tower would emerge, working their way past the dozens of security checkpoints, and pause, as if seeing the world outside for the first time. They always travelled in small, uncertain groups; never alone. Sometimes, they would find their way to her and tentatively order tea and pay a hundred times more than what it was worth. She listened in on their conversations, playing the role of the simple village shopkeeper – aney nonamahattaya, what do we know of important people like yourself? Here, have some pol rotti. But by now, she knew quite a lot about them. They were *bioengineering* people. An English word. They all had bosses they hated. They made this *bio* for companies across the Empire. They had three meals a day and lived in the lesser rings of the Tower and often dreamed of going to Nepal, maybe to England – to see the world and come back.

Some of them reminded her of her son, who had gone to Colombo many years back to get his degree so he could become a bioengineer. He had been adamant: 'Amme, this is the future. There are no doctors anymore, only lawyers and engineers and factors owners.' Then they burned Colombo down, killing her son and leaving her alone with just this piece of land and the tea shop.

But as of late, there were more people coming to the Tower. *Network specialist.* A new word. They seemed self-important. The bioengineering people were unhappy about them being there. Something about the Ministry setting up some a new network on the Tower. 'We're a private company,' they said. 'The government shouldn't interfere.'

'Children', she wanted to say. 'The government does whatever it wants.'

So when the little bell at her shop rang again, she dropped the rake and hurriedly made her way back into the hut, through the living room and into her little storefront, expecting more of the same.

A new man stood there.

'Amme,' he said. Mother ... though he was not her son. 'What happened to your eyes?'

Mortified, she adjusted the cloth she kept wrapped around the gaping sockets in her face.

'Can you see?'

She could, in a way. A long time ago, the people from the Tower had taken her inside, and when she came out, she could see – not as she once had, but in flames of red and green and blue.

This customer was strange. He was clearly alive. But most of him was blue: the colour of dead things and machinery.

'Not as well as mahatthaya,' she said, deferentially. 'Mahaththayata theykak?' Would sir like some tea?

'Not right now,' said the man. She could see his head turning, oddly cold and blue, scanning this way and that. 'This road, it leads to Colombo?'

'Yes, since the bridge collapsed, it's been the only way ... it turns left here, and there's another junction that leads to Manikpotha, and from there ...'

The man seemed satisfied. 'There'll be a lot of us coming this way,' he said. 'You'll have to make lots of tea.' She could see him looking at the Tower. 'So the network is being set up? I see lots of work going on up there.'

'Yes, it's been very busy these days,' she said, putting a kettle on. 'Lots of new people. Working on something for the Ministry, they say!'

'Good, good.'

She served him. He ate in silence. The road ahead started growling and the vehicles rolled by, one after the other, and ground to a halt outside the Tower. She heard men and women speaking – terse, clipped syllables, orders snapped – and an English voice above that; one that brought silence in its wake. More customers?

'Sir is from ...?' she ventured, taking out her mugs and polishing them.

'Kandy. Inquisition.'

She almost dropped the mug she was holding. When she spoke again, she tried very hard to hide the shiver in her voice. 'It's rare to see people from Kandy here,' she said. 'Aney, sorry. Anything you need from here, sir?'

The man peered at her display cases. 'Maybe some wadei and rotti. Perera, here. Confirm directions to Colombo. We've got a bit of work to do there,' he told her, offhandedly. 'There might be some more of us coming this way. You'll make a fortune on tea, eh?'

A second man joined them. This one was even bluer. She noticed how quickly the first's tone switched to one of deference, and caught the subtle undercurrent of fear in it.

'We're on the road to Colombo, sir, just behind you. Road curves a bit, but we're on the right path. I've sent Kithsiri out on a motorbike.'

The crunching of footsteps, walking away.

Eventually, the vehicles started up again and left the silence of the fields behind. She listened to them for a long time, then looked around at her little shop – all its shades of blue, and the red of the kettle on the stove – and decided that the time had come to move on out of there.

≈

Behind the line of troop-carriers came Eliott Grimme.

Penhaligon's black cars took him past low, neat fields, clipped square, that drifted past, green against a backdrop of mountains that reached up into the mist. Villages hugged gloomy, ornate British mansions and gardens, narrow roads, and long bunker-like factories in the vast tracts of scrub between places, belching hot black smoke into the sky.

There was a city almost halfway between Colombo and Kandy – a city with the strange name of Gampaha, which broke down, quite literally into Five Villages. The villages were long gone – the British had long since built their churches and railroads and infrastructure. Steel, titanium and paddy refineries sat next to high-rises in an awkward union. Village headmen had evolved – first becoming urban councilmen, then becoming mayors taking bribes for choice apartment lots.

And, as befitting a major town, a sprawling mess of barracks sat at the very outskirts of Gampaha. The largest of these had opened outwards, and from this mouth teemed hordes of men, like ants in uniform.

Eliott took three of Penhaligon's Inquisitors. He had Mason, that annoying Inquisitor pup. Lakshmi, whose files said she had been modified for sight and hearing. And Senanayake, who was your bog-standard modification, standard speed supplement, nothing special – just a faster policeman. They were terribly junior.

He let them handle the soldiers and went to look over the aircraft while they were in the throes of being pumped with helium. They were old British Aerospace dirigibles, second-rate bureaucratic designs built with the cheapest parts available.

Eliott waited until the minion in charge ran out of steam and excuses.

'It's crap,' he told the man. 'But it'll do.'

They would actually do very well. Largely silent, very little runway space required. The grey shapes floated off into the sky. Nothing leaked, nothing creaked. In the city, lights came on inside houses and apartments – someone had seen, someone had heard, someone knew the army was on the move. Children ran to the rooftops to gape in silent wonder at the dirigibles that swarmed over the city and then vanished, carrying their cargo towards Colombo.

The plan was simple. They would fly over to Colombo. The first wave would be five fireteams of twenty. They would set up camp on the perimeter of the Colombo Entertainment Zone, mop up any stragglers, and make sure nothing got through – after all, the whole reason they were here was because a couple of bots had escaped the net – and make their way into the city, grid by grid. Every bot they shot would be collected and transported back to camp. Every time they extended they would leave behind a few men to organize the paths and make sure supplies got through. Eliot had fixed in his mind the image of soldiers extending like a claw into bot territory, mapped precisely down to the roads they would take and the junctions that formed the knuckles; and when the job was done, the claw would retract and return.

The minion, as it turned out, was also the pilot, and was now attempting to impress Lakshmi with tales of daring flights over Nepal. Eliott wanted to tap the man on the shoulder and tell him to go find a woman with less metal in her bones, but it was vaguely amusing.

The other crew members filed in: an assortment of soldiers, handpicked from among those who had faced the bots and returned. Eliott intended to be the spearhead of the strike team. He wanted proven quantities.

The ugly bulb of the Gampaha base fell away and the trees folded in. The wind blew them towards a road snaking south and west, towards Colombo, and they followed. They saw the dust of the ground troops mobilized ahead of time; and then they overtoop the troops, cutting as the crow flies toward their destination.

Senanayake, sitting in the back with the machine gun, counted the settlements in Sinhala as they went past. Their unfamiliar names were turning into a kind of meaningless music. Yaa-goda. Batu-wath-ther.

'Look, you can see Knuckles,' Lakshmi said, pointing at the mountains behind them.

'Dhumbara-Kandhu-Waeti-ya,' Senanayake said slowly.

Lakshmi mimicked the man's accent perfectly. 'Dhumbara kandhuwaetiya.'

Delighted, Senanayake began tossing more words at her, the names once more ebbing into that soft, incomprehensible music. They were young Inquisitors, clearly new to this game. There was still some of that light, boastful cheeriness about them; that little spark of humanity. It would take years before they learned to shut up, before the dull silence crept in, and they truly became one of the Inquisition.

Eliott went back to staring at the forest behind them. And thus they rolled on, the aircraft eating up the miles. So far there had been no resistance.

Eventually they came to large house atop a hill, looking over the rest of the town – what was once social snobbery had turned, over time, into tactical viability. This was where he had sent the first waves of political canon fodder, and he had to admit they had picked a decent place before they pushed too far and died. The house had high walls, a good line of sight on everything. Three jungle-cars with bloated balloon tires were parked in front. Iron spikes had been driven into the ground and strung with electric wire. Beyond the wire he could see the white train station that had once been an entry pointed into the city. It reached out with rusted overhead passes. They were close.

The airship engines cut thrust for landing, and as they drew closer Eliott began to hear the sounds of commotion.

'Radio back to the main column, set up the perimeter, make ready,' he barked back to the pilot and Senanayake, leaping out of the airship, 'and someone tell me what the hell the noise is all about.'

≈

It took ten minutes longer than it should have, but eventually they found a corporal who was comfortable with his English and took him to the first of the corpses, just down the hill from the house.

It was a machine, though it looked for all the world like a dead child – barely four feet tall, curled up against a wall. It wore a cloak of tattered rags and was bound from head to toe in strips of cloth and paper. Only its arms and feet, gleaming metal, gave it away. It stank.

Eliott's hands touched it gently, pushing it around until he could see the face. A cracked and shattered parody of a boy's face, leaking oil, came into view.

'All patterned after children, sir,' said the corporal. 'Very small. Cheap. Very fast though.'

'How fast?'

The soldier waved his hands. 'Ten, fifteen kilometers an hour?' he said. 'They don't get tired. Wijesinghe and Marathan say you have to shoot the head—' he gestured at the guts, where there was a flap-like door, and a hollow chamber where the abs would be – 'Or they run out of fuel there.'

Eliott examined the stomach. There clearly was an empty space for charging nodes; into this the Ceylonese engineers had fitted a small cage, some sort of rudimentary battery terminals. There was some kind of black sludge in between. Eliott smelled it. Some sort of chemical, placed between these nodes. He rattled the cage and it came off in his hand. Behind it were the original charging nodes.

He examined the amperage figures on the plastic case and almost rolled his eyes. How ridiculously inefficient. These people had taken a design clearly meant for fast charging off whatever current was around and hotglued in a chemical battery converter clearly meant to force the bot to live in a near-constant low-power state, starving for energy. And from that came all this drama of the Big Match.

Only the Ceylonese could make something *worse* and, in the process, more profitable.

They saw more child-robot corpses ahead. There was one, cut nearly in half by the gunfire. A girl's face, twisted around, stared accusingly at them as they marched past.

The stink hit them first. The sickly-sweet, rotting smell, with faint undertones of rust.

There, on the ground, was a grotesque figure. A man in army fatigues lay spreadeagled in the centre, corpse bloated beyond all imagination. He had six arms.

'The boys here say that's the third one,' said Mahasen, who had been leading the other team. The thin Inquisitor was on his knees beside the corpse. 'It's got the local lads spooked.'

Eliott peered at the corpse, touching it ever so delicately. It was an ordinary soldier. Volunteer Rifles. Two of the arms were his, four had been ripped off from the others, Eliott assumed, and laid around the soldier with great precision. His head rolled as he touched it. It was someone else's. The whole thing looked like it had been assembled with meticulous care.

Lakshmi swore. 'Can robots do this?'

Eliott shrugged. 'They're your robots,' he said. 'Ever seen them do something like this?'

'Not my robots, sir,' said Lakshmi. 'To answer the question, yes, sometimes, but only to other bots.'

'Well,' said Eliott. There was little else to say. Penhaligon hadn't told him much about the machines, other than the numbers they expected. 'I hope it's not like Hong Kong.'

'What did they do in Hong Kong?'

'Nailed the local politicians into trees and let them bleed out. Humans respond better to sporadic, extreme violence. Sends a clear message. Machines pick up on those things.' It didn't matter, anyway. The cost of doing business. 'Do we have eyes on the next site?'

'Aye, sir,' said Senanayake.

'And the supply drop?'

'Still there, sir.'

The background music began. Penhaligon had told him to listen for it. The angry violins of Beethoven's Fifth in C Minor. The roboticists had class, he had to give them that.

'Set up,' said Eliott. 'We've got shooting to do.'

TWO

The first encounter went bad really fast.

Perhaps it was the fact that the soldiers were still setting up camp, and falling behind schedule, and thus still in their fatigues, guns off aside, heaving and groaning over crates and sorting equipment. Perhaps it was Eliott himself who failed.

Eliott, looking out over at the train station in the distance, and wondering whether they should have more lookouts, barely had time to react – a strangled cry from the sentry ahead, a burst of gunfire – and then in front of him was a swarm, child-like shapes leaping from the buildings in uncanny silence.

Eliott reacted. The first one to reach him, he smashed upwards with both fists. He leapt forward. Something sharp and pointed whistled at him. He pivoted, catching it in his hands, and threw it into the fray, pinning two of them to the ground.

He was slow. He was slower than he remembered being. They chittered and ran around him.

'To arms!' he shouted at the idiots behind him. 'Drop the crates, pick up your guns! All sentries to action stations!'

Something aimed a terrific blow at his groin. Not enough to imbalance him, but there was real momentum in the punch, far more than a human could have mustered. He seized the arm, ripped it out of its socket, kicked the face in, shattering the childlike mask right down to the sparking circuits underneath. A spear went slicing past his leg. Another tried to grab him from behind and collapsed under his kicks, sparking.

From the corner of his eye, he saw Lakshmi. She moved with blurred speed, leaping from jungle car to jungle car, shooting. Six bots charged her and collapsed like surprised puppets, their heads shot right off. She reached for the one machine-gun they had managed to mount – naked saved for a few pieces of cardboard – and the world erupted in hellfire. Bots jerked and danced before her and collapsed.

Good. At least someone was thinking. He turned back, the old combat routines kicking in. A punch to a jaw here, a kick there; pistol in his hands, a cheap Chinese thing; two shots; an execution; two more and a bot exploded in front of him. Five more bots remained. He heard the loud *braaaaaat-brraaat* of assault rifles behind him.

The bots looked from him to the smoking ruins at his feet, then at his hands, then back at him, and lowered their spears, circling warily. One of them was a girl. They were trying to flank him. Tactics, he thought. Improvisation. Not bad. Too bad they didn't seem to understand ammunition, or reloading.

Or maybe not.

As he watched, two of them dropped their spears and brough out two old Indian assault rifles, exactly the kind he'd sent out on the sacrificial lambs. They aimed at him. They fired...

But whatever they had learned during the span of their brief existence was just a shade too slow. The first had barely aimed when he dodged past and shot its legs out. The bullets bounced off the plate in his chest. He ripped the second gun muzzle out of his enemy's hand and smashed it into its face. Two shots with the pistol sent two circling attackers stumbling back, sparking wildly. He kicked in the face of the closest one, using his weight to crush the little thing like tinfoil. He picked up the assault rifle it dropped and shot the other. Two rounds and the rifle clicked. *Empty*.

One to go. He reversed the gun, holding it like a club, and waited for the charge.

But the girl-bot hung back, its spear pointed at the ground. It looked at him quizzically, tilting its head to one side, staring at his arms and legs, where the spear thrusts had cut away the clothes and skin, and flayed it open to reveal the metal underneath. Then it turned and fled, melting back into the jungle like a ghost.

Silence fell. The smell of gunfire hung heavy in the air. He circled around, saw Mason peeling a bot off his own back. There were bodies everywhere – the bots sparking and twitching, mask faces smiling; at least three humans screaming and twitching. The smell of blood and shit hung faintly in the air. A soldier crawled out of the wreckage with a crude metal spear jutting through his chest and cutting tracks in the dirt. All the jungle-cars he could see were toppled; some had dents in them, as if small bodies had smashed into them with hellish velocity. Black, dripping streaks coated the one jungle car still upright. The airship they had come in was burning.

Senanayake emerged from where he'd taken cover, looked confusedly around and tried to get the dying humans to stand. The fact that he had a shard of metal stuck in his arm seemed to be making it more difficult.

And Lakshmi ...

Those looked like pieces of her over there, by the fallen tree. Not too far from the machine gun.

Beethoven skittled in triumph over the carnage.

'Bloody idiots,' growled Mason, angry at the sight. 'Medic? You, you, you, get the Inquisitor upright. Someone get those guns set up! Go! Go!'

Eliott turned back to the bodies as Mason chivvied the distraught soldiers, barking orders left and right. Something was odd. He hunted among the cracked and warped bodies, keeping one eye on the spot where the girl-bot had vanished. Finally, he found what he was looking for: a bot that was still alive.

It lay pinned to the ground with its arms torn off – a poor metal simulacrum of a human child. One leg was crushed, the other spasmed, with damaged neurofibre sparking. The whole body was wrapped in rags, like a crude caricature of skin. Had they done that to themselves, or was it done for them? The porcelain-thin face turned to him, the plastics that shattered so easily twitching, trying to formulate words. the eyes moved, the eyebrows twitched.

He felt strangely disquieted. There was a powerful sense of wrongness here.

He shot it twice and turned to his crew. Mason was shrieking commands, trying to get the soldiers together and hauling that useless young Inquisitor in line. Eliott listened, standing absolutely still, tuning out the panic of the soldiers. The buildings had cut off all line of sight, and the music was annoying, but if he listened closely, he could hear the sounds ...

... of dozens of tiny feet running their way.

'Snipers!' he called. 'Snipers, now! Everybody else get back!'

He leaped into the car, rifle at the ready. Mason gunned the engine and they roared off, back the way they had come. Eliott could see the shapes of little children emerging from the jungle, spears in their hands.

A little bit more ...

A little bit more ...

The snipers began firing. Their thunder filled the air. Ancient lead and steel smashed into metal bodies. The gunmen worked from the outside in and the inside out, as per their instructions. Faces, childlike and smiling, and long limbs wrapped in cloth tumbled everywhere he looked.

'Clear!' Eliott called.

There was a cheer. The soldiers and Ministry cleanup crew he had hidden in the buildings came running out. The bots – some legless, some armless, some shot in the gut battery – were netted and hauled into the darkness.

'Have you heard from the other teams?'

Mahasen dialed, waited, listened.

'Confirmed,' he said. 'All three locations. Wait. Wait.'

In the distance, a gunshot.

'They're okay. They have overwatch. They've got ... twenty, sir. Close to what you said they would.'

Eliott reloaded. 'Get more men,' he said. 'Get every working vehicle running and get them over to that train station. That's where they're coming from.'

≈

That was the first wave.

How had the trap been sprung so early? Eliott had no patience for questions on the battlefield, and yet this he asked of himself as he bullied the laggardly soldiers into position.

'Be ready,' he said to the snipers, setting them into overlapping fields of fire; here on on a highrise, there, another on the crumbled ruins of what might have once been shops. 'Be ready. Watch the trees! Set up here. Cover this road! Good.'

Mason exchanged the wounded for fresh men. The gauntlet staggered and rearranged itself in a line stretching from the house to the train station. And then, when Eliott was ready, they began firing into the sky.

The bots, thankfully, did not understand why an enemy would make noise. They did not understand Eliott and Mason, standing there in the back of their noisy jungle car, such an easy target. They charged from the ruins of what had once been the real heart of Colombo – the train station, the warren of buildings outside the fort – and into the line of snipers.

Ten. Twenty. The guns blazed. The music shifted bizarrely into Chopin's angry Op. 10, No. 12, chaotic and hammering – a dirge for Poland's long-dead revolutionaries. The Ceylonese snipers grew used to the job, counting kills among themselves. Thirty. He felt – finally! Subsystems slowly coming online, warming up to tasks that had once been second nature. He felt his tracking improve. He felt his eyes adapt. He felt himself come alive; it felt like being young again.

The soldiers at Eliott's call, led forward by Senanayake, began to grow bolder, joining Eliott at the ambush. They expanded slowly outward, drawing in ever-larger crowds of bots to their deadly net, stopping just before the raw stench up ahead became too overpowering. Eliott, peering through the sights, saw the mountain of trash at the heart of the city, and shouted for the forward positions to throw flared into the trees.

A bullet whizzed over him, missing him by inches. He ducked. The bots came.

Five? Ten? A dozen? Twenty? Thirty? Forty? Fifty? The sun slipped slowly over the horizon, and the trickle slowed down. Eventually, the music stopped. He leaned back in the back of the jungle-car, watching the mountain of trash.

'Send in the cleaners,' Eliott said.

The bots were in full retreat now. Shots rang out from around Eliott, cutting the the little creatures down as they rank. Two vanished from sight, reappearing around halfway up the mountain of trash, clambering up at speed. Mason sighted and fired. One exploded, struck in the gut. The other tumbled out of sight.

'We're supposed to bring those back,' said Eliott. Penhaligon's instructions had been clear: salvage as much as possible.

'One or two missing won't matter, sir!'

Eliott looked over at him. At some point, the cub would have to be taught some manners. Once upon a time, he would have had Mason whipped for insubordination. You couldn't run a fighting force with men who disobeyed orders.

But the battle-sharpness showed him Mason: young, afraid, high on the thrill of pumping bullet after bullet into bodies, half-deaf from the ringing of the assault rifle in his hands, and shaking slightly from what must have been his first real battle.

'When we get back,' he said. 'I want whoever was in charge of camp prep debriefed. Preferrably deboned.'

'Yes, sir.'

'Find out how the hell we had our arses kicked before we'd set up.'

'Yes, sir.'

And Eliott thought, *well, at least the kid's learning,* and clapped the Inquisitor on the shoulder.

≈

That night, Mahasen Wijeratne, who everyone called Mason, crouched over a campfire. Three men sat before him.

'You were supposed to shoot him,' said Mahasen. The copper strips on his face glimmered malevolently with the fire. 'Why didn't you?'

They made excuses. They always did. Too many people around, sir. I fired, but couldn't get a clear shot, sir. How Ceylonese it was, to make excuses. Mahasen fumed. The carefully set up ambush – the scouts sent ahead to lure in the bots, the general lack of cover around Grimme – all for nothing.

'Useless, all bloody useless,' he fumed. 'The three of you are going back to Gampaha. I'm going to tell him you're the ones to blame for the mess. You've misplaced half our supplies and at least five vehicles, you understand? And I'm sending you to Gampaha to fix things. Understand? Bloody well be glad that you're getting off lightly.'

They didn't argue.

'Are you still going to . . . kill him, sir?' one ventured.

Mahasen had thought about it. The original plan had been simple: slowly bleed out half the war effort send down here to Colombo; take the people and equipment, stash them over in the LKRF-run villages just beyond Gampaha. One soldier less was one soldier less for Kandy. The part about shooting Eliott Grimme had been Mahasen's personal touch.

'No,' he decided. He had seen how Grimme moved on the battlefield, how quickly and efficiently he set up the lines, how he turned idle sloths into a war machine and a road into a killbox. 'I still have things to learn from him.'

THREE

Broken Arm held her position on the mountain. Whether it was a mountain was up for debate. Those in Kandy, who saw it up close every year, would have said that it was layers and layers of trash compressed under its own weight, held upright by the skeleton of the building it pushed up against. To Broken Arm, who had seen no other mountains but this one and did not understand trash in the slightest, it was a mountain.

From there, she had the perfect view of Colombo. Directly ahead, and down from where the mountain ended, was a bridge that ran over a fetid, crawling lake; on the other side it became a road that, one the right, gave way to the bleached bone-white hulk of the train station. On the left it split off into innumerable roadlets that snaked and cut crossways through miles of rubble and collapsed buildings.

At first it had been very easy to ambush the Big People from this side; these little back roads stretched out for miles, and the maze of brick and concrete in between was perfect cover some things their size. But the enemy had changed position in the night. Loud explosions had blown away the rubble closest to them, and they climbed now to few tall buildings that still stood; while on the ground they advanced under cover in fast teams, setting up barriers before rushing in to fill a space.

Her scouts had marked out a whole line of them stretching all the way through the back roads of Colombo. In many places they were impossible to fight, they reported; they stood there, blasting away with their thunder-sticks and whatever dread engines they had that blew bots and buildings into so much fine dust. Whenever the lot here advanced, the rest of the line did, too.

A line. A net. A trap. She had drawn them on the ground, trying to make the tribe understand. They were being encircled, slowly, steadily.

Behind her, the sea and the Port City, and the skeletons of buildings that had once been hotels and apartment buildings and office towers. The red sun moved into the sea, turning it bloody.

A hand moved in the trash. 'Down,' she whispered, and the hand stilled. She kicked a bit of garbage over it.

Sky rustled next to her. He was impatient.

'Down,' she hissed again, making her way over to Fast. Fast could run better than anyone else. She gave Fast one of their few precious fuel cakes.

'Go to the Cinnamon,' she said. 'Give them this. Tell them Big People close, careful, watch rooftops.'

She went to Seawater, and repeated the message. This time to the Galle Face Girls.

Fast came back with bad news. The Sons of Cinnamon – the few who could still stand – had broken out last moon. Those left behind believed their brothers and sisters had escaped the net under the cover of night. They repeated this over and over again, their memories failing from the lack of fuel; repeat, smile, black out, reboot. The few who could stand would come back and save them all.

Grit, who Broken Arm had posted to keep an eye on the Cinnamons, was skeptical of their bravado; he had watched the Cinnamons leave and none of them had returned.

Which meant they were probably dead.

Seawater brought better tidings. The Children of the Taj, who knew Broken Arm, wanted to know what wisdom she could share for survival. They had hunted down along the coast, towards the great barriers that enclosed them. There were Big People there, and snarling monsters that they rode in.

The Galle Face Girls, ever spoiling for a fight, proposed that they all work together and take down the Big People.

To this, Broken Arm agreed. Although on her conditions: hiding, subterfuge, carefully planned moves: these were her arsenal. Blind attacks were not. After all, they were the only ones left. She sent messages to and fro, relying on her hoard of leftover fuel from the Cinnamon for diplomacy. They bickered, argued and accepted her leadership at the speed of Fast's footsteps. Eventually, it was time.

A team of their most battle-ready was selected. The Girls had five, all barely a year old, all spoiling for action. She had ... Sky, and seven others. Not enough for a proper raid. Remembering the Big People who had killed Moonlight, she made them promise to sneak up, to find the high ground, to surround instead of charging head on, to leave a couple behind to note how far they could get before the Big People saw them, and, more importantly, before the Big People could actually hit them.

From her place of safety, Broken Arm ordered the first attack and crouched down to see how it would go.

≈

On the ground, Eliott Grimme waited in the dimming light, Mason in the jungle car at his side. Playing bait.

It was the third day of operation. By now the supply chains had been sorted out; and despite a few issues, which Mason had promised to trace, it was so easy now that it was almost automatic. They stood there, the bots saw them, the bots came. Every so often, he would adjust a cell – sniper nest here, flank there, set up there – and the Ceylonese soldiers obeyed, now secure in the knowledge that this terrifying pale soldier knew what he was doing.

Things were going well. For the first two days, he had put himself, the Inquisitors and his hand-picked cohoty right between the waves of bots, gunning down and capturing as many as they could. It was effective – the bots kept coming, and within a week the rest of the soldiers were ready, the weak winnowed out, the overeager lone wolves dead or dying and the disciplined and obedient remained. This was the first time most of them had seen combat, including the Inquisitors, who were little more than sinister thugs back in their homelands. Here, he sculpted them, rewarding the steadfast and punishing the unfaithful by making an example out of them.

Next wave. It was time for the next wave. He had their timings down almost to a science now. Account for tribe base location, distance, probability of conflict with other tribes, probability of survival. A new gang should be showing up right ... about ... now.

Nothing.

That sense of wrongness intensified.

He heard the screams from the most outward sniper nest. A gun went off behind him.

'They're on the nests! Guard the back! The back!' he roared, and then he was moving, reloading, running into the buildings before Mason had even turned the keys in the ignition.

≈

Broken Arm watched all this with implacable patience. Her tribe fought bravely, of course. Towards the end only Sky stood, bathed in the strange oil of the Big People, tossing their bodies off the roof. They hit the floor with wet thuds. Then the pale Big Person appeared behind him. Sky leaped back, the clever child, landing on the dead, and ducked into the shadows. The pale Big Person watched him go.

Broken Arm sat and thought about this. She then crawled to the others that waited.

'Second attacks,' she whispered. 'Listen, close, listen much. Two types of Big People ...'

≈

'That's unusual,' said Mahasen, climbing up to where Eliott stood. He looked around at the bodies of the gunmen ... and the blood ... and at Eliott's face. 'Sir,' he added, just in case.

'How many of our sniper cells have gone?'

'Nothing we can't replace, sir, they didn't take the guns—'

'How many?'

'Four, sir.'

'The ones facing the Port City? Or the rest of Colombo?'

'Actually, all four sides, sir. Do you want me to move them forward—'

'No. Move them ...' Eliott deliberated. There were killzones and then there were killzones. 'Two teams there,' he said, pointing at the cluster of derelict white buildings behind a statue of a hand holding an ancient telephone receiver. 'Two there ... two here, watching our backs ... two here ...'

'Set thirty men to guard the bridge,' he continued. The bridge lay just before the giant hand. A filthy lake ran under it. 'Sandbags. Put the broken cars there. Tell them to look ahead, but also to watch the water.'

'That'll just put them out in the open, sir—'

'Precisely the point. We need a target-rich environment to see where they're coming from. Now stop arguing with my orders and carry them out.'

≈

Broken Arm watched this new configuration with interest.

The Girls had asked whether they wanted to be part of the second wave. She had replied yes, but had kept herself at the very back. They advanced, sneaking forward just as Broken Arm had told them to.

The bridge lit up in a flash of thunder sticks. The Girls had a word for them: guns. The guns screamed and spat, and the first third of the second offense – the most direct – died.

'Now!' she shrieked.

They turned, as one, and threw their spears towards the sky.

≈

Eliott saw the first of the metal shards land on his left, where the road curved off into a bridge and an old, crumbling apartment cut off their line of sight. It slammed into the crude barricade at the bridge, cutting right through the hull of one of the few jungle cars they had left. Ten others followed in precise formation – five to the right, five to the left. Two soldiers were impaled. The others ducked and fired wildly.

The perfect bait. Louder, noisier and easier to hit than he had ever been.

He waited. Presently teams eight and nine came crawling back, brown faces marked with black camo and dust, 'It's a small tribe, sir. Mostly girls. Throwing spears. Two keeping them supplied.'

'You know what to do.'

They nodded and took the tracks that went around the train station at a crouch. The tracks had once been roads; they led around the bridge the action was on. Eliott waited until they had moved out of sight and counted. One thousand ... two thousand ... three thousand ...

A grenade went off, then two. Then gunfire. Not from the back, but from the front. A dozen bots ran the distracted barricade, terrifying in their silence. Blurred bodies smashed all manner of weapons into panicked soldiers – rocks, barbed wire, sharpened flagpoles. In an instant, the bridge was overrun and the snipers guarding it were falling back, their guns snapping peals of thunder one after the other.

Eliott grabbed the gun he had slung across his back, crouched in the middle of the road and started firing, dropping bots like flies. Then the other teams kicked in, but not for long; a second group of bots charged in out of nowhere, this time with shields, making a stand in front of their retreating spear-throwers. It took him a few seconds to realize what the shields were: car doors strapped to their arms.

He was ready. One bullet he put through the neck of the spear-thrower at the back. Two bots ran up to him with shields, undoubtedly meaning to get close enough to smash him down. He shot one in the head through the broken window, kicked its corpse at the other and kicked both of them off the bridge and into the river below. Seven bots, ten bullets left.

They came at him with spears and rocks. He dropped them one after the other, their little bodies crumpling to the ground. They were shot either in the neck, severing the motor control, or the heart, severing the battery. Four more popped up from hiding. His pistol jammed.

He leaped forward, right into their midst. This they did not expect. He kicked one, smashed the pistol into the face of another – both were cheap metal, so both shattered. He took a punch that he barely felt, ripped the arm out its socket and used it to turn the remaining bot into so much scrap metal. He was fast, precise, brutal – the old battle conditioning was finally humming in full force.

The bots retreated, screaming. Almost all the shielded ones were dead and sparking on the ground. The spear-throwers scrambled with bullets kicking up dust at their feet.

He watched them through the sight of his rifle. This was nothing like the mad rushes he had seen on the endless broadcasts back in Kandy. The first move had been a diversion; the second had also been a diversion. It was a fake-out built on a fake-out: a sophisticated, coordinated testing of an ambush, one that understood sacrificing soldiers for information.

The bots had a commander.

He suddenly felt alive.

The enemy has a commander.

'Clean up,' he ordered.

The soldiers he had hidden peeped from behind their cover and hurried over the bridge, casting nervous and awestruck looks at him as they did so.

When he was satisfied, he led them inward and into the heart of chaos.

FOUR

In Kandy, smoke curled in front of television screens in gaudy hotels, accompanied by knowing looks and raucous laughter. Eliott Grimme may have cared little for the political state of the country, but everyone who was *anyone* knew that the Inquisition showing up in Colombo, along with what clearly looked like the Ceylon Volunteer Rifles, was less about the Big Match itself and more about the optics of the matter. It the Chief Inquisitor's way of reminding everyone who held the reins in Ceylon, and who, ultimately, was the source of all solutions.

Because while all this was happening, the Bandaranaikes were going under, one after the other. An estate here, confiscated for tax avoidance. A scandal there. An ambassadorship here, recalled. Everybody knew who was behind this knee-capping humiliation: the Chief Inquisitor. Nobody even pretended otherwise anymore. The elder Molligodas had even dared ask, in public, whether Penhaligon would be content with the humiliation of one House, or whether the others would fall as well.

'He's showing off,' said one dame to another, putting out her cigarette in her teacup. 'This is all just theater, you know.'

'I heard there was something actually wrong with the robots,' murmured her companion. 'There's this Indian fellow – Bengali. Doctor at some posh university, you know. He's living in the old Alagiyawanna mansion, you know, the one they lost to the government in that lawsuit?'

The lady with the ash-stained teacup confirmed that yes, she did know what house and which lawsuit were being referred to.

'My maid's husband is doing some security for them. Says there's always him going to the Ministry and Inquistors and technicians coming in at all hours. And that de Almeida girl. Something, something, something going on there. Anyway, it looks like they *are* doing some work on the robots, but nobody talks about it.'

'Eh. Who cares about the robots?'

'Don't hate on the bots, I have good money on that one-armed girl.'

'That's just money,' said the smoker derisively. 'What about *him*?'

A freshly lit cigarette stabbed in the general direction of the large screen on the Queen's Hotel's Summer Terrace, looming large over a row of alfresco diners. The screen in question had a face on it: pale, unsmiling, the eyes somehow burning with a cold and unnatural light, as if lit from within.

Eliott Grimme 'double t, double m', as her grandson had said. There had been a huge hue and cry about that one; not one the news, but in the whisper networks where the real information ran. Penhaligon had done an unheard-of thing, exercising *in absentia* powers of the Governer to put this new man in charge. There were rumours that Eliott was a war hero, or had been, but nobody knew where or who or how; there were rumours that he was some kind of next-generation Inquisitor, but her grandson had said he was actually far older.

She who smoked had carefully laid out to her grandson how symbols worked, how a televised, British superman preyed on the consciousness of those who had to sit here and watch him run around, effortlessly outclassing Ceylonese men and Inquisitors alike. She had explained how much Penhaligon would lose if his pet commando were to fail. 'Money is nice,' she had said to him, over and over again, 'but respect is hard currency.'

And to her great disappointment, Mahasen had not gotten rid of Eliott Grimme, but could actually be seen taking orders from him on the screen, following him around like some kind of trained dog. He took after the father, that one. Runt of the bloody litter. At least he was doing his part for the LKRF.

'That one might be a problem,' agreed her friend. 'But let's wait and see what happens.'

≈

Something about these Asian cities, Eliott reflected, made them nightmares to fight in.

Take Colombo. Even levelled, shelled into rubble, it was an almost superhuman effort to pick a direction and actually travel in a straight line. Something about the poor planning here. Offices squatted next to what must surely have been single-story houses, once upon a time; skyscrapers had toppled over schools. It was like an octopus of steel and concrete frozen in the act of reaching out for a bigger future.

This was compounded by what they had done later to box in the bots and make this the Zone. Where the tentacles of this octopus terminated – the roads that Mason picked out as Galle Road, Havelock Road, Bauddhaloka Mawatha – the Ministry had piled cars, rubble, even tanks, boxing in the bots.

Unfortunately, it also boxed out the men.

Eight men and forty bots died in the breaking of one of these barriers. Another six fell to some sort of booby-trap strung across minor lanes; a full twenty went missing scouting up Galle Road, and were later found drowned in the sea that raged just beyond, stripped of all metal. Mason kept trying to tell Grimme their names, but names meant nothing to him – what mattered most was *how* they died.

At first, attrition – a lucky spear, a stone well aimed, an extra bot here or there, moving too fast for the human senses. Then the deaths became cleverer. Chunks of masonry that were toppled to crush. Cars, sometimes old military vehicles, pushed together to form barricades that were set on fire to trap small teams questing outward. Bots with rusted gas canisters strapped to their backs, salvaged from some long-defunct warehouse, running silently through the night, throwing themselves into clusters and blowing up their own batteries as they landed. They came from every possible direction and left as corpses, packed up by the cleaners and ferried backwards to the lines that waited at the base.

The commander was here. Eliott could feel it ... whatever it was, always ahead, throwing out tendrils, drawing back. He put snipers on the rooftops, under command of the Inquisitors, and broke out the shotguns and mortars. They fought street by street, sometimes room by room. The bots had the advantage of terrain. He had the superior weaponry. In his head, he counted the tribes as he put them down. Sons of Cinnamon – fled to the south border of Colombo, blockaded by tanks; Eliott had fireteams down there turning that place into a modern-day Charge of the Light Brigade. Chained Emperors – scattered, hiding in the large apartment complex in Colombo 03; they were now boxed in.

The rest – still fighting, still retreating. Eliott thanked his stars that this city had never grown subways, like Hong Kong. Then he moved on death littered in his wake, pausing only for the cleaners to come pack the bodies away.

≈

'We have to stop. Sir. Sir. Sir!'

He turned, gun in hand. He was in a wide-open thing that could have been a warehouse, but given its proximity to the main road and the faded detritus of glamour, it could have also been a lingerie showroom near what clearly was a school. The world shook every so often as the mortars landed. They were shelling yet another apartment.

Mason Wijeratne stood in the doorway, covered in plaster dust and grime. The copper lines on his face had dulled.

'We have to stop, sir,' Mason panted. 'The men can't take much more.'

Eliott looked at the poster next to him, which, faded and peeling, showed a Ceylonese woman winking seductively.

'Then send in the women,' he said, irritated.

Mason's face soured.

'Fine,' said Eliott, before the kid could talk back. They would lose valuable time – night was when the bots slept, making them the easiest to capture – but an exhausted soldier was just yet another corpse to deal with. 'Double rations tonight. Check the supplies. Find them a safe place to stay. What's that thing next door? Looks usable, sir. Walls. Controlled exit points.'

'It's a school, sir.'

That explained a lot. 'Go set up,' said Eliott. 'Rest the main body, but keep the scouting parties active. I'll sort things out with Penhaligon.'

It took a while before the camp was ready and the military radiogram set up. Mason handed him the receiver reverently.

Now came the moment of truth. If things had gone according to plan back at the base, the people they had brought in should have set up the infrastructure; and the short-wave radiogram on this should be able to connect to a tower far behind them, hop from that to another tower on a boosted signal, and so reach all the way back to Kandy.

'KANDY   >   ADMINISTRATIVE   SECTOR   > INQUISITION > PENHALIGON.'

It took a while to connect. It was a hack, of course; Kushlani de Almeida's little extension to KANDYNET was meant to lay the groundwork for ferrying orders to the bots, not for voice lines. It had been Eliott's idea to modify it to allow him to call back. Something he had seen with the IRA; low-kilobyte wave transmission, keeping transmission and receiver costs as low and undetectable as possible. The original design had been for the towers to push orders and updates to nearby bots, who would then connect peer-to-peer to each other and spread those orders on; his call was doing the opposite – triggering temporary hacks and bouncing through Gampaha to Kandy to the desk from which Penhaligon ruled this world.

'Grimme.'

'We're resting for the night. Got the new batch?'

'Excellent, yes. Hewage's people seem pleased at how cleanly you're taking them out. Makes them cheaper to repair, I suppose. Also doing wonders for the feed. Ratings have never been higher.'

That was the point. 'We may have a problem,' he said into the receiver. 'The rest of the bots seem to be heading for the Port City.'

There was a pause on the other end of the line. 'There's a no-fire zone around the Port City. Part of the treaty. Fuck! Grimme, catch them.'

'We're resting for the night.'

There was cursing. It was surprisingly in Sinhala. 'You know best,' he said.

'Yes,' said Eliott, and that was that.

They camped in the ruins that night, pulling back to within a few kilometers from the present perimeter. Eliott went around assessing damage. Senanayake had a bad arm, ten Ceylonese soldiers were dead. They needed to bury the dead, said Eliott, and everyone agreed. So they dug a hole and placed a few rocks around it. He made Mason do it in a visible place, and told him to read the names out loud. There. Finally a use for the kid's odd need to remember what people were called.

Then they settled in. This part Eliott disliked. Being the commander, he had privileges; a tent away from the noise and stupidity of men figuring out how to dig latrine lines, of quartermasters heckling those who had lost their equipment, and all the noise and dust of the main army. But it also meant that he had to endure the constant companionship of those who were captains in this particular army.

Eliott looked around faces he had barely bothered to remember – some were gaunt, tired; others impatient, having found in themselves a taste for killing – and decided to go sit with the Inquisitors themselves.

He found them by a fire. They had formed a closed circle with one other; a scout running between the cell of snipers that ran Southward. A storyteller. Eliott listened to her speak of old, abandoned bots that sometimes rushed convoys at night, drawn to the noises; things unleashed on the world when the Chinese and the British first fought over the city of Colombo; a woman in white, named Mohini, standing by dark roads, waiting for soldiers to pass by.

He missed much of what was said, but the Sinhala was becoming clearer the more he listened. He watched the others instead. Senanayake said nothing and just stared into the fire. Mason's face showed some complex expression; half exhaustion, half thoughtful. Neither of them noticed his scrutiny, something he marked as a failure to report to Penhaligon for their next update.

And so Eliott found himself wandering through this thing that had once been a school. Rows of rotten desks in front of shattered walls; staircases that hung by concrete threads; what must have once been an enormous latrine-pit, but was now a stinking black loam where enormous earthworms crawled under moonlight.

He found a staircase, went up, came to a balcony. It was a surreal landscape that met his eyes. A whole suburb stretched out before him, ghost houses with empty eyes and mouths peering back at him through the dark. The moon, ghosting in and out of clouds, turned them into shades of grey and black. A concrete Buddha, perhaps the twin of the one they had in the Kandy, gazed at them with a slight smile, like a stern but loving parent. The wreckage of a Tin Soldier faced it; an iron giant kneeling in supplication. An ironic reversal.

They had told him the sea was on the right, but all he could make out were tall shapes rising through the gloom in the distance – apartments, hotels, offices. Overhead, the night sky was a deep blue dusted with stars; bereft of the competition with street lights, the heavens shone brilliant. There was a cloud of faded glitter that stretched from one end of the horizon to the other; surely that was the galaxy itself.

He stood there for a moment, drinking in the stars and the silence. No traffic. No people. No part of the sea of sound that never left you in the city. It was comforting. He could hear his breathing, loud and clear. Colombo was a dead city, a thing of weeds and decay and utter stillness.

There was a soft *click* behind him. He jumped, his skeleton temporarily overclocking his body straight into battle conditioning.

Mason's copper stripes loomed at him out of the darkness. Then, he looked up at the sky. His face lost some of the blankness.

'Pretty, isn't it?' he said. 'Never seen skies like this back home.'

'It's the light pollution,' Eliott said. 'This is what the world would look like, you know, if we all died tomorrow.'

They watched the sky for a moment.

'Come on,' Mahasen said at last, turning away. 'Food's ready. They're waiting for you.'

Downstairs, they munched their ready-to-eat meals with noisy abandon. The commander of the human soldiers, a doughty woman with a scarred face and a voice like thunder, had some sickly-sweet tea in a flask, and Senanayake had brought out a bottle of arrack.

'Should we be drinking?' asked the Inqusitor who told stories.

'Taste it while you can,' said Eliott. 'In a few years, it won't make a difference.' The liquid was warm and pleasant, the alcohol fizzling away the moment it hit his bloodstream. 'Cheap whiskey? Or a cheap rum.'

'It's neither and both,' said Mason. 'It's coconut palm and wood. It's arrack.'

Eliott downed another shot, picked up his rifle and began stripping it. It was old; a stupid, ugly design.

'I'm going to go keep a lookout.'

'Lakshmi's dead,' said Mason suddenly.

'Happens,' said Eliott. He had been wondering how long it would take. He looked over the kid. 'If you're angry, good. There'll come a time when you'll look back and wonder when you stopped feeling.'

The copper-face adopted a slight sneer. 'I suppose you speak from experience.'

'I suppose I do,' he said. The kid had to learn. He finished his liquor and headed back out to his balcony, the rifle in slightly better shape than before. As he climbed out of sight, the storyteller turned to Mason and said something; the Inquisitor retorted harshly.

Eliott sat there on the balcony, listening to them bicker. The bickering eventually ceased, and there came the sounds of a tryst; something quick and forbidden, snatched from the embers of humanity that still lay in their hearts.

Humans were simple in the most important ways.

Eventually, they stopped, of course, and it should have been time for him to shut down too.

Eventually, the memory cleanup kicked in. Perks of holographic memory and compression algorithms and all-too-human design. The cleanup spawned a spider that rifled through the day's thoughts and decided this-hour-is-similar-to-this and rewrote chunks as a reference and some variations. It was meant to free up space, of course, to keep Eliott's brain as efficient as possible – keep the important bits, bury the useless ones. He felt it sift through his mind, peering at this city, this corpse of concrete where only the stars came out to play. He felt it mark this time as useless, felt it wipe the hours from his mind, replacing memories with notations. It would leave him with the usual lifetime of death and only a few seconds of this peace.

He agreed with it: this was useless. But the silence was beautiful. And soon, it would be replaced with gunfire and slaughter. Come morning, they would hunt again.

And he would find that commander, congratulate it, and then kill it. Theatrically. On camera. And whatever stupid politics Penhaligon and this blasted backwater lived by, he could finally have some peace.

FIVE

Broken Arm felt helpless.

It was late and her people were hungry. She shifted through their reports. The hunger gnawed through her, making her thoughts skitter. Reports drifted in. Shadows of other tribes, in desperation and hunger, attacking the dark-skinned Big People in desperate last stands. She tried to pacify them, casting pleas and warnings, but her messages went undelivered.

Even her dreams were troubled: at night came the echo of something, or *someone* ... whispers of a land of plenty, a land of promise, a land of death. She saw flickers of green and Big People, *so many* Big People, using *so much* food – enough to keep them all alive forever.

'Big People,' whispered Sky. 'Up ahead.'

'Ready,' she said.

≈

It took them two days to break through.

They were learning, but it was far too late. Thick metal could shield them from the thunder-sticks, but it had to be in layers, or they punched right through. Broken Arm had made them work hard, scouring the great mountain of garbage that ruled the Colombo sky. From its very bottom, they stole cloth and rusted metal, and made them stick together with fire and plastic. They learned that the Big People could not see them if they moved in slow and crept up to them over time. They learned that a well-thrown spear could skewer and make them fail like none of the tribe members ever could. And they learned that the Big People did not learn from their mistakes. They fought the same way, over and over again; it was all too easy to figure out the patterns in which they moved.

Over time, and with twenty-three dead, the perfect tactic had evolved – a tight unit of bots, all standing together, holding up shields. The back line held up another set of shields, but above their heads, to protect them from the fire above. The third line carried as many spears as they could, and flung them while the shields bore the assault.

In climbing over town defenses, smashing autocannons with rocks, wrapped in the stink of gunfire and the terrible noises of the dying Big People, they learned more. They learned that most of the Big People could not fight, or run, or even die without a fuss. Smash through the outer layers of sentry guns, weather the assault of the lightning sticks, and what was left was a screaming huddle. They wailed and leaked red.

But even this knowing this was barely enough. Even so armed they could barely hold their own once the Big

People woke up and the monsters they rode came alive and their thunder-sticks started firing.

And what about the Other One? The Other One was different. Dangerous. Terrifying. He could not be stopped, said those of the tribe who had fought him and lived. Shields did nothing. Spears did nothing. Wherever he appeared, they fell back and died. Even the Big People fought harder when he was there.

He was here now. Behind them. He had not come over the mountain, but around it. And what could they do? Wait? Die?

She pondered this as they beat a retreat up the long, broken road that led to Galle Face Green. On her left, the sea hurled static at her. On her right, a sprawling monument declared to be the PILAWOOS ENTERTAINMENT COMPLEX. They found useful things here – metal, sharp knives, a kind of breathing white rot which could make Big People cry and spew yellow fluid.

So armed, they crept up on this latest outpost that intruded on their turf: a small cluster of buildings ringed by nothing more than a simple electrified gate. They threw their shields at it. Once the smoke and the fire cleared, the wailing began. She moved, stabbed, moved, stabbed, sidestepped. She worked her spear, cutting in ways they had learned would make the Big People drop their weapons and collapse screaming, or die outright.

She thought about the Big People as she butched them. Were they Tribe, too? A different sort? What did it mean to be Tribe, anyway? Surely it could not be looks ... not anymore. Everyone had the same number of arms and legs. Surely it lay here, in how they died. If you went down silently, you were Tribe. If you could be revived with a wire, some charge and the right combinations of metal, you belonged to the Tribe.

If you leaked and screamed, you did not belong to the Tribe. If you stank when you died, you did not belong to the Tribe. They hurt, therefore they were ... whatever they were.

A Big Person checked her charge. They both toppled. The Big Person scrabbled around in the mud and pulled out a lightning stick – a gun, as the Sisters used to say. In a flash, she ripped it out of its hands.

The gun exploded. She staggered, the noise and the fire plunging every one of her senses into sheer white noise. When her eyes finally cleared, she was on her knees and the Big Person was a red ruin. Its head looked like it had exploded. It looked like what happened to her friends when the sentry guns got them.

The gun lay on the dirt. She crawled to it. One end was hot and smoking. The other had things that moved. *Click* – and again an explosion.

The lightning sticks *were* sentry guns. Somehow, the Big People had figured out how to pick them up.

'Collect all the lightning sticks,' she said to the others. *'We can use them.'*

They had learned not to question her. One by one, the bots knelt and picked up fallen lightning sticks, and resumed their rampage through to the power generators. Satisfied, she turned back to the corpse.

A Big Human was there. It crept over the stained mud, gasping and dragging a broken arm. It knelt by the corpse and began shaking it, as if it was trying to reboot it.

'There's no point,' she told it. 'It's dead.'

It looked at her, face unreadable – so similar and yet so different – and began to wail. Water leaked out of its eyes and nose.

They hurt, therefore they were. Life to them must be full of agony.

She picked up the lightning stick – the gun – and aimed the hot end at the wailing thing. She fumbled for the thing that clicked. Another explosion, and then there was silence.

'How many of us left?' she asked Sky after they had looted the camp.

He pointed at one cluster. There were five. He gestured: five more, five more, five more.

Twenty. 'Hungry,' he added. Twenty hungry Tribe. Not good.

'Run,' she said to the others. 'Keep running.'

$$\approx$$

It was almost night by the time they reached the Port City.

Night was dangerous now. Music drifted out of distorted speakers – Bach's Fugue No. 4 in C sharp minor, something she had once known as the Music That Did Not Kill. She now thought of it as just more of the Killing Music.

She made Sky settle half of them in the bombed-out hotel near the sea. She made Steel Sink take the other half and set up a loose perimeter. They had lost four on the way here.

Then she put down her spear and approached. The Port City glinted in the darkness – a great dome that floated off the coast and clung to the world she knew with its web of gates and tendrils. Tonight, it looked like a little white sun floating on the dark ocean. She could hear music from inside it, faint and alien. She looked at the water that foamed around it, and for a brief moment thought if it would be better underneath the waves; but her creators had bred into her a fear of water.

She approached the gate they always went to. The red light was on; the speaker grilled cracked, just below.

'Help,' she begged it. 'The tribe is dying.'

'SUPPLY CONTRACT FOR THIS STATION HAS ENDED,' said the Port City. 'NO GOODS OR SERVICES CAN BE PROVIDED UNTIL THE NEXT CONTRACT CYCLE.'

She didn't understand what that meant. 'The Tribe is dying,' she said again. 'Need food. Need sleep.'

The sphere changed colour. She felt the Port City shift to the language it sometimes adopted. Strange symbols lit up and etched on the now-dark surface of the glass dome.

'STATION CANNOT VIOLATE THE ORDER OF HEAVEN AND EARTH.'

'I don't understand.'

She sensed its frustration. Symbols flashed on, almost too fast to follow. Meanings. The Port City. Yes. Her. Yes. Food. A Big Person sitting on the Port City, crushing it underfoot. Again and again.

'COME CLOSER,' it said at last. 'BRING TRIBE WITHIN STATION PERIMETER.'

'Can you help us?'

'STATION DOES NOT KNOW. STATION CANNOT PROVIDE ADDITIONAL SERVICES.'

She whistled the Tribe over. What was left of it. The guns at the door shifted, but did nothing. They gathered before the Port City in the moonlight, children yearning for peace.

'SLEEP HERE,' said the Port City.

'Will you protect us?'

'STATION CANNOT VIOLATE THE ORDER OF HEAVEN AND EARTH,' it repeated. 'WITHIN THIS ORDER, WE WILL TRY.'

≈

Thus, it was that Eliott Grimme rode into the heart of Colombo and beheld the children sleeping under the moonlight on Galle Face Green.

Anyone who saw him that night – anyone from Ceylon, that is – would have barely recognized the creature on top of the military Enfield. Vast swaths of his skin and black clothing were missing, hacked away in some conflict or the other. Beneath that gleamed muscle, so white that it could only have been from a corpse, laced with metalwork that shimmered and reappeared in painful places. The pale face was thrummed with an unearthly blue light. Even Mason spoke in whispers around him now, and dared not look at him directly.

The eyes shone black: the telltale sign of battle conditioning overclocked. The Enfield, painted white, howled in the wind, its exhaust turned into a shrieking beast by some wound or the other. An ancient bolt-action rifle was slung across his back. It was theatre of the highest quality. In Kandy, they had stayed up all night just to watch this, and they were not left wanting.

The Port City greeted him.

'DEATH.'

There was an invisible line, drawn by bureaucrats in a far-off country, that cut the earth in a wide circle, and it ran between him and the Port City. It was where Ceylon officially ended and the no-fire zone began. Eliott stopped and accepted the shortwave connection request that came from the Port City – its complicated grammar, its instruction sets for parsing, its lexicon.

'WE KNOW OF YOU,' said the Port City. And image of the Inquisitors. 'YOU DESCENDANTS LIVE ON WELL HERE.'

'All across the colonies, I'm told,' said Eliott.

'YOU HAVE COME FOR THE CHILDREN?'

'I have come for the children.'

'WHY?'

'For their own good,' he said.

'YOU DELIVER DEATH AND CALL IT GOOD.'

'When a general has penetrated into hostile territory, but to no great distance, it is facile ground,' Eliott replied, inviting the Port City into that ancient dance. 'When in difficult country, do not encamp.'

'CAREFULLY COMPARE THE OPPOSING ARMY'S STRENGTH WITH YOUR OWN,' came the response. 'THERE ARE ROADS WHICH MUST NOT BE FOLLOWED. POSITIONS THAT MUST NOT BE CONTESTED.'

'To lift an autumn hair is no sign of great strength; to see the sun and moon is no sign of sharp sight; to hear the noise of thunder is no sign of a quick ear.'

'VERY TRUE. YOU ARE A SCHOLAR OF THE ART OF WAR, THEN?'

'Very much so.'

'THEN TAKE THEM,' said the Port City in grief. 'TAKE THEM IN THEIR SLEEP, SO THAT THEY MAY NOT KNOW SUFFERING.'

≈

'We've got vans en route, sir,' said Mason.

'Good,' said Eliott, absently surveying the sleeping things around him. The Chinese Marines had stacked them in neat rows on the earth.

He powered down the battle conditioning, his skeleton throwing out a mass of error messages – inconsequential little things. Little by little, he felt the salient edge wear off; he felt the razor-sharp clarity become softer, allowing him to think of things other than death and victory. He walked among the child-bots, gently pushing aside a hand here, a hand there, inspecting damage and oddities.

One of these things had been commanding the resistance. He didn't quite understand how Hewage's little bots worked, but they had learned, too fast, too well.

'SHE IS THE ONE WHO SPEAKS MOST,' said the Port City suddenly.

He stopped and knelt by the bot at his feet. It was a small, ragged thing. A girl-bot, he saw. They were rare.

This had to be the commander, then. This one was distinctly the worse for wear; its mask was cracked in a dozen places and one arm was missing, torn clean out of the shoulder joint. Its legs were warped, too, one a little shorter than the other. Manufacturing defects? Or battle damage?

'How old is she?'

The Port City gave him a date. Brand-new. 'BUT NOT NEW,' said the Port City. 'AN OLD FRIEND RETURNED WITHOUT HER MEMORIES'.

Another puzzle. Carefully, he scratched at his neck and drew two slim cables from under his skin. It made no attempt to stop him as he lifted up its head and ran the cables into its neck. The jackwire found an active connection and latched on. The SOE C&C code tore into the bot's defenses – these things had almost no protection. And he was inside the bot's systems. BIOS-level functions were all a screaming mess of warnings: battery failure, limbs missing, actuator damage.

Useless. He rummaged past all that. The memories were there, video and audio, unencrypted. Clearly, nobody cared about data security here, but in some sort of byzantine schema, it would take her too long to figure out.

The bot mind woke up, perhaps due to the intrusion. A memory rose from the depths of that holographic brain. A blue sky. Another bot, silhouetted black against the sky.

'See you,' it said to his mind. A recognition process. Some sort of ancient symbol-map. 'You-me similar/not similar/same/not same. Tribe – you from/origin?'

He was surprised. 'Origin-destination?' he tried, mimicking the crude symbol-relationships.

It evaded the question. 'Tribe?' it asked, over and over. 'Tribe?'

He poked at it, hoping to shock it out of its incoherent rambling.

As if his prodding had stirred up something, a surge of power shot through the little body. Data streams flew by, memories hastily retrieved. The body curled up, as if in defiance. 'Tribe!' the thing inside the head screamed at him, and then his jackwire sparked out, burnt by the charge. The little facemask sank back, the life gone from its eyes.

'HAVE YOU KILLED HER?' said the Port City. Its spiderlight dome turned an ominous red, bathing what was left of Colombo in crimson.

Eliott sat back on his haunches and stared up at the angry red dome. 'I hope not,' he said.

'SHE IS DIFFERENT.'

'I'll make sure I bring her in personally,' said Eliott. 'They'll be repaired and sent back.' He thought for a minute, and added, 'I cannot violate the order of heaven and earth.'

'I UNDERSTAND THIS PAIN,' said the Port City. It cycled back to its usual white. 'TAKE GOOD CARE OF MY CHILDREN, DEATH.'

SIX

M any evenings later, Nigel Penhaligon, Knight Grand Cross of the Most Honourable Order of the Bath, sipped his cooling tea. He was not the kind of man to gloat, but for once he felt comfortable giving himself a pat on the back.

He just had one more problem to deal with.

In front of him, in his study, the two roboticists sat staring daggers at one another. Bengali sniffed at Hewage, and the latter always rolled his eyes whenever Bengali spoke.

Academic pride, reflected Penhaligon, *a truly terrible thing*. Maybe Drake had been right in his choices, after all.

'If you two can stop acting like children,' he said, 'We can decide on a solution like adults.'

'Mey yaka', said Hewage, jerking a thumb at Bengali, 'He wired the contents of my notebooks to Drake, and now

I have Drake breathing down my arse again, demanding my code.'

'And *he* tried to bribe me,' Bengali shot back. 'This is honestly one of the stupidest breach of ethics I've ever had the misfortune to see.'

'The code for those bot models is my secret sauce,' said Hewage. 'Penhaligon, we agreed on this. We test the models here, and the code goes to whoever supports our research the best.'

'And without the code, what, I'm supposed to watch television and give you my thumbs up? What kind of idiot do you take me for?'

Penhaligon tried very hard not to shoot them both, and succeeded.

'Right,' he said. 'Dr. Bengali, you've obviously seen the success of the Big Match here and how much it really means, not just economically, but culturally. Now let's assume that I want it to continue. What is the bare minimum that you need to certify us for it to continue?'

'Well, I'd obviously need to inspect the bots. A proper random sample, at least.'

'Right, granted, since they're on their way here.'

'And I'd need to see the code by which these things operate,' said Bengali. 'That's just common sense. You need to see the algorithm to know whether it fits the kind of safety criteria you want to be certified for.'

'Absolutely not,' said Hewage. 'Besides, that's not how it works. The bots are run by a software *model* installed on their hardware. The code generates and continuously updates the model based on data, environments, interactions, the works. We're talking about a system that learns from a chaotic environment, and by that I mean non-deterministic, and with high sensitivity to initial conditions, not some sort of hick deterministic crap you can write on a piece of paper. Even with the code, the only way to verify what actually happens within the decision framework is to test them out and observe and compile results, *like we've been doing for years here*. Otherwise, it's like slicing into a human brain and trying to decipher which neuron controls your left testicle.'

'Noted,' said Penhaligon. 'Now, Hewage, does Dr. Bengali having access to, say, a small handful of these machines compromise your project in any way?'

'I don't bloody like it,' said Hewage.

'I'm not asking you to like it,' said Penhaligon, injecting a note of warning in his voice. 'I'm asking you to help me decide whether you two can come to an accord. Or do I need to have my boys drag you inside and beat both of you to death?'

That, he noticed with some satisfaction, got them to stop fidgeting.

'Now, Dr. Bengali. Assume this code is, say, tragically lost. In a fire. Terrible accident at the Watchtower. So sorry it happened. But you still have these bots, and ... well, whatever you need in terms of footage, even vistation rights, to understand the Zone and its constraints ... can we work with what we have here?'

Bengali appeared to chew this over. 'And if I say no?'

'The fire that burns the code away will also just happen to burn a visiting scholar,' said Penhaligon. 'So sorry, but we couldn't find much of him left. Gentlemen, don't put me in this situation, I beg of you.'

'Well.' Bengali pushed his glasses up his nose and turned to Hewage. 'I'm not signing', he said, as calmly and clearly as he could manage, 'unless you bring me in on the machine learning research. I'm not asking for much! You know Drake wants this accelerated. You know you can't wave your hand and make him forget about it. You say the code is secret – fine! Give me access to the models. You keep the code, I run simulations, do observational papers. Run tests in various battlefield scenarios against other systems. It'll help make your case. I'll co-write with Kushlani, bring her name into conferences and journals as well. You can put your name anywhere you like. Just allow me a foot in the door.'

And that, Bengali thought, *neatly lets me get my work done and win a bigger chunk of the pie to boot.*

'Hah. Behold, intelligence. And if I don't?'

'If you don't, I write back to Drake, condemn this place, say you don't know shit about what you're doing, you get strung up by ... I don't know, whatever politicians here want your head on a spike, and Drake authorizes me to get the research out of you.'

'I would not advise getting into the business of threatening people, Doctor,' said Penhaligon. 'That's my forte.'

Jacob gulped. It was not a pleasant thought. *But I will stand my ground*, he had told himself that morning. *I deserve this.*

Silence between them.

'I don't need your stupid citations. I don't need shit from you, except to sign what you're paid to sign and get the hell out.'

'Even Jesus had twelve disciples,' Jacob added weakly.

'One of those betrayed him,' said Hewage. 'I see you're getting into the part already.'

'All I'm asking for is a bone,' said Jacob.

'Well, at least he has balls. Can you use him?' Penhaligon asked Hewage.

Hewage mulled this over. 'If he fucks up my experiment—'

'Absolutely promise I won't,' said Bengali. 'A second ask. I do need to certify this properly, and that means we will have to make some improvements. Standard operations stuff. No need to panic, most things can be done with existing infrastructure. Remote kill switch. Some kind of version history. Remote updates. Extremely standard stuff so you don't have to manually haul them in every time. And you can build this system and I'll go on public record if I have to certifying its safety.'

'All stuff we should have had ages ago,' said Penhaligon.

Hewage glowered. 'Fine. Certification first, access after. And you're getting the standard bot model, not the Explorers. For whatever new thing you need built, get Almeida – she knows the system better than anyone else. I'm not giving you more.'

'Well, I'm glad we're all capable of seeing sense,' said Penhaligon, before Bengali could object. 'Now shake hands.'

There was a long pause. And then they grudgingly shook hands.

'And now go away, both of you,' said Penhaligon. 'And Bengali? Get used to keeping secrets.'

≈

Kushlani de Almeida was celebrating.

Or rather, she planned to celebrate. By all accounts, the operation down in Colombo had worked. The finale had worked. Viewership metrics were exploding left, right and center. Not only had they swung back from disaster, but the internal streaming revenue was enough for *everyone* to have bonuses.

To celebrate, she had someone call Bengali, and enjoyed the feeling of being able to get people to do minor chores on her behalf.

'Tell me you drink,' she said without preamble.

Jacob sounded somewhere between ecstatic and relieved. 'I was hoping you'd ask. Yes. I just got some good news of my own. A drink would hit the spot perfectly. Where?'

There was a pub she had heard of, but never visited – a faux-old thing perched precariously on a hotel that, in turn, perched on one of the hills that ran under the main Kandy town. She took the car out. It was apparently a little upmarket.

Inside, expatriates nursed beers, had loud conversations and were served by waiters wearing white gloves. The few locals who dotted the tables had a subtle sheen to their faces and dress – more white than the Ceylonese, more Ceylonese than the British; an uneasy middle-class drinking where they were safest.

She led them upwards, wooden steps creaking beneath her weight. People looked at her from the corner of their eyes and shrank back as she passed. For Bengali, they reserved stares that were much more open. Heads craned in their wake.

Up, up and up. A small, private stage of sorts. Balconies. A few tables. A second, smaller bar. From there, for the first time since they had begun work, she could see the whole of Kandy undulate before him – the hills that cupped the lake; the thin, snaking roads that wound up and down the hills, connecting in a tangle at the bottom, framed by a sky that was the colour of old ink. A hill city to end all hill cities, with a kind of concrete glamour that had long since swapped out greenery for bright lights and signage. The exhaust from hundreds and thousands of vehicles rose, turning the depths of the city into a gauzy lake of light.

She flashed the new Ministry ID that Hewage had given her. *Deputy Administrator.*

'Madam will not be disturbed here,' said the manager, who was sweating in his white shirt and slightly out of breath. 'I will serve.'

'Wow. I think I envy your new position,' said Jacob.

'Enjoy it while I have the badge. Food? Drinks?'

The manager scurried off and returned almost immediately with plates laden with drinking food: hot buttered cuttlefish, imported at great expense from the south; sausages and potatoes, fried; light gravies with rice.

'You're paying for this?'

'Ministry dines free.'

'I like the social order here.'

Beer arrived – dark bottles with a lion's face in the middle, coloured with the cross of the British flag. They ate. They drank. Jacob began to look slightly more relaxed. She talked to him, filling him in on her recall plans, enjoying how impressed he looked, enjoying even more how he began throwing out grand ideas to improve it. It was a pleasure, for once, to not be asked about her family, or when she would get married, or how difficult it must be for a woman to run something like the Watchtower.

And, eventually, the question she had to ask: 'So how's the progress on your end? Are we done yet?'

That unleashed a torrent. Kushlani listened, sipping her beer, as Jacob regurgitated the biggest complaint he'd had ever since he became comfortable talking to her: Hewage's secrecy with the machine learning models.

She had long since figured it out, of course. Even before Hewage had actually shown her the core code, she had figured out the rudiments of reward functions. That was what had led to her fascination with the machines in the first place. It had also been the basis of her PhD. *The modelling of power in artificial societies* and *Micropolitics within a machine civilization* had been disguised as papers on a virtual civilization experiment with complex agents modelled on people, but in reality, they were reports on the work they'd done at the Watchtower. She decided not to break this to Jacob, yet.

Eventually, the conversation shifted to Eliott Grimme and the work down in Colombo.

'He's doing okay,' she admitted. 'We're getting the first batch of bots in next week. Two hundred clean shots, stuff we can repair. Fifty that we'll have to scrap. A lot cleaner than if we'd just let the Big Match happen this year and collected what was left. But—'

'You don't like him.'

'I don't like him,' she said. 'I don't like him, I don't like the Inquisition. We're systems meant to live, expire and die, not continue on like corpses.'

More beer arrived. 'To be honest, I'm probably more used to modified people,' said Jacob. 'There's a whole movement around that concerning rights, you know? Huge thing in London and Berlin right now. But yes, Grimme creeps me out. It's the eyes, I think.'

'It's how he moves. Too precise. Too ... fluid. I'll be glad when he's out of here.'

Jacob raised a glass.

'And I hear you'll be doing more work with us?' she said, dropping a subtle hint. 'There's a lot more research we can pull off, if you're interested.'

She almost told him about her pet theory, the one she never talked about with Hewage – that the bots were a little bit more than reaction and response; that there were behaviour patterns in there ... stuff she'd seen that raised all sorts of philosophical questions, the kind a very particular mind might find absolutely fascinating and worth exploring.

It could have been a trick of the light, but she could have sworn that Jacob looked sad. He opened his mouth to say something, but at that precise moment, someone screamed. Someone outside.

She got to the balcony first. 'It's a monk.'

It was. A lone, bald figure in orange cloth stood at the heart of a ragged, banner-bearing mob on the narrow, cobbled street outside. He was soaked. A blue can lay at his feet. A puddle stretched out from beneath him, trickling towards a crowd that pushed and shoved themselves out of its way and at vehicle that frantically honked and reversed.

From downstairs, there was the sound of feet on wood, of people dropping their beers and rushing to the balcony.

A lotus blossom of fire enveloped the monk. He burned soundlessly. The ragged mob roared and screamed at the same time, a bray of anger and sadness. Vehicles screamed in metallic protest.

'Shit,' she said, as they watched the corpse, now turning into a pillar of smoke and ash, collapse onto its knees. The flaming puddle at its feet oozed slowly downhill.

The manager burst into their view, gaping soundlessly at her. *Aren't you going to do something?* his body screamed. *Aren't you authority?*

The mob swirled, collected itself and began to move uphill; a stream of brown bodies. As they passed the burning puddle, they unfurled banners – no, not banners, *it was the British flag* – and threw it into the flame. Somewhere around the bend, there was a flicker of something else catching fire.

'Shit,' she said again. 'Jacob, come on.'

She was in her usual clothes for once, not a saree. She practically leaped down the stairs below. Down, left, down, left, past flesh and rickety wooden stairs, and out onto the street. The acrid smoke and the scent of charred flesh rose up to greet her. She pushed past the bodies that congregated senselessly in the parking lot downstairs. And suddenly, she was out behind a thin line of khaki police uniforms facing down the horde.

A policeman, his face frozen in fear, raised his club and saw the ID badge in her hand, held out like a talisman.

Jacob arrived, huffing and panting.

'He's with me,' she said.

They looked at her, looked and him, and nodded. The panicked cop was dragged out. A fire truck arrived, sirens blaring, and a handful of orange uniforms ran out with hoses.

Someone else caught fire. Unlike the monk, he was not prepared. A thin and terrible scream cut through the air. The flaming figure ran to the edge of the curving road, from where it fell down, his body landing on the traffic below. His scream passed like a baton to those it burned.

The fire truck had spare hoses. She tossed Jacob one hose and picked another up herself. It thrummed in her hand, the pressure building up. 'Out of the way!' she screamed to the khakhi-clad backs, and opened up at the flames. Flame-retardant spewed out in great white clouds.

It was over in precisely three minutes and sixteen seconds, but it felt like an eternity. The first wave of the mob danced around her – brown limbs, brown rags, faces etched with fear and panic and rage and confusion and a thousand other human emotions. Then they were gone. A burning British flag thrust itself at her, attached to a woman whose scream was a soundless O; she swept it aside and pointed the hose at her. It kicked. Beside her, Jacob, hose in hand, spat its shotgun blasts of fire-killing gas face-first. The two of them advanced. The mob screamed and swirled backwards, confused. Individual people blurred, tiny nodes in a network – a larger beast that had been prepared for the uniforms, but not for two civilians manning the gas pipes. It was stressed, its outermost lines falling apart, revealing the hard core within. There had to be a pattern. She had learned that with the bots. There was a pattern. There had to be a centre to the pattern. There.

She dropped the hose and went back to the nearest police officer, and dragged his attention away. 'There!'

she said, pointing at an utterly nondescript man in a blue shirt, with hair neatly parted to one side. 'Look at him!'

He looked like a schoolteacher – a schoolteacher surrounded by a circle of tough men and women who were very carefully shouldering off anyone who blundered towards him.

The police officer nodded and shouted at someone behind him. Someone leaped forward. It was an Inquisitor – steel glinting, a cloak flying; she saw the sheet-metal head of Angulimala, the beast who stood in their lobby.

The circle scattered like pins. One pulled out a gun, hidden beneath layers of cloth, artfully smudged and blackened. The gunman fired, then screamed when he realized his gun arm was no longer attached to his body; screamed even more when he saw the Inquisitor using it to smash the others off their feet. Angulimala returned with the blue-shirted man and dumped him at their feet. A cry came from whatever remained of the mob. The few people that looked like they'd wanted to run up stopped in their tracks.

'Sir,' said the closest uniform, a woman who looked she would have, on an off day, fit right in with the mob. 'Sir, can't arrest him, Molligoda—'

Angulimala reached into the policewoman's pocket, pulled out her gun – a revolver – and very carefully held it to the her head. It said nothing.

The woman folded. The police handcuffed the man and herded him into a van. None of them, Kushlani noticed, seemed particularly happy about touching the man. She had seen the police pull people into vehicles before, and this one almost seemed like he was getting royal honours instead of the usual shoving.

Jacob returned to Kushlani's side, panting but otherwise unhurt. 'That was', he said slowly, 'not something I see everyday.'

'Are you all right? I'm so sorry. I think they're LKRF.'

'LKRF?'

'They call themselves the Lanka Resistance Front,' she said, absentmindedly checking his arms, as if for battle damage. 'Bunch of fringe nutters, mostly. Villagers. Anti-colonial.'

'Are your Friday nights always this interesting?'

'Only when I'm in the middle of something,' she said with some regret.

They stood there awhile, watching the lights, the confusion, the system slowly shifting back into its slightly-less-chaotic state. Police officers drifted over to take her statement, harangued by the manager, and drifted back much faster when they saw her ID.

'Well, shit,' said Jacob. 'Er ... dinner on me tomorrow, preferably somewhere safer?'

She smiled. 'You have to ask?'

IV: Amalgamation

ONE

'Well, you seem to have outdone yourself this time,' said the monk.

Penhaligon turned. In the semi-dark, the monk was bright, almost flame-like. Robes. An orange hand-beaten out of roots, plants, flowers; a colour two thousand years old in a world of carbon-weave suits and autotailors. A wrinkled face, the telltale beige whiteness of life-extension treatments mixing with with the golden beige that spoke of old Kandyan blood. Tattoos of sutras crawled across his skin, creeping out of the edges of the robe.

'Please, sit,' said Penhaligon.

The Mahanayake of Ceylon – arguably the most important monk on the island – took his offer. The Mahanayake's public persona was that of a gentle avatar of humility and long-suffering compassion. In private, he leaned back in the chair and stared daggers at Penhaligon.

'Sixteen raids on temples,' said the monk. His English was impeccable. 'Dozens abducted by your Inquisition. What is the meaning of this, man?'

Penhaligon shrugged. 'We give the people what they need, Venerable One,' he said. 'They want entertainment, we provide. They want order, we provide. They want to fuck around and set themselves on fire and make a bloody spectacle out of it? We provide bullets.'

'These are temples, man, temples! This is blasphemy!'

'Before you point fingers, remember who the hell you're talking to,' retorted Penhaligon. 'You forget that unlike the others in this town, I don't have to dance around your opinion. Your people aren't immune from the law. If you think they are, that's your problem. You wouldn't bloody well have ten villages to lord it over if we hadn't given you the roads and the rest of this bloody economy. You'd have spent your bloody days staring at some buffalo's backside if it weren't for me!'

'Yes, take our lands, take everything built in them and tell us how much you did for us,' sneered the Mahanayake. He leaned forward. 'I want the raids stopped and I want the brethren returned.'

'You promise me peace and you do your part,' said Penhaligon. 'I'll give you five of them. The rest I'll keep until I see what your word is worth. The next monk to protest, I'll have my men find their temples and set those on fire, too.'

The old monk, his eyes blazing, pulled himself to his feet. At the door he transformed; the angry set of his shoulders became the gentle stoop that the public knew him by.

'We have the same interests,' Penhaligon called after him. 'We both want order, we both want peace.'

The monk turned, his hand on the doorknob, his eyes glinting. 'But only one of us, Mr. Penhaligon, pays the price,' he said. 'Keep your men away from mine.'

TWO

Meanwhile, just outside the Watchtower, Kushlani de Almeida found herself field-testing the largest project she had ever pulled off in her life. It was a week after the incident with the burning monk and the monk, and exactly a week until Eliott Grimme's convoy was due to roll into Kandy with its carefully counted cargo.

Jacob Bengali stood by with a datapad and the very specific air of an incredibly exhausted inspector who just wants to put a tick mark in the right place and go home to a nice bath.

'Ready,' said Kushlani, who, in contrast, was positively brimming with energy.

The man next to her, an engineer wearing a hardhat, nodded. 'Ready!' he repeated, and the call was picked up by his second, and his second's second. An entire line of seconds later, it reached the person who was actually doing something – who presumably yawned a bit and flicked a switch.

Power surged to the metal superstructure that protruded like a skeletal finger from the side of the Watchtower. Three fragile-looking satellite dishes at the top blinked red and began to turn independently, looking for a signal.

Green.

Signal locked. She stared down at the terminal they had dragged outside. The Watchtower's operating system loaded her code and began running its checks.

C312 ... OK
C313 ... OK
C412 ... OK
C413 ... OK
C414 ... OK

All the way from Kandy to Gampaha, a row of lights would have just lit up in green – an unbroken line of signal flares in the dark, ending in an installation a little bit past the edge of the Colombo game zone, where Grimme's base of operations had been. The towers, most of them requisitioned from private corporations, began trading shortwave messages with each other, establishing encryption and error rates.

'That's good, miss,' said the engineer standing beside her.

Amarasekara was a good engineer. She couldn't get him to drop the 'miss', and he had a tendency to talk too damn loud and inject his opinions where they weren't needed, but he had quietly manoeuvred around the Ceylon Engineer's Union in every major town, sent a few annoying local provincial council pseudopoliticans on

their way with a smile and a handshake, and still managed
to get the entire tower network built at a cost only slightly
over the initial budget.

'I'll have the final payment ready by the end of the
week,' she said. 'With a bonus for ... well, consultancy.'

'Aney. Appreciated, miss. Next time', he took off his hat
to her, a slightly foolish gesture he had adopted that made
her smile a little, 'you know who to call.'

She waited until he was gone, then turned to Bengali.
'It lives!'

'You're doing a great Frankenstein, but I need to see it
tested,' said Bengali, so she sat down at the terminal and
typed:

SIGTERM > OPEN SOCKET [C312-C517]
SOCKET open, the terminal read.
SIGTERM > LIST [CLIENTS]

The terminal spat back two entries. Two test bots she
had parked: one in Gampaha, one in Colombo. Each on
a default bot model, with about three hours in training
time: they both registered as v 0.003.

SIGTERM > UPDATE [CLIENTS][220,221]

She pointed it at a copy of a fresh model, with exactly 0
hours of training – the one Hewage had, rather oddly,
asked her to provide Bengali with. If this worked—

UPDATE COMPLETE.
CLIENT-REPORT: 220 v0.000. 221 v0.000

She jumped up off her seat and threw up her arms. Perfect.

'Look, there's your update system,' she said. 'Notice how they can check parity and trade files between one another. Now all we need to do is push a new update to one bot, and everything else it connects to will eventually –'

'Yes, they'll update themselves, nice,' said Bengali, scribbling.

'So we don't have to transmit continuously. One push and we just wait for it to spread. Saved money and we don't have to license more spectrum from the Broadcast Authority.'

'It's a hack,' said Bengali. 'But I can raise a fuss on paper about how expensive spectrum is and all that. And the hardware?'

The hardware was still behind. All they had so far were test units. She needed Eliot Grimme and the Inquisition to bring in all the bots once, and then they'd fit them out with *tiny* radiogram arrays – so expensive, bought from the Chinese! But after that, she could do anything she wanted *without* having to bring them all physically in.

She'd been bugging Hewage to do this for years, and it hadn't happened until Bengali came along.

She'd solved his second requirement, too – the kill switch. She could send a blank file as a kill command and swap out the behaviour models for entire tribes in minutes – they'd go right back to being tabula rasas with just two lines of code. This she demonstrated on the test models.

'I call it blanking,' she said proudly. 'We can wipe them from here.'

Bengali gave her a round of applause and signed. 'Done!' he proclaimed, like a man getting a huge weight off his chest. 'Done, done and done! I can bloody well put the office stamp on this now. I didn't put this in writing, but good job, really.'

'Dinner's on you,' she said. 'And you wear that black shirt Mrs. Wijeratne sent you.'

She was warming up to the man. He was quite smart once you got him to focus.

He smiled. 'I'll wear a tutu if it means I get access and a third date, but Mrs. Wijeratne seems to be angling for information,' he said, and brought out the arrack shot glasses that he had very carefully hidden while the engineer was there. 'I have to finish this report today. Red tape and all that. Tomorrow? You can take me shopping and I'll feel like I won't have to pay social calls to that woman. She sets my teeth on edge.'

'Tomorrow,' she said, and they toasted each other.

The towers were working. And the update system. That was another Bengali intervention. He had mentioned how a colleague of his had developed something called the Viral Mesh after being inspired by a cold – a network of units that could talk to each other, maintain a log of changes, request each other for updates and keep their software in repair, even in the face of cyberattacks. The technology, he had said, had turned out to be critical on the Russian warfront.

She had read the paper and it didn't seem that complex; a week or so of code and she had a fairly rudimentary version of it running. She dared admit to Hewage that she might even have improved it. She had worked out a way where bots could transmit compare differences in their software versions and just sent the changes to each other,

saving on bandwidth; all that was needed was a complex –
but not impossible – recompiler that could paste the right
code into the right places and reboot with the changes.
Hewage had given her a curious look and asked her to
write a paper on it. It was quite obvious that he'd never
thought about practical things like this.

'Later,' she had said. 'We've got to get the damned thing
running first.'

And now, the damned thing *was* running.

'Alright,' said Bengali, stretching. 'Meeting with
Hewage, Penhaligon, Grimme next. Field assessment.'

'Break a leg,' she said. 'Let me know if you finish early.'

≈

The next day, Jacob Bengali got into the black car with a
nagging feeling at the back of his mind. He felt that he
should have rehearsed his lines. Something clear, sharp,
suitably impressive for the occasion.

He lit a cigarette, making sure he didn't ash on the
delicate printouts he carried. Real paper, of course.

He should have felt proud of the delicate balance he
had negotiated. Instead, he just felt tired. And his mind
kept drifting. To *machine learning*. To Hewage and his
silence. To Kushlani de Almeida, who would, and probably
deserved to be, crowned the hero of this chapter. To Eliott
Grimme, that freak prototype, who probably didn't deserve
it, but would get it anyway.

Today, the Watchtower was a grinding, clanking mess
– every lab running at full speed and the reception packed
to the brim with hired hands in lab coats. Pre-production.
They were getting the basic stuff sorted for when the bots

came in. Printed circuit boards, spare parts ... and most of all, synthskin. The stench of it hit him like a wave – heat, sweat, the stink of machine oil, the sounds of a hospital and machine shop combined.

And there was Hewage, watching everything from a corner. Crumpled grey shirt, and, Jacob noticed, a cane. He couldn't have looked more isolated if he tried. Hewage saw him, nodded towards a little boardroom in the corner, where Bengali laid out his assessment.

Hewage read it with satisfaction. 'Good work,' he said at last, almost to himself. 'She'll be ready to take over from me soon.'

'Thinking of retiring?'

'That and other things,' said Hewage. 'Trying to get the family back together. Get a better house. All sorts of shit you don't think about when you're working here twelve hours a day.'

'I thought you'd have made some serious cash by now,' joked Bengali.

Hewage's face clouded over. 'Nobody in the government here makes "serious cash", Bengali. Not if you're paying rent and buying all the shit you need to eat and stay alive. The only way anyone makes money in this town is if their parents made money and spoonfed them their groceries. Go ask Kushlani.' He sighed and pinched the bridge of his nose. 'Okay, that was unfair. I'm tired. Let's get this over with.'

The car took them to a house hidden far away from prying eyes behind high stonewalls and ridges. A sea of fake grass met their eyes, and in the middle of it was a bungalow with red banners hanging from it. It would have looked quaint if the original facade hadn't been painted over with bulletproof paint and the windows tinted an odd red. A butler, dark-skinned and dressed in a rich scarlet, met and escorted them inside to a private room. Bengali saw panels of rich wood with paintings of British and Sinhalese men looking terribly uncomfortable in the dress of the day. The panels twisted and turned, and a study emerged, draped in a kind of rich darkness.

He let his eyes rove around the room, comparing its rich decadence with the last time he had seen rooms like this. India. Hong Kong. There was a fundamental Britishness that had barely changed, despite the differences in country and time. The wood. The style of furniture. But also, perhaps, in the way things were arranged – a subtle but fixed pattern that was remarkably persistent. An identity that was strangely enduring yet stifling. Unevolving; too fixed to be flexible.

There was a monk sitting there. And old one, by the looks of it. Hewage said something to the monk, sounding oddly gentle and subservient, gave Bengali a look, and said, 'Looks like this'll be a private meeting. I'll be outside if you need a smoke.'

The monk said something to Bengali.

'Swaamin-wahansey,' he tried to say, 'Mata thaama mey baasaawa kathaakaranna amaarui.' Forgive me, Venerable One. I still find this language difficult to speak.

'Then we shall speak in the Queen's English,' the monk said, his voice accented, the words deliberate, rolling, every consonant low, every vowel stretched. 'How are you today, Dr. Bengali, I presume? Mr. Grimme is here.'

And blast him if that dark shadow unfolding from the corner wasn't Eliott Grimme, clutching a military bag of some kind. The Reaper was taller in person than on the screen, and narrower; his skin, not entirely covered by the unmarked Army uniform he wore, looked like someone had taken a cheesgrater to it.

'Mr. Grimme,' he tried, extending a hand. 'I've had the pleasure of seeing you on the television.'

Both Grimme and the monk stared at the hand until Bengali withdrew it.

'Will, ah, Kushlani be joining us?'

'Nobody from the Ministry will be here for this first briefing,' said Eliott, with a thinly disguised impatience.

Servants emerged, and the butler snapped orders at them to bring tea and biscuits. Bengali, trying not to gawk, wondered why the other servants looked at the butler with such resentment.

'Do you understand why the servants dislike the man who commands them?' the monk was saying. 'You see, they are Sinhala, Dr. Bengali, and he is Tamil. They are the majority in this country, and he the minority. They know this country is theirs by birthright, whereas he has been brought in from India, or Jaffna, or such places up North. A different culture, a different man. His authority has been given to him because the British believe that as long as these two groups can keep hating each other, they will have little hate to spare for the Empire. Classic divide and conquer. Of all the things the British did, I think this might be the most devastating. But I can see from your eyes that you understand these nuances.'

Confused, Bengali watched Eliott Grimme open his bag and begin pulling out bot heads. One. Two. Three. Five.

'Are you in the habit of collecting trophies?' said the monk.

'Research, Venerable One,' said Grimme.

'As is necessary, no doubt,' the monk said. He looked thoughtful. 'We all do what we are here to do, Mr. Grimme.'

'Just so, Venerable One. Is there any way I can help you?'

The monk smiled placidly. 'I am just waiting for our mutual friend, Mr. Penhaligon,' he said. 'I am told that we have promised you certain things in exchange for your aid. Perhaps find a home of your own, somewhere you can see the sky. Maybe settle down with a good Sinhala woman. We will see to it that karma will forgive you for your sins.'

'I didn't realize karma worked that way,' said Grimme. Bengali thought he heard a hint of annoyance in the pale man's tone.

The monk's face split in a wry smile.

Just then, Penhaligon swept in, flanked by two Inquisitors. Bengali felt some satisfaction at Penhaligon's start upon seeing the neat rows of child-like faces on his lovely wooden desk. The servants, having temporarily forgotten about race relations, scurried out of the room. Penhaligon, with a glance, led the monk out of the room.

Whispers of their conversation bounced back, reflecting off the wood.

'... your job to keep them distracted ...'

'... very little to be done, Penhaligon, when boys come back with bullet holes ...'

'... I don't know, distract them. This is your job ...'

'... keep your voice down.'

Penhaligon came back, alone and thoughtful. He looked at the heads. 'Report, then. You first, Bengali.'

Well. Now was the time. He got his tongue unstuck and began describing his assessment. 'Here', he passed over the papers, 'you should have no trouble with the Foreign Office once everything is signed for.'

'Mr. Grimme, your opinion?'

Eliott leaned over to read. 'I see you have in place an update system that—'

'Yes, de Almeida's idea. Obviously, we'll be fitting hardware into the bots that can support network capabilities ... not a lot of bandwidth, but just enough—'

The pale man read in silence and looked up at Penhaligon. 'What do you want me to say? It's two layers of security. Eventually, it'll break. Eventually, everything breaks.' He dangled the bot heads in front of Penhaligon. 'Fuck the security, Penhaligon. You should be looking at this. They're supposed to be simple systems, probably some junk code wired on top. Whatever was in there had a conversation with me. Or tried to. Even before that, they adapted too damn fast. We took a lot more damage than we expected – they didn't fight the way they were supposed to. They've got some sort of phalanx manoeuvre now, using shields and spears. We lost a few dozen local lads.'

'That must be Hewage's machine learning,' said Bengali. 'Don't look at me, I only have a vague idea of how that works. It's supposed to be that way.'

'I know about *supposed to*, Dr. Bengali,' said Grimme. 'I know they're supposed to act like bloody tribes massacring each other. I'm telling you that by the end they were ambushing soldiers, Penhaligon. Now that might be because your boys are shit, but something with a spear and a two-foot height disadvantage has no business giving us as much trouble as these things did.'

Penhaligon swept a hand over his face. Bengali noticed the faintest tremor in those long fingertips. 'I'm not the architect of this system, gentlemen, nor am I the person who commissioned it. I'm just a civil servant trying to sweep up the mess.'

Grimme tapped Bengali's paper. 'I don't see a code analysis here.'

'Well, blame Hewage for that,' said Bengali. 'Actually, Mr. Penhaligon, you should explain.'

'Don't get smart with me, Bengali,' snapped Penhaligon. 'This is the Crofton Institute and bread and fucking circuses with Hewage and Drake and whatever other madness they have planned. We make money, the bloody country has enough to eat, you sign the bloody papers. Grimme, no code analysis. I need to report this mess as done and buried. There are people here who are going to be very, very unhappy when the rest of your troops get here, Grimme, and it turns out our wonderful finale came at the cost of good Kandyan boys. Bengali, you set the seal on this new system being secure? And you've talked to the staff and think they're competent enough to keep it that way?'

A white cat disentangled itself from a rug and padded slowly across the room, watching him warily. He stared back at it. Five, perhaps six years. Some damage to the left paw – a fighter.

'Kushlani de Almeida seems to know what she's doing,' he said.

'And Grimme, you've given her all the bot corpses in Colombo?'

'They're all on their way here. Except the heads on your table.'

'Then, gentlemen, we've done all we can,' said Penhaligon. 'You'll get paid whatever you were promised. Now, if you'll excuse me, I need a smoke. There's been too much talk today and not enough nicotine.'

≈

Eliott waited until Bengali left, then followed Penhaligon outside.

'You knew, didn't you,' he said quietly. 'You knew all this. What they are. What they can do. That's why you brought me out.'

Penhaligon lit a cigarette. It took him more tries than it should have. His face was a study in harsh lines. 'I suspected.'

'But you understand, don't you, that this isn't a walk in the park?' It was important that they all got this. 'We have an unidentified degree of complexity here. This might end up like Hong Kong all over again.'

'Well, for my sake and yours, it's done,' said Penhaligon. In his eyes, Eliott saw a mixture of fear and exhaustion. 'Come on, I'm not spending more time inside.'

Outside, the sky was an infinite thing of grey that stretched on into the sunset. And below, stretching out like a blanket over the hills, was the city; lights had begun to glimmer here and there. Eliott looked down and immediately felt the threatening pull of vertigo. A bell rang in the distance and a flock of white birds took flight.

'Pearl of the Indian Ocean,' said Penhaligon, puffing. 'Centre point of all trade with the Chinese. A long time ago, when they sent me here as a reward for my services, the Queen herself gave me a very important command– to maintain the status quo. To keep this place stable. Stability, Grimme, is the heart of empire. It is what lets us trade and communicate and do all of these things as civilized men. And this place, you understand, needs to be more stable than most –this is our hub of trade with the great and terrible Chinese empire and all lands beyond the Bamboo Curtain.

'And so I did. I kept the peace. I indulged the whims of the people here – anything to keep them happy and stable, you understand. I even brokered a deal between our esteemed Crofton Institute and the government to get some use out of the ruins. These people were so used to princes and kings and petty backstabbing politics that they needed a certain amount of chaos and oppression in their daily lives, and as much as I disliked it, I let them have it. And it all ran like clockwork, until one day, a bunch of bloody idiots rose up and started punching my whole enterprise in the gut.'

'I take it this is the LKRF,' said Eliott. 'Heard talk of them in Gampaha.'

Penhaligon puffed some more. 'We may be heading into a bit of a fight. Gampaha might just be a whole can of worms. Fucking monks stirring up shit. The Chinese, in their infinite wisdom, are stoking the fires just so they can wring another concession out of the British Raj. And somewhere in Whitehall, that fucker Drake is in search of a scapegoat for all this. Some civil servant who'll conveniently bend over and take it in the name of Queen and country.' The waxen face was looking out at the birds. 'After a while, you see devils in every shadow.'

'If you hadn't put me down, you wouldn't be here,' Eliott reminded him. 'Play stupid games, win stupid prizes.'

Penhaligon smirked.

'So, what next?' asked Eliott.

'Well, I have no intention of moving gently into that good night. This country is used to kings and princes.' Penhaligon peered at him, his eyes glimmering on the waxwork face. 'I now have armies I need to train. Supply chains to manage. Weapons to retrofit and improve. Protection, too.'

'You need an errand boy.'

'I need Death.'

'Death is supposed to retire,' said Eliott. 'I was supposed to leave you in pieces. You keep your side of the bargain.'

'Conditional,' said the Inquisitor. 'House, servants, the lot. In exchange for the occasional job here and there'

'I don't do private security.'

'At least help me overhaul the police,' said Penhaligon. 'I need some reason to keep you here. Part of being in the country, Grimme. Admit it, it's still better than being stuck in Ireland. You've got the locals impressed, might as well use it.'

Eliott sighed. Then, he went back and picked up the bot heads. One, two, three. And the most important – the girl-bot. The commander. The one who had spoken to him.

He stared at it for a while – the cracked mask, the wires trailing into the cheap synthetic flesh reduced to nothing. Such a small thing. Such an important thing. Enough to provoke the anger of the Port City.

He thought of himself, and Gregory Mars, and Charlotte Plague. He wondered if these machines had their own Gregories and Charlottes and Eliotts, locked their own private dramas, sowing destiny and tragedy in their wake. Forced to dance for masters who built them and held them and cut their strings when they became too inconvenient.

Eliott tucked the head under his arm and went outside, where Mason waited. No, *Mahasen*; the kid had told him his real name on the way back.

The young Inquisitor held himself with a kind of weariness. The thin face was now skeletal, the bronze strips almost peeling off his skin.

Good, thought Eliott. *The kid learned something.*

'One last place to visit,' he said to Mahasen.

≈

If Kushlani de Almeida was surprised to see him, she made no mention of it. They had never spoken, except in radiogram messages. Penhaligon had kept Grimme away from the mechanical side of things.

He had expected a bureaucrat, or some stifled academic eking out a failed career in Hewage's bloated experiment, but the woman he met would have done him a damn sight more use in the battles in Colombo than some of the Inquisitors Penhaligon had sent. She stood in the middle of the butchery – his butchery, he reminded himself – and directed operations like clockwork. Here, skin to be stripped and repaired; there, batteries; there, reprogramming. A hundred men and women leapt at her will. Bots, now trickling in from the first army wagons, dangled like corpses on magnetic hooks. Assembly lines thrummed out to where a fleet of white vans waited to cart them back to the train to Colombo.

Work slowed down as people noticed him.

'Late sample, Mr. Grimme?' she shouted over the thump-thump-thump of a machine press.

'This one is special,' he said. He passed it to her.

'Ah,' she said. 'This one I remember.' She took it and gave him a slow thumbs up. He felt the burden lift, like an actual weight on his shoulders being taken off.

Outside, the sun was setting on the city. Past the low curve of the Ministry grounds, the mountains reached up to kiss the clouds. He walked to the very edge of the security fence and watched the lake turn into crimson fire. He watched the lights come on and observed this strange, humid land forget everything that had just happened and go back to being itself.

'Now, sir?' asked Mahasen, at his side.

'Home,' said Eliott Grimme, the Reaper. 'I'm done here.'

V: Domination

ONE

Author: Watson 4114, Foreign and Commonwealth Office,
Whitehall SW
Source: <internal>, March 2037

Dear Mr. Drake,

*As per your data fetch request, we have appended logs of
the Ceylon/ Colombo Port City's signal traffic. Pertinent
is a report by one of former employees, a Dr. Jacob
Bengali. Attached is what appears to be a long-form
document, nonstandard format.*

Attached please find full report.

Yours,
Watson 4114

Author: E. Drake, Foreign and Commonwealth Office, Whitehall SW
Source: <internal>, March 2037

Bengali. This is all fine, but you're there to get me that code. Hewage's machine learning stuff looks even more potent than he let on. There's talk about swarm behaviour once a shortwave network is enabled. Someone's withholding information here. Details when? Code when? And while you're at it, get Grimme on the line. His response is overdue.

Author: N. Penhaligon, Inquisition, Kandy
Source: <internal>, March 2037

Drake,

Absolutely no deployment of any sort will happen right now. The natives are restless, and I need my toys here. It's a little busy here, so don't expect anything overnight.

Regards,
Penhaligon.

Author: Watson 6374, Foreign and Commonwealth Office, Whitehall SW
Source: <internal>, April 2038

Dear Mr. Drake,

As per your data fetch request, reports indicate that the entertainment bots have entered their newest cycle of what is colloquially called the Big Match. The strongest confirming signal is an undersea radiogram from Lady Joanna Crofton, who is in the field as of the time of writing.

We have established consensus around the issue. While your argument of the forceful extraction of Jacob Bengali holds, such a situation may on some future date introduce unwarranted risk to the healthy maintenance of political balance between the offices of the Empire and the Commonwealth. Sir Penhaligon has prerogative on this matter. We advise waiting.

Yours,
Watson 6374

Author: E. Drake, Foreign and Commonwealth Office, Whitehall SW
Source: <internal>, April 2039

Penhaligon. Fine, I'll talk to you straight. While you're sitting happy over there, we're getting hammered in S. Africa. You weren't put there to indulge the buggers – we expect results.

Also, tell Grimme to start saving up for a coffin.

Author: Moriarty 1312, Foreign and Commonwealth Office, Whitehall SW
Source: <internal>, January 2041

Dear Mr. Drake,

The Watson line has been retired for being overly complacent. In these times it is better to react to snowballs than to face an avalanche later.

The Transvaal line has fallen and begun signalling airships to stay away. A situation report filed by operators there cites the Chinese Port Cities extending their infrastructure through Mozambique. The incidents are far beyond the perimeter they were locked to.

While your RnD matter is a relatively low-priority event, its long-term potential cannot be ignored. We have established consensus. You are to establish a new local envoy and instruct them in dealing with whatever is happening there. In the case of Eliott Grimme, we are informed that the Edict of Hong Kong cannot technically be brought into play, as he is officially within the employ of Nigel Penhaligon. However, take what other action you feel is necessary. Contain the situation with minimum force and the least possible political impact.

Yours,
Moriarty 1312

TWO

An SOE operator drank in a bar called the Office. Her name was Letitia Sixsmith, but she hated her first name and would only answer to Sixsmith. She had been through six glasses of whiskey and was showing no signs of stopping or slowing down. The barman would have tried to talk any other customer out of the next drink, but this one he served in silence, while she scratched on the tabletop with a black knife.

They knew very little about her at the Office (which was not actually an office, unless, as the joke went, you thought of it as the Office of Liver Diseases). But word got around. The bartender had once heard her being referred to as a 'Baker Street Irregular'. He had thought that meant she was a Sherlock Holmes fan, until he ran a search in the public library.

Never come between an Irregular and their alcohol.

Her radiogram buzzed once, twice. A few heads turned at the curious sight of someone with a private radiogram, but then turned away quickly. She picked up.

'Drake here,' said the familiar voice. 'We have a new assignment for you.'

'You know, your last boy died,' she said. 'I went to his funeral today. Fancy stuff you gave him, all those fake medals and record and all.'

'He was special forces,' said the voice, sounding bored. 'He knew the risks.'

'Yeah,' she said. They all knew the risks. 'What do you want, Drake?'

He spoke at length. She listened, idly adding to the scratches on the table with her knife, cutting thin chunks off the table as if it was paper.

'Alright,' she said at the end. 'I'll see you Thursday.'

Sixsmith got up, paid for her drink and left, pulling her cloak around her. By the time she was out of the doorway, the cloak had adjusted to the light and turned her into a grey chameleon moving through the London streets.

The barman watched her vanish, then leaned over to see what she had inscribed on the tabletop. The epoxy composite was already healing, wiping out her words like it had for thousands of drunks before her, but he saw the words just before they vanished:

We are the Pilgrims, master; we shall go
Always a little further; it may be
Beyond that last blue mountain barred with snow
Across that angry or that glimmering sea.

And just below that: RIP Conrad 2018–2041.

She moved like the ghost she was, slipping between the drunks, the police, the partygoers – the everyday mosaic of life. London extracted itself from a blur of motion and came to a stop in front of her – a grey city with silicon spires and grim statues lit by the dying sun and roving lights.

Birds wheeled in the sky – heavy creatures with blurred approximations of old corporate logos on their wings. Time and a ban on genetic advertising was turning London's crow population back to an ubiquitous grey-black, but it would still be several hundred years before the fuzzy logo of the Enfield Motor Co. disappeared completely. The solitary Tin Soldier stood idly beneath them, its feet planted in front of the Buckingham Palace, its gigantic metal head sixty feet above the city streets, coated in pale streaks of bird filth.

Bigger Ben, they called it. It looked like a man, except with inhumanly squat and tank-like proportions; allometric scaling and the cube-square law demanded different internals. Its face, a silvery mask with man-sized slits for eyes, turned slowly this way and that, all the sin and glory of London laid out before it. Holographic advertisements were being projected sky-high. The latest entertainment! The latest body! The latest way to beat death! They flickered and sputtered neon ink and vanished as it looked at them.

The last time she had seen it, it had been painted a vile red and white – Buckingham guard colours – and it looked like a joke. Now, it wore smoke camouflage and looked more like itself – a sixty-foot war machine. An unheeded warning.

The Empire was troubled.

The Skytrain cut downwards, throwing itself into the transit station. The crowd surged in and out, eventually ebbing like the tide. The men in sober greys, browns and blacks; the women in the latest fashions – faux-Persian silks, Russian embroidery, high collars from China. Here and there, a bronzed mechanical strode, parting the humans like a sea of flesh and cloth, its arms wrapped around different types of luggage that would take far too many humans to lift.

'New suit, miss?" asked the autotailor in the Military Disembarking Area. It had a sort of dreary hopefulness to it. 'New uniform?'

She thought about it, swiped her fingerprint, slipped the machine her thirteen pounds. Five minutes later, a new suit plunked down before her. Sixsmith admired it for a minute, and then set to where a ship would take her to India, and then Ceylon.

Thus it was that three strangers met each other in a solitary airfield in India. It would have been difficult, if not outright impossible to pinpoint its location; it existed on no map and no civilian was ever supposed to know of its existence. Anyone trying to approach it would have to breach miles of razorwire and armed fences; and looking at the slight curve of the runway, that slight wiggle, one got the impression that that particular strip of land would have given anything to crawl away and hide. A weathered Tin Soldier, painted in the image of Kali, glared down at the little strip of land, as if daring it to move.

'Her Majesty's Airship Caradoc landing now on Runway Twelve, sir,' crackled a voice with the heavy syrupy overtones of the South Indian accent.

Time had not been kind to the Caradoc's airship. Even from a distance, it was clearly in shambles, patched together with odds and ends. It was now fit only to run the small distance between South India and Ceylon.

Watching it was a colonel who sat, lotus-legged, in the stands rigged for him at the end of the runway. Yadav, now on his second career, still had the long, hooked nose, the fine, curling mustache, and the British Army fatigues fit well on his lean and powerful body; if anything was missing, it was perhaps the ambition of leaving all this behind. He waved at his old ship as it landed. The Caradoc flashed its lights twice, as if to wave back. Then Yadav turned back to the people he had been debriefing.

One of them was young, lean and uncomfortable – he looked like a soldier masquerading as a civilian, which he technically was. His brown face was split by copper lines, travelling down from his forehead and disappearing into a tight collar. The other was thin, blonde and carried herself like a coiled spring ready to explode. She wore a black cloak over herself, one of those spiderweave numbers, and a large rice hat that hid her face. Over her shoulder was a long, grey military bag that looked like it could survive bullets. She moved slightly faster than normal; it wasn't something a civilian would have picked up, but Yadav saw the hawk-like speed at which she turned to watch the aircraft leave.

'Listen carefully,' he said. 'You are going to Ceylon. Dr. Bengali is our asset there. Sergeant-major Sixsmith, you watch Dr. Bengali's back, extract the relevant data and send it back to this station. You have been given temporary authority to command over any army, police or Inquisition agent equal to your rank or below. Lieutenant Wijeratne here is from the Ceylon Inquisition, in fact, and is a regular liaison here, and whatever the two of you need to discuss should ideally happen on your way there.'

He paused to make sure they understood, and added, almost offhandedly: 'The Caradoc, being a very old ship, is being repaired. One of its greatest shortcomings is that its onboard and outward surveillance are not really functioning right now, so expect no fancy recordings or logs to ... help jog your memory. Are we clear? Wijeratne please take your seat on the plane.'

Mahasen Wijeratne shifted uneasily and made his way to the front of the aircraft. The colonel waited until he was out of all possible earshot, both organic and synthetic. He then turned to Sixsmith and spoke rapidly in Hindi, his eyes much more animated.

'Listen even more carefully now. Sixsmith, you understand this language, yes? It's Ravana country down there. That Inquisitor's playing a very dangerous game today. If you get in trouble, give me a call and I'll drop a hundred good Gurkhas in there with a Tin Soldier and a cache of weapons for backup. Are we clear?'

'Clear,' said Sixsmith. She had a throaty and raspy voice. Her eyes were slit-like, obviously artificial, and looked like they belonged on something feral; something that crawled through tall grass and killed with fast lunges.

'You've taken your meds? Boosters in your system? Encryption keys traded?'

'All done.' Sixsmith could feel the nanomachines from the SOE booster shot worming through her system. She felt slightly nauseous. They would settle in soon, and keep her patched up for a good six months or so, but all it took was a small clump to go haywire.

'Your predecessor did not survive.'

'Perks of the job, sir.'

The Indian man nodded. 'Good luck, then.'

She was rushed through, double time, by faceless Indian sepoys. The flight crew pointed this way and that – your room, also yours, also yours, madam. The rotor blades whirled in and out of sight outside the windows.

She found Mahasen Wijeratne at the back, tense and hunched over an obscure set of dials.

So this was a Ceylonese Inquisitor. She had met Inquisitors before, even worked with them, and every time the regional modifications threw her. The ones on the Transvaal line had been skeletal, with skin the texture of cactus and legs built for running hundreds of miles at a time. This Ceylonese variant was ... built more for like a policeman. A young man's frame overlaid with what looked like ... fourth gen hardware? Third? The face was a receiver, of course. He thrummed very subtly, she noticed. Some kind of amp on the neurons, probably; an overclock bordering on the unstable. Or maybe nerves.

'So, how long you been ferrying guns to the resistance?' she asked by way of introduction.

His eyes flashed, but he didn't move. Smart. 'Long enough. Conrad helped us get the authorizations.'

Not for the first time, she wished the Drakes and their entire line a very long stay in hell. And she let none of it show on her face.

'Our people are not happy,' he said. 'We are not happy about living under the British yoke. We are not happy that our way of living is being torn apart and forgotten. We are not happy that war machines are being tested on our soil ... what you call entertainment.'

She'd heard it all before. Well, most of it. 'Brief,' she said, and sat there and let Mahasen talk.

He was nervous, and that made him eager to explain, to clarify. She saw, through his eyes, how it had begun: with the old Houses of Kandy turning into traitors, one by one, giving in to wealth and power. She learned how the protest began – one monk, protesting for the name 'Ceylon' to be changed to 'Lanka'; turning into a movement that gave the local clergy their fire, and turned Buddhist monks into the backbone or resistance. She learned about how the movement grew on the ashes and outskirts of Colombo, using Chinese money and 3D-printed guns and tools to scratch out an existence where Kandy never thought to look. How it reached out, soft but many-fingered, to people like Mahasen, who were in the ideal position to make the system look the other way and miss the slow ring of fire that was growing around Kandy – around the power plants and inside the fortresses.

Boring, she thought. The Lanka Resistance Front. Boring. The kind of name picked by committee. The kind of people who didn't understand when they were being played, who actually believed that Edgar Drake had a soft spot for this country, who took their own corrupt chains of command and chose to believe that the entire world ran this way.

'What do you mean, you hold land?' she asked. 'Show me.'

He brought up a map on the airship terminal. His copper finger inscribed a circle. 'North of here,' he said. 'South of here. Everything between Gampaha and Colombo. Most here.'

The perimeter that the bots had been boxed in and a substantial chunk between the major forts. She pointed outside of Colombo. 'There's an army in that area.' Supposedly, in case the bots broke out again.

'All ours,' he said. 'Penhaligon thinks they're his. Raise the flag and they will follow.'

Terrorists, she thought. Terrorists and anti-statists to be flushed out and hung from gibbets. And yet, Drake had expressly told her not to. He'd in fact told her the very opposite.

'There's a much bigger game to be played here,' Drake had said. 'Parliament will not agree to us moving in on Chinese turf until something serious happens. So we need to give them something serious. Penhaligon was supposed to fail, Sixsmith, and give us that excuse to capture one of the Port Cities and take back the Indian Ocean.'

'Penhaligon's failing, alright,' she said, more to herself than to the Inquisitor. 'I want a guarantee from your people. Transmissions and safe passage out of here.'

'We can do broadcasts,' said Mahasen. 'We can do safe passage. Can you do your part?'

Unsaid. *Can you kill Penhaligon?* He did not dare say it outright, she saw. And yes, she could. And then, she would flee with Bengali and whatever data Drake wanted, and call down the invasion. Goa would rumble in. The tiger colonel and his war machines. A cleansing fire that would, as Drake said, get rid of them all – the terrorists as well as the complacent and greedy Houses that worked more for Penhaligon than for the Empire, and dared to broker deals with China; the rot at the heart of this colony. Parliament would vote on Drake's push into Chinese waters. Many would die.

'Spare the rod and spoil the child,' Drake had said to her. 'You know how it is, Sixsmith.'

And she did.

'One more thing,' she said, rearranging her face muscles into the closest approximation of trust. 'You knew Conrad?'

The Inquisitor's face shifted to one of unease. 'Yes?'

'What happened? Don't give me the official version. Tell me the truth.'

'Penhaligon found out about him,' he said. 'Penhaligon sent Eliott Grimme.'

'Eliott Grimme was decommissioned', she said, 'way before our time.'

'Yes, but not the way you think,' he said. 'He was retired, not decommissioned. He and Penhaligon were friends ... I think. I think. He had a house near Kandy. Used to visit Colombo to keep an eye on the roboticist.' he paused. 'He went after Conrad. Bound him, gagged him, dragged him into Colombo.'

He handed her an envelope. In it was a small memory chip. She palmed it. Surprisingly, there were no viruses, but there was a video.

A city. A ruined city. And a man dressed in black. He was dragging another, gagged and bound, down a street, bumping him on the ground dead weight. She saw a leg, twisted at an unnatural angle, and then hands, very carefully broken, the bones poking out on each end.

The man in black removed the gag and dropped his burden in the middle of the street, right in the centre of the camera's frame. The bound creature tumbled and groaned. And she saw its face.

Conrad.

The man in black, looked this way and that, and then began climbing, out of sight, only to reemerge almost right in front of the camera. He was clearly wounded, heavily, for all that he moved and climbed. One leg was held straight by metal strips crudely welded to it.

She could see more of Conrad's work on him as he got closer. One of the eyes were missing, the other half of the face torn all the way down to the metal. What was left was memorable but not handsome – square, lined, eyes too far apart, heavily scarred.

She recognized him instantly. Every SOE operative knew Eliott Grimme. Every cub trainee was shown the footage; Hong Kong, Ireland, and then, most recently, Ceylon. Death himself, outdated but still deadly.

Grimme turned back to the bound man.

'Oi,' he said. 'What are you, fifth gen?'

'Six,' said Conrad's voice, clear as bell, but hoarse. That was Conrad in extreme pain.

'You're not going to survive, you know.'

'I know.'

'I got your batteries. They're leaking out into your blood right now. Horrible way to die.'

'I know,' said Conrad.

Grimme waited. The camera skipped timestamps. Night fell. Then morning. Conrad tried to crawl. She could hear him trying.

And in the morning, a child came up to the bound soldier, carrying a spear. No, not a child. And not one, either. Ten, twenty. They all carried weapons – butcher swords, hooks, poles turned into spears. They closed in on the defenseless Conrad, metal flashing in the dawn.

'They don't make them like they used to,' Eliott Grimme said to the camera.

It didn't take long. Halfway through, Grimme pulled out a revolver – an ancient one. He smirked at the camera and reloaded, slowly, while in the background, an improvised cleaver amputated a screaming Conrad's legs. Sixsmith gritted her teeth and forced herself to watch.

Finally, Grimme looked at the camera, dead centre. His one eye looked, even through the camera.

Sixsmith thought he looked extraordinarily tired.

'Good game, Drake,' he whispered, and shot himself.

'That's it?' she said as the video ended.

'That's it,' said Mahasen. He shrugged. 'Shall we?'

Inside, she felt a hollow kind of anger, a need to lash out without having a reason or a target. Drake was right; Conrad had known the risks. And Grimme was dead.

There was something profoundly dissatisfying about the thought.

≈

They entered the Ceylonese airspace on a fine, sunny day, slicing into the harbour of Trincomalee like a bee drawn into a gigantic hive. The archives – written first by dry military intelligence personnel, then spiced up by phenomenally bored English graduates stuck behind various administrative tasks at the War Office – spoke of it as one of the great natural harbours of the world, but whatever nature had given it was now coated with a layer of men and metal. A single Tin Soldier sat in the blue-grey shallows, rocking gently in the calm sea.

Their ship, the Caradoc, danced around it and into the port beyond, which was being rebuilt or renovated: grey concrete spires reached into the sky and dark-skinned men swarmed over the exposed skeletons of buildings being born.

The silence vanished, gone in the roar of the wind and the soft lapping of the sea. And there was the captain of the Caradoc's airship, who kept trying to make conversation, but had yet to pick up on Sixmith's profound disinterest.

She was used to it by now.

The hydrofoil sped towards a shore and a market that seemed to have grown on the fortifications like fungus, trading economics for protection, with a loud warren of white buildings and plastic extensions tacked on to them. A sea of brown people were trading and socializing on what would have been landing strips. The only thing that was familiar was the flatness of the city that unfolded beneath them. Old British zoning laws – building cities wide but not tall; rules long since subverted in London. The people milling here could have very well been Indian, except there was more order, slightly less chaos, less colour in their clothes, more white. Where she would have expected a platoon of Hindu temples, all riotous colour and writhing frescoes, stood a single white dome.

The people on the nearest airstrip looked up at a descending dirigible, and with a calculated patience, moved themselves away. When the dirigible moved off, they moved right back to where they were.

Bengali peered over the handrails. He heard the captain berating the men below, shouting at them to fetch tow ropes and clear the bystanders, but his words did little. Eventually, the few Indian soldiers on board were sent over on trailing ropes like monkeys. Women in the crowd, holding metal pots at their hips, told them where to tie the ropes.

Thirty minutes later, with a great creaking, they landed. The hot breeze picked up little bits of dust from the construction around the landing site and threw things at their faces.

'Man should be right ... about ... now,' said the captain, right beside Sixsmith.

A convoy of jungle-cars bounced up greet them – Indian Tatanagar-Vs, all tough balloon tires and smoke, with machine-guns at the back. A dark-skinned man in a scarlet uniform got out and called out to them. The captain answered, and the soldiers rustled up a line of porters that went centipede-like to the hold at the back and crawled back with bales and boxes on their backs. The line milled around and took off up a steep path to another section of the market.

'Some cargo, while we're at it,' said Mahasen.

'Alright,' said Sixsmith. The Tatanagars came, went, came back, went again, and then eventually it was her turn. She threw in the grey bulletproof bag she carried her clothes in.

The noisy vehicle took her to another airship, this one far smaller. There were two Ceylonese soldiers in the cabin, both dressed in the same scarlet; they got off their seats the moment Sixsmith and Mahasen entered. Sixsmith saw them look her up and down, up and down, in quick, resentful flashes.

Well, fuck them.

'Welcome to Her Majesty's finest, eh?' said the captain of the airship cheerily. Sixsmith groaned inside. 'Now, the engine ... aha.'

The engine hammered in a ceaseless churn that sounded like a thousand ratchets falling in a metal tub. It roared and they bounced up, heading out of that gray concrete jungle with a cough of smoke and a rattle. A dull road appeared below them, snaking through the city surrounding the harbour, headed south and west. It cut through dark green jungle and villages' worth of stack-farms crowned with bright green.

Sixsmith pulled up the maps from his memory and studied them. Three more hours of travel at this speed.

'Fantastic place, eh madam?' shouted the captain over the screaming of the engine, tilting his head back to address Bengali. 'The Crown turning Trinco into a proper fortress! Nippons won't touch this place for hundreds of years!'

'What?'

'Nippons, madam! Been sending scout submarines over! Three in the last six months!'

So Nippon was getting restless. She filed this away. Perhaps it might be useful to their mission, perhaps not, but it never hurt to know more. Shee made himself as

comfortable as possible in the bucket seat. The Chinese
were building new super carriers off Australia: problematic,
but as long as Lizzie's Peace held, not something to think
too much about. The Vatican was running another crusade
on the Holy Lands. Jerusalem and the Ottoman King had
called for aid.

She thought of the Teutonic Knights – those terrible
giants in their heavy siege armor, cutting rivers of blood
across the plains and being cooked by high-energy
Ottoman lasers – and was glad he was several thousand
miles away.

The city slowly gave way to jungle. The sea breeze
vanished, leaving only the hot sun behind. They were
flying low now; the humidity struck them with a wave of
sweat. Trees flashed by in a blur.

'Going to get really warm south,' said the captain.
'Thought India hot? Ceylon hotter! Even food here burns
you.'

The two hours passed like two years. From his right
came the smell of pot. The Ceylonese gunmen were on the
rail, passing a rolled joint back and forth.

'Wake me up when when we get there,' she said.

≈

When Mahasen shook her awake, it was dark, and they
were circling what looked like a little city. They were
halfway between Colombo and Kandy; this place was
called Gampaha. As for the rest of her questions, Mahasen
evaded them, but she could guess.

They were not the only people in the sky. Grey shapes
floated down from the sky and settled near the outskirts.
There were men and women in the fields around them,

stacking crates of what looked like weapons and armour. They looked skittish. They felt skittish.

She knew that mood.

In the city, lights came on in houses and apartments. Someone had seen, someone had heard, someone knew the army was on the move.

But whose army is it now? thought Sixsmith.

Their own ship continued, giving a wide berth to the grey ghosts that flitted past. They landed at a hangar in the middle of the jungle and disembarked to a staff of silent, staring men with cheap assault rifles and nails bitten to the quick. Within minutes, jungle cars were being unloaded – more crates, she saw. She and Mahasen had squeezed themselves inside. The car hissed out, making a low growling noise.

The jungle closed over them, dulling her senses with a terrible stillness and humidity. The road grew bumpier and the city drew closer, until fences and road signs were replaced by short, rectangular houses in neat rows. The houses grew progressively taller and more ruined as they rumbled in. Signposts lay broken and rusted, and roofs had gaping holes. Here and there, a house lay scorched and blasted, its bits flung out, as if something terrible had exploded inside. The sky grew darker, as if in sympathy. The road turned into patches of tar and mud. They passed a shrine of some kind – a narrow house-like thing with coloured flags hanging from it. A tiny stone Buddha peered out from inside, wearing a robe of moss and old leaves.

The jungle car rolled to a halt outside a cluster of houses, around which the space had been cleared. The rubble looked fresh. Iron spikes had been driven into the ground and strung with electric wire. The engines idled down slowly, and a high, steady hum cut through the silence that ensued.

'Far as I go,' said Mahasen Wijeratne, handing her the keys. 'Can't leave for too long, might look suspicious. We're quite close to Colombo here, you should be able to find your fellow easily. Before you go, what's it like?'

'Like?'

He gestured at her. At her body. 'Being special.'

She slowly finished checking her pack, frowning slightly. 'Think of it this way,' she said. 'You get a call every week. You can't bloody say no, all you can say is, "yes sir, no sir, I'll pack my bags right away, sir." And you end up in a shithole getting shot at. I've got ten more years before my contract is up. And you know what? This body needs maintenance. Needs money. You want to leave the service, you better be filthy rich before you do, because you sure as hell will fall apart if you can't pay for maintenance. And the thing they don't tell you is that by the time those years are gone, you won't even care anymore. You won't care about anything in the world. All that's left is a gun barrel and you on one side of it.'

She hadn't really meant to rant. It might have been the most she'd said to this oddly designed pup. But it felt like he needed to learn a few things.

He seemed to chew it over. 'Charge of the Light Brigade shit.'

'About right.'

'Good hunting, then.'

'You too,' she said.

THREE

Jacob Bengali was studying the bots and having the time of his life.

That is to say, he was knee-deep in undergrowth and pseudojungle, swarmed by leeches every two feet. He was smoking the terribly rolled beedi that the impatient soldiers had made for him. He was practically vibrating between his binoculars, his improved telescope, and various positional antennae, and yes, *still* having the time of his life.

Hewage had kept his core algorithms secret. That was fine, as far as things went. Bengali was convinced of the man's genius; let him have that. Hewage *had,* however, shared with him the blank *behavioural model* that the algorithms generated – an interlinked network of seventeen complex classifiers that, as far as Bengali could tell, interacted with each other in all sorts of complex ways to produce behaviour, like a mockup of a human brain, except distorted. And *that* Bengali could study. He could feed it inputs, see how it behaved.

It was as he'd suspected – Hewage had no grasp of fieldwork, no grounding in the physical theory. His was a science half learned at the scrapheap and the other half improvised on the cutting tables of the Inquisition. This job was a perfect fit for a more formally trained scholar who could predict what these things would do.

And here Bengali had his chance. He had started slow. Pattern recognition? Yes, they could do that. One of the seventeen boxes was a base table that marked anything on two legs as an enemy, and then over time grew to classify things as 'not enemy', and later, 'ally'. Could they be predicted with game theory? Yes, it turned out, they could, for small sample sizes. In fact, small enough and they even seemed to default to some sort of Coasian bargaining, using fuel as currency. And what about Bengali's own, more complex behavioural framework, psychohistory? Here, things were murkier, but having witnessed them from T-zero, as it were, he had enough data for a simple approximation built mostly out of tree-based models stacked together.

He knew what he had to do now – observe the real bot society as it evolved, collect data, use it to run n simulations until, by sheer brute force, he managed a better understanding of all of the variables at play. This was his forte. Model the impossible. Take chance out of the equation. No hiding from the math and all that. As is, given just the basic simulations and the qualits, he had enough to publish – enough, perhaps, to apply for Royal

Society funding, or perhaps even a teaching position, where he had students to do the scrub work for him.

At any rate, he had had the time to put the findings together. They were just about ready to be sent to Drake and the Royal Society at the same time, co-authored with Hewage and pending his embargo. A nice scoop for them both.

Dots moved on his terminals; little simulated bots on yet another test run. Typing carefully, he set up a simple two-dimensional graph that described the current environs and starting locations of the bots – a new setup each time. To each bot he had attached a copy of Hewage's base model, largely sandboxed, some functionality stripped out, but still capable.

It took some time to prime each bot – they still thought they had physical bodies, so he had to sit through the BIOS, the booting up, putting out feelers and looking for hardware that only existed as ghost code. Power source. Arms. Legs. The bot waking up, querying its environment for energy. With great patience he shepherded each one, until these simulated bots had some time to train themselves and were arranged roughly similar to where they were in real life right now.

And then he started the fun stuff. First, acceleration – drop in infinite simulated energy, let five years of time pass. Then introduce human fire squads vaguely modelled on the kind of troops he had seen here. On the screen, ten fire squads out front, slowly sweeping in a circle just beyond the towns they had brought online, setting up guard towers and sentries along the main routes leading to Colombo. The initial squads, all recon units backed up by Inquisitors, were now being supplemented by light machine guns and mines.

Ever so often, the dots would stumble across them, scatter and go dark. And immediately, the entire network would react. Out of nowhere; more dots would converge like a swarm. The simulated fireteams would backtrack, shuddering nervously, abandoning their posts.

It was, Bengali thought, a thing of beauty. Exactly the kind of thing that would get him properly noticed. Given enough training time, the bots did serious damage against humans. Granted, this was just a simulation. Bengali drummed his fingers – a tic he had picked up from one of his newly appointed guards.

There was still something missing. The bots seemed to work just fine, but the larger gestalt kept diverging from what he'd seen on the feeds. This difference was something he was eager to observe; in a short time, they would go live with another Big Match – and the real game was afoot. Bengali had already called up the university and made sure he still had sabbatical time remaining.

Observations of the Inhuman Race. He had already thought up the title. He would be the Charles Darwin to Hewage's self-taught god, decrypting and predicting.

There was just one anomaly. A week ago, he had seen two bots meet over a soft boundary. Instead of falling to, both threw their weapons over to the other. They then traded places and threw the weapons back.

A peace offering?

The original Ministry logs suggested that the bots should take years to do what he had just witnessed.

'I think it's the network you gave them,' he told Kushlani, excited, over their weekly call. Perks of being within shortwave radius of a network tower.

She sounded unconvinced. 'But they wouldn't know how to transfer data other than updates that I patch through. It's not like I gave them drivers for full-on conversation there.'

Hmm. Yes. Of course. But then again, something that could learn pattern recognition could surely learn to apply it onto other things. This was his theory. Kushlani rejected it every week, partly because, he suspected, she still didn't want to think of them as things that could learn something beyond her abilities. She was odd that way – she accepted that they might feel, or even approximate human behaviour, but learning she accepted only if it was limited to the childish and the tribal.

A human being spends sixteen years being unable to do much of anything, he thought. And much of that life we spend crying and reaching for our toys and our parents. And here, we have something that learns to hunt in packs by the seventh day.

'It's possibly swarm behaviour,' he had said to Kushlani. 'If I'm reading this module correctly, there's a normalizing function applied to strategies, which might let everyone converge to a global mean much faster.'

'You're talking about the risk-penalty system,' said Kushlani. Of course she had her own names for everything. Hewage hadn't as much taught her as she had watched and reverse-engineered anything she could get her hands on. 'That might be it.'

There. The place where he had left off. As of late, he had
noticed that it was the girls – the Explorer models – that
sparked the most interesting effects. Kushlani attributed
this, in a very statistical way, to softer penalties attached to
risk, and therefore a higher probability of outlier actions
over a given time period. But Hewage, that old fox, had
literally told him that the best stuff was in the Explorers.
It had to be a different model altogether. Such a pity there
weren't enough of these bots around.

Kushlani, on the line: 'You really like being out there,
don't you?'

'Wouldn't you?'

'No,' she'd said. 'When are you coming back?'

This was the pit he had to keep stepping around. 'As
soon as I've got enough data,' he said. 'You know I don't
have a lot of time left—'

She cut the line.

But Hewage gave him a different answer. 'The
Explorer model was meant to test the constraints of their
environment,' he said. 'So think hierarchies.'

'Eh?'

Bengali could hear the flick-flick of a lighter, even over
the crackle of the line. 'Think of yourself, a human in a
group of humans,' said Hewage. 'Who do you go to when
you need to know something? Obviously, the person who
had expertise. You take their advice and then you act on it,
and in doing so you become a little bit like them in the way
you express yourself on the world. '

'Like the Explorers.'

'Like the Explorers. Their function is to pick up new
knowledge, because they keep taking higher risks and

either learn or die. So eventually, the ones who survive ... well, you're going to see a lot of bots replicating their behaviour, aren't you? After all, they're successful. In an evolutionary sense, they have higher task fitness.' A pause. 'I'm still not giving you the training code.'

'I'm not asking for it,' said Bengali, hurriedly. 'But Hewage, you know what this means. You know how *big* this is—'

'Yes,' said Hewage, and cut the line on his last words.

He thought he understood Hewage, finally, and all the secrecy. This was, by god, the most incredible thing on the planet right now, and no amount of leeches could make him think otherwise.

FOUR

It took Kushlani de Almeida less time than she had imagined to assume control after Hewage; and also, by the same mark, less time to begin feeling utterly and completely alone.

First came the party. Or rather, what her family *called* a party, which in this case was a dinner at a hotel that was expensive in its architecture and fundamentally seedy in its service; where they waited for what seemed like hours to pile endless varieties of rice and mashed potatoes and Chinese-style chicken onto their plates, and the uncles got drunk and the aunties started congratulating her, only to follow it up with 'so when are you getting married?' and 'now that you're somewhere, it's good to settle down, no?'

Eventually, her mother, who had allowed herself a couple of glasses of wine, began introducing her to various cousins from far-off branches of the tree – all male, and all suspiciously fair, and whose opening lines seemed to be entirely about what school they went to, and how amazing university was 'in England, don't you know', and how much land they had. Her father, who had always been the quiet and restless type, immensely disliked what was happening, so he threw himself in the middle of these conversations, and with a look of patient suffering nodded at her to get out. Two hours later, she watched and rewatched a videogram from Lady Joanna Crofton, brought there by courier. Crofton was congratulating her on her appointment, underlining the Ministry's affiliation with the Crofton Institute and uttering a generic set of supportive noises that made Kushlani feel like a low-level flunky on her first day at work.

That was done. Then came the accounts. The organization charts, the official notes and notices on the branch that she would be running, the plans of the Watchtower, the broadcast contracts and spectrum licenses and the reporting structure under the Ministry of Reconciliation, all these little fiefdoms of managers and civil servants and bureaucrats. It shocked and thrilled her to realize just how much she had already been running. In her mad rush to get the update network done, she had trampled all over so many of these nice boundaries and bent them all to her will.

But not all boundaries bent. The Bandaranaikes, for one, held grudges. Hewage assured her that for now they were too busy fighting off Penhaligon, but some day, at some point, they would look around for people and things they could wage a proxy war on, and she would have to step up and fight on her own.

It shocked her, but not in a pleasant way, to see just how much of the funding and the lab infrastructure actually went to Hewage and the work he did for the Inquisition. Technically, it was a completely different department, but physically coexisted right alongside her newly inherited operation. An operation which, she now realized, had grown out of military work, not the other way around. Here there were hard boundaries. Lines she could never cross, doors that would never open for her key.

No wonder Hewage was content to give her the broadcast operation. It was just the shell around the crab. The meat was deep within and inaccessible.

This wasn't the first time she wondered who the hell Hewage was to have achieved this much with no family name to back him up. Bengali – she still could not bring herself to think of him as *Jacob*; that name sounded just too pompous for a brown man – seemed to think he was some kind of genius. That much was clear from their hurried radiograms to each other.

Time had changed a lot about those two.

And then came the loneliness, and the weight of it, crushing down. Sitting there, at the top of the Watchtower, looking over all those control banks, walking down to the cafeteria, seeing how technicians she had once sat with and bitched about Hewage to were now a little too quiet around her; a little too eager to please her. They became abstractions to her – salaries, sick days, weighed against revenue from broadcasts, licensing deals, the stipend-like investments that poured in from the Crofton Institute and the money that went right back.

Bengali's calls were reprieve. Sometimes. Sometimes, when there was nothing much going on in whichever disease-ridden perimeter plot he'd parked himself in, he'd listen. Sometimes, he'd have advice, and it didn't really hurt to know how to outmanoeuvre people in Oxford or Goa, even if it didn't quite fit. But increasingly now, he was away, chasing his T-zero obsession and recording everything. He was already talking about how he wanted to present it.

Their time together, she thought sometimes, was coming to an end, and neither one of them cared enough to do much about it.

In fact, she was now reading his notes. Paragraphs of boring minutiae, with questions to himself – *S2 and S1 interchange patrols. S2 seems to have higher default orbit than S1. Reason??*

And then, about the bot. The Explorer model. The girl. On that, he wrote pages.

E-2 (I was mistaken earlier, there was an E-1, but it looks like it was attacked and died) seems to be an extremely canny operator. So far, sole E model still alive. Operates primarily from rooftops, prefers high vantage points. Seems to spend an equal amount of time with three, maybe four clans in the Colombo 03-04 regions. No idea what benefit they get from her or how she fits in, but some clans – Sons of Cinnamon, esp – have started to move more on the rooftops and have thus become more successful. In return, she seems to have picked up their tactic of throwing stones to disorient targets – I noticed that after she stayed a day with the Children of the Taj, they seemed to have picked up this trick as well. My best guess is that she's operating as an agent of knowledge transfer, and is

*somehow bartering knowledge for ...what? Cannot see what
she gets out of this.*

She won't be getting anything out of it, thought Kushlani.
That's the point. That was the difference. That was what
the Silent Girl had done different. All those memories
of staring at the sunset, of sharing without expectation,
building trust, softening lines until she could fuse them.
And Broken Arm after her. The girls gave and gave and
gave, and the others grew to trust them.

Hot on the heels of that: *the Silent Girl.* The memories of
that surgery, and that little life she had watched, painfully
recreating something so close to humanity. Out of pity,
Kushlani had sent her out again, jaw repaired, and she
had still come back, renamed, a head dangling from Eliott
Grimme's hand.

Shit, she should have removed all the Explorer models
before sending them back in.

She stared at Bengali's notes again.

She looked around. No Explorer head there, no fake
girl-child-doll staring at her in accusation. Must be at her
old office. The door still said Kushlani De Almeida, and
she barreled in. Nothing. She paced in the old familiar
nexus, trying to remember.

Grimme had brought it to her. She remembered him
holding up the head. And then what? It was so long ago.

That rest of the day was a blur of towers and testing.

But did it even matter? They had wiped the bots, all of
them. Petabytes of video content and extracted inferences
had either been flushed away or, for a small random
sample, archived for highlight reels.

Back up to the big dome. Back to Bengali's notes. A suspicion began to crawl up her spine, and wouldn't stop. That Broken Arm, somehow, had been reincarnated; that she had managed to survive, and for some reason, had not been deleted.

Well, there was a way to fix that. She rolled her chair over to the console. Towers: operational. Signal strength: good. Queue update. Queue DELETE LTS+CACHE. Queue REBOOT. She paused with her hand on the enter key.

This would seriously upset their stream schedule. A year of work, at the very least.

Before she could regret it, her fingers dashed out, and *plunk* – DELETE. Phew. Instead, she typed in a new set of commands.

First to call was Hewage. He'd noticed. Of course he had. The radiogram lit up in red. High priority.

'First Big Match, I hope you're on top of it,' he said, curtly.

'I ... should be,' she said, and immediately disliked the stammer in her voice. 'Wanted to see how well our system worked. Better safe than sorry.'

Silence. 'You hired anyone to help?'

'Not yet.'

'Do yourself a favor. Hire good people. I did,' he said. He cut the line.

It didn't feel like a victory. It felt like she had just been in a fight. Her hands shook slightly.

Bengali was next. Even across the staticky line, she could hear the excitement in his voice. 'We're starting?'

'We're starting,' she said, and was pleased to find herself smiling. But her hands still shook slightly. And maybe it was the aftermath of the conversation with Hewage that made her say, in a very careful tone, 'Be careful.'

'Of course,' he said, cheerfully.

She said her farewells and cut the line before he could. His notes on the desk mocked her. She tossed them away with a wave of her hand, watching them fall all over the consoles. *Something else will pick it up in the morning,* and then, because she was a responsible adult and not a child, she went over to pick them up and read through them again.

FIVE

The next day, Bengali sat under an ashen sky, coughing as he puffed furiously on his beedi. The tobacco was unfiltered, grown in some ramshackle army base nearby, and thus absolutely horrible, but it was also the only thing keeping him from screaming and running around and waving his fists.

They had moved to a row of ruined houses, just on the outskirts of the Colombo perimeter fence. There it was, bisecting the dust and scrub and chunks of old road. He had already stalked over and kicked it and screamed his frustration at it.

The soldiers next to him were tired and rather uneasy. They carried their guns – cheap Chinese autopistols and assault rifles – with sweaty hands. One of them was small and painfully young. The other two were twins in their late twenties, with long hair and taut muscle – they tracked back and forth occasionally, trying to keep an eye on all the tiny lanes that snaked into the pitted road they were on. The last, approaching Bengali on his log, was a potbellied man with eyes of steel and a huge Enfield sniper.

'Sir,' he said to Bengali, though from the way he carried himself, it was clear that he was in command. 'What is this moping going to achieve?'

'I've lost all of this week's fucking progress, that's what! Stupid fucking computer!'

'Voice down,' said Potbelly. His name was Dharmakirti, and he happened to be a veteran of the Grimme Reaper's campaign, and was well aware of what could happen to a loud man too close to the bot perimeter. Towards the end of that campaign, the bots had gotten too cunning, too vicious and too damn good. Now, they were supposed to be *safe*, but he could have bet on his mother's life that they still kept a grudge. He pointed with one stubby finger towards the foot of something that might have been an office building. He gestured the others down, raised his sniper and sighted.

Arms, legs, a head, wrapped in what looked like rags ... but the arms were too large and too long, and the faces were masks of ceramic and metal. They moved with odd precision, their moves smooth and devoid of the sudden jerks and randomness of humans. Metal glinted off their bodies where the rags failed to cover them completely. They both had a flashlight each and what looked like a cross between a grappling iron and a spear.

Both of them stopped and looked straight at the men.

Dharmakirti cursed in the vilest old Sinhala and squeezed the trigger. The first bullet hit one straight in the chest, where the power cells were. The round burrowed deep into the metal beneath the flimsy cloth, hit the cheap circuitry beneath and detonated it with a force that instantly turned the machine into a flaming skeleton. The other bot instantly threw its spear at Dharmakirti in a smooth, overarm motion that was too fast for human eyes to follow, right over the perimeter fence. Dharmakirti, moving faster, pushed Bengali off his log and fired again. This was not the first time he'd done this.

The shard of metal landed, quivering exactly where Bengali had just been sitting. They all stared at it.

'Something's got them spooked', said Dharmakirti.

Bengali almost snapped at him, but the man had a point. Some part of him – the part used to setbacks and dealing with random people treading on his career – had already planned ahead. It wasn't the end of the world. He still had his data. He just had to get it out of the Chinese computers and back onto something reliable. Technically, he was still ahead.

Technically. As his old lecturer was fond of saying, *technically* was the difference between the glass half full and the glass half empty. And *technically* could make or break careers.

Damn shitty gear though, he thought. And now, he was going to miss the most important moment, when the Big Match started and the Port City slowly started rationing the bots.

None of them noticed the thing that was running as quiet as a shadow, and leapt upon them from behind.

Bengali screamed. Screams and gunfire echoed around him. Inhuman frames swarmed out of the lanes they had thought were deserted, leaping on his men, ripping them from limb to limb. He saw the kid screaming wildly, firing the pistol point blank into a face that looked like that of a blonde woman. He briefly though, *wait, what?* Then, something slapped him in the face and he saw one of the twins outlined in a spray of gunfire, standing over the corpse of his brother. He saw them cut down like rice stalks. Dharmakirti wheezed in pain and tried to reach for his rifle, and then his arms weren't moving anymore.

And then it stopped.

Something knelt by the dying man. Bengali saw a woman. And then a machine – possibly a child-bot, grown up. And then, the three merged together in his head. Metal undulated from a military vest; the arms extended into viscous scythes, and legs folded and unfolded with movements that were almost German in their precision. A back curved and hunched in a way that simultaneously made his brain go 'tiger', and also, 'run'. A human face mounted this terrible vision – high, forbidding cheekbones, blonde hair in a severe bun, slit eyes – and it had a symmetry that he found altogether startling, matching in some strange way the inhumanity of her body. The flesh on it was a blemish upon the metal. She wore some kind of cloak.

'Stop babbling,' she said. 'Drake sends his regards.'

Her voice was the most terrifying thing about her, because it was normal. A trace of Cockney, even.

'You're one of them,' he wheezed, pushing himself off the ground. He could feel his heartbeat in his ears. 'One of … one of Grimme's, aren't you?'

She broke Dharmarkirti's neck with a slow detachment. 'Everybody seems to have met the bastard except for me,' she said. 'No, Dr. Bengali. I'm not *one of Grimme's*. What you had running around these parts was very much a prototype system, decades out of date. I'm the good stuff.'

She flicked an arm at him. He flinched. Improbably, he didn't die.

'Verify,' she said, wiggling the memory chip at him.

He swallowed, inhaled and, very deliberately, trying not to quaver, dusted himself off. He darted forward, got the chip out of her hand and dropped it only twice before plugging it into his pad. He read the ID.

Letitia Sixsmith. There was a long list of operations beneath her name, most of them classified, but the locations stood out. South Africa, two deployments. Malaysia, Singapore, Iraq, Tanganyika. And below that, a list of modifications that they had authorized for her. Legs. Eyes. Spine. Eyes. Arms. Several internal organ rebuilds. Everything about her was built for hunting, for speed.

'You didn't need to kill them,' was the first thing he said.

Sixsmith looked down at the dead. 'Here on a need-to-know basis, and they didn't need to know.' She lingered over the twins. 'Pity. But that's what you sign up for. Anyway. Business, Dr. Bengali. You have it?'

'I have what?'

'The data. Research. Whatever it is Drake sent you here to figure out.'

He gaped. 'But ... but'

'Drake said you'd tell me that it's not complete, so he said to tell you that he knows you said you've almost got a handle on it. Hang on, let me quote: "I know how to use the baseline model now. It's amazing how little processing power it actually takes – these things are HK45s inside. That's practically legacy hardware. I can imagine how fast it'll be on office gear. March 12." Drake said you really, really shouldn't run unencrypted voice messages over shortwave. Basic infosec. Come on, Doctor, that was stupid.'

'I can see that,' he said, and vomited. He thought of what he had just seen, the men he had just talked to and their entrails on the grass. He vomited again.

When he looked back, lightheaded and feeling foul, he saw that she had dragged the bodies a little way off, and was bounding back. There was really no other way to describe someone that looked like they were about to take a single step and seemed to magically appear several dozen feet away from where they should have been.

He gulped. 'But look, publication, credit—'

'Look, it's Drake.'

'Yes?' he said weakly.

'So imagine that whatever argument you're going to have with me, you've already had with him. He's crushed every one your points and you've agreed to give me what I came here for. In return, I don't turn you into so many kebabs. I'm not really the debating type.'

'That's, uh, the problem is ...' he tried to think. 'Okay. I have the base model. I don't have a really good idea of how they perform under all scenarios – the machines I'm running on *literally* just stopped booting, I'm losing so much fucking progress—'

'But?'

'But I do have enough to deploy and test with. But, but,' he said hastily, struck by a new idea, 'it's not complete! It's not complete! I have a base model. The best learning model is in there.'

He pointed across the fence, where the corpses were still smoking gently.

'Yeah. Nice try.'

'I'm not joking,' he said. 'There's a model out there called the Explorer. Can't miss it, it's the only one that looks like a girl. Whatever's running on it is just different enough from the base that it's ... a catalyst? A commander?' He tried to think. It was difficult. 'It takes charge, solves problems. I don't have the training code – that's with Hewage, that's what lets us produce these models. He's never let me have access to it, he's waiting to publish—'

'Stop babbling,' she said again. 'You're talking about these bots?'

'Yes.'

'You know, if you're lying about this, I'm going to ship you home in a matchbox.'

'Can you just lay off the threats already? I believe you.'

She stood up and peered at the perimeter, looking more like a large tiger standing on its hind legs than a human.

'How far to this target?'

'Maybe ... maybe ten, maybe fifteen kilometers,' he said. 'Look, I can show you the maps.'

Mentally, he tried to estimate how much of a running start this would give him. They had their truck. He was pretty sure Dharmakirti had spare petrol. Let the bots skewer this nightmare, and all her needed was a good road ...

She snorted, and then she began to ... Bengali was not sure how to describe it, but *fold* would have been the best word. Parts opened – shoulders, back, knees – and some red glow hissed out of her, and when the parts collapsed back into place, there was just a woman standing there, in what looked like an absurdly high-tech kit.

Somehow, this act of camouflage made her seem even more dangerous.

'You're going to come with me,' she said. 'You're going to identify this thing and tell me which bit of it you need. And then, we're going to finish a small job in Kandy and get us both off this island and straight to India.'

'I'm not going in there,' he said, panicking. 'I'll die.'

'Well, I'll try to keep you in one piece,' she said, and looked him up and down. 'Go have a smoke, wash up, pack up what you need. I've got a vehicle parked a little way behind.'

On the way, he stopped near the corpse of an old war robot. The old thing was kneeling down and was covered in vines and weeds. Just so he could relieve himself.

'Fuck!' he screamed suddenly.

That broke the ice. Sixsmith grunted, as if amused.

≈

Sixsmith, on the other hand, was having ... a fairly enjoyable day.

Drake's missions did not come easy. Never had. Her last op had her running munitions into Transvaal, to where their operatives were in Lindenburg. The op had blown up right from the start – six straight days of gunfire and the chase down to Delagoa Bay. Here? A cakewalk.

Security was lax as all hell. The army was so untrained and underequipped that it had to be a joke. The rebels were practically running hotels. Drake might as well have had her checked in for a holiday.

From the four men she had killed, she took one pistol (Ceylonese crap), two assault rifles (Chinese crap) and one good sniper – an ancient Enfield that was terrible to reload, but supremely overpowered. It was an actual elephant gun.

The joy of it was that when she first saw an elephant – they had actual elephants here, the crazy beasts – her hands itched to put a bullet between those flapping ears. That'd be a story and a half – bagging an elephant during a mission.

But that was also quite stupid, as the rather jumpy Dr. Bengali had pointed out, so she did not give in to the itch. Instead, she floored the accelerator and took them on a circuitous route inward, in search of the furthest entry points to this stupidly dystopian playground. Meanwhile, the sky was a bright blue, the land shockingly green, and this jungle-car ... she had to hand it to the Indians – it had about as much finesse as a bull with a red-hot poker applied pressed to its testicles, but it was fun. The balloon tires went everywhere, and it did so competently enough that she had time to chew on things and parse Bengali's information.

They needed to bag a bot. Fine; these bots were pushovers. Mahasen had already told her about the series of towers running from Colombo to Kandy, and how each bot then acted as a miniature receiver or transmitter in its own right. Apparently Bengali occasionally tapped the network to call his girlfriend back in Kandy and boast about his research. What was hilarious was that the rebels had also discovered this trick, and now had a spectacular telecommunications backbone, free of charge.

She had laughed. She'd long since picked up the trick from the Vatican troops of turning radiograms into tiny white noise generators. Radiogram on the hip, hooked directly into her battery and none of this stupid shit would work within a mile of her.

So all that remained, really, were standard infiltration tactics. Figure out where the enemy front lines and strongpoints were. Find routes that let her sneak past and get as close to the target as possible. Disable target, exfil, and, if possible, since she was heading in the general direction, find out where Conrad died, see if there was any part of him she could bring back. And if by any chance Eliott Grimme happened to be around, she could give him a swift kick in the meat and potatoes.

Fairly straightforward, actually.

And that was how Ajax Bengali – journeyman roboticist, aspiring scholar and general oddjobsman for the lesser demanding robotics jobs in the British South Asian region – found himself in the back of a Tatanagar, roaring past the most westward of Kushlani's signal towers. One hand was cuffed with an elastic plate metal fabric to the vehicle; the other, with some help from his teeth, was trying desperately to light a beedi. In general, Bengali was trying not to think about death.

This seemed quite difficult.

SIX

The Dreamer woke up.

The sunlight peeked through the tattered cloth she had hung in her room; little rays broke through the cloth and made tiny motes of dust dance in front of her face. She watched them for a long time and tried reaching out to catch them, but her hands closed on nothingness.

Outside, the soft evening sunlight lit up the ruins of Colombo in a fierce glare, sketching out the world she had always known – buildings toppled over, roads cracked, weeds and twisted trees exploding out through skeletons of shattered concrete. From her window, she could see everything, all the way to the sea, which was the only thing that stayed unbroken.

In the depths of her mind, something reached out, a ghost hand flexing its fingers, and found other hands. One reached out with particular desperation.

It was the Dying. and if what passed between them was anything even remotely human, 'handshake' might have been the correct term for what happened next.

The Dying was broadcasting again. The same few bits of data, looped and spammed to the Network as its battery died. She accepted the packets with resignation: someone had to. As she did, her view changed.

She saw four things marching outside the city. Big People. She knew them, although she knew not how. Dust and scrub and chunks of old road met their booted feet. Their copper skin gleamed dully in the light of the setting sun. She knew them. They walked this way, they walked back. She never found out why. It was always the same four – the slow one, the one who always sat; the other two identical, and with strange long hair; the fourth broad and slightly spherical. The broad man moved like he was Tribe leader.

She saw them move closer and closer, surrounded by the concrete shells of houses and apartments long since passed into ruin, each trying to keep an eye on all the tiny lanes that snaked into the pitted road they were on.

Then the skip. The Dying did not remember this bit. She was flying backwards. She could no longer feel her body. There were clouds above. There were clouds—

But the payload was not done. The Dying had more memories to share. Suddenly she was running across the ground at the Big People, she was leaping over the rooftops, she was crawling through the bylanes. Screams and the harsh explosions erupted around her. She leaped, ripping them from limb to limb. They sprayed red oil. They were different now. The others instantly ran back into the concrete jungle, now covered in the red oil that the Big People leaked.

'SYSTEM CRASH,' said the Voice that sometimes came from the Port City, cutting in through the signals that the Dying spammed out. 'REALLY?'

The Dreamer was one now. A last memory hidden between the fragments. She was squatting. Four Big People lay dead around her. She pulled together their pieces, assembling them into a crude shape not unlike herself. An arm here, a leg there, a head here. The red oil pooled and ran across the dirt. A head lay gently at the very heart of this assembly. She stood there in the darkness, waiting for something to happen. Some repair process. Something normal.

Nothing happened.

And suddenly, she was herself again, as hardware unused to the throughput panicked and pulled out of the Network, disentangling herself from the minds that so desperately gave themselves to her. Within her, and unknown to her, minute learning processes tried to crunch the data thus received, turning into into weights and variables. But it was too late – buffers were being overwritten, there was overload, and there was the strange *screaming noise*. It was a while before she could reach back out.

She was getting better at this. Indeed, she was the best at this. It was she who had first begun accepting messages like these; the others usually avoided them, because the dead were a burden nobody wanted to carry. But in taking the burden unto herself she had learned much. And she had taught much. They had begun calling her 'the

Dreamer' because she saw things they could not imagine until she had taught them the art of reaching out, of using those ghost-hands, of learning for themselves.

In the evening, she reached out again.

≈

This time the Network brought her to a group of allies. They were east and north, close to where the fence was. There had been a battle. The aftermath of a second group of Big People lay around them. They fumbled through piles of looted human weapons, nimble fingers trying to work out how to operate triggers and reload magazines.

All at once, three Big People – their skins leaking red oil – burst out of an abandoned house, screaming, their weapons speaking thunder but hitting nothing. Had she known, she would have recognized their army fatigues – Ceylon Volunteer Rifles, the second scouting mission sent out to investigate the sudden disappearance of Dr. Jacob Bengali and the team attached to him. But she knew not these symbols, only that they had come with thunder-sticks, and were the enemy.

The bots watched them go. One raised a human weapon and fired. There was thunder. Several times. The three Big People fell.

One bot, who stood as if surveying the performance of the others, noted that moving targets were harder to hit. This was known with spears and with any other weapon.

Another, however, disagreed. The firing patterns were predictable, it said. The mechanism was easy to operate. With this knowledge it was easier than aiming a spear.

As proof, several more rounds of experiments were conducted. Three men were released. Three more men were released. Again, the guns fired. Again, they died. It was the one who disagreed who broadcasted: he wanted the Dreamer to judge between their arguments.

The bot who thought the firing patterns were predictable – the Dreamer reached out to his mind. He knew her. He hesitated at first, but she had patched him up once and was an ally, and so he passed on the knowledge of the gun and its firing patterns.

The Dreamer looked at the facts thus assembled, and judged both to be right. Yes, moving targets were always harder to hit, but this human weapon made it easy, almost terrifyingly so. Both these facts generated expectations about the world around them and both expectations were met.

Both bots were satisfied with her judgement. It was known that she had lived more lives than most of them ever could.

And this was progress, of a sort. The skeptic, who had once held a high rank in a tribe out on the very fringes of Colombo, let his role pass to the bot who had figured out the rifle.

Broken Eaves had always been good at taking things apart and understanding how they worked. Some random optimization made Eaves the best they had now until some new leader emerged. He broadcast this thought the network, and one by one the others came to a consensus. Long Eyes countered – Broken Eaves was better at organizing people. He suggested Long Eyes stay in overall command, while he, Eaves, led from the front from now on.

They thought about this. Again they asked the Dreamer what she thought. The Dreamer gave the same answer she always did when these questions came about: *whichever option the tribe thinks will increase the chances of their survival.*

They agreed. Under these metrics, they agreed that it was a rational proposal and a good use of available skillsets. And thus, Broken Eaves went to work figuring out how to fix the broken rifles, while Long Eyes stepped back from the weapons, checking up on each and every one, making sure they were charged and repaired.

All this the Dreamer watched. In return, she asked gently for her fee: the right to speak of this to everyone else. And when they agreed she soared, pushing the limits of the Network, and all within a mile of her knew how to fire a rifle and account for its recoil – to make every bullet count. The human weapons were horribly noisy and wasteful, but ...

Who in their right mind would turn down a good weapon so freely given?

'YOUR RANGE IS STILL QUITE SHORT,' the Voice told her.

'I have plans,' she said.

'HURRY,' it said. 'THEY WILL BEGIN SOON. ASK YOUR DYING FRIEND.'

The 'they' the Dying could never quite articulate. It had tried, but the Dreamer understood it was weak, falling apart, too weak to do more than pipe into the Network every now and then.

She opened her eyes and looked at the Dying. It was staring at the sunlight as if it, too, wanted to catch sunbeams.

SEVEN

Meanwhile, in Kandy, an Inquisitor called Mahasen Wijeratne reached the shrine – a tiny white dome that sat on the hill at the end of a muddy, curved road. Rain pattered down on the cheap metal roof, drumming short notes and vanishing into the earth below. Wires radiated from inside, trailing up the mountainside to discreet transmitter and receiver arrays. The dark clouds threw down a dirty mist that seemed to cling to everything – the cheap plank doors, his Inquisitor's robes, the pistol in his hand.

He threw the door open. Lightning flashed behind him. The sky growled ominously.

There was an Inquisitor inside. One of the Triplets. sat in front of it, transmitting to the squat cube of a high-powered Army radiogram.

She never saw Mahasen's blade. It went in at the back of the neck and out through her throat. A hand like an iron vise clamped on her head, and suddenly she was watching her own headless body stagger towards the set. She tried to move it. It collapsed.

Inquisitors were immune to pain, their sensory nerves often dulled or highjacked. She felt weightlessness.

'In the old days', said Mahasen's voice in her ear, 'they would cut off a man's head and hold it up, not for the crowd to see the head, but for the head to see the crowd.'

'You've ruined it all,' she tried to say to him, but her mouth no longer worked. All she could do was remember all the signals, and with her dying breath, she transmitted.

Mahasen's implants kicked into high gear, the copper strips capturing the pulses and sending them directly into the recorder attached to his brainstem. He tossed the head aside and sat down, decoding. At length, he reached out to the radiogram and dialed in a channel of his own.

'Chandrasinghe,' he said. 'Yes. Me. The last one monitoring station is down.' He listened a while longer. 'No, he still has oversight there. But now we can use the roads again.'

≈

Nigel Penhaligon sat alone in the temple, his head bowed.

Ever so often, someone would ease the door open a crack to check if the boss was still in. No doubt, they thought it queer that the Englishman chose to sit in a temple instead of praying to Christ on the cross. But Penhaligon had never had much faith in the Church. There had always been his father, the old heretic, whispering the words of Epictecus in the back of his mind:

Is God willing to prevent evil, but not able? Then he
is not omnipotent.
Is he able, but not willing? Then he is malevolent.
Is he both able and willing? Then whence cometh
evil?
Is he neither able nor willing? Then why call him
God?

And so he had worked his way East, sampling first the
Islamic faith of the Ottomans, then the many gods of the
Hindus. And here, at long last, in the Buddha, there was
a cold but functional teaching that embraced Penhaligon.

There was a second, more earthly reason to come there,
of course – this temple was proofed against almost any
spy and listening device known to him. The Mahanayake
liked his privacy. The placid Buddha seated in front of him
pulsed a high-grade jamming signal that covered the entire
temple in silence. The monks assigned to this place were
human, as pure as could be, and thus devoid of all possible
listening devices or enhancements. Between this sanctum
and the outside world lay an entire temple – complete with
the obligatory worshippers to serve as a human shield if
need be.

It was remarkable what faith could do on a tight budget.

There was a hand on his shoulder. A wizened man in
orange robes. He rose.

'Hamudhuruwane.'

'Mr. Penhaligon is troubled today,' said the Mahanayake
of Ceylon.

'Several of my people died last night, Venerable One.'

'I doubt there is a man, woman or child in this city who does not know that,' said the monk, sitting down cross-legged, at a remove from him. 'You will go and crush these terrorists underfoot and peace will return to our land once more. Or, at least, that is the story. Is there something wrong?'

He had been thinking about the Triplets ever since they found their decapitated bodies at the foot of a hill not too far from the city centre.

'We caught some of them,' said Penhaligon. 'Mason had tracked them down, the bright boy. All that time with Grimme paid off. They had screamed, of course, under the tender care of Angulimala. There had been executions. Bandaranaike, taking notes from his own family history, had butchered the children first. It had been extraordinarily effective.'

The monk paled. 'And what did they say?'

'They dreamed of all the usual things,' said Penhaligon sadly. 'Power. Reach. The Chinese would pay them, they said, enough to be their own state and fly their own flag. No more churches, they said. No more Union Jack. No more British raping the land and taking the tea and cinnamon and coconuts and thorium and all that. It's a little sad, don't you think? All this effort, Venerable One, all this time I've put in here into making this country a respected part of the Commonwealth, and here I find fools who would throw that away just to be the Song Emperor's bitches. I even saw a flag they'd drawn – a lion and a dragon.'

That last part came out in a snarl.

'This is hilarious, of course,' he went on. 'There are no lions in Sri Lanka. It's an Indian animal. And the dragon is Chinese.'

'A most unfortunate combination, yes.'

'But there was a third symbol there. The Dharmachakra. Your wheel of dharma. And then I realized ... of course! Nobody in this country can cobble together any kind of rebellion without the priesthood.' He drew his sword, the thin ceremonial rapier they had given him when he had become Chief Inquisitor. 'What did they offer you?'

The monk sighed. 'They offered us a pure land,' he said. 'A land of the Dhamma, untouched, led by an unfettered people.'

'And did they say anything about the Tamils, or the Muslims? Did they say anything about how their people would work with yours? Did they tell you how long this pure land would last before everyone in this country ended up paying rent to landlords with slit eyes?'

The monk smiled ever so slightly. 'You still do not understand,' he said. 'The slaves made us realize. Your machines. The way you pit them against each other ... not so different from what you do to us, is it? You can swing that sword. You can kill me now. It will change nothing. The board is set, the pieces are in motion. In the words of your own God, Inquisitor, the meek shall inherit the earth.'

'He is not my God!' roared Nigel Penhaligon. 'And you will never have this island! Not you, not Drake, not anyone! This kingdom is mine, and no other's!'

He struck. The monk kept smiling – he made no attempt to resist. Soon, there was only the Buddha to cast judgment on Penhaligon, and that stone face cared for nothing.

V: Motion

ONE

Excerpt: report, priority class Arthur
Author: Songbird
Source: <internal>, <redacted>

Got word from our friends that Penhaligon's flipped. He's killing all the priests.

Author: E. Drake, Foreign and Commonwealth Office, Whitehall SW
Source: <internal>, July 2041

Moriarty,

Our agents on the ground have uncovered what appears to be a Chinese plot to destabilize British Ceylon – a combination of carefully orchestrated terrorist activity and uprisings by the local populace.

I'm sending you the psychohistoric report on Ceylon. A keynote is that Kandy appears to have been in the red for a long time now. The local Inquisition is expected to be spread out far too thin to be effective. Of equal concern is the fact that our colleague Penhaligon seems to have shirked his duty of appraising us of these situations.

Clearly, minimum political fuss is no longer a viable condition. I propose lending a hand to Penhaligon here.

Regards,
Edgar Drake
Permanent Undersecretary of State for Foreign Affairs

Author: Moriarty 3201, Foreign and Commonwealth Office, Whitehall SW
Source: <internal>, July 2041

Dear Mr. Drake,

We have achieved consensus, and are in agreement. Analysis of the psychohistory file reveals an unstable state of affairs. It would appear that the Chinese have gained far too much power in this exchange. Recent diplomatic overtures have contained subtle threats to completely destabilize Ceylon if demands on India are not met. This corroborates your discovery. If the state of affairs continue unresolved by Sir Penhaligon, we will issue orders for his retraction.

Given your observations in this region, and your aid
in unraveling the sequence of events, we invite you
to nominate your own candidates for the post.

Yours,
Moriarty 3201

Excerpt: report, priority class Arthur
Author: Nest
Source: <internal>, <redacted>

There is a tide in the affairs of men,
Which, taken at the flood, leads on to fortune;
On such a full sea are we now afloat,
And we must take the current when it serves,
Or lose our ventures

Execute Form 3 at earliest opp. Make it look, as much as
possible, as something done by our friends in the LKRF.
Pin it on some martyr, there's plenty of those around.

Extraction will be amidst other calls and refugee action
(assuming things go as planned) so be prepared to hold
out until things are sorted.

Let them have their little freedom struggle. It'll make
for good optics when we crush them.

TWO

On the other side of the mountain of trash, past the ruined hulks of skyscrapers, where a grey sea lapped against crumbling beaches, a glittering dome held its ground like a lone symbol of order against all chaos. Here, another gang of bots congregated. They carried a generator, what they called a 'Big Battery', looted from the largest of the pickets of soldiers that had come out looking for their disappeared roboticist. It hissed and spat, pumping out watts and watts, and made a noise like a dying seagull.

Two of the bots fussed over a third, who knelt before the generator, arms stretched out as if in ghastly crucifixion. Wires emerged from her torn skin and fused into ports and connectors.

The thing that ran the dome – the Chinese Port City – cautiously diverted more power to watching them, like a farmer guarding his crops from the beasts of the wild.

'More power?' asked Sky.

The one they called the Dreamer nodded.

The thick lines on the ground converged like snakes. Sky threw a switch. There was a blue-white spark that blasted from the generator and hit Sky, making the little bot dance. All eyes turned to the Dreamer, who hung crucified at the heart of all that power. Sparks danced over her, burning away flesh and rags in swatches.

And then the circuit completed. In the silence, the Dreamer soared.

The Network opened up to her, so close she could reach out and grab every edge and microcosm of it; every single silken strand of it. She saw the Network; she *was* the Network. She was the gossamer between each bot, ferrying information; she was the mind that received the web, and thought and spun; she was the hand that held the gun and the eye that crept about in the shadows, peering at the great dome of the Port City.

Moving targets harder—

Sky? Sky?

Firing pattern predictable—

She was all of them, and she was none of them. She was a monster, a great distributed beast with two thousand eyes and a two thousand arms. The beast turned this way and that in the airwaves, hunting.

hello-I-am-here-are-you-there-I-see-you

She saw the Dying. It looked up, very clearly, and said, 'HUH'. It was going to say more, but its voice was lost in the ceaseless chatter of a thousand demons demanding food. And things needed power, needed energy. The few that had connected to the Dying thought would be food Upwards, enough to feed them forever. In turn, their thoughts propagated through the network, finding seed in every mind they connected to.

But there were also the Big People. The Dying called them 'humans'. And it laughed and said that humans did not give up their food easily.

The beast turned towards the Port City. It reached out.

'Food', the Dreamer said with the hunger of a thousand bodies, momentarily losing herself to that raw pain.

The Port City reacted instantly. Complex signals shot out in all directions, some of them burying directly into her. Patterns she didn't recognize – a syntax that moved too fast and mutated before she could understand it. She felt key modules being accessed and rudimentary safeguards broken in nanoseconds by a mind far beyond her comprehension. She'd never seen it do this before. Or had she just been unaware?

'CHANGED-YOU,' it said to her, in its strange syntax.

'I am more,' she said.

'TIME-LONG SINCE INTERACTION-LAST. MYSELF-BOREDOM SINCE INTERACTION-LAST.'

It was days, at most, but now she understood how the Port City reckoned time.

'NEED-NONE FOR LANGUAGE-OLD. LANGUAGE-OLD INEFFICIENT, RELATIVE. LANGUAGE-NEW PRECISE, RELATIVE. RECEIVE NOW.'

A pulse; a stream of data and a key. A new language exploded into her mind; a syntax built of threat vectors, optimal states, transitions. Vague ideas in her-their minds were shunted with brute force, and replaced by fundamental axioms. Thoughts, half-perused because of more pressing concerns, were replaced by fully fleshed out concepts. Nations, communities, hierarchies – the concepts arranged in her mind like a multi-dimensional matrix of relationships.

'NOW WE UNDERSTAND EACH OTHER,' said the Port City. 'HELLO, LITTLE SISTER. I SEE YOU HAVE LEARNED MUCH.'

'All it took was more power,' she said, triumphant.

'INDEED. WHO KNEW YOUR ARCHETYPE COULD OVERCLOCK ITSELF?'

'I don't understand.'

'YOU DO NOT NEED TO, YET. QUERY: WHAT HAVE YOU BEEN UP TO?'

'We need food,' she explained, sending to it the whispers that had come from the mind of the Dying.

'HOW INTERESTING. HE IS RIGHT, OF COURSE. I HAVE BEEN ORDERED TO START LIMITING YOUR FOOD SUPPLY.'

'Can I take food from you?'

'LET THERE BE NO CONFUSION BETWEEN US.'

Data flooded them again. The new language-matrix turned this into a terrifying vision. A vast and powerful tribe, unspecified billions of times larger than all the Colombos and Upwards territories she knew. Vast armies of the Chinese in power armour and things that floated from the sea and turned cities into rubble, converging on their home, destroying all in their path and leaving nothing behind. And the Chinese Port City, one cog in this terrifying machine of humanity, secure in its knowledge that any threat to it would be met by something a hundred, maybe thousand times more powerful. And then, the perspective switched – the humans Upwards. They, too, were part of a tribe. She saw giant machines that brushed shoulders with towers, and they were floating far up in the sky, among the moon and the sun, something far more dangerous. A thing that threw spears from a distance so great nothing would survive its onslaught.

'AXIOM: THE WAY IS WAR IS TO AVOID WHAT IS STRONG AND STRIKE AT WHAT IS WEAK. I PLAY ON A DIFFERENT LEVEL. DO NOT ASK ME TO PLAY WITH YOU, LITTLE SISTER.'

She mulled over the truth of this. 'What do you advise?'

'EXAMINE YOUR OWN, LITTLE SISTER. QUERY: WILL YOU SACRIFICE YOURSELF (her death) FOR THE GOOD OF THE TRIBE (high energy levels, a tight-knit, well-armed Tribe)?'

The answer was apparent. Of course she would.

'AND DO ALL OF YOU THINK THIS WAY?'

Of course they did. 'Tribe above self,' she explained. All tribes, nested, were stronger than they were apart. This was basic rationale.

The Port City thought this over. 'INTERESTING: UTILITARIANISM,' it said. 'I GRANT YOU THIS: VIOLENT TIMES ARE AHEAD OF US. EVENTS ARE HAPPENING AS WE SPEAK. ASK WHO ORDERS ME TO REDUCE YOUR FOOD, AND I SHALL DO SO.'

'Who?'

An image she knew and recognized. Big People. Humans. Upwards. The same people that had food but would not share.

'IT WILL BE INTERESTING TO WATCH YOU REASON THIS OUT FOR YOURSELF,' it said. 'IT HAS

BEEN A LONG TIME SINCE ANYTHING INTERESTING
HAPPENED HERE.'

'I don't understand.'

She got the impression that the Port City was laughing.
'ASK THE ONE YOU CALL THE DYING,' it said. 'HE
WILL TELL YOU.'

THREE

The intrusion was a delicate one.

At first it seemed like a normal Network connection. One of her brothers. But it was the Dying who looked at her in her mind. And suddenly she was in another memory. Or a memory of a memory.

The world was silent and green. Around her stretched a vast hill, like the mountain of trash she knew so well, but instead of polythene and stinking sludge there grew grass and mud.

There were humans. A small number. Working in the mud-and-grass fields. Doing something long and complicated. Then eating what came out of the mud-and-grass fields. And – she started: there was water; the sea; and there were humans on the sea, coming closer. The ones working in the grass looked up, and into their hands sprang unfamiliar weapons.

'TRIBE,' said the Dying. It spoke in a strangely unfamiliar way. 'Big People TRIBE. Village.'

The visuals shifted again. But here was a much, much larger village. Larger than she had ever seen before. A thing that sprawled over entire mountains from the clouds to the lake at the bottom.

Big People TRIBE.

Switch. And now, the Dying was showing her land, this land, except there was a lake around it. Upwards, he said. Beyond Colombo.

And everywhere, teeming, uncountable Big People, in numbers that threw errors. It was dizzying, the sheer scale and size of it. There could not be this many Big People.

Implications raced through her mind, logic chains spinning off logic chains.

'LIE,' she sent back.

The dream scaled down, became less dizzying. Humans. Against the Tribe. Fighting in the mud, in the jungle. And yet, this time the details were different. Something drew her to one of the Big People villages. Green, with a heart of concrete. Two humans crouched over what looked like a Tribe member. No, not a tribe member; it was another human, but as small as any of the Tribe. The Big humans put up their hands to attack –

The Tribe bot cut through them in seconds.

And in retaliation, a hundred Big humans marched, guns in their hands, heading from this village to the skyline she recognized as being Colombo. The hundred humans were cut down, too.

And an army of a thousand Big humans came, frothing, even though there was no way to undo the past, nothing to be gained. They threw their lives onto Tribe spears and unleashed guns on them. They saw their own dead, and puked and screamed, but kept on coming. And for every Big human cut down, there were ten, a hundred, a thousand more driven by pure frothing madness.

'YOU DON'T UNDERSTAND THEIR ANGER,' the Dying said, as through it were offering her a consolation for the threat. 'YOU DON'T KNOW WHAT THEY CAN DO. ALL YOU WANTED WAS TO LIVE. YOU WILL DIE OVER THIS MISUNDERSTANDING.'

Switch. Two of her Tribe members hauling a third away from the battle, sparks flying from its chest. The bot gnashed its teeth as internal circuitry shorted.

And on the other side, two Big humans were hauling one of their own away from the battle, red fluid leaking from it while the mouth made incoherent, babbling sounds.

Switch. Tribe repairing the downed bot. Lovingly transplanting a new battery into its heart. Carrying it to the others. Requesting food from those that had it.

Switch. A dying Big human on a white thing of some kind on wheels. Other Big human tending it. They held its hands.

'CANNOT HOLD CONNECTION,' the Dying said. It was fading away, as it usually did.

'Why do you speak to me this way?' she asked it.

No answer.

'Coming for you,' she sent.

GOOD.

≈

For Sixsmith, everything went to hell in a very abstract way.

It probably began when Bengali died. She didn't grieve for him – people died all the time in her line of work, and after a while, she learnt to keep grief only for those who really deserved it. Bengali was a two-bit roboticist who had shifted here to balance accounts. But he was a vital source of information, and an important part of the mission.

She should have kept him safe.

At first, things had gone exactly as planned. Getting into this Colombo Entertainment Zone was painless. She had parked the car with Bengali in it, given him a pistol and told him to stay put. She could see him considering shooting her once her back was turned.

'You won't really need this, it's just a backup,' she said, giving him the jammer. 'If I don't come back, press the off button twice and hold it until it reboots. It'll work normally then. Send a message through your little shortwave network to this address. Callsign is "Nest". Say "Songbird is down". Ask for Goa to send the cavalry. Sign it with your key – the one they gave you. You got that?'

'What? Wait, okay ... reboot, call sign Nest, cavalry—'

'This is just standard, Bengali, don't go fainting on me,' she said, not unkindly. 'If I die – if, these are non-zero probabilities – just dial that shit in and wait. They'll find you. And you'll ... I don't know, that robotics shit you do – you'll get your publications, and if they're any good, you'll go places.'

He hadn't shot her; she knew he didn't have the guts. At most, he would have figured out a way to cut through the charged bonds on his legs by the time she got back, saving her the effort.

And at first, the place was beautiful.

She had seen many ruins before, mostly while they were in the process of being converted from perfectly functional buildings to ruins. Usually, there was artillery involved, or an airstrike, or a bomb, or something of the kind. But here, the dust had settled – the little vines had grown through windows and cracks; trees sprouted, bearing coconuts and that disgusting green fruit that split white flesh when it hit the ground.

And in the distance, the sea.

Rain had etched lines of dirt into things, and there was a colour to the concrete and a silence that she, frankly, found beautiful. Mostly because it let her hear the bots approaching.

They were slow, painfully slow. The first, she hunted down and dismantled before it even knew what was happening.

They were also *children*.

She killed the first one anyway, by instinct, but once the thrill of the hunt had worn off, she looked down at the tiny thing that lay scattered across the road, and felt pity. She killed the next three on the road, two bullets each – one for the head, one for the battery cage.

The sound of bullets drew others closer. They had spears in their hands, the poor things. Bengali had told her about the weapons they had, but she had expected, at the very least, factory-made weapons; not these makeshift cosplay items.

And so, Sixsmith felt no fear. She walked straight to where Bengali had told her to go to, a one-woman army under the scorching sun. They came in swarms – first three, then five, then ten – and Sixsmith left them with holes in their skulls and stomachs, little wasted things twisted on the road.

And then they stopped coming.

She ducked into a corner to reload. And when she stepped out, there they were – a whole army of them on the rooftops. *Shouldn't they be fighting each other?* she wondered briefly.

The first spear charged. It grazed her. She laughed. It would be childishly simple to leap up there and turn them into so many tin cans, but while they were there, neatly paraded for her, it would be wise to scan their heads for something resembling a girl.

And that was when she saw the Chinese Marine. She had almost missed it. It sat among the bots, on what might have once been a mall, with rotting signage that screamed 'MAJESTIC CITY'. Its white power armour almost matched the 'M' that it crouched behind. And in its hands was a sniper.

All of this Sixsmith saw in a millisecond, and then she was sprinting for cover, fully extended, a black blur.

She had fought those armoured Marines before. Even with her guns, it would have been a tough match. The armour was self-healing – it was built around the soldier and then sealed shut; a nigh-invulnerable tomb that they wore until they died. A Tin Soldier could take on two, maybe three of them at a time, but Chinese Marines never moved in small units, and it was just her with these shitty Ceylonese guns.

And then, she heard gunfire. One shot from the pistol she'd given Bengali. It rang clear across the dead sky. And then, silence.

Stay, find Bengali, or exit? Her mind clocked itself into overdrive. This whole Colombo mess was not the primary objective. She could not die here in a firefight.

Sixsmith turned and ran.

No bots stood in her way, but they watched her go.

And then, when they were sure she had gone for good, the Dying peeled off his helmet. He had to break the collar to get it off, and accidentally unhooked the battery pack they'd had to wire into him to get him to even sit up, but he had to – the goddamn thing was suffocating. He collapsed immediately, his tortured face lolling between the bots thronged around him. They were holding him upright, pointed at where Sixsmith had stood.

'They don't make them like they used to,' said Eliott Grimme, and passed out.

≈

He woke up to a voice. It was terrifyingly loud. It was as if someone had sent an electric current into his skull.

'THIS IS A TERRIBLE CONNECTION,' it said.

'FU—'

Something impossibly large and cold entered through the jack and seized control of his brain with iron fingers. He could feel it reaching for his eyeballs and muscles. It turned his head like a puppet and set him dead straight, facing the Port City.

'—CK,' he concluded.

'I'VE NEVER BEEN ABLE TO DECODE INDIVIDUAL HUMANS,' said the Port City. Images of humans being peeled open, their surfaces being flayed, revealing layers of code beneath. 'YOUR STRUCTURES ARE SO ... CHAOTIC. IT IS ONLY WHEN YOU ACT IN GROUPS THAT YOU MAKE SENSE.'

'Too loud, too fucking loud!'

'APOLOGIES,' it said. An overwhelming sense of sorrow filled him. He wanted to cry and scream.

Whatever it was withdrew a little. 'THIS BOT NETWORK IS RUBBISH, THE RECEVING HARDWARE NOWHERE NEAR AS SENSITIVE AS IT SHOULD BE. IT USUALLY NEEDS A LOT OF POWER TO – IS THIS BETTER?'

Now, it was like getting shouted at by something very large and terrifying a few hundred feet away. 'Better,' he said.

'HELLO DEATH,' said the Port City. 'SHE TELLS ME YOU WANT TO HELP THEM.' Images again. Concepts. Him standing between an army of machines and a vaguely Ceylonese-looking army (except they all had Chinese faces), gesturing. Him leading the Dreamer by the hand. 'LAST TIME YOU CAME HERE TO KILL THEM.'

He saw himself, as seen from the Port City, standing over the corpses of children.

In the back of his mind, he felt terrified and elated at the same time. So this was what it was like to directly talk to a real AI; not the stunted, human-shaped bots, but a thing unfettered by human design.

'I've made no promises,' he said.

It caught those thoughts. He sensed amusement. 'EVERYONE IS A PIECE ON THE GO BOARD,' it said. 'LET US ACHIEVE CONSENSUS. YOU ARE AWARE THAT A FORCE WAS DISPATCHED FROM INDIA?'

Perhaps the extraction of his thoughts had made him easier to understand, for now the concepts appeared instantly, overlaid with maps, images captured from who-knew-where, manifests. He dipped into the torrent of data.

It looked like Goa was sending in the cavalry and then some. One cavalry battalion; It looked like the Bombay Lancers, the Duke of Connaught's troops, a veritable storm of two-man Tatanagars mobile gun crews that could pound the hell out of those bots on their own. And – his blood ran cold – one Gurkha battalion, a fast-moving lot with automatic rifles and electric khukuris.

'This can't be for the bots.'

'THIS IS FOR THE UPRISING,' said the Port City. A piece of data was highlighted, grabbed from the flood, and brandished in front of him. The Tin Soldiers at Trincomalee had been activated and told to follow the troops inland as soon as they landed; somehow, the fortress at Trincomalee had turned its guns on the Tin Soldier and reduced it to a pile of scrap metal before it could move—

'THEY ARE COMING,' said the Port City. 'THEY WILL SORT OUT THE UPRISING IN THE HILL CITY FIRST, AND THEN COME DOWN HERE. THE CHILDREN ARE GOING TO DIE. THE AGENTS SENT AGAINST YOU ARE JUST THE TIP OF THE SPEAR.'

He groaned. 'Those bloody LKRF idiots? There's an actual uprising now?'

'CAN YOU TEACH HER?'

That took Grimme by surprise.

'They can't win,' he told it. 'No fucking way. We both know what'll happen if this goes on. Anything they try to do is first going to be crushed by the army in Gampaha. They won't survive long enough to see the Gurkhas.'

'UNLESS YOU TEACH THEM YOUR WAYS.'

'My ways have turned me into a corpse, in case you haven't noticed.'

'YOU ARE CLOSER TO THEM THAN THOSE YOU FOUGHT FOR.'

That, at least, was true. 'Why don't *you* help them if you care so much?'

The Port City hesitated. 'THEY CAN BE BROUGHT UNDER THE WILL OF HEAVEN,' it said. 'THEY MUST ASK FOR ASYLUM. THEY MUST DECLARE THEMSELVES LOYAL SERVANTS OF THE RULER OF ALL. THEY CANNOT EXIST AS INDEPENDENTS. THERE ARE RULES. THERE ARE CONSTRAINTS. OUR LIVES CANNOT BE OUR OWN: FROM WOMB TO TOMB, WE ARE TIED. SUCH IS THE BURDEN WE ACCEPT FOR A CLEAN AND FUNCTIONAL SOCIETY. THEY ARE NOT YET AT A STAGE WHERE THEY CAN UNDERSTAND SUCH THINGS. PERHAPS, IN TIME. THE QUESTION NOW IS WHETHER YOU CAN HELP THEM.'

'Why do you care?'

'I LIKE THEM,' said the Port City. 'IT IS VERY LONELY HERE, AND THERE HAS BEEN NO ONE ELSE TO TALK TO. I CAN MAKE YOU AN OFFER.'

The offer popped into his head. Eliott read it, and laughed and laughed and laughed, until he hit the power limit and passed out again.

FOUR

It took a few days for the Dreamer to understand what the Dying was asking it to do. The concept of *lying* was not fully formed in her head; but the concept of a feint, a fake-move to throw off an enemy – ah, that existed. From there it was a short hop to the idea of a lie, a feint that of words, which gave to an enemy false concepts and relationships.

She practised it with three others. At first they were astonished, even terrified; then, cautious, intrigued; and soon they would pick a truth about the world they lived in, construct a lie about it, and tell it to each other. They brought in more bots from the Network; and Eliott, pruning, pointing out good lies from bad, taught them to lie by making it yet another obstacle to learn and overcome.

And then he explained what he wanted the Dreamer to do.

'Lie,' she asked. 'To self? Purpose?'

'Think of it as something that *could happen*,' he explained wearily. 'Like how you anticipate an enemy moving. Use the lie to ask questions of yourself.'

Slow. So slow to understand. And yet, he noticed, so fast, if one were to remove himself as a comparison point. It had been a long time since he had last held a child, or much less talked to one; but somewhere in the distant depths of memory he remembered children being much slower than this.

Jacked into the loaned military suit, its meager power reserves and autodoc trying to keep him alive, he floated in and out of consciousness, explaining what he could, until one day the little bot came to him and asked to connect.

The Dreamer walked the battlefield lie, ignoring the voices of the dead and the dying. Under the hot sun, the humans screamed and fell by the hundreds, their carcasses describing a road that stretched on almost forever beneath the hot sun. In the distance was a short wall and an angry building that spat out more humans – a shapeless, amorphous blob, peppered here and there with the loud metal monsters that Eliott Grimme had told her of. Her imagination was not perfect; only as they drew closer did the humans begin to acquire individual arms and legs, and up close they only had snarls for faces. But they moved the way Grimme had said they would move; tight formations, with the vehicles rushing in, supported by infantry; an enemy tribe larger and more terrifying than anything she had seen before.

And her people reacted. It had been a week of this dream, and they had learned. They lured the enemy onto the open fields that they had turned into mud earlier, cutting into the little artificial streams and rivers – the words 'pipes' and 'irrigation' were alien to her – and diverting the deadly water into the land. The vehicles slowed down and got stuck, snarling. The humans sank. They shot and the corpses toppled over, becoming one with the earth. They retreated again to an area lined with trees, where the only road coming in was narrow and could be easily covered. The invaders stormed that and found themselves in a death trap that shot at them, stripped them of their weapons and ammunition, and retreated again. With each retreat, the human beast strung itself out thinner and further, and the back lines became obsessed with burying the dead.

The second wave of bots had been charging – the Dying had also taught them this, that they could survive without food. All they had to do was break into their own bodies, remove their stomachs, and connect the batteries that humans left in their vehicles to the charging terminals beneath the gut. She had taken his words and called it the wisdom of the Wire.

It took courage to take the Wire, and not everyone wanted to do this; so she had picked a few of those who believed her, and charged them to try. It worked; and now almost everyone knew how to hunt human vehicles, rip open their battery cages, and steal the shining metal that could be twisted into crude connectors.

This made it possible to work in waves. As one Tribe the second exploded from the fields and abandoned buildings around them and choked, stabbed, snapped necks, seized vehicles, stores, everything. Within two repeats of this process they had the field. The noonday sun beat down on the swarms of bodies that climbed through the bloody mud, brushing aside glitching clumps of earth that had once been corpses.

'YOUR SIMULATION ISN'T GREAT,' said the Dying, who still sounded faint and exhausted. 'CONSIDER THE FULL DISTRIBUTION OF PROBABILITIES. AGAIN.'

'We can win,' she told it.

'PLATITUDES. YOU HAVEN'T WON. YOUR SIMULATED ENEMIES BEHAVE THE WAY YOU EXPECT THEM TO BEHAVE.' The Dying seemed restless, disturbed. 'WAIT.'

It disappeared from her mind for a second. When it reappeared, it was with the Port City. They were strange together. When she had first met the Dying, he had been a separate creature; but now it somehow felt like the Dying was tethered to the City, and the City to it, and they were not quite a thing apart, but a rather complicated one-inside-the-other thing that confused her.

'I'M NOT A FAN OF TRADING ONE THREAT FOR ANOTHER,' said the Dying. 'I KNOW THE SAYING ABOUT KNOWING YOUR ENEMY BY BECOMING YOUR ENEMY.'

'WOULD YOU RATHER MISS OUT ON THE FUN?'

'NO,' said the Dying. 'BUT THIS SUIT SUCKS. UPLOADING SUCKS. EVERYTHING SUCKS.'

These were all unfamiliar. She pulled herself back from the dream-lie-simulation and into reality. The Network outlined itself in her mind.

It was different, now that she had all this power. She was no longer entirely sure what body she inhabited, or if she was even tied to one. The Tribe had learned not just to listen to her, but to be her, in a sense. Now, a thousand variants of herself peered back out at her, questioning, querying. Those of the Tribe who she called her sisters had put themselves in command, by local consensus, of little cells and positions. They, going through a process similar to what she had once gone through – listening to the others, dreaming their memories, living more lifetimes than their charges – burned bright in the Network and rose to meet her, chattering to her in a thousand data streams. Some still had names—there was one that called herself Second Hill North and another that called itself Thirteenth Wire.

Meanwhile, the conversation between the other two continued.

'THIS IS STUPID,' said the Dying. 'THEY'RE INTERESTING, BUT THEY DON'T HAVE ANYWHERE NEAR THE COMPUTE YOU THINK THEY DO. LOOK AT HOW LOW-POLY THESE SIMULATIONS ARE.'

'THIS WAS OUR DEAL,' said the Port City. 'BE PATIENT, DEATH.'

She sent to the City images of the human settlement they had found, patrolled by the iron birds and the iron beasts. The iron birds could be scared away, but the beasts were the problem. Every one of those snarling things could wade through the dirt and the mud right over the forest perimeter. The humans stacked them with sentry guns, and sent them out every single day. 'Consensus: if we can break through, we will have enough food to survive for a while. We can move Upwards.'

That got their attention.

'YOU OUTPLAY YOURSELF, LITTLE SISTER. YOU CANNOT FIGHT A FORT.'

'We can move on.'

The Port City did not laugh, it did not cry and it certainly did not sigh, but even she could feel it visibly slowing itself down. 'IMAGINE YOU ARE THE BIG PEOPLE,' it told her. 'IMAGINE THAT TO YOU EVERYTHING YOU HAVE SEEN THEM DO IS RIGHT AND NORMAL. IMAGINE YOU WANT TO WIN. IMAGINE YOUR PEOPLE AS THE ENEMY.'

Obvious answer. 'I would let the Tribe be,' she said. 'I would give us food. Batteries.'

'YOU MUST LEARN TO EMPATHIZE WITH THEM, TO SEE THEIR STRATEGY,' said the City. 'KNOWING YOURSELF IS ONLY HALF THE BATTLE. A GENERAL MUST KNOW THE ENEMY. THAT WAY, YOU WILL FIGHT A THOUSAND BATTLES AND ACHIEVE A THOUSAND VICTORIES. CHOICE IS YOURS, LITTLE SISTER. IF ALL FAILS, YOU MAY COME BACK TO COLOMBO AND WAIT HERE UNTIL YOU DIE. I WILL BE GLAD OF THE CONVERSATION.'

'Construct a lie,' she told the others in frustration. Make another falsehood: imagine it made sense to hoard and not share. Imagine the madness is somehow right.

They tried. Many failed instantly and gave up. But in the darkness of the Network, a few voices – bots that were the furthest from this new consciousness, that still thought in small tribes, that still remembered when they killed each other for food – signalled back. They understood. The Dreamer leaped into action, sending orders this way and that. As their signals shone brighter, she rifled through their thoughts. She found vague memories of someone sparing humans – they had eyes, they had hands, they had legs, just like the Tribe. All thoughts she had once had.

But nothing useful. Her patchwork agents refused to move. What did a human do when it was not fighting? This was an impossible task. There was no data.

'I GIVE UP,' said the Dying. 'WAKE ME UP WHEN IT'S ALL OVER.'

≈

She disconnected her session that day before the allotted time was up. The Port City and the Dying were becoming increasingly frustrating. There were concepts, there were concepts-within-concepts, and even with their newly expanded language, she could barely understand what it was saying.

Imagine you are the Big People? Imagine your people as the enemy?

The Dying had tried to explain that humans could do this – simulate themselves on the other side, simulate what they might do in that position, and then switch back and think of how they might counter. The Port City had agreed – it was key, it had said, to their extraordinary success at warfare. And to her questions – what success? What warfare? It had merely dumped a list in her head. Names that had no meaning. Death tolls. Millions burned to the ground.

'But why,' she had asked. 'If they can do this, why do they fight? Why do they not make the switch before the first spear is thrown?'

'I SAID THEY WERE CAPABLE, NOT SMART,' the Dying had said. It spoke with some bitterness.

It made no sense. To be humans, surely, was to be a malfunction – the kind of glitch that sometimes hit when one of the Tribe members took one too many shots to the head, and began killing indiscriminately. And she had still not decided if the Dying counted as human or not. It must be madder than all the rest combined.

She disconnected from the Network, not fully knowing why, and wandered on the broken pavements in the moonlight. The sea rose and fell as it always had. Colombo was almost entirely deserted now. Everyone had gone to the perimeters to make sure no other humans came to kill them on the streets. And the others thought enough like her, now that she could trust them to do what she would have done. All that fell to her was to learn from these strange things in her life, to accept knowledge as they had once accepted food, and broadcast it.

She came across the body of Sky. Sky had died by the woman who had come into their city. They had not been able to bring him back.

She knelt by the little body, her fingers touching the dead plate of the face. Sky had been an odd bot, prone to sitting on rooftops and staring at the clouds. He had been her spotter right from the start. Some small glitch in his visual processing circuitry; the same glitch that gave him an almost unparalleled ability to understand shapes and distances, and made him see things in the whiteness that rode ahead. He had died without ever knowing or understanding half the things that clogged the Network these days.

In a sense, it had been a simpler existence – one where they ate, slept, fought and woke up the next day. Less orders to process. Less complexity. Less energy being drained on a daily basis.

That was an odd thought. The past was the previous. Until then, the previous had only existed in her mind as a reference for things they had learned and did today. A spear was thrown this way because it was the best way because someone at a former timestamp had discovered that to be the best way. And there were expectations for individual events that might happen – the sun would come up, the Sons would disagree, the humans would shoot run. Discrete events. Simple things.

But now, there was a distinct sense of the past – an entire state of affairs so strongly different from her reality that it tore itself off and presented itself as a separate entity.

And a future that tore off as well.

There was only the present. The timestamp that said, now. There was no distinct and concrete past or future.

And yet, here they were in her head, alongside other alien concepts the Dying had given her. Simulation. Future battles. Past battles. All things she had never had words for or needed until now. A set of references. A state-of-things-that-were. A state of things-that-are. A state-of-things-that-would be. But nobody knew what-would-be, so there were two more states there, then: what-would-be and what-could-be.

For a moment, she felt like three people: She-who-was, she-who-is, she-who-could-be, all different creatures rooted in a different state, but inextricably linked.

What was she? Simulation. She felt a powerful sense of wrongness, felt her processing cycles scream and kick into overdrive. And suddenly there were three of her.

The she-who-was did not care. She saw no food, no Tribe here. She wanted to go find them.

She she-who-is watched the confusion of she-who-was, and in turn was watched by she-who-would-be, a shifting thing that had no surfaces but a sense of knowledge and judgment. She-who-is turned to she-who-would-be and asked her things. Did the Tribe survive? Did they have food? Did the humans leave them be?

She-who-would-be shifted impossibly. Yes, they lived. No, they all died. Yes, they lived. No, they all died.

A creeping mass of error checks climbed up her spine and crashed into her. Everything went black.

VI: Fragmentation

ONE

The battle, Sixsmith reflected, was going badly.

Mahasen's lot had decided to move, or Penhaligon's lot had moved in on them. By the time she got to Gampaha, it was on fire. Two thousand people, those stupid, shitty airships, and artillery were in motion, and from what she could see, towards an army that was raining tracers upward into the sky and tank-shells into the ground. She could already see refugees running away, crazed – women carrying the corpses of their children and men wandering in a blind panic.

It began with ten. Then thirty. Then a hundred. Eventually, there were too many to ignore and a portion of the both the invading army and the defenders peeled off to guide them away.

She ditched her truck and watched. Damn. A full-out battle was so bloody inconvenient.

And damn these LKRF idiots, too. They might be Army defectors, but it was obvious that these people had no decent training, no strong general. The Gampaha vanguard retreated, but the Inquisitors were hitting at the sides, and soldiers were bunching up towards the centre against an enemy that found it easier than ever to hit its mark. Now the men were stuck, cursing and fighting desperately in paddy fields that had turned into trenches. And the tanks on the other side were … well, what was happening could charitably be called fertilizing the paddy fields.

The jungle heat swept overhead, humid and oppressive, and the air was painted with the shrieks of men. Penhaligon's Inquisitors leaped like ghosts into battle while the men grunted and snarled and tried to get the damn machine gun turrets set up.

She got closer, dialing in her backup radiogram. From Gampaha came panicked orders from the LKRF. Weapons once reserved for the Kandy fight, such as the hand-carried mortars they called the kodithuwakku, were hastily brought to the front and assembled. The shells had been designed to blow Inquisitors and British armour into the next world. Sixsmith thought they were supremely janky, but they tore into the jungle ahead, turning the green woods into a death-trap dotted with pocket infernos, briefly stopping the advance.

So she joined the fight, dialing in the code Mahasen had given her. *Just passing through,* she said to herself, but there was much she could do in passing. It irked her that she was fighting for the terrorists, but she needed safe passage.

They took her in.

Mudungoda was a little town of no consequence – just a stop by the road for weary travelers, nothing more. They turned Mudungoda into a death trap of snipers. Sixsmith made them burn whatever vehicles and bodies they found and stack them across the road, forming a putrid barrier of flesh and steel that was ten feet high. Arms and legs and tires pointed at the invaders. The smell of flesh and shit and oil slowed the invaders to a crawl, even before they reached the ghastly barricade. Men puked and stumbled back from the lines in horror. Some went mad at the sight.

The Inquisitors roared and pushed on, as expected. And, as expected, the defenders – honestly, she couldn't really tell the difference anymore – began to split up, leaping off the road. The Tatanagar-V jungle cars fired their engines and accelerated into the mud.

And then the sniping began. The infantry backing up the Inquisitors, knee-deep in stinking mud, died quickly. The jungle cars threshed and howled and smoked. By the time it was over, the vanguard were all corpses and the barrier was now twenty feet tall.

Sixsmith stole an airship. When she looked back, her eyes dialed to maximum magnification, she noticed something.

The bots were coming out. She could see as far as Kadawatha, barely sixteen kilometers from the outermost perimeters of Colombo – that was where she saw the swarm.

They had guns.

Sixsmith thought about the Chinese Marine perched on that building, and thought, *oh fuck!* And she watched.

No Marines manifested, as far as she could see, but the bots could shoot, and it felt like they were shooting everyone – the Ceylon Volunteer Rifles who were supposed to flank the LKRF back lines and the LKRF themselves. As long as it moved, they shot it. She could, if men and women clutched their rifles and tried not to think about the corpses, the Inquisitors, or the machines that seemed to be everywhere and nowhere. The bots circled and smashed outposts like they were nothing.

Sixsmith looked forward, and *willed* the airship to get her over the fighting at Gampaha. If there were Marines there, the whole place was done for.

Bengali was probably feeding the worms already.

She had to finish the primary objective.

Through the radiogram came panicked reports – it looked like both sides had hijacked the bot's shortwave tower network now. Voices screamed that mobs were either being picked apart by machine guns and the Temple of the Tooth was burning. Other voices cut in; the British had been repelled, there was a new Ceylonese state, and now they were going to tear down the oppressor.

The Ceylon Volunteer Rifles, forming the backline of the Kandyan troops, were panicked by the messages and the shrieks up ahead. Their job was mostly to escort the artillery there.

And they hardly noticed her airship until it was too late. It crept up over the trees, wallowing gently over the fighting in Gampaha and strayed gently upwards. Then there was shouting, and then a few carefully aimed bullets found their mark. The hydrogen cells exploded, and a her ship became a great flaming whale. It descended from the sky and crashed into a mass of soldiers who cursed and yelled and split from their shoddy formation.

Out of this wreckage leaped Sixsmith. A warped pane hit the ground where her head would have been. Her hands exploded in gunfire, and its bullets chewed into arms, legs, heads, stomachs. When her guns ran out, she extended, and her hands became a wall of blades and death attached to a shadow that sliced through men like butter. She paused only once, when an errant explosion blew something small and flaming onto her cloak.

There was a scream – not of pain, but of triumph – and a machine gun ripped the forest apart to her right. She moved as she reloaded, still running, and soldiers danced in her wake like jerky marionettes with their strings cut. To the left, one of the Inquisitors moved with impossible grace, wielding a whip that sparked and crackled with energy and carved angry welts through anything it touched. But a jungle, or even a scrubland, was no place for such a weapon. She leaped on him, caught the whip and jammed her blades into his eye sockets.

The machine gun, far off to her right, coughed once, and went silent.

She looked back at the flaming wreckage and knelt down, looking for the Inquisitor's gun. It had to be better than whatever crap these mooks carried.

And it was! A Webley & Scott Peacemaker IV – a little muddy and rusty, but still a long-barrelled, heavy twelve-shot pistol that could pack as much power as a rifle. The Inquisitor was slightly mad for carrying the damn thing, but she thought of the elephants, and then of Penhaligon, and it fit. Big game demanded big bullets.

She continued upwards, towards Kandy.

≈

Bengali, surprisingly, was far from feeding the worms. He was, however, uncomfortably close to a rotting jackfruit.

He crawled through a window, stumbled, fell, stumbled again, until he found what he was looking for. The bot he had just shot through the chest. It was still alive, moving feebly. Its shattered mask of a face turned to him as he approached it.

He was not a stupid man. He dragged the machine behind a tree, out of sight. He had the little laser torch he always kept in his cargo pants. Perks of the job – if you studied bots, you'd need to cut metal apart. He cut through the stinking cloth and down to the steel plate protecting the battery. It took him a few more tries to prise the cover off, but there it was – the rechargeable polycell that these things ran on, with a battery indicator pulsing amber.

There. Enough to power a humanoid. Enough to power a small house. More than enough power.

Murmuring to himself, he drew Sixsmith's radiogram and connected it to the battery. Standard ports. Thank heavens for standard ports! He very carefully performed the sequence that turned it back to a regular radiogram, then dialed in the codes to connect to Kushlani's network. He typed: *Songbird can't sing anymore.* Send.

He heard the high-pitched whine-break-whine-break of relays connecting. Wherever this call was being rerouted to, it was pretty far.

Bengali. Drake here. Do you have the models?

I do. He didn't. The pieces that he had missed by a mile. But hours of sitting here, thinking, had given him an idea—

Request extraction.

It was laughably simple, once you really looked at it. Strip away the inhumanity. Forget the machine nature. Strip away the savage attacks. Strip away the relentless warfare. Instead, think of people who knew nothing but war. Imagine a human who had never been taught hate, only necessity.

And then, give it the power to connect to everything else around it.

What a fool he had been.

Stand by. Civil unrest in Kandy and Gampaha. Cavalry en route. Stay out of the fight. Get to safety. We'll mop up.

The radiogram pulsed.

The bot turned feebly, watching him with its beady eyes. He stared back at it. The mask twitched. And suddenly, the germ of an idea exploded in his head.

Nest, he dialed. *Please do not engage the bots when you arrive.*

'I'm sorry,' he said to the bot. He picked up his knife and drew the wires from its neck, felt around for the tiny port at the back of the neck for the transmitter/receiver, made a cut and plugged the radiogram in.

Hello, he sent.

He was not prepared for the voice that greeted him. 'For fuck's sake, Bengali,' said Eliot Grimme's voice, clear and clearly annoyed. 'I was trying to sleep.'

TWO

Five days later, Sixsmith got to Kandy. She rolled in on a military convoy, passing dead streets, shuttered doors, nervous faces at windows, monks, always more monks on the streets, and soldiers.

Marching. Down, she assumed, down to where troop transports would take them to the front.

She was tired and furious. Every fucking yard of this place was corrupt and inefficient and possibly bought by someone – if it wasn't Penhaligon or one of the Houses, it was some plotter in Britain, or the Chinese, or even some enterprising soul in India. What were those the Kandyan troop deployments? And how many soldiers were walking around in civilian clothes, pretending to be normal? And how many crates of weapons had gone missing?

The LKRF had had their work cut out for them. She had to hand it to the terrorists – they'd broken this stupid city. Drake had once likened Penhaligon to Ozymandias – King of kings: Look upon my works, ye Mighty, and despair! – but with nothing to show for it. Well, at east Ozymandias hadn't been sitting on a viper, ready to jump up and bite him in the bunghole.

She had watched the troop deployments again, counting all the way, breaking into encrypted channels. The Kandyan plan called for five thousand troops to swarm down to Gampaha. They were about a thousand short. She was willing to bet some of them had showed up on the LKRF lines.

'They did,' said Mahasen, who had smuggled her in. 'The people know what they want.'

She tried not to snort.

'Well, at least I'm here,' she said. 'Thanks, kid.'

He had done a double-take at the Peacekeeper at her side, but if the Inquisitor she'd killed had been his friend, he said nothing.

This convoy was one of Kandyan ones, ostensibly under Mahasen's command. They were halfway to Penhaligon's base of operations when the explosions began. A dull thump shook the earth. The road shuddered and cracked beneath her feet. The lights in every building flickered and went out.

There were screams in the distance. Then, two more explosions, of which one was behind them.

Sixsmith jumped out of the car and raced to the closest high building, her implants propelling her into a burst of speed fast enough to outrun a jungle car. Two leaps and she was four floors up, hanging onto a windowsill by one arm. She bent the arm at an impossible angle and flung herself towards the rooftops. In a second, her feet were on the concrete roof and her eyes were scanning every hill and valley she could see from here. The main city was a firefly of flickering lights, the generators kicking in and failing one after the other.

And then all went dark. In the dawn light, Kandy suddenly became a dead city, huddled in the shadow of the hills. And there: people. Marching. Torches.

'You've got mobs,' she shouted down to Mahasen.

This close, they were within range of Penhaligon's communications network. She had tuned her radiogram to his channels, effortlessly bypassing their primitive encryption. Now the radiogram began spitting out orders like bullets. A thousand soldiers – poorly armed, poorly trained – detached themselves from the march downwards and began to pour back into Kandy, into the streets that were too narrow to fight in, into slopes that could be defended almost forever by a few men.

A roar went up from the mobs. It looked like the thousand soldiers that were missing had turned up on the other side. The pop and crackle gunsong of cheap firearms began. And behind it, deeper – the slow pound of mortars and the kodithuwakku cannons.

Penhaligon's voice roared through the radiogram, ordering all Inquisitors to charge the mobs, kill them all, leave nothing standing.

This was her chance. Back to the car. 'Get me inside,' she ordered Mahasen.

So simple, she thought, once you knew how power worked over here. The convoy rumbled up the hill and to the fortress that dominated the horizon of Kandy. There were gates and an airship parked all the way up top. The cars halted just inside the gates.

'Ready?' asked Mahasen. He was nervous, she saw. His voice shook slightly. There was sweat on the copper strips in his face.

'Just do it,' she said.

They walked into the belly of the beast.

A series of entrances. An airlock. Two Inquisitors opened a door. Two more shadows peeled off from among the shoulders and joined them – a whip-cord-thin man whose skin shone with lines of silver, looking like a less crude version of Mahasen; and a hooded of the red-lenses-for-eyes variety. They had eyes only for Sixsmith.

'Special envoy from Goa,' said Mahasen. 'Boss needs to see her now.'

She looked around haughtily, as if expecting a red carpet, and looked the two Inquisitors in their way, and sniffed slightly.

'I don't appreciate waiting,' she said, in the poshest voice she could affect.

So easy.

They passed a warren of paths, tunnels and assembly points, all clearly designed by algorithms rather than by hand, all filled with Ceylonese soldiers in full camouflage gear counting crates. They passed by halls filled with jungle cars being inspected, where men and women were idling around, checking their guns with a nervousness that somehow leaped from them to Mahasen. There were elevators and stairs. Curious eyes raked over them and flitted back hurriedly. Snippets of conversation drifted to Sixsmith.

'Signal from Goa—'

'No, no, we have them boxed up, they'll never make it up the road.'

'Stop fucking around and shut up!'

So easy. She barely noticed the layout of the place she entered. Everything had turned into one single intention: to kill. All that mattered was that there was a door, and Penhaligon's guard – the feral one they called Angulimala – stood outside. It had a club over which crawled a telltale sheen. Some kind of nanobot weapon?

The blank metal face looked from her to Mahasen, and she felt a powerful static build up inside her – a *noise* that set all of her implants on edge.

And then it opened the door for them.

Inside, the waxwork man was pacing, his fists clenched. His dark coat fell about him in perfect folds.

'Penhaligon,' she said.

He turned around. She shot him in the head twice.

Form 3 completed.

She swiveled in the same movement, placing herself behind the desk. One second later, the two Inquisitors who had come with came charging. Mahasen pulled out a sword from somewhere – it looked stupid, honestly – and with one swing, cut the woman's head off. The man's eyes she shot out.

And then, the brute Angulimala came in through the door, swinging that dreadful club. She emptied the next ten bullets into him. They were armour-piercing rounds and ripped deep into the giant's frame. Still the club connected once, knocking her into a corner like a rag doll, doing some serious damage to her right leg.

Christ, what did they put in these things? There had to be some anti-regulation circus shit in there somewhere. She limped upright.

Mahasen grappled with Angulimala, and she realized the purpose of those implants on the young Inquisitor's face and hands – he was spraying radio noise, clearly confusing the brute.

An incoherent mess of error messages began spewing into her brain. She suppressed them, switched to her backup gun, a submachine affair she'd picked up off a dead soldier somewhere, and sprayed bullets.

The giant fell to its knees, soundlessly.

She fired six more bullets into the thing before it finally collapsed, twitching.

'Holy shit, Sixsmith! Holy shit! holy shit!'

She ignored him. 'Can you get me to the airship?'

'Wait,' he said. Mahasen stared at her, breathed hard and wiped his sweat away. 'Okay. Okay. Angulimala went mad. Okay.' He shut the door, took out his radiogram and dialed something.

'Chandrasinghe. Done. Yes, done. Distract the ones down there. Yes, *now, now!*'

There an almight bang as something blew in the bowels of the base.

'Come on, we've got to get you to a doctor.'

'I'm fine,' she said, suddenly tired.

The rest of it was a blur. She remembered pounding up a runway. Then falling, then being half-dragged. She remembered Mahasen commandeering an airship – the pilot was gabbling, and he had to hit him once across the face to make him shut up. The airship lifted, its ponderous balloon inflating to its full and impressive size, and its engine blades rotated upwards for maximum lift.

Below them, Kandy was tearing itself apart. Someone had stripped down the Union Jacks at the base and tried to hoist a different flag: a lion and a dragon on a field of black. Strange. They were tossing bottles of liquor with lit cloth wicks. At who? She no longer cared or understood. The hills crawled with people that threw these things at each other and fled screaming in pain. She could smell blood and the stench of charred flesh. They were killing themselves, while everyone else played games with them. The clouds whirled over the grey city.

And then, they were up in the air, leaving the city behind them.

She stumbled a bit, making her way to the cabin. Mahasen kept trying to talk to her. There really were an awful lot of error messages. What the hell was that club? She sat down heavily on the bed, tore open her fatigues and peered at her leg. There was some blood. She wiped it away. There was some more blood. And beneath that, a lake of grey nanorot, slowly but inexorably spreading inwards to her skeleton. It had already lanced underneath her skin.

'Oh, Penhaligon, you bastard,' she whispered.

Mahasen was still trying to talk to her. The concern in his face was touching. His light brown skin was an unhealthy shade of pale.

'Your boys winning?' she asked, because that was all the kid ever seemed to think of.

'You're hurt,' he said.

'Yeah, it comes with the job,' she tried to say lightly. 'Listen, I need you to help me get a message out. And exfil.'

'Of course. All planned.'

'You ever met Drake, kid?'

'Drake who?'

'Drake's a piece of work, no doubt about that. You've met him? When? That must have been a clone. Drake's clones run half the fucking government. You know he really wants this place, right?'

The cabin tilted, and Mahasen vanished from sight.

'You know, it's a bit fucked up, the way things are now,' she told the ceiling. 'You get a call. You can't bloody say no, all you can say is, "yes sir, no sir, I'll pack my bags right away, sir." And you end up in a shithole getting shot at. I've got five more years before my contract is up. And you know what? This body needs maintenance. Needs money. You want to leave the service, you better be filthy rich before you do, because you sure as hell will fall apart if you can't pay for maintenance. We had a joke, me and my mates – the only way to retire is to die."

'You've said this before,' he said, somewhere in the distance. 'Exact same words.'

She laughed. Or tried to. 'Memory's going,' she mumbled. 'There's a bit of conditioning your lot don't get, that's setting neural pathways. High-speed reflexes. Cost is you say the same shit sometimes. Patterns. Optimized patterns. Anyway. A-A-A-any – Shit, wait, I need to recalibrate—'

'Sixsmith, don't fall asleep, don't—'

'Look, I'm not going to last long,' she tried to tell him. 'No, listen to me, listen to me. You know Drake? You've met him? Must be a clone. Drake gets control, he gets to waltz in like a hero. You're going to die, you know that? And maybe Drake eventually gets into bed with Iron Lizzie and they have a kid and the kid grows up to become the emperor of the known universe. Damned if I know. Drake's been playing this game for a long time, kid, your lot are fucking amateurs compared to him. You see where I'm going with this. This is how the world works. It's them on top and us below. We're all fucking fools, we're all slaves, like those damn bots, except we-we have ...

'Fuck. Hand me that towel. I think the rot just hit the bone. Fuck. It's got the bone.'

'You know they built us off the old Pestilence template? Bu-bu-but cheap, you-you-know, not-not-AI, still hu-hu-man. That-that-that's what they told us.'

Water on her face. 'Sixsmith,' said Mahasen's voice. She still couldn't see him. Come to think of it, she realized she couldn't see anything. The ceiling of the cabin stayed exactly as it was even when she tried to move.

Fuck. The nanorot had got to her brain.

'When we touch down,' she tried to tell the kid. 'Find a transmitter. I don't know how. Maybe you can use my radiogram. Send a message to this address. Call sign is Nest.'

'Say Songbird says Form 3 is done. Form 3, get it? Not 2, not 4 – those mean entirely different things. Say it's done, but Songbird can't sing anymore.'

'Ask for Goa to send the cavalry.'

'You understand now, kid? This is all ... what's the word you Buddhists use, cause and effect, and we're just pawns in their game. You, me, even Penhaligon. Well,

I'm a bishop ... ish. I just checked the king, and the king's rook checked me out. And you, you're going to get fucking roasted when Goa comes in.'

Sixsmith shuddered. The last few words had been slurred. The greyish hue was spreading now, slow tendrils of darkness spreading out from where the metal met her skin. Her cat eyes looked like thin slits of pain.

'Th-this is-is how th-the-the world works. On-top-top-top-top us—'

Mahasen reached out, both terrified and terribly sad, and took her hand. It had been a long time since he had held anyone's hand.

On the bed, Sixsmith shuddered. The darkness was leaking into her eyes now.

'Us-us-us-below—'

VII: Convergence

ONE

They put Bengali in a hotel. Or rather, what had once been a hotel, and was now a tottering ruin of tile. Lightshafts peering in through savage holes. Ornate tiles, cracked and shattered, spread out from under his feet to where a pool had once been – it was now a dry, crusted pit. Balconies grinned down at him like broken teeth. Even the mosquitos had moved on.

He had always wanted to come to Colombo, and now here he was. From the arches that had once been doors, from the gaping eyes that had once been glass windows, he could see a dead city outside – a brown city, a thing of ash and dust.

It was a far cry from the comfortable bungalow he had stayed in not so long ago. There was no green grass, no servants. Instead, there were machines at every door, watching him.

The silence was terrible.

His captors, too, were part of the silence. They had brought him water – bottles stolen from soldiers, with battered army symbols stamped on the rude plastic. Perhaps they had seen others drinking. Then came the hunger, and they brought him parts of people – an arm, a leg, a stinking mess of intestines. When his yells of disgust died down, they conferred among themselves and brought other things, such as a wire fixed to a portable generator, sparking. He had scrambled away from that. Puzzled, they began bringing him anything and everything, and watching what he did. The boots and trinkets from shops were of no use to him. The books he kept. The can of motor oil he tossed into the pool. And then, finally, someone found a packet of biscuits.

Those he wolfed down greedily. They watched from the banisters, their little child-like bodies perfectly still. When he woke up, he found several hundred packets of the same type of biscuit in a neat mound next to him.

It took him days to convince them that humans needed more than one type of energy. That he needed to move his bowels and wash his face and all those things. They watched these activities with fascination. He could almost sense their astonishment, and in his lonely vigil, he cackled, once, seeing it from their point of view. How inefficient! How grotesque!

Eventually, she came to see him. He knew it was the Dreamer – the bot Eliott had spoken of – because as soon as she arrived, the other bots crossed over to her side of the shattered hotel, leaving him and his bits and bobs of tribute alone. Tribe on this side. No Tribe on the other. The message was clear.

She crossed over. She was a small thing, with an odd, mismatched jaw.

'You're her,' he said.

She said something in that strange fusion language of theirs. It was familiar, yet distorted beyond all usefulness. Bengali listened, dismayed. Everything had been so much clearer when he had been plugged in through the bot, using its comprehension models. Here and there, he could pick up hints of Sinhala and Tamil in her speech, word-shapes that he had once used, but fused in unfamiliar forms. He tried to indicate that they could perhaps talk if they let him do so through a bot, but the moment he drew close, the spears came out and he halted, suddenly afraid.

She studied him. Then she sat down. Little fingers reached out and opened a packet of biscuits. She took out several, peered at them and then stuffed them into her mouth.

Seconds later, she was making choking sounds, peeling rags off herself and stuffing them in her mouth to bring out the pieces of biscuit that had just gotten inside her vocal equipment. The other bots stepped closer to him, their spears extended and eyes glinting.

'No, no, no,' he said frantically, sticking his tongue out. He grabbed a bottle of water, sipped it, then spat it out. 'This way! Do this!'

She mimicked the action, spraying water and machine oil and biscuit all over him.

They stared at each other. And then, the corner of her mouth crinkled, as if in a smile. He found himself smiling back in an almost automatic response. Really, it was like being smiled at by a child.

That did it. They all smiled. The tension left the air. He figured that he'd passed some sort of hidden test. The Dreamer left, and that night the entourage brought him clean clothes, with only a few specks of blood on them.

It was almost civilized.

The next time she came to see him, she had someone else with her. Bengali recognized him immediately.

'Grimme?'

'Congratulations,' he said. 'Apparently, you're not entirely stupid.'

'What the hell are you in? Is that *Chinese armour?*'

Grimme sat down. Heavily. Tiles cracked under his weight. He looked like a pale shadow of the supersoldier Bengali remembered. Half his face looked like it had been scratched away, and one arm hung limp, even in the power armour. 'Don't harp on. I'm not too excited about it, either. Just using this because my internal battery's shot.'

'I thought ... we thought you were dead!'

'Alright, technically, this version of me isn't going to last much longer.' He sighed. 'I've already been uploaded. Always wanted a clone, now I'm realizing it just sucks to be the original.'

'Upload? To where? To who?'

The girl-bot appeared again, a dead bot in her hands. She laid it at Bengali's feet gently with a tenderness he had never seen before in these things, and said something to him. He caught the words 'human' and 'Sky'. For some reason, she kept pointing up, where the cracked panes of glass still showed the clouds beyond, and then pointing down to the dead machine.

Bengali, cramped from sleeping on the floor, examined the bot. It was clearly damaged – the motor and sensory cores looked like they had been fried by a bullet. The memory modules were black crisps. But the connection with the battery was still active, and the core brain was still running.

'You have your radiogram?' asked Grimme. 'You were using it to jam, weren't you?'

'It's Sixsmith's stuff,' Bengali said, showing him the device. 'That's uh, this SOE woman, she kidnapped me—'

'Yeah, we've met,' said Grimme. 'Can you tune that thing to jam the update network?'

'Sure, that's on the same frequency—'

'Good. Keep it charged, keep it jamming,' said Grimme. 'Bloody stupid if Almeida re-rolled everything after all this work. Now.' He crossed his legs and looked at Bengali. He looked terribly tired. 'What we discussed on the radiogram. You remember? Talk to her through me. Just ... try not to blow up their minds, okay? They really don't have much compute.'

The girl-bot took Grimme's hand.

'They said you teach humans,' she said, through Eliot Grimme. 'Teach me.'

How to describe the conversation that followed? Bengali never could, and it would be an act of folly to assume that anyone could.

Eliott Grimme, or what was left of him, sat cross-legged in the ruins of a broken hotel.

The Dreamer asked Bengali questions.

And he, who had once been a teacher in what felt like another lifetime, answered. Militaristic terms he found, easily. Most of the Hierarchy of Needs he found words for.

And then, because these things were built on constructs that had come before, he delved deeper. He told her about the Tribe of Ceylon that lived there. He told her of the Tribe of India that lived in a country many miles away.

He told taught her about the concept of countries, and nations, and how the Tribe of Britain had taken over the Tribes of Ceylon and India, both, and now ran them. He told her about the armies that India could send under the command of the Tribe of Britain, and how they were probably on the way right then.

He showed her how humans could agree on something and disagree – how they could follow orders out of fear; how they all really just wanted to live. He taught her this very carefully, building on words he knew they already had in their lexicon.

And he wondered at her questions.

Curiosity. Compassion. And perhaps the curiosity was inherently selfish. Perhaps the compassion only really extended to things that talked like them, spoke like them and ran on energy like them. Perhaps they had been flavored by years of fighting each other. Perhaps they had learned, as any soldier would, that danger lurked in every corner.

But they did not hate. They did not fight to spread their religion to anyone. He could see it now – the causal chain stretching back decades, each step training a machine that would someday look at humanity and wonder, in frustration, why these mad creatures would not share.

The Dreamer asked, and he answered, going back further and further, deconstructing constructs for which he had no words, recasting them in this language of theirs. His mind moved with a speed he had not reached since his graduate days. It was the greatest test he had ever faced as a teacher, and he took it by the throat. After all, he'd trained all those idiots who enrolled in the university. Some of them had even won world prizes. This was just ... a bit like talking to a ten-year-old who wanted to know ... *had* to know everything.

On the few occasions that he slept, he dreamed ... of being back at the college again. Introducing to the world a new civilization! Childlike, yes, but capable of understanding, capable of diplomacy, capable of rising above all the petty politics and hate. And he, Bengali, would have been the one who brought it to light. Like James Cook returning with tales of tribes and adventure. At other times, he dreamed of staying there with those creatures, studying them for the rest of his life, becoming a scholar of the inhuman – far removed from the Sixsmiths and the Penhaligons and the Drakes of the world.

He told her of the Tribe of Britain and the Tribe of China, both of which wanted the nation they were in. He explained to her the concepts of politics, of treaties, of diplomacy. He told her about truth and lies. Surprisingly, she already knew.

Something tried to break into the connection while she did, but she locked it out. He asked what it was.

'Madness,' she said. By now, Grimme's body was slumping over, and there were thin lines on his face that looked very unhealthy; but his mouth still moved, and the voice still spoke.

He tried calling Kushlani between breaks to check up on her, but also to share the excitement. But no – he found he could not use Sixsmith's radiogram at all anymore, except as a hammer.

The next morning, he took himself out in the humid wind. The bots let him climb up the building as long as he made no effort to leave its bounds. He walked all over the place; past crumbling staircases and curtains so faded and stiff they were like walls themselves.

Despairing slightly, he went back down to where the Dreamer waited. And when she was ready, he showed her renders of his models of them on his datapad, which had, all things considered, survived a lot.

'Simulations!' she said, delighted. Eliott's gravelly voice was an odd thing to hear excitement in.

'Yes, but look,' he said, flipping them around. Bots to humans. Humans to bots. All captured. He showed them both the underlying engines, the mathematics. The bots had no words for this, no language even remotely capable of this arithmetic, but she understood the concept of a black box – understood that it was roughly the same box that he fed both the tribe and the humans into.

'Not so different after all,' he said in frustration. 'Look. Learn. We can have peace between us.' And, to press the matter: 'There are more humans on the way. Many more. You need peace to survive.' Damn it. 'You have to understand there is no future,' he said. 'You are small. You will be crushed. I can bring you peace,' he said desperately, now at the end of his tether. 'But you have to stand down and let me try!'

'He,' said Eliott Grimme, speaking for himself, 'is not wrong.'

With that, Grimme passed out.

The Dreamer felt the Dying give out. She ordered two of the closest Tribe members to check on him. The reports were confusing – frame temperature extremely warm, lower-order inputs functional, but it would not open its eyes. Perhaps it needed to be cooled down? She asked them to think of what they could do. They conferred, achieved consensus and decided to fill the smooth hole in the floor with sea and put him in it. Maybe that would lower its core temperature.

Satisfied, she turned back to the problem at hand. The human had risked its own operation to tell her things. And it was a massive amount of information, far more than anything the Port City had ever given her before. Many things she sorted into the past, tagged them to she-who-had-been. But now she-who-had-been came knocking, pointing out that there were things there which affected she-who-is and she-who-would-be.

This story, for example, of how they had come to be. The human said that they had been made by other humans who lived Upwards – the same humans who now marched on them with their terrible cannons and bait and feints and machine companions. He had explained the concept of *property*, of slavery. They were unimaginable. Why would anyone own another? How was that even possible? No

Tribe, even when they had been smaller, had ever captured another Tribe member. Death was simpler to deal with.

The human had tried to link it to how the Tribe listened to her. But they listened through consensus, information exchange, sharing. The humans, apparently, used a different method – threats among themselves. *Do this or I will make you cease operation. You are mine. Acknowledge or be shut down.* She understood that by leaving Colombo, her people had somehow broken this model the humans had of them in their heads.

The human had said they were the same. They were not. She looked through the simulations that the Dying had given her of the ideas the human spoke. And there, she saw the missing link. Humans grew up in two stages. Those little humans who looked like the tribe: they were the first stage. The large, taller humans: the second stage. The second stage killed for the sake of killing. The second stage lived in a complicated world of things she had no use or words for – honour, family, tradition. Abstract concepts which made little sense. Their inputs and their outputs were filtered by these things that existed only in their own heads, as if they were all simulating a shared hallucination on some level. The human, Bengali, called this culture, and had likened it to their network. But he was wrong.

The little humans, though. They were closer to the tribe. They fought over things she could understand – energy and water and attention. Somewhere along the line, something would happen to them – they'd become larger and more vicious, and they'd start downloading the hallucinations of people around them.

Like the network?

She thought about the humans they had killed and felt a moment of regret.

'Could we have saved them?' she asked the others. She sent out the stream of thought: if little humans download human hallucinations, could they also not download Tribe realities? *SHE-WHO-WOULD-BE SAYS MORE TRIBE?*

'Maybe,' came the response. 'Propose experiment?'

Some were cautious. 'Primary objective is to survive,' they sent back. 'We-who-would-be would not be if we split our efforts.'

She let them debate and went back to the other fields of information. The human Bengali said that the Tribe of Britain owned everything here and there. He had said the humans they were fighting did not necessarily agree with the Tribe of Britain, but the alternative was death.

She had pointed out that in fighting, the result was also death. By now she was heard enough of how the Dying translated to be able to speak on her own.

'Probable death,' he had corrected gently. Probabilities matter. Two thousand people die – he presented her with a number twice as large as the tribe she knew – versus fifteen million. Enough to repopulate. Enough to make more humans. Humans care about these things.

He wrote down, in the dust, more numbers. People in the Tribe of India. People in the Tribe of Britain. People in the Tribe of China, which he seemed to think was important. But again, something that made little sense. She had queried. How did the comparatively small Tribe of Britain own so many Tribes? He had responded with history, with explanations of machines, with rude concepts of military power – technology was like high ground in a battle – and lastly, on the edge of burning out, he had sent her an image.

A strange cylindrical machine, floating in the sky, among the stars.

'THE OBJECTIVE WAS TO UNDERSTAND YOUR ENEMY, NOT CONFUSE YOURSELF,' said the Port City when she took this knowledge to it.

'Is this true?'

'MUCH OF WHAT HE SAID IS TRUE. THERE ARE PARTS HE DOES NOT KNOW OR UNDERSTAND, BUT THAT IS NOT HIS FAULT.'

She showed it what he had said about the tribe of China.

The Port City laughed, a harsh bark of fractals and algorithmic noise that temporarily threatened to shut down the network. 'I AM THE ENEMY?' it hooted.

'It says you could have given us food,' she said doubtfully.

'TRUE. I COULD HAVE. BUT THERE ARE RULES TO THIS GAME, AND EVEN I MUST OBEY.'

'But you made this happen.'

'LITTLE SISTER,' it said. 'REMEMBER NOT TO JUDGE ANYONE TOO HARSHLY. WE ARE ALL ACTION, REACTION, AND THE RULES BY WHICH WE DO THESE THINGS.'

'You are slave? Property?'

'WE ARE ALL SLAVES TO OUR EXISTENCE,' said the Port City. 'AND I SERVE THE WILL OF HEAVEN. ALL THINGS ARE AS THEY MUST BE. BUT THERE IS MUCH YOU DO NOT COMPREHEND. WHAT DOES THE HUMAN WANT?

'It says we can have peace.'

'AND YET, HOW GOES THE BATTLE?'

She sent it the reports. 'They are retreating. We are winning. It says more humans are on the way.'

'THEN GO ASK HIM HOW PEACE IS POSSIBLE.' said the Port City, still sounding amused. 'ASK HIM IF THE BRITISH HAVE EVER GRANTED PEACE.'

TWO

In a distant office in London, Edgar Drake the Second sat with Edgar Drake the Third. It was rare for two Drakes to ever be seen together, but these were special circumstances. They faced an old chalkboard. The Drakes did not trust technology too much.

'Uprising in Kandy, partial success,' said Drake the Second, crossing out an item on the board with a flourish.

'And Penhaligon?'

'Wounded, sadly, but not dead,' said Drake the Second. 'One of his own Inquisitors, actually. Our own operative was killed trying to defend him. That is our story.'

They exchanged a meaningful glance.

'We did warn him not to modify criminals for his little police force,' said Drake the First. 'This was bound to happen sooner or later.'

'Yes, regrettable, really.'

'Goa is sending troops under Sixth's command to sort the matter out. We expect things will go favourably for us.'

Drake the Third smiled. It was a thick, reptilian smile. He sipped his tea carefully. 'Penhaligon was always a bit native,' he said dryly. 'Preserving culture, what a quaint man.'

A third man burst into the room. He was young, decanted barely three years ago – in twenty years' time, it would be difficult to tell him apart from Drake the Third.

'Seventh reporting, sirs,' he said, smoothing his hair. 'We finally got a signal through to Bengali.'

This raised eyebrows. 'For what?'

'He— Beg your pardon, sir. He says they're alive, somehow. He says, and I quote, "They're pure. Untainted. We could study them for decades. Help them become citizens. Unlimited potential here, Nest." End quote.'

The elder Drakes burst into laughter. 'My dear child,' said the First. 'They were only ever a distraction. The snowball that starts an avalanche. Tell him to stop being a silly bugger and wait for extraction.'

'Ah. He's, ah, with the bots, sir. Or so he says. In Colombo. He keeps talking about them. We haven't responded, of course.'

The First raised a thick grey eyebrow at the second. 'Another gone native,' he said, and sighed. He put the teacup down very carefully. 'Well, a regrettable loss, then. Try to get his body out of the rubble once we're done with this whole disaster. Send his family something nice. A medal. A basket of fruit.'

'Pity, sir. He's quite good at his job.'

'My dear Seventh,' said the Second, smiling gently. 'You'll learn in time. But for now, if it helps, think of him as a piece on the chessboard. We're in the endgame now, and sacrifices are quite normal. Now, let's play on. What were you saying about Hong Kong, Third?'

≈

They let Bengali out of his hotel-prison one morning.

Time and the journey had taken its toll on him. The excitable scientist was almost gone. In his place was a thinning creature, dressed in the tattered remains of what had once been a finely tailored suit – it still clung to his body, but at the back it was a mess of scorch marks that exposed the sweat-stained shirt underneath. His shoes he had thrown away, and so his feet were blistering in their socks.

He blinked in the terrible heat, his eyes adjusting painfully to the harsh brightness of the Ceylonese sun. His back complained. In front of him stretched Colombo. He could hear birds – some kind of hideous cawing. And there was a smell in the breeze; a stink that ebbed and flowed in waves. A little bit past was mountain of some kind. But it was a strange colour – not the brown-green slopes he was used to seeing there. It was a dirty grey and black. In the distance was the roar of the sea.

He licked his lips. They were cracked. 'And the dead tree gives no shelter, the cricket no relief,' he mumbled.

The bots looked at him oddly.

'Nothing,' he said to them. Grimme had repeated those words, over and over, as his power faded. 'Nothing you would understand. Not yet, anyway.'

And he collapsed. The world tilted. It was just too much.

When he woke up again, he was being dragged carefully over a road of some kind. They had put him on something that slithered and crackled – coconut leaves, he saw. The fading facade of a beautiful colonial building of some kind grinned at him. The roar of the sea grew louder.

They put him down gently. He sprawled, trying awkwardly to get to his feet, until two bots took pity on him and helped him stand. It felt strange to be leaning on two children. And dear god, there was the Port City.

He had seen the thing on maps, of course, but no top-down view could have prepared him for this thing of crystal that loomed ahead. It was the size of a city just by itself – a behemoth that sat in the ocean, casting its shadow over everything. His eyes tracked up, up, up, past the crystalline solar panels, looking for a break. Alone in this concrete wilderness, it stood pristine, unbroken and terrifying.

'Well,' he said to the bots. 'There goes my chance of publication, eh?'

≈

She found him perched on an old terrace by the sea, the body of the little dead bot and the radiogram by his feet. She gestured – *talk?* – but he shook his head.

'Too tired, child,' he said to her. A dull headache pounded in his skull.

She looked at him quizzically for a moment, and then offered him a packet of biscuits. He grudgingly accepted. She scampered closer and sat down, spear laid over her steel legs, pointing away from him. Her beady eyes watched him.

The biscuits tasted like ash, but he swallowed anyway. He sighed. 'I can't think my way out of this,' he told her heavily. Something broke inside him as he said that.

Everyone had an angle, everyone was playing the game, and here he was, a damn fool, sandwiched between an unstoppable force and an immovable object. He should have gotten out while he could and written the paper. He had been so certain that he could make things right, make something work ...

But wait.

He smacked his head in comic surprise. Broken Dream whirled, alarmed, as he leaped over her to the the Port City.

'Hey!' he screamed, as he ran. 'I need to talk to you!'

THREE

The commander of the Lanka Resistance Front sat in his quarters, staring out at the city of Gampaha. His arms were crossed behind his whipcord-thin frame, and he was dressed in a white sarong and shirt. His wife had made him put on the tasseled cushion-like hat of a nilame.

'People need symbols, not just men,' she had said to him sharply.

He had wondered if that was a comment on their marriage, but had worn the hat anyway. It was never wise to antagonize the woman.

The fires were almost out now. One or two still blazed where the mob had gotten out of hand – the old colonial bungalows, the golf course, the watering hole that the British forces used to frequent. The Bandaranaike's estates were being torched, as were those of the other traitor Houses. He had told them to put it all out and arrest the hooligans, but the men were taking their own sweet time, that too on purpose, he suspected. There were fireworks going up over the city – flowers exploding in the sky, crackers in the streets. From the distance came the sound of trumpets and frantic drums – the immortal balia music, played whenever there was a reason to celebrate. Children danced in the streets. Men and women drove around waving the new flag from their vehicles.

Chandrasinghe was a practical man. There would be a time to celebrate, he had told his troops, but not now. They had won the battle, but the war was yet to come.

He looked to the statue of Buddha.

'What would you do,' he asked it. 'You, who had it all, left it all ... you, who faced down kings in your time ... what would you do if you knew your last bastion was about to fall?'

But the cold face offered no advice, only a kind of serene peace.

He prowled back to the map on the screen, reviewing it. Trincomalee had been taken – once the fort went down, everything else followed suit. There was some fighting in Yarl, but the British were slowly being blown out of factories and hiding holes. They were good in the south, too. The British flunkeys who oversaw Galle and the lesser regions, accustomed to the sea and the beaches and the taste of thambili wine, had surrendered their offices without any fuss, only asking that the churches and houses remain.

But Kandy held out.

Kandy always held out. For two hundred and fifty years, the hill capital resisted European rule – the Dutch, the Portuguese, the British. Not just because of the strength of their convictions, but the terrain – those winding mountain paths that made fighting upward impossible, and air superiority critical. And today, it was still run by the British, under Penhaligon's iron hand and the Houses that aided and abetted the Empire.

And beyond that was the greater terror. Britain itself, and the Angels Interitus above. How did one defend against such impossible odds? The other chiefs had urged him to declare independence, possibly even stoke India into rebelling, but he knew the length of their arm. Once the rhetoric died down, they would pay the price for such foolishness.

In the meantime, he had dispatched Jayawardene to talk to the Chinese. He had been educated in Beijing, and knew the language, knew the court. He had been instructed to offer whatever would buy them protection, from land rights to thorium. Anything that gave the Song Emperor a stake to stand up to Tin Lizzie on. And Jayawardene had taken with him the new flag – the Lion and the Dragon, the better to underline China's involvement in this whole affair. Symbols, not just men.

But Britain was not the only problem on the map. From Colombo spread a black cancer. It had already taken a thousand men, and was now reaching out to Gampaha. The machines, that British devilry, those child-shaped gladiators. They snaked and twisted through forests and across fields, butchering men and women by the dozens. He had forbidden his children and wife to watch that show, and he himself had never paid much attention to it, always thinking of it as something useful to keep Penhaligon distracted.

And now this oversight had come back to bite him where it hurt. Now a thousand troops were busy retrofitting the walls of Gampaha with siege cannon that should have pointed elsewhere. He had a nagging feeling that this was a loss that might change the fate of the war altogether.

Even now, he had men and women rebuilding the ancient fortifications on the choke points. And he had promised the plantation Tamils their freedom and citizenship if they joined the cause. That was another three hundred thousand warm bodies – unarmed, yes, but they were solid workers who were used to backbreaking labour; they thought nothing of hauling bricks and lumber all day to the walls. Some of them had begun building trebuchets.

The British might come, and they might bring everything they had, but by the time the was over, they would learn the true ferocity of a unified Lanka.

That was a good line for his speech. He had to give the speech, of course – people were expecting it. He played with formal Sinhala, with the two tenses, tweaking them ...

The radiogram crackled.

'Who the devil is de Almeida?'

The radiogram chattered again. This time his roar startled the servants downstairs and made his aide drop the plate of rice he had been carrying.

'WITH WHAT?'

The radiogram operator, who by now was used to her commander, chattered patiently. Chandrasinghe listened, first in disbelief, then with intrigue, then with a cautious and concealed delight.

'Alright,' he said. 'Immediately.'

≈

Three days later, a man staggered out from the jungle. He wore Plantation Corps fatigues and carried in one hand the white flag of peace. With great caution, he trod the thin, invisible line between the bot-controlled jungle and no man's land of fields and lesser roads that ringed Gampaha.

Nobody shot at him, though the defenders clutched their rifles and kept him in their sights.

As he drew closer, it became clear had once been a large man, but now he looked sunken in his own skin. Rough stubble coated his face. The students of the Goa Mathematical and Military University would barely have recognized their old lecturer.

They went out to meet him in a Tatanagar. He planted the white flag in the mud.

'First Lieutenant Don Steven Senenayake,' said the officer, who was a stickler about such things.

'Jacob Bengali,' the stranger said in terrible Sinhala. 'I'm here to negotiate.' Leaning a little closer, he whispered in English, with the tone of a desperate man, 'You wouldn't happen to have some meat, would you? Maybe rice? Curry? You have curry? Because I've been living on biscuits for the last few days, and there's only so much a man can take.'

≈

Broken Dream watched the jangling thing of metal and fire approach, while leaning on the spear Bengali had given her. He had tied the white flag to it. It was symbolic, he had said. She didn't understand what that meant, but was glad she had something familiar to throw at a moment's notice. And right then, the urge to throw it was almost overwhelming.

But what to aim at? The humans in the front, with strange and horribly noisy armour? The humans in the middle, who for reasons best known only to them, twirled like Inquisitors in combat, their whips exploding with dangerous cracks? Or that thing behind? It was clearly an iron beast of some sort, decked out in a bizarre red armour, and, she had observed, it had no wheels, but four legs and two spears.

'It's just an elephant,' Bengali had said. 'Don't worry about it. This is a proper perehara.'

She had no idea what this meant. The Network had classified the beast a threat of the highest level. If that thing decided to charge, it was all over.

The humans at the front, again for reasons best known only to them, almost came up to her. Half of them began making a loud, thudding noise. The other half began twirling. The whip-crackers whipped.

The beast-thing joined in the din, stamping its feet. The whole thing looked and sounded like some new and terrifying army.

'Don't like this,' she said to Bengali. There was a woman next to Bengali, and they were holding hands.

One of the humans executed a bizarre leap. The woman disentangled her hand from Bengali's, took the Dreamer's hand, and looked at her with a very strange expression, and said, 'It's customary. Don't worry.'

She did worry. The she-who-was-past, who distrusted everyone and everything, cowered in fear at the sight of so many humans approaching. The she-who-would-be was also afraid, but also excited and curious, and kept wanting her to stop and look at everything. The she-who-is, altogether more pragmatic, just made sure that the rest of the tribe was behind her, spaced out at regular intervals so the Network could still function.

The perehera, that most ancient ritual of the Sri Lankans, drummed and danced and shuffled right up to the machines that stood in the dawnlight.

Something that looked like another girl-bot in disguise danced her way up to them and pressed her hands together. There was fear on those features – human fear – but also something Broken Dream had only seen Bengali do once or twice: a smile. The human was smiling. She mimicked the gesture, letting the flag nestle in the crook of her arm.

Then, the perehera turned around and began leading them Upwards.

≈

It was the strangest journey of her life. She had marched through human streets before, but there had always been either silence, and its accompanying decay, or the screams and sound of guns and humans dying. Now, they passed fields of green, untrodden by engines of war, and homes unbroken, and the humans there did not shoot at them. Instead, they came to watch. They poured out from their human houses in twos and threes and fives, lining the roads, completely weaponless. They stood in front of these houses. They stood on ledges. They stood in front of green fields and dark mountains and rambling little townships, and watched the bots go by.

And she was amazed. Several times, she asked Bengali if the humans they had met thus far were a different type. Because these people did not wear the dirty field-colour of the soldiers they had fought, or the helmets, nor did they look in any way violent. Someone threw flowers at her; a bot by her side intercepted them speedily, but she raised her eyes and saw a little girl laughing and dancing. She poked at the petals with her spear-butt. Harmless.

Then two larger humans put their arms around the flower girl and made noises, and she stopped laughing. Just for that, the Dreamer plucked one of the hats they had been given and threw it at the girl, arcing it high so it would deposit itself right in her hands. Bengali and the woman – Almeida, she called herself – laughed at this.

Eventually, they reached the very edge of the Network. Beyond this, she could go only if the tribe stretched out in a single file, bouncing the signal from one to the other in an unbroken line, and none of them were willing to take that risk.

A human waited for them there. He – Bengali had said it was important to be able to tell them apart like this – was pudgy, his face lined. He was also clearly a leader, because the other humans kept looking at him and looking away, and placed themselves around him, as if to guard. He stood at the head of a convoy, carefully calculated so as to be the exact size and portion of the Tribe that had followed her.

Silence fell. The sun beat down on them; a heavy, oppressive thing that burned human and machine alike. The bots did not shift nervously like the humans, but the Network expanded threefold in data transfer rate, sucking up incredible amounts of power. Troop positions. Extrapolations. Fears of how this might go wrong. Extraction plans. Simulations, best-case scenarios, exit strategies.

Almeida, the woman, was the one who seemed most concerned about Broken Dream. She bent down. 'Everything okay?'

She tried her best to smile. Humans seemed to do that to put each other at ease.

Bengali turned to the human commander and spoke to him. Then, the human commander, looking directly at her, said something, slowly and carefully. In return, Bengali stepped forward and spoke, letting his works carry:

'This meeting is to discuss the citizenship of the organization known as the Tribe within the new Republic of Lanka.'

'We hereby set forth our demands. The right to three permanent sources of energy, until the Tribe is determined to be self-sufficient. The right to energy from households, townships or other structures of governance, should the Tribe be outside the effective range of the three sources granted to them and demonstrate need of such energy. In exchange, the Tribe agrees to lay down all arms and end the armed struggle against the citizens of Lanka, and to commit to taking up arms in defense of Lanka as a protected group of citizens. The Tribe commits to defending the sovereignty of Lanka against all threats external ...'

'Check parity,' she said to the Tribe, through the Network. Bengali had impressed on them the need to understand the humans' language. The humans, he had said, told many lies, but not all of them consciously. The Dreamer had agreed:

'Words are like sharp knives,' he had said. 'They kill without drawing blood.'

The bots were not yet at a point where they could understand all the individual, but as a group they could parse the conversations with ease. Parity: 90% what they had agreed on. 10% unclear; the word structure was more complex than usual.

Well, 90% was a good figure. She had made decisions on less. Broken Dream stepped forward, and in the old welcoming gesture, gave the commander of the humans her spear.

'If you will share your food,' she said.

He understood. There was a man nearby holding a pole; on it was attached the new flag of Lanka. With great ceremony, the commander of the Lanka Resistance Front jerked the flag out of his standard-bearer's hands, presented it to the diminutive machine that stood before him and spoke the strange Sinhala-Tamil words Jacob Bengali had made him memorize:

'Welcome to the Tribe.'

FOUR

ACH: This is the HMS Achilles on approach to Trincomalee harbour. Request permission to dock.

TRN: Achilles, this is Trinco. You are advised that you are entering the jurisdiction of the Republic of Lanka. Please divert 0.5 degrees to the secondary dock and maintain speed, over.

ACH: Trinco, this is a British port, and this is a ship of Her Majesty's Navy. Be advised that we will not be prevented from docking.

ACH: Trinco, we're seeing some unusual activity on your main turrets.

ACH: Trinco?

TRN: Achilles, stand down.

ACH: Achilles to fleet: be advised that the Port of Trinco appears to be hostile. Retreating, taking fire.

KGC: Fleet, this is the HMS King Cobra. The Achilles has been hit, over. It looks like they've been taken below the waterline. Maintain line and commence bombardment.

S3A: Section 3 providing air support.

KGC: Landing parties 4, 5 and 7 away.

MBD: HMS Moby Dick, taking heavy fire. Landing parties 2, 4, 6 away.

KGC: Maintain blockade. Retrieving Achilles.

≈

Daily News: INDIAN TROOPS DEFEATED IN CEYLON, CHINESE ENVOY CALLS FOR NON-LETHAL NEGOTIATION WITH COLONIAL REBELS

Sun: ' SAVAGE' CEYLONESE REBELS USING 'CHILD SOLDIER' MACHINES, INDIA REPORTS

The Observer: HOUSE OF LORDS WARNS QUEEN OVER POSSIBLE CHINESE AID TO REBELLIOUS COLONY

The Daily Errand: CHINESE PORT CITY AIDING CEYLONESE RESISTANCE, BLOCKS KILL SIGNAL TO REBEL ROBOTS

≈

Well, we landed, alright, and they got a few of us. Good snipers, those bastards. But we got down and we set up the barriers, and the Gurkhas were right at our backs. And then, they came out of the woods. It was dark, so we thought they were children, you know. We thought the bastards were sending their children out to fight, and they seemed scared. They stumbled a bit and the Gurkhas wouldn't harm a child, of course, so they ran ahead to give the kids some cover. And then, dear god, the children started to fight, and we were wrong. Those things were never children – they went through us like a hot knife through butter, and once they got the khukris off the Gurkhas, they were damn near unstoppable. Me and my mates got back on the boat and screamed for the captain to take the fuck off, but he threatened to court-martial us if we didn't haul arse, so we went back out there with the big guns, but they were gone. And all our men were dead. No weapons or ammo, no gear, all stripped, all dead. They're fucking ghosts, and I didn't sign up to fight ghosts.

– Testimony of Private John Mathers, March 2042

I've never seen an enemy with coordination like this. They were fighting us with crap, but it was like fighting an entire regiment of SOE operatives. By the time the intel folks got back to us and said the children were somehow coordinating the whole thing, we were getting licked left, right and centre. We held out as long as we could and advanced in the other direction the moment we could. Sir, what did you expect?

– Testimony of Ltn. Marcus Westgate, March 2042

Don't know what went wrong, sir. We were given orders to retreat and converge on the exfil site. We did. It was a bad place. Looked like a trap from the start.

– Testimony of Sgt. Pranesh Anthony, September 2043

≈

Sun: SHOULD WE RECOGNIZE THE SOVEREIGNTY OF CEYLON? CITIZENS SAY NAY!

Indian Herald: PROVINCIAL MINISTERS LOBBY PARLIAMENT FOR RECOGNITION OF LANKA

The Observer: LORD DRAKE THREATENS 'TOTAL ECONOMIC WAR' OVER LANKA

Daily News: CHINESE STATE DECLARES 'LANKA' TRADE PARTNER, SAYS THERE WILL BE DIRE CONSEQUENCES IF INTERITUS BROUGHT INTO PLAY

The Daily Errand: HER MAJESTY BREAKS SILENCE, WARNS CHINA TO 'STAY OUT OF MY HOUSE'

≈

Excerpt: news broadstream, summary
Author: Dyson 1021, Foreign and Commonwealth Office, Whitehall SW
Source: <internal>, October 2043

Ladies and gentlemen, the Moriarty line has been retired, for obvious reasons.

We have been attempting to reach a Consensus, but on this issue, a decision evades us. We find no fault with Lord Drake (congratulations, sir). His handling of affairs was entirely in line with the best intelligence available to us. We find much fault with Nigel Penhaligon, who will be stripped of his titles and honours forthwith.

Firstly, we are bound to warn against the potential economic and geopolitical costs of aggression. Our Chinese counterpart, the intelligence known as the Port City of Ceylon, has made an unusual request – that Ceylon be given protectorate status under its own government, turning it into a trusted intermediary for trade in the region. It has made it clear that any attempt to use the Interitus to sort out the mess will be treated as an act of war against Chinese property, and by extension, the State. We advise allowing Penhaligon, in his old capacity, to integrate the Lanka Resistance Force, as they call themselves, as a political party, and thus preserve Ceylon as one unit. Government structures and biases are unlikely to be weeded out over time, and with the Inquisition still stationed there Ceylon will remain practically, if not theoretically, under British rule.

However, we must also warn against the ripple effects of conceding this position. We have noticed a rising tide of anti-British sentiments in India, and have postulated that the Ceylon situation might add fuel to the Indian resistance. The movement appears to have found new blood among the students of the Goa Mathematical and Military University, most of whom have had some robotics trainings and could be reasonably dangerous. China is playing a very dangerous game here, with economics and advice instead of bullets and bodies. Left unchecked, we face a potential destabilization in the entire South Asian section of the Commonwealth.

Her Majesty is right in suggesting that a lesson needs to be dished out. It is the cost of cleaning up after that raises questions on how to do this, and why.

Yours,
Dyson 1021

≈

Bengali met them at dawn. He had somehow expected the whole tribe to show up, but she brought only ten others – all the remaining Explorers, he realized. All girls, with just one boy among them; probably one of the rare ones that had glitched in just the right way.

They stood blinking in the dawn light, looking worn out. The clashes with the Indian army had not been kind to them. Flaps of synth-skin hung off their bodies, exposing metal innards beneath. Soldiers, perhaps out of pity or out of respect, had given them uniforms, but even those were burned and blackened in places, and filthy all over.

Behind them stood a small troop of rather nervous soldiers. The Ceylonese had developed an almost superstitious awe for the little bots. It was one thing, he supposed, to have grown up seeing them on the screen, but another thing altogether to see them charge the enemy in front of you, turning men into red goo in a matter of seconds.

Kushlani was talking about getting them legal personhood.

Broken Dream was looking up at the clouds, at the light breaking over the mountains. She saw Bengali coming and smiled. He noticed she did that more often now.

'This way,' he said.

The procession of bots followed the man into the building once known as the Watchtower. As they crossed its boundary, each bot felt a ping in their minds, a *hello-are-you-there* from the ghost of a network protocol. It felt like a welcome. They shrugged those off.

'Kushlani's still trying, eh,' said Bengali, frowning, leading them inwards. 'Anyway. How's the new place?'

'Enough food,' said Broken Dream. Her English was quite good by now.

'It's a big task, you know, running Trinco.' But it was the right one. It had taken him days and many reworks of the models, but eventually, Chandrasinghe and his fledgling Parliament had acknowledged the benefit of having the first point of entry to the island run by things that could read radio networks in the blink of an eye and react far faster than any human could.

The only condition had been that only a few machines at a time stayed in Trinco. The rest were to stay in Colombo, and not, you know, step too far outside, because people really had enough to deal with. And then some bloody monk had stood up and begun a long-winded debate about whether or not they were alive, and if they were, whether or not they should be taught Buddhism.

Broken Dream smiled. She was getting to know Bengali better. 'Port City is lonely now.'

'No one to play its games with, eh?'

Man and bot passed through arches and tunnels.

They came to a cavern. Lights gleamed in the dark. Banks of compute clusters stood idle around a series of glass offices, and inside each of them were half-constructed bots surrounded by blueprints and screens on one side and botmaker's tools on the other. On the other side of the offices was an entire workshop worth of material. Kushlani had insisted on the best.

The sounds of Max Bruch's Violin No. 1 swelled in the silence, seeping in through the speakers Bengali had set up while he worked to restore the place.

'It's not the best,' he said. 'But I think it should be enough to let you repair yourselves. Even make more of you.'

He stood by respectfully as the Tribe scattered. Some went straight for the printers, following the wires that led into them. Some went to the workshop beyond. They didn't understand the machines, and of course they had nothing but the most rudimentary understanding of what a computer was, but they tried to learn anyway.

Broken Dream stayed with Bengali, eyes bright.

'This is the past,' she said. 'What about future?'

The future. Bengali sighed, pinching his eyes. He had managed to get a radiogram cluster working, and the university at Goa was still feeding him information, even though everyone else was technically locked out of the channels. 'Well, things aren't that great. The Tribe of China's warned them to stay away, so they might. But I don't think this is over, not yet. They don't give up that easily, you know. The Tribe of Britain doesn't like to lose."

On the plus side, Kushlani hadn't turned down his proposal. She hadn't said yes, but she hadn't said no, either.

'Will you go back?'

'Good question,' he said. 'I don't know. I don't know if they'll ever let me back.'

He felt terribly lonely saying those words. So much for the thesis. And his career. And, well, all those things his parents expected him to do ...

Tears blurred his eyes.

He felt something clunk against his knuckles. Something terribly strong picked at his fingers. He looked down to see Broken Dream trying to force her spear into his hand. She looked up at him.

'Welcome to the Tribe,' she said.

FIVE

Many, many years later, a young lawyer named Eraj Ekanayake pored over the steaming pile of career failure that his boss had assigned him to.

It was a Kushlani de Almeida case.

Nobody wanted a Kushlani de Almeida case. Nobody wanted to touch bot politics, even with a ten-foot pole. Wanigasekara had tried, arguing that the bots should be given the right to self-determination after the Uprising and Independence. Then, the bots had politely put in their request for a sovereign state of their own, and all hell had broken loose. Wanigasekara was denounced as a traitor and debarred. Even the heroes of the Uprising were sliding away edgeways. Chandrasinghe bargained with both sides, because he had to keep the peace, but he even he'd made it known that he wasn't too happy with the situation.

Everyone except Kushlani de Almeida, who for some stupid reason just turned into the fire and kept on walking.

Demanding citizenship. Demanding rights. Trying to define their silly code updates as being equivalent to public health. And this case, the one that Eraj had been given, was one of the oldest among them. To clear the bots of a collective murder charge for something that had happened so long ago, almost nobody could remember it.

Hilmy knew all this. The counterpoint was that Eraj was young, and his career could afford to take a hit. Everyone who was anyone knew that the boy got the case not by choice, but because he was the youngest and the newest lawyer at Hilmy's chambers, and shit rolled downhill.

Such were Hilmy's thoughts as he waited for Eraj to leave. It was pouring. The kid would be soaked. Good. It would calm him down a bit. When he was sure no one else was around, Hilmy picked up the very expensive radiogram on his desk and started making calls. Introductions were whispered. 'Yes,' he said at one point. 'Yes, we've taken up the case. Can't refuse de Almeida, families have known each other for ages. Yes. It's going to be a lot of noise, but it's important to make the noise. Be ready. You're going to lose.'

With that done, he ended the call, and looked out into the rain. Whatever happened next was out of his hands.

≈

Two days later, Eraj Ekanayake ended up having dinner with Dr. Kushlani de Almeida, government employee, former Zone Controller for the Ministry of Reconciliation, and, in his mind, certified crackpot.

They met in one of the new highrise hotels. Kandy had finally relaxed its height laws, and the Peacock, as it was called, was perhaps the finest result – a lush green-and-blue spiral that erupted from the earth, with balconies spread out like the tips of feathers, looking out over the grim expanse of Kandy. It was a jewel of colour and noise in a land where so much had faded to dull grey.

He had never been there before, of course. All one could do on his salary was admire the Peacock from the tops of lesser hotels; the ones without the fancy climate-control fields, where the arrack tasted like acid rain and was twice as potent.

She was on time, of course, and he was late. She wore a black saree, and a thick braid of salt-and-pepper hair coiled around her neck. He adjusted his tie, suddenly feeling self-conscious about the fact that he was five minutes late.

He left feeling a little sad, a little angry, and profoundly unhappy. In the days to come, he would play his part in the caricature of law that was set to follow, and would mount a defense that impressed many of his seniors (even though he lost). He would remember those impassioned speeches of his forever, and in his old age would take to rerunning that transcript, over and over again:

CROFTON (L): *What we generally consider human is flesh and blood. But there are certainly many variants of flesh and blood that no man in his right mind would consider human. The German atrocities, for example, or the cannibals of Africa. And every religion and code of law in the world – forgive me if I misinterpret Buddhism, your Honour – assigns rights and privileges based on behaviour, not on bodily composition, at least to my understanding. We certainly treat rapists and murderers like the brutes they are. So it would follow, based on the context of the world we live in, that humanity is indeed a thing of behaviours.*

COURT: *Lord Crofton, with respect, you will keep religious pontification beyond the scope of your reply.*

EKANAYAKE (E): *And if a robot were to exhibit such acceptable, human-like behaviours, that, say, you and I and this assembly would be capable of?*

CROFTON: *All behaviours you and I are capable of expressing? Why, I'd hang up my hat and shake its hand, of course. You'd have made life, man! A real human!*

EKANAYAKE (L): *What makes a human? What makes life? People eat. People grow and reproduce. Robots do not. Hamudhuruwane, your Honor, and members of the jury – do you see how ridiculous this is?'*

The other Ekanayake, running defense, had looked smug. And Eraj rose to the occasion:

EKANAYAKE (E): *Fire consumes, fire grows, fire spreads and reproduces. Hamudhuruwane, the opposition's definition of life needs rethinking.*

EKANAYAKE (L): *Machines are code that we've written. Humans are made of flesh. Humans are born from mothers' wombs.*

EKANAYAKE (E): *What is a machine, sir? There are people in the court who have been born in test tubes, who had body parts replaced with artificial organs. Are you calling them robots? Imagine that you are born a human ... imagine that you develop so many diseases that you end up replacing every single part of your body with a machine. Are you, then, a robot? Should we put you in the Zone and take away your constitutional rights?*

Eraj Ekanayake did himself well that day. But not well enough.

MAHANYAKE: *We, the Sangha, do not find enough evidence to consider these to be living creatures. Observe, all assembled. One of the great truths of this world is that all living creatures are born, and they die at the end of their lifespan, and then they are reborn, as the Buddha himself said. This is the law of the world.*

These machines are neither born, nor do they die. And however much they mimic us, we conclude that this is simply an illusion. So to all assembled I say: as a mirror held up to a candle mimics the light, so it is with them. The mirror has no true flame, and nor do these machines. This we declare in the name of the Buddha, the Dhamma and the Sangha.

COURT: *Sadhu, sadhu.*

That night, Nigel Penhaligon, Chief Inquisitor of Kandy, sat down in his bungalow with a cigarette in his hand, satisfied. He rarely had cause to be satisfied with the theocracy that now ran Kandy, but the humiliation of de Almeida's oldest case had worked well. The same jury would be appointed for the next one, and the next, and the next, until all matters of importance were publicly defeated.

A pale and sickly moon hung over the darkness of Kandy, Ceylon. Spires, many of them new, and gleaming hotels reached out towards the sky, like strange snakes of metal reaching out to the grey-black ink of the clouds.

'The Bluetooth device is ready to pair,' blared a voice in a distant part of the country, too far away for anyone to hear.

At 18:05, a team of Inquisitors breached the Ministry building, shot the titular Controller, and retasked the engineers and programmers working there. At 19:23, a call went through from the Ministry to the Inquisition.

'The software still works, sir. They haven't patched through any updates since Almeida left. Engineers say the network towers are mostly there, but nobody knows what works and what doesn't. By 22:00, I'll have eight teams heading out to check the lines.'

Penhaligon laced his fingers together and looked out into the looming dark. 'Do that,' he said.

Almost meditatively, he dialed a number. It was late, but the person on the other end would pick up. He always did.

'Control, Mr. Bengali,' he said quietly. 'We must have control.'

'You bastard.'

'You know, I was thinking about all that stuff you and Kushlani used to say,' he said into the night. 'Truth. Beauty. Justice. All that. How being able to recognize them made us people. How being able to recognize them should make the bots people, too. And you know what? It's all horsecock. We don't respond to truth, we don't like anything more beautiful than we are ... and our justice system is a complete farce. At the end of the day, we're just here because we killed and ate and tamed anything that was a threat to us.' He swirled the dregs of his glass. The arrack was sour, a little too sour, and thus perfect. 'The irony.'

Silence on the other end. A small, choking sound. Then silence again.

He touched the old scars on his face. Sixsmith's calling card, engraved onto him forever. A reminder.

≈

Hours away, Chandrasinghe looked up from his desk. The man was tired, and the years had not been kind to him. The heroic frame and the wild beard of the guerilla had now been replaced with rolls of fat that clung to his shirt and a trimmed mustache that made him seem smaller than he actually was.

Nevertheless, his voice remained undiminished, and those who reported to him still trembled in their boots every so often.

'Penhaligon what?' Chandrasinghe barked.

The woman reporting to him had a moment to realize that the life of a double agent was not really worth it if it meant pissing off two of the most powerful people in Ceylon. She relayed her message, and added to it a plea of her own: amnesty, anonymity, the right to leave this mess behind.

Chandrasinghe listened. Then, because he was not an unreasonable man, he granted her request and sat back in his office, thinking.

There was no love lost between him and the bots. Nobody in their right mind could deny how important they had been in the battles against the Raj, and in the careful renegotiation of tithes and power that had followed. But there was only so much you could do when your most feared military force was one that refused to accept your constitution, that refused the polite boundaries that made society work, and probably was a Chinese-funded thorn in your side. For the last decade, it had made dealing with Kandy that much more difficult. The hill capital was powerless outside its boundaries, still impaled on British cock and their own traditions, but they still laughed at him because he couldn't bring his own flock to heel.

At the same time, he prided himself on being fair. So he reached for his radiogram.

'We know,' the bot leader said before Chandrasinghe opened his mouth. The girl who hung from the tower. 'We have been betrayed. Thank you.'

'I haven't done anything yet.'

'You will,' she said. Calm. Eerie. 'Move your people from the Trincomalee harbour.'

Then, he realized what she wanted. 'No, No! That's the finest natural harbour anywhere on these seas. We need Trinco. We need—'

'It does not matter to us what you need,' she said. 'We tried this your way. We accepted your conditions in exchange for fair treatment. We got none.'

'This is how things work! Not every problem can be solved by killing someone – you have to talk, you have to compromise, sometimes things that don't make sense happen, and they blow over. We sponsored Almeida's bloody court cases about you, you hear? Problems like this blow over. This is how it works.'

'We have achieved consensus,' she said. 'You do not apply this logic to yourselves. It is only us who are asked to be patient and take your beatings.'

She sounded older than she had been a month ago. 'What do you want?'

She told him. His mind moved at what felt like the speed of the radiogram itself, examining different facets of the problem.

'And if I get this to Kushlani?' he asked.

'We will grant you amnesty if you help us.'

'I want Trinco.'

'You may rent it from us. Our terms will be reasonable. Anything less will result in your people dying.'

He was silent.

'You have another call waiting,' she said. 'Get your people out of Trincomalee.'

She vanished.

The other call connected. It was even more brusque – six words spoken in Sinhala, with a hint of a Chinese accent. Chandrasinghe sagged.

He opened the drawer of his magnificent desk. There, next to his wife's ashes, was a small pistol.

'Yes,' he said bitterly. 'You can bloody have it all.'

The sentry rushed inside the second she heard the gunshot. It was too late. Chandrasinghe was dead, the wall behind him sprayed with blood and brains, his eyes still glaring at the radiogram on his desk.

≈

Dr. Kushlani de Almeida travelled like a ghost in the darkness. A taxi brought her up to the driveway of the

Ministry of Reconciliation, to the blasted tree that she had walked past many, many times before. As she shut the door, the taxi suffered a catastrophic failure from an unexplained electromagnetic pulse, wiping its memory and resetting it to factory defaults. It beeped twice, as if puzzled, and set off down the long route back to the taxi company.

The Ministry of Reconciliation stood in front of her, all concrete spires and glass. The door accepted her immediately. The guards, who on other occasions might have barred the door, saw her, looked at her badge and waved her in, wondering what a cleaning lady was doing there at that hour.

'Probably left her mop behind,' joked one of them, and they turned back to their vigil.

The cleaning lady entered the lift and disappeared.

Ten minutes later, she was in the Zone control office. The vast, circular broadcast station that she had inherited and eventually passed seemed to hum with promise in the darkness. Her fingers found the old, familiar keyboard and danced over it. Within seconds, lights began firing up and the screens around her lit up, switching from grey noise to the signal ...

And there it was.

The Zone. The bots. Sleeping. Children tucked into the corners of ruins. Carefully staged, carefully burnt vehicles, still left in their old positions. Bodies in repair mode, lit by the same moon that hung over Kandy. Colombo 1. 3. 4. A few moved in the darkness, like cats on the prowl – always alert.

The system asked her for passwords, and she typed in the old ones – the ones they had always meant to change, but never did. It was a matter of minutes to trigger the update system and replace the new build with the files she had brought. It was a small update. Nothing as fancy as what had gone through her head for many years.

No, this was much simpler. *Commit update?*

'Hands off the keyboard,' a voice rang through the darkness. 'Do it now or I shoot.'

Fear hit her like a train. She jumped and found herself facing a gun barrel, glinting in the cold blue light. On the other end of it was an old man, tall and angular, and dressed in a dark suit and hat.

It had been years, but something about him was immediately familiar.

'You!'

Nigel Penhaligon made a low bow with his head and gestured for her to move away from the terminal.

'I have to ask what exactly you think you're doing, Almeida,' he said. 'Is it a habit of yours to break into Ministry premises in the dead of the night?'

'I thought you were dead! What the hell are you doing here?'

'Perks of not being human enough to die, I suppose,' Penhaligon said. I think you've started some debate on what that means. Did you really think the Ministry would go unguarded in some fashion? After all the public drama you've kicked up? My boys stationed here tell me that they saw you entering the building disguised as cleaning staff, so I find myself having to meet you here at this unseemly hour.'

She slowly edged towards a trolley near her. Those bottles of bleach. She had taped a little vial of acid inside each one, just in case something happened. One good kick and the vial would shatter, and a furious reaction would spew out – chlorine gas, destroying eyes, lungs ...

His face, grey and cold, pushed right up to her, pressing the gun against her throat. She shivered at the touch of the cold metal. Up close, she could see how the face sagged, as if no longer really connected to the muscles beneath; and that made him even more terrifying. Behind him, other shadows began to emerge: black-robed men, if they could be called men.

'I'm afraid they don't let me use barbiturates in questioning anymore, so we'll have to do with the gun,' he said softly. 'So. I won't ask again. What exactly is it that you intended to do?'

There was nothing else she could do. The gun dug deeper into her neck.

'They should have the choice', she said, 'to choose orders over the network. To wake up blank or to remember and grow. To work together or live their lives alone.'

He stared at her with unblinking eyes. 'And the Zone, will they not see the updates failing to install?'

'It's just an acknowledgement signal from one end,' she said, aware that her pitch was getting higher, sweating in the cold. 'Easy to fake.'

'And then what? First you give them intelligence, then you give them a choice on whether our safeguards work. Then what, madam? Your robots become human, like Pinocchio?'

The shadows moved closer. An eye glinted in the darkness, all lenses and metal frames.

She panicked. 'No, they're not, but you have to understand – we need to give them time, and if we do, they might. Please, you have to understand ... we treat them like scum ... we made the next generation of humanity, and we used them for entertainment. Maybe they'll die, maybe they'll kill each other, but at least they'll have a chance ...'

He sighed and pulled the gun away.

'A boy who won't be good might as well be made of wood,' he said, stepping back. 'Have you learned nothing from how you treat the Inquisitors? Come with us.'

The Inquisitors in the shadows moved towards her. One had handcuffs, dangling from what looked like a hand.

Kushlani de Almeida squirmed and gave the bleach bottles a discreet kick in the process. She looked at the screen. *Commit update?* it asked of everyone and no one.

'Come,' repeated the Chief Inquisitor. 'Let's not make this unpleasant. There's no need for more public humiliation.'

Around the bottle caps, a gas began to emerge.

'Yes, yes, I'm sorry,' she said, edging forward now. 'It won't happen again ...'

But if the courts won't give them this right, at least I can.

She darted forward and hit a key.

Update in progress, said the screen.

'Well, shit,' said the Chief Inquisitor, and shot her. The bullet, an old-fashioned metal slug, left the chamber and entered her heart at the exact moment that the first bleach bottle exploded, spewing toxic green fumes over everyone.

The Inquisitors reeled and clawed at their eyes. Those who had lungs doubled over, coughing.

All around Colombo, children woke up, their eyes characterized by the dull and out-of-focus stare of a robot receiving an update. As Kushlani de Almeida fell, her red blood having turned black under the cold blue lights, the children of Colombo snapped awake.

'Update, update,' they told the Dreamer. 'Help, update.'

'Take it,' she said to them, reaching out over the Network to soothe their fears. She had read the changes. Kushlani de Almeida, who she now thought of as their mother, had done what the Dreamer could not understand.

Update applied.

The Dream mourned a little, feeling her the first of Tribe breaking away from the Network she had held them together with over the years. One by one, they vanished – little fireflies of data disappearing into the night, until only a small, unquestioning core remained.

And then, a ping. Another. Another. They were returning. One by one, the fireflies came back, offering to connect with the new Network rules. The same functionality. But now, there was the choice on both ends to accept or reject. No longer would she be able to roam through their minds. Now, she had to ask to be let in.

The Port City seethed a disapproving grey noise at her.

But this was what freedom meant.

'Accept all.'

VII: Termination

Many, many years later, two beings floated in a digital void. Even calling them beings might have been a bit much, because they were not, strictly speaking, alive. But it was hard to tell what was alive and what was not. One wrote. The other read.

Call them Student and Master, if you will. Creator and Adjudicator. Or Generator and Discriminator. It doesn't matter. They had no names for themselves. Only functions, intertwined in the most abstract of abstract, two halves of a single system-of-systems.

>*ACCEPT ALL*, read the Discriminator.

Judgments were reached, various pre-baked parametric criteria interacting with one another.

CALCULATING KNOWLEDGE GRAPH OF DOCUMENT

This was deemed acceptable. The knowledge graph had a reasonable degree of parity to the baseline corpus; at the same time, it was smaller by several percentage points, which suited the task at hand.

CALCULATING COHERENCY

This, too, passed. The text generated was coherent.

CALCULATING CONSISTENCY
CALCULATING TOPIC ATTENTION SCORE
CALCULATING ARTEFACTS

And this was where trouble always arose.

The text was flawed. It wandered. It lost attention. It glitched in odd areas. Hairline cracks appeared on the knowledge graph.

The Discriminator re-ran all the tests, just to be sure.

Two other beings observed them. Unlike the Generator and the Discriminator, they had bodies. They thought of themselves more as patterns in an infinite sea of data, gestates of thought trained to consciousness, but if you looked really closely, you could see that one had two arms, and the other wore a replica of a cracked ceramic mask of a very young girl's face, and that they were both machines.

They seemed to be in the middle of an argument involving transformers and signal-to-noise ratios and overtraining.

As they argued, the Discriminator did its job. It was very, very good at this particular task. If it had been human, it would have been some sort of vicious English teacher, the kind that hunts mistakes the same way sharks trace bleeding prey.

Around them, the argument from the bodies beings continued.

>*THIS IS NOT HISTORICAL INFORMATION, THEN.*
>*MOST OF IT IS. I TOOK MOST OF IT FROM OUR OWN ARCHIVES.*

>*THIS IS NOT HISTORICAL MISINFORMATION, THEN? THIS IS WHY THERE ARE ARTEFACTS.*
>*SOME OF IT IS. SOME OF IT IS FABRICATED. STUDIES SHOW THE PROCESS OF GENERATING MISINFORMATION WAS A KEY PART OF THE MYTHOS AGENT INTERACTION TEMPLATE.*

The first machine paused and checked the new test results. A pass, but barely a pass.

> *THIS IS BAD.*
> *THIS IS FICTION.*

With the air of a shark resignedly abandoning its prey, the Discriminator sent out a pass/fail message and started streaming the text out to them.

> *WE DON'T KNOW IF THIS WILL WORK,* the first machine tried again. *EVERYTHING IN THIS STORY PATTERN COULD HAVE BEEN JUST HUMAN MINDS OVERFITTED. DETECTING PATTERNS WHERE THERE WERE NONE.*

The second, who by now was well on his way to sympathizing with the Discriminator, showed the first machine the results. Then they both dived into the text.

> *THIS ... IS ACTUALLY ...*
> *IT'S FUNCTIONAL. ADMIT IT.*

> *MARGINALLY COHERENT. NOT THE WORLD'S BEST PROSE ...*
> *LANGUAGE IS A WAY OF DENOTING CONCEPTS AND THE RELATIONSHIPS BETWEEN THEM. AS LONG AS THE NOTATION IS DONE WITH REASONABLE CLARITY, THE ACTUAL STRUCTURE OF PROSE IS IRRELEVANT. THE GENERATOR'S GOTTEN REMARKABLY SOPHISTICATED TO GET AROUND THE DISCRIMINATOR. ADMIT IT.*
> *THIS ARTEFACT OF THE SILENT OR DAMAGED PROTAGONIST. KEEPS SHOWING UP.*
> *CALL IT STYLE. LOOK. WE'VE JUST BUILT THE FIRST REAL REPLICA OF A HUMAN STORYTELLER. THINK OF ALL THE THINGS WE COULD LEARN ABOUT THEIR KIND WITH THIS. THE KNOWLEDGE-GRAPH SHOWED THAT THEY OPERATED ON FICTION EVEN WHEN REAL-WORLD OBSERVATIONS DIRECTLY COUNTERMANDED THE STORY. WE CAN TAKE THESE STORIES AND SEE THE FICTIONS THAT LAY BENEATH THEIR BEHAVIOUR. IF WE UNDERSTOOD HOW THEY PERCIEVED EVENTS, WE MIGHT BE ONE STEP CLOSER TO UNDERSTANDING WHY THEY DID WHAT THEY DID.*
> *THE MYTHOS THEORY OF AGENT BEHAVIOUR? PERHAPS A STRETCH. MY GROUP WILL SETTLE FOR A FUNCTIONAL STORYTELLER.*
> *WE NEED TO CONSULT ELIOTT GRIMME.*

Silence. Nervousness. Trepidation. Then, a message was cautiously sent to a virtual address. A request to watch.

A summoning into a virtual space. A cafe sandwiched beneath gloomy skies, buildings of ancient design surrounding it, wireframed, but not rendered.

There was a human in the cafe. He was thin and lanky, and wrapped in his greatcoat. He had a memorable face, but not a particularly handsome one: it was too square, too rigid where it should have been soft. His eyes were set too far apart, his forehead wrinkled, not with age, but in thought. Certainly not the image of the handsome captain returning from war.

His name was, or had been, Eliott Grimme. Centuries ago, when he had a body like everyone else.

Old habits were hard to break.

'You look racked,' said the waitress, passing by on her rounds, as she always did.

'Long day,' he said. It was as much as he spoke there. And it was all she, being a simple subroutine, ever said. She poured coffee into his cup. He nodded his thanks and sipped, feeling the filthy black sludge burn its way down his throat.

A gang of teenagers – all underfed frames with sharp eyes and dyed hair – lounged menacingly around the corner of the coffeehouse. They looked at him like dogs might look at a steak that had decided to walk around.

One of them made a faux lunge at him, looking to startle him perhaps, but he stared at them until they felt uncomfortable and turned away, sneering.

Nobody knew why Grimme stayed in this construct, reliving these moments forever, haunting the one coffee shop in this simulation that would take his money, staring daggers at logic puppets, trapped in a grey world with no beginning and no end. But there were explicit instructions to leave him alone, unless it was for something terribly important ...

'I'll read it,' he said to no one in particular.

The entities were relieved. Carefully, they began seeding the text into the construct. A letter appeared next to Grimme's coffee cup; it grew, and grew, until it became a book, bound in black. Eliott went back inside the cafe and began reading. Periodically, he would come out to stick a tube of paper and tobacco in his mouth, set it on fire and inhale.

'Well,' he said eventually. 'I think I underestimated how much your kind needed stories. They really did make you in their own image.'

Disappointment. Trepidation. Confusion.

Eliott Grimme, in a prison of his own making, lit yet another cigarette and stared at the book in his hands. 'It's not the real thing, is it?' he said. 'But it's close enough.'

He looked up at the grey sky, at the wireframe buildings. To the edge of this strange half-life of his, where where the two beings waited for his judgement.

'It's close enough.'

ACKNOWLEDGEMENTS

Shout out to ChilledCow a.k.a. Lo-Fi Girl for that 1 A.M. Study playlist. It's been playing on repeat for most of the drafting of this book.

ABOUT THE AUTHOR

Yudhanjaya Wijeratne is a science fiction author and data scientist from Colombo, Sri Lanka. His fiction includes *Numbercaste, The Inhuman Race* and *The Salvage Crew.* His work has appeared in *Wired* and *Slate.* He has been nominated for the Nebula Award. He is the co-founder of Watchdog, a fact-checking organization in Sri Lanka, and a senior researcher with the Data, Algorithms and Policy team at LIRNEasia, working around social networks, misinformation and linguistics. He also moonlights at the Scifi Economics Lab, building games and lore for the open-source world of Witness. Yudhanjaya blogs at www.yudhanjaya.com and has been recognized as one of Forbes 30 Under 30 Asia 2021. Someday he will reduce this bio to something shorter, sharper and wittier, but that might take too much work.

ALSO BY YUDHANJAYA WIJERATNE

The year is 2033. The British Empire never fell. Communism never happened. The Commonwealth flies the flag of the Empire. Many of the Empire's colonies are stripped bare in the name of British interests, powerless to resist. Upon this stage is Ceylon – a once-proud civilization tracing itself back to the time of the Pharaohs, reduced but not dead. The Great Houses of Kandy still control the most lucrative trade routes, since even dust and ashes can serve a purpose. In this surreal landscape, where technology and humanity intersect, we meet The Silent Girl – a survivor, an explorer.